Strong
Force

About the Author

René Roberts is a number-cruncher by day and storyteller by night! She was born and raised in South Africa, the most beautifully diverse country in the world, but she recently moved to Rotterdam.

She left her forwarding address to the muse and hopes she finds her way to the Netherlands. René loves all forms of art, good food, theatre, and music. She doesn't like technology, breaking a sweat, or writing author bios (which makes her sweat). She remains committed to her wife and in service of their beautiful cat.

Strong Force

René Roberts

BELLA
BOOKS
2022

Bella Books, Inc.
P.O. Box 10543
Tallahassee, FL 32302

Printed in the United States of America on acid-free paper.

First Edition - 2022

Editor: Heather Flournoy
Cover Designer: Heather Honeywell

ISBN: 978-1-64247-387-2

PUBLISHER'S NOTE

Acknowledgments

The end.

These two magical words signify the end of a journey that can be solitary, volatile, beautiful, exhilarating, tiring, and fulfilling. Sacrifices are made by committed partners and resentful cats. I would like to thank my partner, Charese, for always being my fiercest supporter and accepting the fact that some of my time will always be spent with fictional women vying for my attention. I also apologise to our cat for not serving at her paws at all times. Thank you, Heather, for cleaning up when things got messy. You made my first experience with an editor a pleasant one!

CHAPTER ONE

Flicking down her visor, Shae McPherson assessed her appearance. She needed a haircut, and her new base didn't manage to hide the dark circles under her eyes. She winced and dug around her bag in search of something to remedy the situation. Unfortunately, her bag didn't contain a good night's rest, so she turned to the lip gloss, applying a thin layer. Pressing her lips together to distribute the gloss evenly, she rolled her eyes.

"Dr. Ramsey is probably bald and fat. What do I care?"

Stepping out of her car, she let out a sigh as she made her way to the heavy front door.

"Who in South Africa still has a knocker on their front door?" Shae mumbled under her breath.

Lifting the offending knocker, she shook her head as she banged it against the dark wood.

A stocky old woman with a smile as broad as her hips opened the door. She peered over her spectacles and held out a puffy hand.

"Good morning, Mrs. McPherson. Please come in."

Shae couldn't help but smile at the friendly receptionist.

"Morning. It's Miss."

"What's that, dear?"

"I am Miss McPherson. Not married," Shae said and displayed her naked ring finger as if she needed to prove it.

The receptionist made a disapproving noise and shuffled down a passage, beckoning Shae to follow her. The old house sported the most beautiful wooden floors and high chandeliered ceilings, and it could easily pass for a museum instead of a consulting room in Johannesburg. The smell of what could only be freshly baked scones permeated the air and made Shae's stomach growl.

At the end of the passage, the door to a spacious room stood ajar.

"Dr. Ramsey, *Miss* McPherson just arrived," the old lady announced.

The emphasis on her title didn't escape Shae and she felt silly for having corrected the sweet old lady. There was some shuffling inside the room before a tall woman stood in the doorway. Her black hair was in a tight bun, accentuating her high cheekbones. She had piercing blue eyes and a sensual mouth resembling that of Cate Blanchett. Dr. Ramsey was a lucky man to have this beautiful creature on his couch, Shae thought to herself.

"Miss McPherson. Welcome. Please have a seat. Ella, could you please bring us a pot of tea and some of those fresh scones that have my mouth watering."

Wait. What? This tall beauty was the therapist? Shae battled to hide her surprise.

"Yes, I am Dr. Ramsey. Don't worry. I often get that look. The fact that my mother insisted on naming me Adrian keeps my life interesting at the best of times."

Clearing her throat, Shae shook the outstretched hand of the goddess that she now assumed would start prodding and poking around her psyche soon. Suddenly, therapy didn't seem like the worst idea ever. She stepped into the room and performed a quick scan. Wall-to-wall mahogany shelves were crammed full of books and a plush maroon rug covered most of the floor. In the middle of the room, a small coffee table stood surrounded by two leather recliners and a matching two-seater. The walls were decorated with abstracts in warm earthy colours. A Zen garden dominated the one side of the room, and a beautiful fireplace the other.

"This is not quite what I expected," Shae said as she nervously clasped her hands in front of her stomach.

"What did you expect, Miss McPherson?"

"Can you please call me Shae? I am Miss McPherson at school all day," Shae said as she shifted around on the stiff recliner.

Ella entered the room carrying a tray with a pot of tea and the most beautiful scones Shae had ever seen. Taking the tray from her, Dr. Ramsey instructed her to close the door behind her. Let the prodding begin, Shae thought.

"Help yourself to these scones, Shae. I guarantee it will be the best part of your day. So, what did you expect?"

"Not this."

Adrian poured two cups of tea and slid one across the table before she meticulously buttered a scone like a skilled mason would smooth cement over a brick. She then layered it with strawberry jam and sunk her perfect teeth into it hungrily. Closing her eyes, Adrian made a satisfactory noise in the back of her throat while Shae sipped on her tea and stared at her own untouched scone.

"Go for it. You'll be a changed woman," Adrian said and dusted crumbs from her chest.

"I just had breakfast," Shae lied.

Adrian slipped into doctor mode as she opened a folder and started scribbling in it. Shae sighed and placed her cup on the coffee table before she wrapped her arms across her chest protectively. The room was quiet for a few moments before Adrian suddenly looked up, crossed her legs, and shifted in her seat.

"So, Shae. You say that this is all unexpected?"

Time to measure my words carefully, Shae thought.

"I don't think I had any expectations, actually."

"We always have expectations, Shae. Even when we don't realise it. Most people expect to crash on my couch."

Shae pointed to the two-seater and shook her head.

"That is not comfortable enough to crash on. Now that you mention it, if I had any expectations, it would have been to sit comfortably," Shae said as she squeezed the stiff armrests.

Adrian chuckled softly.

"I find that people don't really challenge themselves when they are too comfortable. Also, these are new. I renovated a short while ago."

Shae nodded slowly, picked up her cup of tea, and sipped carefully.

"That's not why I'm here, though. I don't need to challenge myself."

Adrian started to chew on the back of her pen and momentarily stared out the window at the vast gardens outside. From what Shae could see, the scene outside was just about as pretty as they get in the City of Gold. In the absence of picturesque mountain ranges or the unmatched beauty of the ocean, Gauteng residents with an appreciation for all things beautiful tended to grow luscious gardens. Shae deduced that Doctor Adrian Ramsey had to be one of those residents, making the best of what Johannesburg, the commercial hub that it was, had to offer.

"Why are you here, Shae?"

"My boss didn't tell you?" Shae asked.

Adrian refocused her attention on Shae.

"Mr. Foster is not my patient. The instruction was to assess whether you needed professional support. He mentioned that there had been an incident at school that might have left you traumatised. I'm afraid that's the extent of my knowledge."

Shae crossed her legs and shifted deeper into the recliner. She pictured Mr. Foster trying to articulate while staring at Dr. Ramsey's assets. It was no secret that beautiful women made him uncomfortable. Shae's good friend, Fiona, took great pleasure in making their principal blush whenever she had the opportunity—usually in front of the students' parents.

"I am here to humour Mr. Foster. The incident that he referred to happened almost a year ago, and I am completely fine. I guess I need you to set his mind at ease," Shae said and drained her cup.

Adrian nodded a few times and scribbled in the file.

"Seems the topic of the day is expectations. *You* expect me to set his mind at ease. *He* expects me to assess your mental health."

Shae's arms were crossed over her chest again.

"What do *you* expect, Doctor?"

Adrian smiled brightly and dropped her pen in the folder on her lap.

"I thought you'd never ask. It's actually very simple, Shae. I don't expect you to bare your soul to me, but I do expect you to give this a shot," Adrian said.

Nodding slowly, Shae started chipping nail polish off her thumb, tapping her foot against the leg of the coffee table. She inwardly cursed herself for committing to this nonsense, but Mr. Foster had made it quite clear that she had run out of options. She still felt that these drastic measures were unnecessary. Mr. Foster had a way of overdramatising everything and she certainly did not agree with him about her performance at work. Was she traumatised? At first, she definitely had been, but by no means was she neglecting her students. Mr. Foster was being neurotic.

"Look at it like a first date," Adrian said.

Shae cocked her brow at that.

"You can start by telling me a little bit about yourself," Adrian continued.

Shae rested her elbow on the armrest and her chin on her closed fist.

"You probably wouldn't have said that if Mr. Foster had given you the heads-up. I'm a lesbian," Shae said defiantly.

Shae studied the doctor's face intently, but she didn't register anything. Dr. Ramsey didn't seem affected in the least. She closed the folder on her lap and dumped it on the coffee table as if she'd lost all interest in recording any facts about Shae McPherson.

"I don't happen to think that one's sexual preference defines you. Either way, you should still treat this like a first date. Just talk about yourself, and after our time together you can decide whether you'd like to see me again."

Shae uncrossed her legs and wiped her palms on her thighs. Why she was suddenly anxious, she had no clue. She stared at Dr. Ramsey, but her words simply refused to form sentences. Adrian smiled at her and started rolling her ring around her finger.

"What's it like teaching at Willowmore?"

"It's very rewarding. Do you know much about Willowmore?" Shae asked, feeling a little more relaxed.

"I don't, actually."

Shae pictured the smiling faces of her students. Over the years, she had formed profound relationships with each of them. She had been privileged enough to see some of her students grow from awkward children into remarkable teenagers. Forming deep connections with her students was a natural result of spending the majority of her waking hours with them.

"It's the best public school in the province," Shae said.

Adrian nodded slowly but didn't say a word. It was in these silent moments that Shae felt like she was under a microscope and assumed that Dr. Ramsey was dissecting every word she uttered, which made her shift around uncomfortably.

"I suppose every mother thinks her kid is the brightest. I mean, I don't have statistics to back up what I just said."

Adrian studied her carefully and sighed when Shae visibly started squirming.

"Look, Shae. I know that this is uncomfortable. Nobody sits in that chair completely at ease. There's a reason people avoid seeing therapists."

Standing up, Adrian crossed the room, opened a window, and watered a succulent that was the centrepiece of the windowsill. By the time she took up her seat again, Shae was somewhat more relaxed.

"I don't mentally record every word you say, Shae. Not everything has hidden meaning, so please relax. I can assure you my purpose is not to expose you to anyone."

Shae stared at her for a long time before she picked up her untouched scone. She broke bite-sized pieces off and almost groaned as her taste buds exploded. Dr. Ramsey was paying close attention. She might not weigh every word, but Shae was not ignorant. She knew that any good therapist must have perfected the art of observation. If she was going to retain any semblance of control, it was crucial that Adrian realised that Shae was no amateur when it came to the science of human behaviour.

"You're thinking that I'm very controlled because I didn't groan in satisfaction. Do you have your receptionist bake these as part of your assessments?" Shae asked.

Dr. Ramsey chuckled at that.

"I wish I could be that calculated. Ella bakes because she doesn't like having idle time. It's a perk. She gets therapy for free!"

Damn. That chuckle seemed so sincere. Shae felt a little silly for trying to challenge Adrian. From what she could tell, Adrian was kind, and she probably didn't deserve her antagonism. She sighed quietly before she started talking.

"I don't love my job despite what happened, I love it because of what happened. It just reaffirmed the importance of the role that educators play in the lives of troubled teens. It's why I was drawn to this profession."

Adrian still wore a poker face. Shae understood perfectly; having studied some psychology, Shae knew the importance of maintaining the delicate balance between seeming detached and engrossed. She often used the same technique on her students to lure them into speaking more freely.

"It takes a village, as they say," Adrian said, nodding. "What do you do for fun?" she asked.

She clearly didn't want Shae to dwell or take a step backward, hence the change in direction of the conversation. Shae felt somewhat comforted by the knowledge that this Dr. Ramsey was no fool. She obviously already realised that it was too soon for them to rip off the Band-Aid. Shae smiled and cocked a brow.

"Nice diversion, Doctor."

Adrian mimicked a bow as far as was possible in a seated position.

"It depends on my mood, really. Sometimes I build architectural models in the quiet of my den. Sometimes I play beer pong with a bunch of unruly friends," Shae said.

Shae pointed to the folder as she leaned forward in her seat.

"Come on, Dr. Ramsey. We both know you are dying to scribble a few notes in that folder."

Adrian wiped some lipstick residue off the rim of her cup and captured some strawberry-speckled crumbs on the tip of her index finger. She stuck her finger in her mouth and sucked lightly, an innocent action that had Shae slightly aroused. She blushed inwardly—she hoped.

"What do you reckon I would want to note, Shae?"

Shae perceived it as a challenge. She sat back in the recliner and crossed her legs. Linking her fingers, she cupped her joined hands around her right knee.

"Patient displays signs of manic behaviour. Possibly trained in psychology to some extent. Defiant behaviour at times—investigate occurrence of Oppositional Defiant Disorder as a child."

This time Dr. Ramsey made a show of being impressed. She pursed her lips, raised her perfectly shaped eyebrows, and nodded slowly.

"Noted, *Doctor* McPherson." Adrian smiled, making air quotes around the title.

It was now Shae's turn to mimic a bow, which she performed with gusto and a big smile. Therapy, it seemed, was going to be much more interesting than Shae had expected.

CHAPTER TWO

"Mom, can you please ask Avril to stop staring at my steak with that look on her face?"

"What look, dear?" Mrs. Ramsey asked absentmindedly.

She was concentrating on carrying two bowls and a glass of wine to the table. It was family night at the Ramseys' and that meant chaos. Adrian's sister Avril had two rowdy boys with the rare gift of moving every single obstacle out of its place within the first five minutes of entering any given space.

"Like my steak had slit the throat of baby goats," Adrian said and playfully shoved Avril away from her.

Avril leaned on one elbow and poked the other one in her sister's side.

"Do you realise that somebody fed that poor animal for the sole purpose of ending up on your plate?" Avril asked with wide eyes.

Norman Ramsey entered the dining room and kissed his wife on the cheek before relieving her of the two bowls.

"Elbows off the table, Avril," he said and shook his head.

Adrian smiled triumphantly at Avril, hoping that she was invoking flashbacks from their childhood. Norman didn't admit to it readily, but Adrian had always been his favourite and Avril had hardly ever walked away the victor when they were at each other's throats.

"God, if I was a serial killer, I could have axed the whole lot of you!"

Plunking herself down next to Adrian, Easton started picking beans off her plate. At twenty-one, Easton was the youngest of the three Ramsey daughters. The three of them couldn't have been any more different from each other and family night was never uneventful with the colourful cast of characters.

"Were," Adrian said.

Both of her sisters looked at her, frowning.

"You're not a serial killer, so, grammatically you should say that if you *were* a serial killer, you could have axed us all. And get your dirty hands off my food," Adrian said and pretended to stab her sister with her fork.

Avril and Easton shared a look, shaking their heads.

"Tell us, Dr. Ramsey, what does it say about our baby sister's mental state if she pictures axing her entire family?" Avril asked and shoved the pepper shaker in front of Adrian's mouth as if it was a microphone.

Ally Ramsey grabbed the pepper shaker and finally took a seat next to her husband.

"It means she might just be as deranged as you," Adrian said and made a show of biting into her juicy steak.

Avril's two boys, Jayden and Jonah, were chasing each other around the table, all the while giggling. After watching them for a while, Avril sighed audibly and dropped her chin to her chest. The boys were completely unaware of their mother's frustration.

"Would it make me a terrible mother if I sprinkled their peas around outside? It's guaranteed to keep them entertained for a while," Avril said.

Easton loaded her plate with the fruits of Ally's labour. It was quite a spread, and being that Easton was a cash-strapped student who lived off canned food, Adrian supposed that it was even more of a feast to her.

"I say go for it," Easton said.

Shaking his head, Norman handed Avril two small plates so she could dish up for his grandsons. After Avril's divorce four years ago, Norman had stepped up to the plate and served as a father figure to the two boys. Their own father had run off one morning, never to be seen or heard from again. Despite happily raising three girls that he absolutely adored, Norman had always wanted a son. Needless to say, he had been overjoyed when Avril had gifted him with two grandsons. Unfortunately, he was a total pushover and the boys had him wrapped around their little fingers.

An hour later, the boys had been bathed, the kitchen tidied, and the conversations exhausted. Avril shared a rare quiet moment on the couch with Jayden and Jonah. They snuggled up against their mother, flanking her on each side, as she read them a story. Adrian kissed her cheek as she passed her on her way to the porch where she joined her parents for a nightcap.

Norman had his arm wrapped around his wife and she was very close to drifting off, resting her head on his shoulder. Offering Adrian some warmth, he lifted his other arm the second he spotted her in the doorway. She wasted no time and snuck in under his arm, linking her fingers with those of her mother resting on his belly.

"Now this is what I call being blessed," Norman said as he pulled them both closer.

Ally let out a contented sigh and Adrian smiled in the semidarkness.

"It's so good to have you back, my girl."

"I was never gone, Daddy."

A moment of silence passed between the three of them and all that could be heard was the crickets and the bullfrogs serenading under the stars.

"It sure felt like it for us, honey. That man isolated you from everyone you held dear," Ally said, echoing what Adrian assumed were her father's thoughts.

Adrian couldn't argue the facts.

Frederick was everything her family made him out to be—and worse. The divorce had been everything but amicable, but it was in the final stages and Adrian could breathe a little easier. She was not ignorant. She realised that it would take long months, possibly years, to work through the trauma of being married to a narcissistic control freak. Gradually, Adrian had worked up the courage to set the divorce in motion, and knowing that she had had the strength to do that, she had no doubt that she would find a way to pick up the pieces of her life once this chapter was closed.

"I know, Mom. I'm just glad it's almost over."

"You've reached an agreement?" Norman asked quietly.

"You could say that."

Norman knew better than to try and pull information from his daughter. He simply nodded and waited for her to offer more.

"He figured that I would want to clean him out. He had his attorneys draw up an agreement that leaves me with the bare minimum."

Still Norman didn't rush her.

"You should have seen his face when I signed on the dotted line without hesitation."

Norman chuckled at this. He squeezed his daughter's arm and Adrian felt assured that he understood the gravity of the situation despite his laughter.

"It was the most gratifying moment of my entire marriage."

Ally let out a noisy yawn and leaned across her husband to peck Adrian on the cheek.

"I'm not one to swear, but good fucking riddance," she whispered.

She stood up and disappeared inside the house. Having watched her mother for years, Adrian had come to the conclusion that Ally loved the daily routine of her life, taking care of her family. It was time for her nightly errands, which consisted of tucking the boys in while Avril had some time to herself, making sure that Easton went to bed instead of crashing on the couch, and drawing her husband a bath.

Adrian sighed audibly as she felt the alcohol untangling the tense muscles in her shoulders.

"Tough day at work?" Norman asked.

He shifted so that he could look Adrian in the eye.

"You could say that." Norman nodded quietly and rubbed her shoulder. "I started seeing a new patient today, a feisty teacher," she said.

Running his hand through his greying hair, Norman stared off into the darkness. He sipped on his sherry and Adrian ruminated on the rock he was for her. Shifting closer, Adrian rested her hand on his thigh.

"This teacher is in good hands," Norman said.

"Thanks for the vote of confidence, Daddy. If only it was mirrored by my patient."

Norman stood up and leaned against the porch railing, facing Adrian with his arms crossed over his chest. Adrian had such love for this man who had been ready to carry her through fire since he'd first held her in his arms thirty-seven years ago.

"Your patient will come around."

"This one is pretty guarded, Daddy."

Norman nodded and sighed quietly.

"Aren't they all when you first meet them?" he asked.

Crossing her legs, Adrian bit on her lower lip and she pictured Shae insulting her furniture and stubbornly refusing to express her enjoyment of what were only the best scones in the Southern Hemisphere.

"Yes, they mostly are."

They weren't all defiant, though.

"Things will shift when your patient realises how helpful you can be," Norman said.

Adrian remembered the look on Shae's face when she had confidently stated that she didn't really need the help of anyone—she was simply humouring her overzealous boss.

Norman was now leaning his arms on the porch railing, no longer facing her. Adrian joined him staring across the yard at the garden that had gone from an oasis in the light of day to something ominous, shrouded by the cloak of darkness that nightfall had draped across the expanse.

"No, I think it will be quite a while before we even reach that point. She needs to trust me first."

"Will you be okay, Adrian? You know you've gone through so much lately. It's perfectly acceptable to take a break if you need it."

Adrian wrapped her arm around her father's back and kissed his temple.

"Daddy, you would be a terrible therapist with that big old heart of yours. I'll be fine. You know what? She'll be fine too. I'm *that* good," Adrian said, winking.

CHAPTER THREE

"So, did he finally ask you out?" Shae asked the blushing young girl sitting across from her.

She figured the timing was perfect since the attention of all the other boys and girls were focused on the Pitchnut board. They were all huddled in the centre of the room, some clutching their knees against their chests, others with legs crossed and eyes covered, no longer able to handle the tension of the final stages of the game.

Shae had initiated the Friday afternoon get-togethers for her students. She had wanted to create an escape for the unfortunate minority of students who didn't excel at sports or perform well academically. The turnout on that first Friday two years ago had been disappointing, but Shae had been committed to the cause, and gradually more and more students had started to show up. Over time, Shae had bought them a few board games, a dartboard, and even a secondhand pool table.

"Yes, he did. We're going to the movies next weekend."

"That's wonderful, Trish! I am so happy for you. Just don't let your grades drop, because you'll force me to rip out his heart through his belly button."

Giggling quietly, Patricia shrugged.

"No, Miss McPherson. That will never happen," the spotty teenager promised wholeheartedly.

Shae squeezed her shoulder as she joined the crowd around the Pitchnut board for the final showdown. They all cheered as the resident Pitchnut champion, Archie, sunk his final piece and claimed his prize—a shopping voucher that Shae had purchased as award for their monthly competition.

Two hours later, the last few people sauntered out of the room and Shae waved until they had disappeared around the corner. Looking around the room, she felt a sense of pride at how her students took responsibility for keeping their den organised. What they called the Zen Den was actually a Wendy hut that Shae had found at an auction. She had encouraged the kids to paint it as a crafts project and the result was a den fit for a hippy, covered in bright flowers.

She headed to the back of the den to fetch her car keys and as she turned around, her best friend, Fiona, stood in the doorway. Fiona's black hoodie was pulled over her hair and her whitewashed jeans clung to her legs. The blood drained from Shae's face as she clutched her heart and started shivering uncontrollably. Seeming to realise her mistake, Fiona slipped her hoodie off her head and held her hands up in the air, palms facing her friend.

"Jesus, Shae! I am so sorry. I don't know what the hell I was thinking. Are you okay?"

Leaning against the wall, Shae slipped to the floor as her legs gave out. She closed her eyes and concentrated on gaining control of her breathing again. She fought down the nausea and flexed her fingers as the panic attack gripped her a little tighter. Fiona approached her carefully, talking to her softly.

"It's just me, buddy. Thoughtless old me. I'm just going to sit down next to you, okay?"

She settled in next to Shae and reached out to her slowly.

"Just take deep breaths. In through your nose and out through your mouth."

Shae followed her instructions like an obedient child, and the relief was almost instantaneous as the oxygen finally reached her lungs. After a while, she could feel the needles and pins settling in her hands and her stomach stopped doing flip-flops. Wiping the tears from her cheeks with the back of her hands, she banged her head against the wall softly, feeling frustrated with herself.

"Hey, hey! Please, stop that, Shae."

Shae rolled her head from side to side as she felt the tension making itself at home in her shoulders.

"I'm sorry. I should have taken this stupid hoodie off before I came in. I forgot that I move like a cat sometimes," Fiona explained as she gripped Shae's hands.

Swearing under her breath, Fiona wrapped her arm around her friend's shoulders and pulled her closer. Completely out of character, Shae leaned her head against Fiona's shoulder and shamelessly accepted the comfort.

"I have to snap out of this quickly, Fiona. I have an appointment."

"There is no way I'm letting you drive like this," Fiona argued.

Shae pulled her fingers through her clammy hair and let out a sigh.

"It's not my first panic attack. I will be fine. Just help me up if you don't mind."

Fiona helped Shae to her car and promised to check in with her later. She apologised profusely again and offered to drive her across town to her appointment, but Shae declined. She assured her friend that the drive would serve her well and allow her to clear her mind and calm her nerves. By the time Shae parked her car, she was relatively calm, but the attack had left her drained. Seeing the concern on Ella's face as she reported to reception, she slipped into the bathroom to splash her face with cold water minutes before Dr. Ramsey called out her name.

"Shae, please have a seat. How are you today?"

"Just fine and dandy, Doctor," Shae replied sarcastically and regretted it immediately.

She realised that by acting this aggressively, she was probably achieving the opposite of proving she didn't need professional help. She was simply too exhausted to get her guard up where it was supposed to be. Normally, she would take a nap after an attack, and she was irritated with Dr. Ramsey for standing in her way.

"I'm glad to see that you're agreeing to a second date," Adrian said. "You'll notice that I'm not subjecting you to the scones test today. I do have a pot of tea, though. Can I get you some?"

Shae's tongue was plastered against her palate, but the nausea hadn't completely passed and tea seemed like a tall order.

"Could I trouble you for a glass of water instead?" she asked.

"It would be no trouble at all," Dr. Ramsey said.

She left her office and minutes later appeared with a glass of cold water with a slice of lemon in it. Shae nodded her thanks before she drained the glass and placed it on the coffee table. She touched her cool hands to the back of her neck for a few seconds before leaning into the recliner.

"Thank you. Can I order a steak and vegetables for lunch?" Shae asked.

Noticing Adrian's confused frown, Shae pointed to the lemon.

"You serve freshly baked scones and you just happen to have fresh lemon to slip into a simple glass of water. I'm just wondering what you serve for lunch."

Another bout of nausea nearly overcame Shae, and she realised that she had drunk that water too fast. Leaning back against the cool leather of the recliner, she closed her eyes. Feeling pebbles of sweat breaking out across her forehead, she clenched her hands together tightly in her lap. When she opened her eyes a few minutes later, Dr. Ramsey was staring at her worriedly.

"Shae, you might not believe me, but Mr. Foster has no sinister intentions with you at the end of this. I personally don't believe that your job is on the line."

Shae sighed softly but didn't say a word.

"Are you in dire need of professional help? Will your life fall apart if I don't save you from yourself? Probably not. You have to be here, though, because you agreed to it. You might as well benefit from it. I can assure you that there are most certainly things that I can help you with."

Shae rubbed her hands across her face as her heart rate picked up.

"If only you can allo—"

"I had a panic attack," Shae interrupted.

Adrian allowed a few beats of silence before she continued.

"The fact that you look utterly exhausted makes sense now," Adrian said. "Do you need some more water?"

Shaking her head, Shae cleared her throat and wiped at her brow.

"No, thank you. It normally takes a while for me to recover. A good night's sleep might do the trick."

Adrian studied Shae closely and Shae envisioned her consulting a tattered textbook, flipping to the chapter on panic attacks and offensive patients to refresh her memory. Adrian stood and poured herself some tea before she reclaimed her seat across from Shae.

"You're a strong woman for still making it here. Most of my patients are left immobile by panic attacks," Adrian said, reassuring Shae that she was not alone in her suffering.

"I know the drill by now. Control your breathing. Flex your fingers. Realise that it will pass," Shae explained.

Probably sensing that Shae was slowly cracking the door so a tiny sliver of light played around her feet, Adrian capitalised.

"Would you say that it happens often?"

Shrugging, Shae started to twirl a strand of hair around her index finger. Her hair, normally ash blond, was darker and stringy, the one physical sign of the aftermath of an attack that she hated almost more than the attack itself.

"Define often," Shae mumbled.

"Once a day? Once a week? Once a month?" Adrian suggested.

Shae's hazel eyes widened.

"God, no. I guess it doesn't happen too often. The attacks are triggered by certain events, which makes it harder to control."

"If you're able to identify what sets it off, you can probably try and avoid it most of the time," Adrian offered.

Shae nodded in agreement. A long silence followed before she took a leap.

* * *

"My attacker wore a black hoodie and skin-tight jeans. Being around teenagers for the majority of my waking hours complicates avoiding that image," Shae said.

Adrian waited patiently, accustomed to maintaining the delicate balance between being supportive and being intrusive. In her line of work, she had come to understand that the extent of achievement was a relative concept. For certain patients, simply getting out of bed was sometimes a brave accomplishment. Every step forward was a step in the direction of healing, however small it might be. It was key to acknowledge every little victory.

"Just by being able to identify your triggers, you take so much power out of the attack. You know that already, don't you?" Adrian said.

"Yes, Doctor. If you live with a beast, you get to know it quite well."

Adrian was struck by an image of her soon-to-be ex-husband gripping her wrists.

"Don't I know it."

She chastised herself the moment the words left her mouth. Judging by the fact that Shae was no longer staring at her feet but actually making meaningful eye contact for the first time, her interest had been piqued.

Adrian warred with the therapist in her. It was an unspoken rule—don't connect with a patient on a personal level. What complicated the matter was the look of utter desperation on Shae's face. In that moment, Adrian was certain that Shae would retreat if she didn't validate her suspicions. She folded.

"What? You think therapists have perfectly happy lives behind their picket fences?"

Needing to escape Shae's intense stare, Adrian made an unnecessary adjustment to her tea. Taking her time to stir in two spoons of sugar, she could feel an unexpected blush slowly creep up her neck and spill onto her cheeks. She pretended not to see Shae's amused grin when she stood up to open some windows.

"It's a little stuffy in here," Adrian explained.

Always defiant, Shae tipped her head to the side.

"Is it really?"

It was time for Adrian to get back on track. She reclaimed her seat and sipped on her tea, making careful eye contact across her cup.

"Tell me about your sleeping patterns."

By the smirk on Shae's face, Adrian could tell that she enjoyed witnessing the composed Dr. Ramsey off-balance for a moment.

"Well, that generally depends on the woman I'm with. I don't really have a pattern. You could say that I'm well-balanced, equally comfortable in the giving and receiving department."

The lapse in Adrian's composure was fleeting, and Dr. Ramsey was back to wearing her poker face.

"Sending them home before midnight allows the sheets to air and prevents me from having to fight for the right side of the bed," Shae continued.

Unmoved by Shae's inappropriate elaborations, Adrian drained her cup and wiped her palm across her lips in an effort to clear them of any sticky residue. She dragged an imaginary line across her brow with the back of her pen before she started rolling it between her thumb and index finger.

"Do you sleep fitfully once you've sent them home?"

"It depends on how good the sex was. Obviously, the ideal is to be utterly exhausted," Shae replied with a glint in her eye and a cocky smile tugging at the corners of her mouth.

"So, if you're not physically depleted, you sleep fitfully," Adrian said.

"Which happens quite often, since I have boatloads of stamina," Shae said, unwittingly stepping into the trap.

If there was something that Adrian was certain of, it was the fact that a patient's stubborn pride almost always served as a tool. Shae didn't disappoint. She scribbled notes in the file.

Irregular sleep patterns.

Panic attacks.

"Do you want to tell me about the attack?" Adrian risked steering the consultation into serious territory.

She purposefully didn't look up from her notes, allowing Shae some time to consider what she felt safe to divulge. After a few minutes of silence, she looked up to find Shae studying her closely. She was caught off-guard since she expected Shae to be peering out the window or down at her feet. Adrian couldn't quite identify the emotion in Shae's eyes, but she was moved by it.

"Where would you like me to start, Dr. Ramsey? Should I start by telling you how he locked me in my storeroom at school and tortured me for four hours?"

Adrian refused to blink. She was witnessing a breakthrough, and very little in life excited her more.

"Or do you prefer the part where I had to bargain with him not to rape me?"

Closing the folder, Adrian shifted her elbow to the armrest and rested her chin on her thumb, all the while maintaining eye contact. Shae seemed to be getting angrier by the second.

"Do you want to know what it was like staring into his cold, blue eyes when he finally slumped to the floor, leaving his brains behind against the wall?"

Adrian's heart started to hammer in her chest as Shae leaned even closer, her eyes wild and her fists clenched on her knees. She tried to control her breathing, knowing that she could not afford to show her patient that she was terrified in the moment.

"Should I admit that a part of me was relieved when he let out his last gurgled breath? I realised that I was possibly dying, bleeding out in that room, and what could potentially have been my last fucking thought was a hateful one. I was glad that he was dead."

Adrian relaxed slightly as Shae covered her eyes with her hands and sank back into the recliner.

"In what could have been my final moments, I didn't care that he had only been eighteen years old."

Shae cried softly behind her hands.

"I was glad that it was over."

Adrian let her cry for a few minutes before she tentatively placed a hand on her knee. She just left it there for a few seconds. When Shae finally looked out from behind her shaking hands, Adrian patted her lightly, smiled encouragingly, and left the room. She returned with a glass of water and a box of tissues.

"Do all your second dates end in tears like this?" Shae asked as she accepted the water.

Laughing, Adrian placed the box of tissues in the centre of the coffee table.

"It's been a while for me, but I do recall a few disastrous second dates," she admitted.

Sipping on the water, Shae plucked a tissue from the box and dabbed at the smudges of makeup under her eyes.

"Well, it hasn't been too long for me, but I generally look a little more attractive on my second dates. No sweaty palms, tangled hair, or puffy eyes," Shae said.

She let out a long sigh and rested the glass on her thigh.

"Now that I think about it, the better second dates normally end with sweaty palms and tangled hair," she said.

Adrian simply smiled.

"Yes, Dr. Ramsey, it's my favourite diversion technique. Humour, not sex. At least, not all the time," Shae said and winked.

Frustrated by her newfound tendency to blush like a teenager, Adrian decided to set some boundaries. Despite the obvious breakthrough, Shae had a lot of work to do in these sessions and Adrian needed her to commit to the process and take it seriously.

"Shae, you did really well today, and I think you can do even better. It's offensive when you don't take this process seriously. Do you realise that I devote my time to you?"

Shae grinned at her before sipping on her water again.

"You're so busy trying to get under my skin by making inappropriate comments about your sex life that you don't even realise that this can be beneficial to you. I'm committed to this, but if you decide to come back here for another session, I expect you to be here for the right reasons."

Shae drained the glass of water and chewed on the slice of lemon, wincing.

"Dr. Ramsey, the real question here is why. Why do I get under your skin?"

Adrian just gaped at Shae as she made her way to the door.

CHAPTER FOUR

Shae scanned the crowd of people around her.

Plunge had started out as a small coffee shop a year ago, but quickly shaped into a hideout for many local people, so the owner identified an opportunity to extend its trading hours and acquired a liquor license. Currently, Plunge was a coffee joint-slash-pub-slash-lounge with an eclectic mix of patrons.

A definite side effect of being stoical was the fact that people tended to underestimate the intensity of Shae's suffering. For some time after the attack, Shae had been terrified to go out in public. She had been on the edge of becoming a recluse, hiding away inside the four familiar walls of her house. Going to work was not optional, but as soon as the last bell would sound, she would rush home and lock herself in.

Shae's mother, Audrey, had always been distant and it was no different after the incident. She had stayed with Shae for a week after she was discharged from hospital. Taking care of all the practicalities, she cooked meals that were left untouched, ironed clothes that Shae had no intention of wearing, and tended to Shae's animals. Audrey's modus operandi had always been to run away from any situation she didn't have the courage to face. She had clearly figured that reliving the horror of the incident by talking about it would only serve to trap Shae in the past. She encouraged Shae to move forward as quickly as possible.

Not a word was spoken about the incident, and Audrey had left Shae to her own devices as soon as she saw an opportunity. Conditioned by a fierce single mother to be strong at all times, Shae had returned to work within three weeks after her discharge. In her absence, Fiona had repainted her classroom and reshuffled the desks. The tiles and the ceiling had also been replaced in the storeroom. By the time Shae had walked into the classroom, it looked vastly different from the gruesome crime scene that she had been carried from weeks earlier.

Despite this fact, Shae's heart had been gripped by a cold fist of fear when she had entered the room upon her return. Had Fiona not been beside her that first morning, Shae probably would have fainted. It had taken every ounce of courage Shae had possessed to keep returning to that room every day, but she had refused to be a victim. It had taken months for Shae to feel relatively safe at work, and she still avoided being alone in that room.

Plunge had been her first attempt at socialising after the attack. Initially, the crowd had been quite young and Shae had suffered many panic attacks brought on by innocent teenagers dressed in the same style as that of her attacker. Determined not to become housebound, Shae had embarked on a journey of discovery. She had done extensive reading and research on the matter of post-traumatic stress disorder. She had always believed that in order to slay your dragon, you had to know your dragon. She read every book she could find on the subject, performed every exercise, and considered every form of treatment—except for psychological analysis.

Plunge was her way of assessing her progress.

Sitting at her favourite corner booth right now, she felt proud. The panic attack she had suffered the week before had been the exception. Fiona should have known better than to sneak up on her while she was dressed like that.

"Hey, Shae."

Fiona's cheeks were rosy. Part of her weekly Sunday ritual entailed meeting Shae for coffee right after her jogging session.

"Hi, crazy person. Do you know what else gets your cheeks all rosy and is much more fun?"

Fiona slid into the booth across from Shae and pulled her fingers through clammy hair.

"Tennis?" Fiona asked.

"Not really what I had in mind, but in your case it would probably involve hairy balls. How was your run?"

Within minutes, their regular waiter delivered two steamy cappuccinos, two chicken mayo pancakes, and two slices of French toast. Wordlessly, Shae swopped one slice of toast for one of Fiona's pancakes, a testament to their comfortably familiar relationship.

"Tell me, Fi, what's it like, straight sex? All that friction and no climax?"

Fiona flipped Shae the bird before digging into her breakfast. She gave Shae an update on the adventure that was Fiona's life. Teacher by day, socialite by night, she had a busy life, and Shae often frowned upon some of the bad choices Fiona made. She was fearless and had no concept of boundaries.

"Don't dis it if you haven't done it, buddy," Fiona said.

Wincing, Shae pretended to shudder at the thought.

"I haven't stuck needles in my eyes yet, but I'm pretty sure I won't enjoy it, Fiona. What are your plans for today?"

Pouting at Shae, Fiona attempted sensually sucking the syrup off her fingers, but she only managed to look like a glutton on crack.

"Passion, Shae. That's the plan."

Frowning, Shae chucked her used serviette at Fiona.

"On a Sunday? Sometimes I wonder why we are friends. My mother would not approve," Shae said.

"Who are you kidding, Shae? Your mother would love me more than she loves you, which is why you refuse to let me meet her."

Being more of a variable in Shae's life than a constant, Audrey never quite stuck around for long enough to meet anyone of importance to Shae.

"It's not very easy to get that woman to stay in one spot for longer than a week. Besides, she does not simply hand out buckets of love, Fiona."

Fiona burped as she slid her empty plate across the table.

"Perhaps you should take that up with your shrink as well. How is that going?"

Signalling the waiter closer, Shae ordered a Coke Zero for herself and a Sprite for Fiona.

How was therapy going?

Shae pictured Dr. Ramsey blushing and shifting around in her seat uncomfortably. The image made her feel equal parts guilty and aroused. When she finally looked up, she was met by a frowning Fiona.

"Well, Miss McPherson, had I not known you for so long, I would probably not pick up on that little twinkle in your eye. Spill."

Shae knew that indulging Fiona would be the worst mistake she could make. There was no way on earth that she would let on that she was attracted to Adrian Ramsey. Mentally, Fiona was awarded a few brownie points for being attentive, though.

"Nothing to tell, really. She's trying her best to help and if I'm being completely honest, I am trying my best to get in her way," Shae explained.

"She? Your shrink is a hot woman?"

"Who said anything about her being hot?" Shae asked.

"Oh, you didn't have to. I know you so well. So, why are you being an ass to her?"

Shae had been trying to figure that part out for the better part of two weeks and hadn't come up with the answer, though she had managed to narrow it down to a few possibilities. Firstly, she could simply be taking out the anger she felt toward Mr. Foster on Dr. Ramsey. If Mr. Foster really planned on getting rid of her, Dr. Ramsey could be his secret weapon. There was no way that she was going to lose her job without putting up a fight.

It could also be that the idea of receiving therapy made Shae feel like a weakling. She had overcome many a challenge in her life and had never had to turn outward to do so. She found the mere fact that Mr. Foster had insisted on therapy insulting. The part that made all of this a little unfair was that poor Dr. Ramsey had been the object of her frustration, and she realised that her anger was misplaced.

Then, there was always the possibility that Shae was in fact not being hateful by flirting with Dr. Ramsey. Maybe she wasn't trying to get Dr. Ramsey to admit defeat. It was quite possible that she was trying to get under her skin because she found her disturbingly beautiful and utterly mysterious.

"I don't know. I've just been very resistant. I'm probably just pissed at Foster."

"Look, Shae. Regardless of how you may feel about his decision, this is not going away. I think the easiest way to get past this is to let it happen."

Shae cocked a brow at Fiona's sudden burst of pensiveness.

"It's a little like anal sex. It might be uncomfortable for the first few inches, but you'll breathe a sigh of relief once it's over," Fiona said and shattered her fleeting moment of maturity.

"There she is, the inappropriate foul mouth I know and love," Shae said.

They finished their cold drinks and chatted about the week ahead, which for Fiona entailed a lot of training. She was a brilliant teacher, but an even better hockey coach. She had been trying to get Shae on board for years, with little success. The closest Shae came to being active was playing the odd game of golf. She'd much rather bury her nose in a book, which was exactly what she planned as she bid Fiona farewell that morning.

CHAPTER FIVE

"Dr. Ramsey?"

"Sorry, Ella. You were saying?"

Adrian had been in a miserable mood all morning. In fact, the mood had followed her home the previous Sunday night when she'd woken up on her parents' couch, wrapped in Jonah's blanket and clutching Jayden's teddy. Her divorce had been finalised the previous week, and despite being relieved, Adrian had also been emotional. The sense of failure that followed the finalisation of her divorce had caught her unaware.

Three days later, Adrian still felt off-kilter and Ella was starting to lose her patience with her. It was evidenced by the narrowed eyes peering over her spectacles and the tapping foot in Adrian's doorway.

"Miss McPherson is in reception. Do you need a moment?" Ella asked. However, her face told Adrian to pull herself together.

"I'm good, Ella. Please send her in."

Adrian swivelled her chair away from the window she had been staring out of. She slipped her compact mirror out of her drawer and unnecessarily wiped her fingers across her perfect brows. She hastily applied a fresh layer of lipstick and shut the drawer as Shae entered.

"That colour is perfect for you," Shae said as Ella closed the door behind her.

"Thank you, Miss McPherson."

Shae seemed surprised to see a smile tugging at the corners of Dr. Ramsey's mouth instead of the poker face she usually reserved for the incessant onslaught of flirting.

"It's Shae, remember?"

"I do. Have a seat, Shae. How have you been?"

Her grip was strong as she wrapped her fingers around Shae's own. Shae bit down on her lower lip and Adrian wasn't sure if she was trying to stifle a laugh or biting back some clever retort about a woman with a strong handshake. She sat down opposite Adrian and smiled.

"An ass, Dr. Ramsey."

"Excuse me?" Adrian asked as her blush intensified.

Shae's smile turned to a chuckle.

"I've been a complete ass since I started seeing you. I realised it this weekend and I hope that you'll accept my sincere apology."

Battling to hide her surprise, Adrian cocked a brow and cleared her throat.

"I really am sorry, Dr. Ramsey."

"You can call me Adrian. I accept and appreciate your apology," Adrian replied.

"Wow, first-name basis in only a few weeks. I bet we'll be down to terms of endearment in a month," Shae said.

Adrian sighed lightly but didn't say a word.

"That was just a joke. I do tend to make inappropriate jokes— even when I'm not being an ass," Shae continued.

Opening the folder that had been sitting on the coffee table in anticipation of Shae's arrival, Adrian scribbled a few notes. She finally glanced up at her patient and flashed her a quick smile.

"Noted," she said. "Do you want to tell me why you were antagonistic in your prior sessions?"

"I've thought about it, and I think I was just really angry with Mr. Foster for sending me here."

Adrian nodded quietly, hoping that Shae would elaborate on her feelings. She had already identified the fact that Shae was in the habit of diminishing her feelings, which certainly wasn't healthy.

"So, my anger was misplaced. I realise that I have no other option than to just get through these sessions, despite the fact that I still don't believe I need them."

And there was that stubborn streak again. Adrian scribbled more notes.

"It's exactly that," Shae said.

Adrian paused and looked at her then.

"The scribbling. The notes. The reports. That's what makes this so uncomfortable," Shae continued.

Studying her patient carefully, Adrian thoughtfully tugged at her bottom lip, pulling it away from her teeth. Suddenly, she closed the folder and dropped it on the table. She made a show of slipping her Appelboom Montblanc fountain pen into the inside pocket of her tailored jacket.

"Better?"

"Don't you think that if I happen to say something of importance you'll remember it once I leave?" Shae asked.

Adrian nodded in agreement. "You're absolutely correct. I will make notes in your absence when I feel the need. Deal?"

Seemingly more at ease, Shae sat back in the recliner and crossed her feet.

"I suppose the logical starting point for these sessions would be the discussion of what Mr. Foster calls 'The Incident,'" Shae stated.

"Only if you're ready to discuss it with me."

In Adrian's experience, reliving a traumatic event almost always invoked the same emotions in her patients. Observing Shae closely, Adrian could tell that it was no different for Shae when she wiped her palms across her thighs, leaving faint sweat stains on her light jeans.

"Shae, have you spoken to anyone about the attack before?" Adrian asked as she leaned forward and placed a tentative hand on Shae's trembling knee.

Wordlessly, Shae shook her head.

"Can I perhaps just slip away to get you a glass of water?"

Shae nodded and wiped at her brow as Adrian stepped outside. Adrian returned with a pitcher of water and two glasses.

"Thanks, Dr. Ramsey," Shae said as she accepted the drink.

"It's Adrian, remember? Take your time."

Shae took a few sips from her glass and drew lines through the condensation as she started talking.

Devon Nelson, an eighteen-year-old boy, had enrolled in Willowmore mere months before the attack. He had been labelled a weirdo by most of the teachers, but Shae hadn't had much contact with him. He hadn't taken any of her classes, and none of her students had ever mentioned him. Looking dishevelled, Devon had showed up at the Zen Den two weeks before the attack, and Shae had encouraged her students to make him feel welcome. He partook in the dart games and chess matches that had been scheduled for that week's entertainment. According to Shae, she had found it very difficult to connect with the strange boy and had mostly left him to wander around the den, figuring that he would open up to her when he felt that he could trust her.

He hadn't shown up at the Zen Den the following Friday. It had been a normal Friday afternoon for Shae. The students had enjoyed an afternoon of Pictionary and Rummikub and Shae had locked up the den after the last students had reluctantly made their way home. On her way to her car, she had realised that she'd left the papers that she had been meant to grade that weekend behind in her classroom. She stopped by the classroom, and as she opened the door, a cold hand had slipped around her neck, crushing her windpipe.

Devon had shoved her inside and immediately locked the door. He had dragged her to the storeroom at the back of the classroom and locked the sliding gate, trapping them both in the small enclosure. Then the bargaining started. Shae had begged for her life while Devon had frantically quoted from the Bible, pacing the small room and tugging at his hair. There had been no reasoning with him, and he had continued to subject Shae to the most unbelievable acts of violence. The whole dreadful incident had ended with a bullet in Shae's thigh, another through the young man's skull, and a terror-stricken teacher hunched in the corner of a room that seemed to grow smaller by the second.

By the time Shae had recounted the horrid details of the day that had changed her life irrevocably, Adrian was clinging to her own glass of water in an effort not to cover her mouth in horror. There was a thin layer of perspiration across Shae's brow. Not once did Adrian interrupt her. Now that Shae had finally stopped talking, Adrian lifted her brows and shook her head slightly.

"Shae, I actually understand your resistance a little better now. Having lived through that kind of horror and still maintaining the kind of functionality that you do, you must question what I can possibly add to your healing process."

Adrian closed her eyes and shook her head again.

"What you managed to do on your own is nothing short of a miracle. I am astonished."

Shae relaxed against the recliner, then shuffled around uncomfortably. "Sorry about sweating all over your expensive furniture, Doc."

Attempting to regain her professional composure, Adrian drained her glass and sat taller.

"That's why they call it the hot seat, I suppose," Adrian said.

She needed time to absorb the details of what she had just heard, but her patient was sitting in front of her, probably feeling exposed and more vulnerable than ever before. Part of being a good therapist was the ability to store information in the back of your mind. Folders and folders of misery sat on a shelf of unconsciousness only to be extracted once she was alone—mostly when all she wanted to do was to escape from the darkness.

"Maybe we can swop chairs next time," Shae said.

"I doubt that that chair can get any hotter. In fact, the worst is over, Shae."

Shae shrugged and stared out the window.

"I hope you won't underestimate the magnitude of what you've just accomplished, Shae. Carrying a burden like that around for so long could not have been easy."

Shae leaned forward in the recliner and winced as her shirt clung to her back.

"Do you know how many people discover sweat glands they never thought they had from sitting in that chair?" Adrian asked.

Shae scrunched up her nose in what Adrian assumed was disgust.

"Now you're thinking that you're lucky I just renovated!"

"Pretty much, yeah," Shae admitted.

"I personally don't know why people find it so humiliating. Sweating is as natural as urinating, and we're not embarrassed to do that," Adrian explained.

Shae's legs were stretched out in a more relaxed pose than Adrian had witnessed before.

"Everything in life serves a purpose, and sweating is no different. It's not simply a by-product of exertion," Adrian continued.

"Now you're just tempting me to be inappropriate," Shae mumbled.

"Sweat glands host stem cells that assist in the healing of wounds. Coincidence? I think not."

Shae rolled her eyes at Dr. Ramsey.

"Come on now, Doctor. Don't tell me you really believe that the very unsexy stains down my back is busy healing me from emotional scarring."

Bearing a look on her face that begged Shae to prove her wrong, Adrian shrugged and smiled.

"You don't believe in coincidences?" Shae asked.

Adrian sucked her lower lip into her mouth as she really considered the thought for a while.

"I don't think that I do."

Shae nodded slowly, and when she spoke her voice seemed so small.

"Then you agree that Devon picked me for a reason. It's no coincidence that I left those papers behind and had to go back for them. It's no coincidence that for once, none of my students offered to stay and walk me to my car."

Adrian was caught off-balance by the unexpected turn the conversation had taken.

"It's no coincidence that my girlfriend was out of town and wouldn't notice that I hadn't returned home. It's no coincidence that the janitor had knocked off earlier than usual, only to return at ten that night, leaving me weeping and trembling in a puddle of blood that soaked into every part of my being for four hours straight."

Adrian linked her hands on her lap, secretly digging the nail of her right thumb into the soft flesh of her left palm.

"It's no coincidence that I had left my cell phone in my car. It's no coincidence that Fiona didn't join us at the Zen Den that afternoon like so many afternoons before. It's no coincidence that there was not one fucking soul in the vicinity of the school to hear the gunshots go off!"

Slumping forward, Shae covered her eyes as heart-wrenching sobs racked her body. Adrian closed her eyes momentarily and willed her professionalism to make an appearance and remind her that this was no time to feel her patient's pain. She took a deep breath, and instead of laying a hand on Shae's shoulder like she wanted, she cleared her throat and held out the box of tissues.

"Still don't believe in coincidences?" Shae asked as she blew her nose.

Adrian didn't have to think about it very long.

"No, I don't. I know it would probably feel good thinking that it was all just a coincidence. That way we can stop trying to find purpose or meaning. We both know that that's the hard part—making sense of it all."

Shae nodded and sighed lightly.

"If it's all just a coincidence, we don't have to do the hard work. We don't have to pick up the pieces and put ourselves together again," Adrian said.

Shae wiped the back of her hand across her puffy eyes.

"People who believe in coincidence also like to say that time heals. Time doesn't heal, Shae. Doing the hard work does, and that is why you're well on your way."

Pointing at Shae, Adrian leaned forward.

"You, Shae McPherson, are brave enough to do the hard work."

Laughing weakly, Shae made a show of performing the most pathetic fist pump Adrian had ever seen.

CHAPTER SIX

"So, you want to give this thing a name?"

Shae leaned back in what she now referred to as the hot seat. Crossing her legs, she started nibbling on her bottom lip.

"Shae, it's always had a name. I just think if we call it what it is, it's easier to deal with," Adrian explained.

Staring out the window, she clasped her hands together in her lap. Her brow was furrowed in concentration as she thought of ways to make Shae understand the relevance of identifying the demon that had been breathing down her neck.

"Do you have an ugly ginger kid in your class?"

"Excuse me?" Shae said, frowning.

Adrian shifted gears.

"There used to be a girl in my sociology class called Victoria. She had frizzy red hair and her entire face was covered in freckles. To top it off, the poor woman was morbidly obese."

Listening intently, Shae repeatedly rolled her middle finger around her thumb—a sure sign that she was paying close attention.

"Needless to say, poor Victoria kept to herself and had very few friends. Eventually, I was paired with her for an experiment, and avoiding her was no longer an option," Adrian said.

"You avoided the fat, freckled chick because she wasn't popular?" Shae asked.

Adrian was abashed, and Shae was clearly amused to see the familiar blush creeping up her neck.

"I'm a therapist, not a saint. Once I'd spent some time with Victoria, I learned that not only was she hilarious, she was also one of the kindest people I've ever met. We became great friends, and I purposefully paired up with her for every other assignment that year."

Bobbing her foot up and down, Shae flashed Adrian a smile.

"What a pair you must have made, the striking raven-haired student hanging out with the freckled Oompa Loompa."

The blush was back in full swing, and Adrian's ears felt like they were glowing.

"I think you're missing the point," Adrian said.

"You think that naming my affliction will be beneficial to my healing process."

Adrian nodded slowly. "I really think it will."

Shaking her head, Shae took a deep breath as Adrian slipped a pamphlet across the coffee table. In bright yellow letters, her diagnosis glared at her: PTSD. Reluctantly, she picked up the pamphlet and shot Adrian a piercing look.

"Did you find this abandoned in a drawer, Adrian? Or did you pick it up especially for me?"

Adrian hadn't expected Shae to accept her diagnosis without putting up a fight. Most patients preferred not to attach a clinical term to their struggles, because it generally tended to substantialise it. A clinical term was definite and required action.

"I happen to have a stash, Shae, because PTSD is not uncommon and I also happen to treat a few patients who suffer from it."

Shae seemed irritable and her playful mood had suddenly vanished.

"PTSD is something that soldiers suffer from, Adrian. I didn't flee for my life, dodging landmines while trying to outrun armed gunmen. I witnessed a crazy kid who meant nothing to me commit suicide."

Adrian braced herself for what was probably the worst part of every treatment cycle. Patients often had a temporary setback once a therapist validated the extent of emotional injury that had been inflicted. Sometimes, perceiving something as horrible was more manageable when it hadn't been confirmed to be every bit as horrible by a third party, especially a trained therapist. In the mind of the patient, there was always the possibility that he or she might be overreacting, or that the mind might be fabricating things that were not real.

Adrian's professor always explained this phenomenon by explaining the concept of reaction. He often used the example of a child's reaction being determined to a large extent by that of a parent. Often, children gauge the intensity of injury by assessing the level of panic apparent from the behaviour of a parent. A child will storm into a room with blood spurting from his forehead in a moderate state of distress. How a parent then reacts to the child will determine whether the level of distress is heightened or alleviated. A fainting mother signals to the child that he has reason to be concerned, while a calm mother signals that there is no real danger to fear.

Similarly, if a trained therapist validates the existence of your challenges by giving them a clinical name, the level of panic could be heightened.

"How is that any different from what you experienced, Shae?"

Shae's eyes widened as she leaned forward in the recliner.

"Are you kidding me? My ordeal was over in a few hours, while these soldiers are tormented for months on end. They are deprived of basic needs for extended periods of time with only their fear to keep them company."

Nodding in silence, Adrian allowed Shae some time to connect the dots. She was confident of Shae's level of enlightenment, and she had no doubt that she needed little more than a shove in the right direction. She wasn't disappointed.

"Fine. I was also disconnected from the world for a few hours and perhaps deprived of basic needs."

Pointing to the pamphlet, Adrian smiled.

"In my professional opinion, you can really benefit from the treatment usually associated with PTSD. All I am asking is that you familiarise yourself with the condition and consider the treatment."

Shae poured herself a glass of water from the pitcher occupying the centre of the coffee table. She smiled when the omnipresent slice of lemon slipped into her glass.

"You know what else goes well with lemon?" Shae asked.

"Tequila?"

Shae cocked a brow. "Oh, Dr. Ramsey, you dark horse. I was going to say Kola Tonic and lemonade," she said.

"I am not above bribery. Let's make a deal. If you agree to subject yourself to some PTSD treatments, I will have an entire pitcher of Kola Tonic and lemonade sitting in that spot every week."

Shae looked at her through narrowed eyes, clearly considering the generous offer. In Adrian's mind it was quite simple: the treatment wasn't really optional, so Shae might as well benefit in every way possible.

"Talk to me about these treatments. I am not about to be bribed into something I know nothing about."

Dr. Ramsey took her time explaining the various types of PTSD treatments. Starting off, she explained the purpose of what was called Prolonged Exposure Therapy, also known as PET. This type of therapy was also referred to as Talk Therapy. Shae would be required to talk about her trauma extensively, wording her emotions and fears repetitively in an effort not to avoid her fears, but to relive them in the safe environment controlled by her therapist.

Next, she spoke to Shae about Cognitive Processing Therapy. The objective with CPT was to eliminate any negative feelings, such as guilt, that Shae might be experiencing as a result of her trauma. The patient is required to explain all the negative thoughts or feelings that might be halting the healing process, while the therapist is meant to challenge every one of these thoughts. The ultimate result one would attempt to achieve through CPT would be for the patient to change his or her thinking about the trauma, replacing negative thoughts with more uplifting ones.

Adrian paused for a while, allowing the information to sink in.

"There was always going to be too much talking involved, I suppose," Shae said.

"I would add ice to that pitcher," Adrian said to sweeten the deal.

Shae leaned back in her chair as Adrian explained the last two types of treatment. Eye Movement Desensitisation and Reprocessing involved the introduction of sound or movement while the patient talks about certain memories of the trauma. Focusing on an external sound or movement eventually allows the patient to think of the same memory without feeling the fear. The last treatment was called Stress Inoculation Training. This was what Adrian identified as the maintenance plan after having successfully completed one or all the other treatments. SIT was the process of training the patient to manage stress and problem-solving in a healthy manner.

Sighing deeply, Shae leaned back in her recliner, rested her right foot on her left knee, and slipped her hands under her thighs.

"Wow, that's quite a bit of information, Doc. Do I even still need that Holy Grail of a pamphlet?"

There was a knock on the door before Ella peeked around the door.

"Sorry to disturb, Dr. Ramsey, but I think we have an emergency."

Adrian's brow furrowed and she sat up straight, her face etched with real concern.

"Adrian, I'm sure we can continue this discussion next week," Shae offered politely.

Thankful, but torn, Adrian winced. "Are you sure, Shae? I am so sorry to do this to you."

Standing up, Shae gripped the pamphlet, pointed at the pitcher of water, and winked at Adrian.

"Certainly. Just don't forget the ice, Dr. Ramsey."

Shae was almost knocked to the floor as an unruly, clearly unkempt, teenager burst through the door. Adrian managed to wrap her arm around Shae's waist just in time to steady her. She apologised profusely and ordered the offending girl to take a seat and calm down.

"I am fucking calm!" the girl shouted.

"Could have fooled me," Shae mumbled as she took her leave.

* * *

"He can't fucking do this!"

Taking a deep breath, Adrian closed the door and headed to the credenza in search of Jax's file, taking a minute to compose herself. She didn't appreciate Jax's rude behaviour and needed to remind herself that reacting to her outburst with anger would not serve either one of them well. She cleared her throat and turned to Jax, who was now draped across the recliner like a wet towel. She was seated sideways, feet dangling from the one armrest, her head resting on the other. She stared at the ceiling through angry slits.

"Hi, Jax. Please calm down and tell me what upset you enough for you to burst into my office and slam into one of my patients."

Jax didn't honour her with even as much as a glance in her direction.

"You mean the weak fucking dyke that almost landed on her tight little ass?"

Adrian was shocked. She was baffled that Jax had been able to identify Shae's sexual orientation in what must have been two seconds flat. She hated stereotypes, and people like Shae made the idea of practicing it seem completely ridiculous. Nothing about her gave the idea that she was a lesbian.

Adrian had always found the mystery of figuring out a woman's sexual orientation quite sexy—until Frederick had ridiculed bisexual women by pointing out that even in Greek mythology, Iphis had to be turned into a man before Ianthe could marry the love of her life, because "inarguably, the dick stays slick." She had vowed that Frederick would never discover that she had once considered herself among these "ungodly fence-sitters" as he liked to call them.

"Yes, my learned *therapest*. It takes one to know one."

Jax's favourite pastime was creating her own derogatory dictionary. Adrian was often referred to as a *therapest* who dished out *diagnonsenses* for a living. She always figured that Jax would be a wonderful artist if she ever decided to put all that creativity to good use. Adrian certainly had her work cut out for her with Jax.

Less than six months ago, Jax had stormed into her office in a similar fashion, followed by her desperate mother. Jax had been suspended from school for wearing a shirt in support of the "Free the Nipple" campaign, but that was just the proverbial final nail in the coffin. She was a very outspoken, anger-filled teenager with no filter. She said whatever she wanted and never considered the consequences of her actions.

It hadn't taken Adrian very long to identify the root of Jax's deep-seated anger. She loathed her emotionally abusive, military father. Everything she did or said was aimed at challenging his authority and "rocking his fucking cage" as she freely admitted. Adrian had yet to live through a session with Jax where her father wasn't the main topic of discussion and the object of her misery, which was why her sexual orientation hadn't been revealed until now.

"What has you this upset, Jax?"

"Fucking shrinks. I bare my soul to you and you fucking divert the conversation!"

Shaking her head, Adrian jotted the date down in Jax's file.

"Jax, you are yet to start a conversation today. These outbursts are the opposite of a conversation. Instead of being heard, you're being placated. So, let's just calm down and really talk for a few minutes."

Jax rolled her eyes at the ceiling since she was still not making eye contact with Adrian.

"So, would you prefer talking about your sexual orientation before you tell me what caused your earlier outburst?"

Jax started picking the remnants of black nail polish from her thumb.

"I'd prefer talking about the hot piece of ass that occupied this seat before me," Jax said as she pretended to sniff the seat of the recliner.

"Would you like it if I discussed you with any of my other patients?"

Adrian mentally rapped herself across the knuckles as she momentarily lost her composure. For some reason, Jax's inappropriate carnal references to Shae McPherson unsettled her. Jax finally sat upright, kicked her shoes off, and hugged her knees to her chest. She seemed so much smaller than when she had charged into the office a short while ago.

"I'm indifferent."

That was the last thing Jax Wesley was.

"I'm an indifferent, out-of-control, rude lesbo. Now fix me, Dr. Frank-N-Farter."

Adrian smiled at her. This kid was sixteen years old and she was referencing a character from *The Rocky Horror Picture Show*, a movie that was released in 1975. Jax was by no means a typical teenager. She often referred to herself as being stuck in the wrong era, with the wrong parents, in the wrong country. She had a tendency of being a little dramatic.

"That was one of my favourite movies, actually. I don't really mind being likened to the great Dr. Frank-N-Furter. After all, he knew the secret to life itself," Adrian said.

This earned her another dramatic eye roll.

Leaning forward and dropping Jax's file on the coffee table, Adrian pointed at her.

"You're in luck, young lady. Despite this aggressive bravado you insist on displaying, I really like you and I think you have immense potential. For that reason, I will share the secret to life itself with you."

For the first time since Adrian started treating Jax, she displayed an emotion other than anger. She seemed vulnerable and even just a little hopeful.

"There are not very many things in life that you can be sure of. Regardless of who you are, life deals you an equal hand of cards. It has nothing to do with Lady Luck. You will live through some horrible things, but you can count on some wonderful things crossing your path as well."

Adrian was pleasantly surprised when Jax still didn't deliver her habitual eye roll.

"The key is to talk about it. All of it. The good and the bad. You talk the shit out of it."

Whispering from behind a cupped hand, Adrian smiled.

"Don't tell anyone, but that fancy degree on the wall, just about nine years of studying and many more of treating patients from all walks of life dealing with all kinds of problems, culminates in that one line of wisdom. You talk the shit out of it."

CHAPTER SEVEN

"Thanks, Easton. I really appreciate the offer, but I won't be able to make lunch. Take Avril with you."

Since Adrian's meltdown a few weeks ago, Easton followed her around like a shadow. Adrian adored her baby sister, but she also missed having her privacy. She was fully aware of the fact that Easton had faked an argument with their mother in order to keep an eye on her. Easton had spent every night for the last two weeks on Adrian's couch.

"But Avril gags when I order meat," Easton complained.

"Just ignore her. You'll be fine."

"She also licks her straw in what she feels is a very seductive manner when we end up with a male waiter."

Adrian winced.

"That's a little harder to ignore. Maybe insist on a female waiter?" Adrian suggested.

"Well, clearly you're not going to budge. See you tonight, Adrian."

Adrian disconnected the call only to dial her mother's number. It wasn't very long before Ally's cheery voice sounded on the other side.

"Mom, you have to take back your child. I need my couch."

"Hi, baby. Already? Can't you keep her for another week? Her indentations are just starting to lift from our couch."

Adrian put her mother on speaker while she applied fresh lipstick and powdered her nose. She reached for the stack of folders that Ella had left on the corner of her desk this morning. The folder on top indicated that her next patient was Shae McPherson.

"No, Mom. The only time I am by myself now is when I poop."

"Really? You are so lucky! Easton actually likes soaking in the bath while *I* poop," Ally said.

Adrian jumped in her seat when she heard a chuckle from the door. Shae was leaning against the door with her arms crossed over her chest.

"Mom, I have to go. Please call Easton."

"I'll think about it. Love you, Adrian."

Adrian disconnected the call and waited for Shae to take her seat. She shuffled around the folders, hoping to find her self-respect somewhere in the pile. Mentally cursing Ella for not announcing Shae's arrival, Adrian grabbed Shae's folder and headed to the seating area.

"Your mother is so delightful," Shae said.

"Hi, Shae. That she is. I'm so sorry you had to hear that. I'm not sure why Ella didn't see you in today."

Spotting the pitcher of Kola Tonic and lemonade in the centre of the coffee table, Shae smiled and filled her glass.

"Would you like some, Dr. Ramsey?"

Declining the offer, Adrian sat down in her regular spot and watched her patient slugging down her sweet drink like she'd been trapped in the desert for days. Something about the way Shae groaned in satisfaction made Adrian feel like she was missing out on a special treat.

"On second thought, I could use some sugar," Adrian said as she filled another glass.

"You mix a mean drink, Adrian. Thank you."

After taking a few sips, Adrian had to agree. She was glad that Shae had agreed to experiment with some treatments in return for the special treat. She'd never gone through this much trouble for any other patient.

"I have to admit that I outdid myself this time."

Finishing her drink, Shae removed the slice of lemon from the bottom of her glass and started nibbling on it. Adrian let out a breath as she placed her glass on the coffee table and crossed her legs.

"I suppose this is where I live up to my end of the bargain, hey?" Shae said.

"Yes, I think so. I figured we should try the PET if you're ready," Adrian suggested.

There was silence in the room for a while as Shae warred with her feelings, and Adrian steeled herself for what she expected would be one of the most gruelling sessions she'd ever had. Both women lifted their gazes at the same time.

"So, this PET is what they call Talk Therapy? Where do I start? I mean, I told you exactly what happened."

"PET is more about remembering physical details of the attack in a safe environment. Naturally, we tend to shut down any memory of the events that traumatised us. This behaviour is not conducive to healing, and that's why therapists encourage patients to relive the finer details of the event in a space that is detached from the scene."

Clicking her knuckles, Shae seemed a little paler than moments before.

"Shae, PET wouldn't make one bit of sense if you don't feel safe here with me."

Shae took a deep breath and discarded the slice of lemon.

"I don't mind spending a little more time on getting you ready for this," Adrian offered.

"No, Adrian. I do. I feel safe here."

Smiling, Adrian nodded slowly. From experience, she knew that it was very unlikely that Shae would start this difficult conversation without being prompted. She touched Shae's knee to draw her out of hiding.

"What were you wearing that day, Shae?"

Shae turned her gaze to the window.

"I had returned from a hockey trip earlier that afternoon. Fiona is the hockey coach and she had convinced me to accompany her on a tour to help her supervise the girls. I hadn't had time to change, so I showed up to the den in my chino shorts and a blue golf shirt."

Adrian reached for the folder and suddenly remembered that she had agreed not to make notes in Shae's presence.

"Shae, would it be okay if I made notes now? I just want to capture the details, so I can refer to it when I need to. I don't want you to have to repeat yourself if I don't deem it beneficial to you."

Shae was still staring out the window, but she nodded at Adrian's request.

"What colour were the chino shorts?"

Suddenly, Shae turned her attention to Adrian. Adrian was surprised to find her scowling, and the sudden mood swing indicated to her that she'd already hit a nerve.

"What fucking difference does it make?"

"It probably doesn't," Adrian lied. "But since PET is about the details, we should make sure our account is very specific."

Shae shook her head and shifted in the recliner until her entire body faced the window.

"White. The chino shorts were white."

Adrian nodded as the significance of the colour of Shae's shorts became more evident. If Shae had been wearing white shorts, she was probably more traumatised by the stark contrast of the crimson colour of the blood that would have been covering her shorts shortly after the shooting. She scribbled a short note.

"What shoes were you wearing?"

Shae filled her glass again and pushed the ice around the glass, staring at the amber liquid.

"I'm not sure that this was a fair trade-off anymore," Shae said.

Adrian took a deep breath and picked up her own glass for another taste. She made a show of wiping her mouth afterward.

"I don't know, Shae. This is a pretty awesome drink."

Sighing, Shae rolled her eyes.

"Humour me, Shae."

Shae sucked an ice cube into her mouth and rolled it around her tongue while Adrian picked invisible fluff off her pants. Adrian was fairly certain that Shae was not fooled by her feigned indifference.

"Dr. Ramsey, we both know that those pair of pants are as clear as your conscience."

Adrian's cheeks coloured and she swallowed softly.

"I'm not perfect, Shae."

Shae clearly regretted her comment the moment she recognised the flicker in Adrian's eyes as pain. Leaning forward in the recliner, she touched Adrian's arm lightly.

"I'm sorry, Adrian. That wasn't meant to be hurtful. I guess I still get personal when I try to distract attention from my own discomfort."

Shrugging, Adrian accepted what she considered to be a sincere apology from Shae. She resolved to grow thicker skin. She couldn't afford to let her professionalism slip in the light of her own personal tragedy.

"So, do you remember what shoes you wore?"

Sitting back in the recliner, she faced Adrian head-on and looked her in the eye as she mentioned as many detailed facts as she could recall from that day. Those facts ranged from the type of shoes that Shae had been wearing to the texture of the hairs on the back of Devon's hands. After a long while, Adrian took a moment to assess their progress.

"How did that feel, Shae? Talking to me about what happened?"

Shae explained to Adrian how initially, she had felt a tightening in her throat as she painted a picture of the day that had changed her life irrevocably. Her palms had been sweaty and her scalp had been prickling as she described Devon in the finest detail. She admitted, though, that there had been less of a reaction from her body by the time she recounted the events that had unfolded when the paramedics had arrived on the scene to transport her to hospital.

"Shae, have you been able to recall most of these things before?"

"Actually, I'm not sure. I don't think I ever really felt safe enough to think about what happened. I just always figured that thinking about it was pointless and destructive."

Shaking her head, Adrian finally closed the folder and slipped her Montblanc into the breast pocket of a striped dress shirt that fit her like a second layer of skin.

"Quite the contrary, actually. I will go out on a limb and say that today's session has already made a difference," Adrian replied.

Draining her glass, Shae pulled her fingers through her hair.

"Hold your horses, Doctor. That was far from comfortable for me."

"Shae, having these conversations will never be comfortable for you, but it will be less painful the more we talk it through."

Studying her nails, Shae attempted to change the topic.

"Do you ever get tired of the power suits?"

Adrian looked down at her pants and tugged at the jacket that she always felt rounded off this particular dress shirt perfectly. For a moment she considered humouring Shae, but then she decided that keeping the momentum of their session going was more important.

"The next time we talk about the incident you'll probably remember other details. It's like working your way through the layers of an onion."

"I hope you don't," said Shae.

"Excuse me?"

"The suits. I hope you don't get tired of them. If I'm going to be tortured on a weekly basis, I will appreciate more benefits from it than a well-mixed drink."

Adrian blushed despite her best efforts at staying in control. She gave Shae a look that was meant to remind her of her commitment to keep their chat appropriate. It was met by a chuckle and a shrug from Shae, who held her hands up in the air, as if to surrender.

"Hey, I never promised you perfection, Adrian. I warned you about my tendency to be impolite."

Taking the final sweet sip from her glass, Adrian recrossed her legs and cleared her throat.

"Well, Shae, I happen to be a perfectionist. That means I can't close your file at the end of this if I don't feel like I've changed your life for the better."

Glancing at her wristwatch, Shae seemed almost disappointed to find that her time was up. Picking the final slice of lemon from the pitcher and sucking on it lightly, she leaned forward.

"That snug dress shirt has already done just that, Dr. Ramsey."

CHAPTER EIGHT

Staring out the window, Adrian absentmindedly ran the fingers of her right hand across her ring finger that used to carry an extravagant eight-carat diamond ring. Frederick had taken pride in spoiling her with exorbitant gifts—whether it was after her taste was never of consequence. A knock on the door startled her.

"Penny for your thoughts?"

Shae was wearing black skinny jeans and a white tank top. A pink-and-white-checked shirt with three-quarter sleeves covered the tank top that spun across her breasts. Her blond curls were held together loosely by a silver clip that had its work cut out for it. A few strands formed into a curl that had managed to escape on the one side now brushed her cheek. Shae blew at it lightly through one corner of her mouth, only for the stubborn curl to return to its original position.

"Really?" Adrian asked.

"Absolutely," Shae said as she plonked down in the recliner.

For the past two months, Shae had sat in that same recliner, pouring her heart out to Adrian. She hadn't missed one session and she had surprised Adrian with her commitment to the treatment plan. Discussing the attack in the finest details on several occasions had served its intended purpose, and Shae had reaped the benefits. She had admitted that not trying to escape the memories of that fateful Friday afternoon and gently allowing them to pass had been the easier and healthier route.

The second part of her treatment, Cognitive Processing Therapy, had been significantly more difficult. During CPT sessions, Shae was required to identify any negative feelings surrounding the attack that possibly halted her healing process. The most pivotal moment of this part of the process was when Shae realised and confessed to Adrian that she felt guilty for not being able to convince Devon not to take his own life. The part where Adrian had to challenge these feelings of guilt and turn it into something positive was proving to be next to impossible. It was a work in progress.

"Come on, Doc. I already pay you quite a bit of pennies so you can have unrestricted access to mine."

Feeling particularly positive, Adrian momentarily forgot that Shae was a patient and not a friend.

"I was thinking about my wedding ring and how it symbolised my entire marriage."

Adrian realised that her regret at the slip of professionalism was probably visible to Shae as a blush crept up her neck. She cleared her throat and immediately started watering her succulent, a sure sign that she was in distress.

"How that poor thing is still alive is beyond me," Shae said.

Adrian turned to her, a puzzled look on her face.

"Every time you treat me like a human being instead of a subject, you water it. You know it can only handle sips of water at a time, right?"

Adrian wiped the droplets of water off the plump little leaves and returned the succulent to its resting place on the windowsill. When she took a seat, Shae had poured them each a glass of Kola Tonic and lemonade. Ruminating on Shae's observation, Adrian sipped on her drink. Finally, she smacked her lips together and shifted in her recliner.

"I do that?"

"Sure you do. I'm going to assume that the absence of that whopper of a ring means that you are now divorced?"

Nodding slowly, Adrian mentally repeated the term that now defined her relationship status. *Divorced*. It didn't feel as terrible as she anticipated; it felt liberating in some way.

"Divorced. Yes, that's me," Adrian said.

"Oh, come on, Doc. I'm sure if the tables were turned, you'd be telling me that a legal term doesn't define me."

"Look at you, *Doctor* McPherson! When did you get this enlightened?" Adrian chuckled.

"Adrian, you know I am absolutely perfect and just come here for the drinks, right?"

"Don't forget the tight suits," Adrian said.

They were interrupted by an aggressive banging on the door, which startled Shae so much that she almost spilled her drink down her own shirt. Leaning forward, Adrian squeezed Shae's shoulder and apologised, wondering what the hell Ella was being paid for.

"I'm so sorry, Shae."

The next moment, Jax stormed inside.

"How fucking cosy! I can't say that I blame you for crossing the line with this one, Dr. Frank-N-Farter," Jax said as she pointed to a still visibly shaken Shae.

Paying Jax no attention, Adrian gave Shae an apologetic smile.

"Are you okay?" Adrian asked.

Wiping her clammy brow, Shae offered Adrian a weak smile.

"Yeah, I'm good. Where's the fire, young lady?"

Jax helped herself to Shae's abandoned drink and dropped onto the two-seater like a bag of potatoes. She burped as she drained the glass and made a show of wiping her mouth.

"The fire? Oh, it was about to be ignited between the two of you before I walked in. Talk about a fucking spark."

Jax turned on her side and made herself comfortable on the couch, all the while blowing bubbles with her gum and staring at Shae. Shae calmly rested her chin on her palm and smiled at Jax, which seemed to infuriate the teenager.

"Jax, you are going to have to wait outside, I'm afraid," Adrian said.

Arms crossed, she stood while Jax continued the staring contest, refusing to break eye contact with Shae. Adrian assumed that Shae had the advantage of years of training in her profession. Bad-mannered and frustrated teenagers shouldn't scare Shae one bit, and she had clearly accepted the challenge from Jax.

"Actually, Dr. Ramsey, I don't mind her staying."

"Shae, that's not how this works," Adrian explained.

"Perhaps the great Dr. Ramsey prefers to get on with whatever I interrupted earlier," Jax teased.

Awarding Jax the staring contest trophy this time, Shae shared a look with Adrian that begged her to trust her on this one. Reluctantly, Adrian took a seat and turned her attention to Jax.

"You're quite right. I would prefer to get on with my session from earlier, Jax. Shae turned up at the scheduled time and deserved my undivided attention. Being the kind person that she is, she's now decided to share it with you. So, if you're going to stay, please be respectful."

Rolling her eyes, Jax turned on her back and resumed her bubble blowing.

"Has anyone ever told you that you're like super dramatic and shit?" she said as a bubble popped and collapsed around her mouth.

Shae smiled at Adrian and slipped a piece of lemon between her teeth. Adrian closed her eyes momentarily, drawing on her reserve of self-control in order to act in a civilised manner toward Jax even though she really didn't feel like she deserved it.

"So, how are you today, Jax?"

"Peachy, Doctor A."

Jax turned to Shae.

"The A is for annoying, not amazing."

Shae responded with a calm nod but didn't say a word. Suddenly, Jax sat up, hugging her knees to her chest and clearly not caring that her Doc Martens were scuffing the couch.

"Is she always this talkative?" Jax asked Adrian while pointing at Shae.

"I teach at Willowmore. I'm used to rowdy children and I've found that shouting at them doesn't work, so I sometimes try keeping quiet instead. Shocks them into submission sometimes."

"I'm not a fucking child, LouAnne Johnson," Jax said.

Again, Adrian was taken aback by Jax's appreciation for old movies. *Dangerous Minds* was released in 1995, at least six years before Jax was born. She could tell that Shae was equally impressed by the smile she offered Jax.

"Willowmore is indeed a public school. Do you think only poor kids attend public schools?" Shae asked.

"I think I'd rather be finger-fucked by a cow than to attend a public school."

Adrian winced. Eight months of exposure to Jax's foul mouth had not desensitised her, but she refused to let Jax know how much it grated her.

"You strike me as a Curro snob. Am I close?" Shae asked.

"Is she allowed to fucking insult me like this?" Jax asked Adrian.

"This is literally uncharted territory, since none of my other patients have hijacked other people's sessions. So, I guess we'll make up the rules as we go along," Adrian said.

Jax returned to a horizontal position.

"Yes, I go to Curro. They have real teachers there."

Shae chuckled and pointed the index fingers of both her hands to Adrian, letting her know that it was over to her. Adrian mouthed her fake thanks to Shae and took a deep breath before addressing Jax.

"How are things at home, Jax?"

"Hitler is now threatening to take away all of my privileges if I don't stop smoking at the dinner table. He kills me, that man. The concept of compromising is like the fucking G-spot to him—he just can't get a handle on it."

Jax's father was often referred to as Hitler, Stalin, Amin, or Putin. Despite the fact that Adrian had never laid eyes on the man, she had a clear image of him, an image that she had constructed by combining the features of the top four villains in the history of evil. She would imagine an insanely rich, very short, black dictator with a toothbrush moustache wearing stacked shoes to appear taller in the hopes of overpowering his daughter, who was, at times, more devastating than the Cold War. Adrian had suggested group sessions with both of Jax's parents present, but Jax threatened to chew off her wrists.

"Maybe you can smoke outside after dinner next time?" Adrian suggested.

"I told him how it works, Doc. If he is allowed meat on his plate, knowing that I find it completely repulsive, I should be allowed to have a cigarette, which he happens to find repulsive."

Shae chucked the drained piece of lemon aside and crossed her arms over her chest.

"I would love to argue with that logic, but Jax has a valid point. Don't you think so, Dr. Ramsey?"

Adrian peered at Shae through narrow slits. How dare she side with this obnoxious teenager? Careful not to disturb the perfect bun at the back of her head, Adrian repeatedly dragged her index finger through her hair and across an itchy spot on her scalp. Finally smoothing her hair down, she let out a quiet breath.

"I think that Jax is entitled to her opinion, but so is her father. Compromise would indeed be the key here. I'm not sure you can compare eating meat to smoking at the dinner table, though."

The daring smile on Shae's face told Adrian that she hadn't scored any points yet.

"How is it not the same thing? Jax, I'm assuming, is a vegetarian and the meat on her father's plate offends her. It possibly even ruins her appetite. I'm sure the smoking does the same to her father, but why is this not a fair compromise?"

Shae had a twinkle in her eye, and she didn't even attempt to hide how much fun she was having with this.

"Where have you been my entire fucking dreadful life?" Jax said as she high-fived Shae proudly.

Feeling that things were slipping out of her control, Adrian shifted in her seat and took out her frustrations on the click mechanism of her pen. Clicking ferociously, she turned her attention to Jax.

"All sixteen years of it?" Adrian said.

Jax slipped into a semiseated position, legs dangling over the armrest. She shot Adrian a death stare.

"Yes, Jax. We all seem to be forgetting that you are a minor and that you are, in fact, in the care of your parents. Unfortunately, that requires you to abide by their rules, unless they are being unreasonable in their requests."

Shae winced in disagreement and earned a raised eyebrow from Adrian.

"I believe Jax feels that this particular request is unreasonable. Perhaps she doesn't feel like her own request is unreasonable either. Why should she sit there and bear witness to something she despises?"

Shae was seriously getting on Adrian's nerves. What the hell? The smug smile on Jax's face didn't ease her frustrations.

"Doc, you probably want to stop clicking like your life depends on it. Coming from a little bit of money myself, I happen to know that you can feed a small village with the money that paid for that Montblanc."

Adrian offered Jax a fake smile and stopped clicking.

"She's right, you know. Having my dinner elsewhere if he fucking insists on eating animals is not an unreasonable request."

Determined to show both Shae and Jax that there was in fact a better way to deal with this trivial little issue, Adrian stared at the ceiling. She pretended not to notice that the two collaborators were chatting away. She could hardly believe that Jax was having a normal conversation, in a calm tone and without dropping the f-bomb every five seconds.

"Okay, you mentioned compromise earlier. So, why not suggest the following compromise to your father. Perhaps your father can commit to trying a vegetarian dish every other day. That means you don't smoke at the dinner table on those nights. Could that work?" Adrian suggested.

Jax stared at Adrian as if she had grown a second head. Giving her some time to toy with the idea, Adrian focused on Shae, who was still wearing a smug smile. When Adrian refused to return her smile, Shae stuck out her lower lip, silently begging for forgiveness. She would have to earn it.

"Well, Jax. You have to admit that Dr. Ramsey's idea doesn't completely suck. You could cook Hitler a meal that nothing had to die for. Teach him a better way of living, one meal at a time."

Jax sat up straight and tugged on her untied shoelaces while chewing on the inside of her cheek.

"I love those boots, by the way," Shae said.

"They really are come-fuck-me boots, hey?" Jax said as she winked at Shae. "And you, Dr. Frank-N-Farter, might have come up with a clever idea for a change. I'll give it a shot this week and report back. Are we having another threesome next week, then?"

Adrian had been toying with an idea for a few weeks, and this presented an opportunity for her to run it by Shae and Jax simultaneously. She regretted not discussing it with Shae before, but she decided to risk putting her on the spot like this. Besides, Shae wasn't really her favourite person at that moment.

"I actually wanted to start doing a group session next week. How would you guys feel about attending such a session?"

Picking at her cuticles, Shae shifted in her recliner and rested her right ankle on her left knee. In the past few months, Shae had slipped into a more relaxed version of herself around Adrian, and this particular pose struck Adrian as confident in addition to successfully avoiding eye contact. When Shae finally looked at her, the annoyance was evident in her big hazel eyes.

"You can both think about it. No pressure. It would be a small group of people just having a chat once a month. I would obviously lead the group in discussions, and you would continue with your individual sessions as well."

Jax flopped back into a horizontal position and ran her hand over the spiky blond hair on the one side of her head. The hair on the other side of her head was black and styled in long layers—the girl's hair was as complicated as she was. Adrian would expect Jax to have an abundance of tattoos and piercings for dramatic effect, but Jax, with her porcelain skin, was everything but predictable.

"The minute I get a fucking AA meeting vibe I'm out of there, Doc."

"It will be far from that. I promise," Adrian vowed.

CHAPTER NINE

"Just tie the ribbon already, Adrian," Avril said.

Adrian had been trying to tie the ribbon of a huge red balloon to the chandelier when she spotted what she was almost certain was a hickey on Avril's neck. She now stared at it with wide eyes and a dropped jaw. Avril wasn't able to hide it since she needed both hands to hold the ladder steady.

"You little minx!"

"Adrian, keep your voice down! I will push you off this ladder."

Adrian hastily tied the ribbon and descended the ladder in a rush, hoping that there would be a quiet moment to interrogate Avril before the rest of the clan showed up. At that very moment, Easton walked into the dining room with flowers in one hand and at least three gift bags in the other. Adrian shot Avril a look that said that this was not over. Pecking Easton on the cheek, Adrian took the flowers from her and pointed her in the direction of the gift table in the corner.

It was Ally's sixtieth birthday, and the Ramseys' dinner table was covered in all of Ally's favourite treats. Adrian had baked the cupcakes, mini Swiss rolls, and pecan nut tartlets herself, while she had arranged for a caterer to do the rest. For once, she wanted her mother to relax instead of serving her family.

"Wow, Avril, that's some hickey, girl!" Easton shrieked.

"I've always wondered what my life would be like if Mom had faked a fucking headache the night you were conceived," Avril said to Easton.

Arranging the gift bags on the table, Easton turned to Adrian and rested her hands on her hips.

"Do you think I should rescue what little dignity she has left with my magic concealer after she spewed such hate at me?"

Avril collapsed the ladder and stormed out of the room in a huff.

"Just give her the concealer anyway. Rise above, little one," Adrian said as she left the room in search of her father.

She found him on the bench under the giant oak tree in the backyard where she used to play hide-and-seek with her sisters. On that same bench, she had caught Easton smoking for the first time. Not long after that, she had hidden behind the tree to take pictures of Avril and her boyfriend making out on the very same bench. She had bribed Avril into dishwashing duties for weeks with those pictures. The three sisters' initials were carved out on the back, and Norman was now running his fingers across the indentations.

"There you are," Adrian said as she slipped under his arm.

"Have Avril and Easton had their first argument yet?" Norman asked as he squeezed her shoulder.

"You bet. What's up, Daddy?"

Norman let out a long breath and kissed her on the temple.

"Not much, kiddo. How are you doing? Are you finding it difficult to adjust after the divorce?"

An image of her home flashed into her mind. She had chucked out the queen-sized bed she had shared with Frederick and replaced it with a smaller sleigh bed that she had fallen in love with at first sight. Frederick had insisted on displaying his coveted *Guernica* on their bedroom wall. *Guernica*, Picasso's anti-war masterpiece, depicted a bloody attack, but Picasso had used only black and white. The absence of red in the monochrome painting represented Picasso's protest against violence following the bombing of a town during the Spanish Civil War. Adrian had referred to it as Frederick's *Fifty Shades of Grey*—in his absence of course. She had taken it down without replacing it with something else. The blank spot above her headboard represented a clean slate to her.

"Oh, Daddy. It's been so liberating. You remember *Fifty Shades of Grey?*"

"That bland, overpriced piece in your room?" Norman asked.

"The one and only. I took it down and propped it up against the garage wall, unwrapped."

Shaking his head, Norman chuckled.

"I missed the rebel in you."

"I missed her too, Daddy. Well, she's back," Adrian said and winked.

"How are things at work?" Norman asked.

"Things are great. I just have a restored sense of focus and it seems to be benefiting my patients as well. I'm even making headway with the one patient I had little hope for."

Well, technically, she had Shae to thank for her breakthrough with Jax. She smiled as an image of Shae popped into her mind—the relaxed version of Shae, her blond hair more tousled and her hazel eyes less guarded. Despite the horror of what had happened to Shae, there was lately either a smile on her face, or one was threatening to break through her serious façade. Shae McPherson was forever chasing the next smile, and Adrian was pleasantly surprised by the new and improved version of her.

"Would that be the feisty teacher?"

"No, I am referring to a troubled teenager that I started seeing some time ago."

"That's great. It must be so rewarding changing the lives of your patients." Norman pinched her cheek and pulled her closer. "How is that teacher doing now?"

"She's a changed woman, Daddy. Honestly, every time I see her she seems to be doing a little better. In fact, she played a pivotal part in the breakthrough of this other patient. She certainly has a way of connecting with people."

Norman simply smiled as his daughter's face lit up.

"You should have seen this, Dad. This girl is angry, self-righteous, and bitter. She refuses to let me near enough to actually be of any help. For months, I have tried everything to connect with her. The teacher, charismatic woman that she is, chats with her once and suddenly the child agrees to group therapy, something I have suggested more than once."

"That's just wonderful, dear. Is she married? She sounds like a perfect match for Howard."

Adrian was suddenly slightly irritated with Norman. Why was her father always trying to set Howard up? Howard was the son of her father's best friend, and admittedly not a terrible catch. She just couldn't see Shae with someone so ordinary and dull. Shae was quite a looker. Besides, as far as she knew, Shae was not even remotely confused about her sexual orientation.

"She's a lesbian, Dad, and matchmaking doesn't form part of my professional services."

"Who's a lesbian?"

Easton had appeared out of nowhere with a glass of whiskey for Norman and a glass of wine for Adrian. She was dangling a cigarette from the corner of her mouth and Adrian tutted in mock disgust as she accepted what she hoped was a smooth merlot.

"Easton, put that thing out. You know Dad doesn't like it."

"Please, don't, baby. I have to check on your mother anyway. See you girls inside."

Waiting for Norman to disappear around the corner, Adrian took the cigarette from Easton and dragged on it. Closing her eyes, she slipped farther down the bench and returned the cigarette.

"You'd never say that you're almost forty, smoking behind Dad's back like that."

Adrian slapped her sister's thigh.

"I am nowhere near forty, brat, and I'm not smoking. It was just one little puff in the name of defiance."

Easton rested her hand on Adrian's.

"Tell me more about this act of defiance."

"I used to love smoking. Do you remember that? Then Frederick forced me to stop, because he couldn't be seen with someone with such horrible habits."

"Might be the only good thing that prick ever did for you," Easton mumbled.

"So, a few days after my divorce was finalised, I bought a packet of cigarettes and I smoked them all—in his study. I ashed on the plush carpets and I put my cigarettes out on his mahogany desk."

Chuckling heartily, Easton offered Adrian another drag, which she refused. If she was being honest, she also didn't care for the habit of smoking anymore, but being reminded of her newfound freedom was a heady feeling that she had grown to love.

"You should shag someone on that desk for good measure."

"I just might," Adrian said.

"So, who's a lesbian?"

Adrian decided to take that drag after all. Easton turned to her, and it was obvious that her interest was piqued. It was no secret that Easton was sexually fluid and had also dated on both sides of the fence before. Before Frederick had filtered into every fibre of her being, Adrian had spent hours with Easton ranking female celebrities according to their "fuckability."

"My patient. Have *you* made up your mind yet, or are you still deciding?"

"It's not a decision, Adrian. Love is love. It's not bound by trivial things like gender. Do I really have to remind you?"

Adrian tapped on the end of the cigarette and watched as the ash wafted to the floor. Easton slipped her fingers into her dark curls and massaged her scalp. While Adrian had Norman's straight black hair, Easton had inherited their mother's curls.

"Speaking about lesbians, did I tell you that one of my friends is actually dating our seemingly straight and very married professor Sylvia?"

"You're on first-name basis with your professors now? This friend could only be Carla. That girl has always been irresponsible."

Carla and Easton had been inseparable from kindergarten and had been labelled "Double Trouble" by Ally since the age of seven. Since Carla had been a regular visitor in the Ramsey household, all three sisters had a relatively strong bond with her.

"Carla is a little fickle at times, but I have a suspicion that this could be the real thing," Easton said as she stubbed out the cigarette.

Adrian nodded in silence.

"So, is she hot?"

Frowning, Adrian stared at Easton.

"Your lesbian patient. Is she hot?"

Shrugging, Adrian started plucking weeds from a pot beside the bench. She yelped when Easton poked her in the side.

"Easton, you are being quite inappropriate. Have you been spending too much time with Avril?"

"Who is she? Maybe I know her," Easton said as she wiggled her eyebrows suggestively.

Chucking the unearthed weeds into Easton's lap, Adrian winked at her and walked off.

"She's out of your league, Easton. That's all I'm going to say," Adrian said across her shoulder.

Adrian joined Avril in the dining room where the final platters were being arranged. She pointed to Avril's neck and gave her a thumbs-up sign. Clearly Easton had worked her magic with the concealer and their parents would be none the wiser. Finding out who Avril's love interest was would be at the top of Easton's list—or so Adrian was hoping. Ally finally made her appearance and was greeted by loud cheering and the twins' version of "Happy Birthday."

Jayden and Jonah looked adorable in matching dungarees that would probably soon be covered in some sweet and sticky substance. Norman had an arm wrapped around each boy and was beaming at Ally, who was moved by the boys' heartfelt but off-key singing. Easton pointed out that the boys clearly inherited their mother's talent for singing.

Once Ally had opened all of her gifts and the champagne had been poured, Norman held his flute in the air and proposed a toast.

"To the love of my life. When I look at our girls, I am filled with such gratitude. When I look at their mother, I'm simply dumbfounded. Thank you for choosing me to share your life, for always making me believe that I was worthy, and finally, for always forgiving me when I wasn't. Happy birthday, Ally!"

CHAPTER TEN

"So, you hung me out to dry last week," Adrian said as soon as Shae settled down.

Shae had been caught in a rainstorm and her shirt was drenched, clinging to her skin in places. Flicking her fingers through her hair, she wiped her hands on her jeans, all the while smiling at Adrian.

"Did I, Dr. Ramsey? I thought that I was giving you a hand. Shit, I must look like a mess."

Adrian watched as Shae tugged at the back of her shirt to separate the material from her wet skin, but the motion only caused her shirt to cling to her breasts instead. There was a real possibility that Adrian had only started admiring Shae's physical attributes as part of her "let's break all of Frederick's ridiculous rules" campaign, but she honestly had no idea. Those breasts were probably perky enough to make her notice regardless. She might not be blind, but she respected her profession enough to chastise herself for even noticing.

"You look just fine," Adrian said.

"Sure, Doc. I look like I'm heading to a wet T-shirt competition, and judging by the look on your face, I'm in the running to win."

Adrian was getting used to Shae's flirtatious manner, but she kept admonishing her in order to keep those boundaries clear. Still being mildly annoyed with Shae for putting her on the spot with Jax the previous week, she felt even less like humouring her.

"So, what was the deal with Jax? It could have backfired badly, Shae."

Leaning forward in her recliner, Shae rested her hand on Adrian's knee, shaking it lightly.

"It didn't, Adrian. She signed up for group therapy after all. You can thank me now."

Giving Shae a look that said no thanks would be given, Adrian disappeared from the room only to return minutes later with a towel, which she dropped in Shae's lap before settling in her usual spot.

"Your hands are freezing. Just dry off the worst," Adrian said.

"It's not the cold hands bugging you, Dr. Ramsey. It's my ample bosom betraying how cold I am."

Adrian rolled her eyes, but the blush creeping up her neck probably didn't escape Shae.

"Are we ever going to start this session, Shae?"

Gathering her hair, Shae draped it across her shoulder and squeezed the excess water out. She dabbed the back of her neck before she nuzzled the fluffy towel, inhaling deeply. Finally, she drooped the towel around her neck and let out a contented sigh.

"I'm all ears, Adrian," Shae said and flashed her a broad smile.

"Your problem is that you are more mouth than ears. Shae, it really was a huge risk letting Jax interrupt our session and then teaming up with her against me. I've been working so hard at earning her trust."

Shae rubbed her palms together and finally rested her clasped hands between her thighs. Biting down on her lower lip, she rested her cheek against the towel, eyes locked on Adrian.

"Okay, fine. I admit that it was a risk, but, Adrian, you'll never get anywhere if you don't take any risks."

"Really, Shae? You think I've never taken any risks? I married a controlling sociopath. I think that's pretty risky. It doesn't mean that it was a good idea."

Adrian immediately regretted her mini-outburst and reminded herself that Shae was a patient. It was just almost impossible keeping things professional where Shae was concerned. She was always busy crossing a line since she either had no concept of boundaries or simply didn't care about them.

"That explains the shift in you after the divorce. I didn't mean to offend you, Adrian."

"Shift? What do you mean by that?" Adrian couldn't resist.

Shae readjusted the towel around her neck and crossed her legs, slipping into her usual pose.

"Predivorce Adrian was more controlled and reserved. She even looked different. She kept her shirts buttoned all the way to the top. Her smile didn't always reach her eyes."

Adrian was intrigued.

"Postdivorce Adrian is more comfortable in her skin. She rocks those higher heels, and I am relieved to see that she does in fact have collarbones."

Adrian absentmindedly touched her collarbone and peeked at her shoes. She had to give it to her—Shae was nothing if not observant. The interior of her house wasn't the only thing being transformed. Adrian's newfound freedom after the divorce was final had manifested in her physical appearance. She had made what she had, up until now, considered to be subtle changes to her wardrobe, and there was a certain lightness to her being that was unmistakable. The fact that Shae had picked up on it shouldn't have surprised Adrian the way that it had.

"I forgot how perceptive you can be, Shae. Just try to remember that I am still the therapist here. The therapist in me says that you were irresponsible last week."

Adrian held up her hand as Shae started to protest.

"Clearly, in this instance your reckless behaviour benefitted Jax and for that reason I will lay it to rest. We will not be repeating that kind of session, however."

"No more threesomes then?" Shae asked.

Adrian shook her head and flipped through some folders that had been stacked on the coffee table before Shae had arrived. Uncrossing her legs, she arranged the folders on her lap and by the time she looked up, her authoritative smile announced to Shae that they were officially in session.

"How was your week, Shae? Any panic attacks or insomnia I need to know about?"

"Nothing to report, Doc. As far as the insomnia goes, I've always battled falling asleep, even before the attack. So, please don't measure your run rate according to my sleeping patterns."

Resting her elbow on the armrest of the recliner, Adrian held her chin between her thumb and index finger, staring at Shae through narrowed slits.

"My run rate?" Adrian asked.

"Yeah. Your performance. Your rating."

"You think I'm chasing a good run rate?"

Shae seemed baffled. She shifted in her seat and started toying with her damp hair.

"Why wouldn't you?" Shae finally asked.

Adrian was often taken aback by Shae's perspective. It seemed like everything in Shae's world was about keeping score. There was an objective, a planned route, and a bag full of tricks that would get you there. She very rarely had questions, and almost always had the answers. Sometimes, Adrian had to remind herself of how Shae had ended up in the chair across from her. She was certain that Shae would never have crossed her path had that disturbed young man never registered at Willowmore.

"This is not an exact science, Shae. The objectives are different for every patient and so is the treatment plan."

"I can imagine, but in the end you either reach that objective or you don't," Shae replied.

Her hair was frizzy and her lips had a faint blue tinge to them. Adrian was tempted to offer Shae her jacket, but she could only imagine the teasing that would evoke.

"It's not that simple. The goal keeps shifting throughout the process, which means the plan keeps changing. Along the way, there might also be setbacks, in some cases undoing a lot of hard work and sending you right back to the start."

"What is the objective here, Adrian? What is your goal for me?"

Adrian couldn't concentrate and decided to risk the teasing. Dropping the folders on the coffee table, she retrieved her leather jacket from the back of her office chair. Shae didn't disappoint; she had a smug look on her face as she draped the offered jacket across her shoulders. She tucked her nose under the collar and made a show of inhaling Adrian's perfume.

"Don't make me regret that act of kindness, Shae. You tell *me* what the goal is. Why are you here?"

Shae toyed with the zip of Adrian's jacket, never losing eye contact with her.

"Please don't be cute, Shae. Be serious for just a second and tell me why you are here."

"You think I'm cute?" Shae teased.

Adrian rolled her eyes and started shuffling through the folders again.

"I think you try to deflect the attention from any serious matter by being flirtatious and getting under my skin. It won't deter me from asking the hard questions, though. I'm sure you know that by now. So, why are you here?"

"I came here because I went through a very traumatic ordeal that left me somewhat off-kilter and in need of perspective. I am here because I trust you and you give me that perspective."

While Adrian didn't expect the seriousness of Shae's tone, she welcomed the approach. She really wanted Shae to be as invested in the process as she was herself.

"Do I flirt with you? Yes, I flirt with beautiful women all the time, Adrian. Trust me when I say that I am as focused on getting well, as you need me to be. In fact, I need your opinion on something."

Fully intrigued now, Adrian leaned forward in her recliner, ever so slightly.

"Shoot," Adrian said.

"Well, I don't know if this is a very good idea, but I've been thinking about doing some research on Devon. I know so little about this man that changed my life in so many ways. Do you think I'm insane?"

Leaning back in her chair, Adrian rubbed her chin and stared out of the window.

"What do you hope to achieve by doing this, Shae?" Adrian asked after some time went by.

She liked to look at things from all angles, consider all possibilities, and then offer her thoughts, so she wasn't in the habit of rushing a response simply to appease her patients. She realised that the process could be annoying to Shae at times.

"I hope to find more meaning. I don't know if that makes sense to you," Shae explained.

"I'm sure you know about the restorative justice programme that is often introduced in prisons all over the world. The objective is for offenders to meet the family of their victims and make amends for their actions. It gives them a platform to voice their apology and possibly gain the forgiveness of these families," Adrian explained.

Shae nodded silently.

"Now, I have patients that have participated in such programmes. Some of them benefitted greatly from it, while others experienced huge setbacks because of it. I believe the reason for these vastly different outcomes lies in the objectives," Adrian said.

"I can see how this would be similar to restorative justice. So, you think the reasoning behind the initiative determines whether I'll be devastated or uplifted in the end?"

"I do. So, just be very clear about your expectations, Shae. I would hate for you to be devastated all over again. You are doing so well at the moment that I'm just feeling a little hesitant to give you the go-ahead for this."

Shae sighed deeply and rested her head against the back of the recliner, snuggling into Adrian's jacket. For a few moments, both women were quiet and thoughtful. Adrian was mentally running through her cupboard, trying to identify which outfits had earned her the name of Postdivorce Adrian. She was also wondering which other articles of clothing would look as good on Shae as her leather jacket. The worn jacket was the perfect addition to her tight black jeans and knee-high leather boots.

"What kind of questions should I be asking myself here?" Shae interrupted her thoughts.

Why you don't own a jacket exactly like that one? Adrian would rather die than let Shae have some insight into her immediate thoughts.

"Well, you could start with a few easy ones. Why would knowing more about Devon make a difference? Am I ready to have an understanding of who exactly he was? What are the pros and cons of digging into this?"

Adrian appreciated the fact that Shae always took her suggestions into consideration. It demonstrated the complete trust that Shae had mentioned earlier, and it warmed Adrian's heart more than it should. For some reason, Adrian wasn't able to distance herself from Shae as successfully as she did with her other patients. She was more invested in Shae's wellbeing than was recommended by the masters of her profession. She would focus on shifting these feelings into safer territory. Remaining professional and objective was very important to Adrian.

"Thanks, Adrian. Let me think about it and we can talk about it next time."

"That's a great idea. I hate to bring it up, because I know you're not crazy about the idea, but please be reminded that I'd like for you to attend the group session next week," Adrian said.

They spent some time discussing the upcoming group session in more detail. When the session came to an end, Shae slipped Adrian's jacket off her shoulders. She lifted her shoulder to her nose and inhaled deeply. Leaning over Adrian, Shae draped the jacket across the back of her recliner. She paused, her mouth right next to Adrian's ear.

"I've been hoping to leave this office with your perfume all over me."

It took Adrian a good ten minutes to wipe the silly smile off her face. Wipe it off she did, determined to reinforce those healthy boundaries.

CHAPTER ELEVEN

Adrian rearranged the scatter cushions for the umpteenth time. She had transformed her sunroom into a session room in anticipation of her first offsite group therapy session. She had decided to have the session at home since such a change of scenery allowed her to study her patients' behaviour in a more natural environment. It was surprising what the absence of a clock on the wall, a stiff recliner, and file cabinets could do.

If anything could put her patients at ease, it would be Adrian's sunroom. Low, comfortably worn futons invited you to take a load off. Her brightly coloured scatter cushions in all shapes and sizes gave the room a festive atmosphere, and all the futons had a full view of the garden. When Frederick's servants had still tended to the garden, it was an immaculately trimmed affair. Adrian now allowed the morning glory to creep up the bench by the pond, and against the back wall the ivy was celebrating its newfound freedom as well. Gone were the trimmed green hedges, replaced by birdfeeders and bursts of colour.

Right at the back of the yard, the only remainder of Frederick's fascinations was waiting to be uprooted. Years ago, when they had just bought the property, Frederick had designed an intricate maze. At the time, Adrian was fascinated by his eccentricities, and she could picture their kids running through the maze. She couldn't have predicted that she would often try and hide in the same maze, when she needed to escape his belligerent tone at the extravagant dinner parties he hosted. More than once she had sat in the middle of that maze with tear-streaked cheeks and a very heavy heart.

The only reason she hadn't arranged for it to be ripped apart and removed from her property yet was because she hadn't figured out what she wanted to do with that space. She also often imagined him leaning against the entrance of the maze with his arms folded across his broad chest, watching the ivy that he hated so intensely covering the entire back wall of the garage. It gave her some pleasure to imagine the look of disgust on his face.

Leaning against the sliding door, staring at the maze, Adrian flipped the imagined image of Frederick the bird.

"Fuck you, Freddie."

"I spent the majority of last night wondering what you are like in your own personal space," Shae said.

When Adrian turned around, Shae was sprawled across one of the futons, clutching a cushion to her chest.

"I have to say, I kind of like the foul-mouthed cheeky side of you, Adrian."

"What if I had a huge Rottweiler in my backyard?" Adrian asked, clasping her hands behind her back.

"Do you? Is his name Freddie by any chance?" Shae asked.

"I don't, but you took a risk sneaking into my house."

"Is it sneaking if the front door is wide open? Who is Freddie, and what has he done to deserve your scorn?"

Adrian took a final peek at the maze and headed to the small bar that was situated in the corner of the sunroom. She had prepared freshly squeezed orange juice, fresh cheese scones, and the trusted pitcher of Kola Tonic and lemonade with lemon slices. She poured Shae some and handed her the glass with a smile.

"Welcome, hoodlum. Next time, knock."

"Who's Freddie?" Shae asked again as she sipped on her drink.

"Freddie is a phantom in my maze. Maybe I'll tell you about him one day," Adrian said.

She winked at Shae and moved the pitcher of juice and the scones from the bar to the coffee table. She was expecting her other five patients any moment and for some reason she was nervous being alone with Shae in this setting. Actually, if she was being completely honest, the thought of being alone with Shae in this room excited her as much as it terrified her. Shae was yet to take her eyes off the doctor.

"Maybe you can show me your maze as well," Shae said.

Shae pointed at the pitcher of Kola Tonic and lemonade that still sat on the bar. "I don't mind sharing that with your other patients, you know. I do mind sharing you with them. So, you owe me."

Adrian responded by adding the Kola Tonic and lemonade to the refreshments on the coffee table. It was so hard ignoring the alarm bells that started ringing when she admitted to herself that she was also a little saddened that she wouldn't have one-on-one time with Shae today. Soon, this room would be filled with people needing her attention and guidance. This was no time for Shae to distract her.

"I'll be right back. I have to meet the rest of the guests at the front door since I doubt anyone else would have the audacity to trespass," Adrian said.

At that exact moment, Jax stepped into the room and plonked herself down next to Shae.

"Wow, Dr. Frank-N-Farter, all the crazies certainly bought you nice digs, hey."

"Good afternoon, Jax. Please make yourself comfortable."

In the doorway stood a beautiful redhead with striking blue eyes.

"Hi, Dr. Ramsey. I'm Maddison, Jax's cousin."

She held out her hand to Adrian, but her eyes were locked on Shae, who flashed her a brilliant smile. *Is she flirting with this perfect stranger?* Adrian shook her head slightly as she shook Maddison's outstretched hand firmly.

"Hi, Maddison. It's nice to meet you. Are you joining us, today?"

"God, no. I just want to know what time I can pick up that little shit," Maddison said, pointing to Jax.

Jax didn't lift her gaze from her phone where she was flipping through various images on Instagram, but she did stop scrolling to flip Maddison the bird. Maddison chuckled and winked at Shae, obviously flirting with her. Suddenly, Adrian was eager to get rid of her.

"Great. We should be done in two hours."

That certainly caught Jax's attention. She threw her hands in the air and looked at Adrian with wide eyes.

"Two fucking hours? You are kidding, right?"

"I'm afraid not. It's a group session, Jax. That means six patients will be allotted twenty minutes each."

Jax held her thumb and index finger, shaped in a pistol, against her temple.

"No worries. I'll pick her up in two hours. Have fun, ladies!" Maddison said.

She waved at Shae before Adrian walked her out. It turned out the journey to the front door was just long enough for Maddison to make enquiries about Shae.

"Is she also a patient of yours?" Maddison asked and pointed across her shoulder.

"Excuse me?"

"The blonde with the stellar boobs, is she your patient?"

Adrian could certainly tell that Maddison and Jax were family. Maybe insolence was a family trait of theirs.

"That would be confidential. Now, if you'll excuse me, I have to get ready for the session."

One by one, the other four patients arrived and gathered in the sunroom. Once they were all comfortable and sipping on their drinks, Adrian sat down next to Shae and explained what she had in mind for the group session. To start the session off, she wanted each patient to introduce themselves to the group. She received four nods, one eye roll, and one bright smile.

Basil Thompson was a sixty-three-year-old retired colonel who had lost his leg in combat. When his fourth wife sued him for divorce, he knocked on Adrian's door for help. What he thought would be couples counselling turned into PTSD treatment instead. Adrian had identified that his failed marriages were only the symptom of the debilitating disease at the heart of his problem.

"Hi, everyone. My name is Colonel Basil Thompson and I've been seeing Dr. Ramsey for six months now."

He knocked on his prosthetic leg and chuckled.

"I lost my leg in combat. I also lost three and a half wives."

Adrian noticed that Jax was still engrossed in her phone, pretending not to pay attention to the people around her. At least

Shae had persuaded her to remove her earphones a bit earlier. The fact that she had to bribe her with cash was beside the point.

"I'm sorry. Did you say three and a half?" Shae asked.

"I did. The good doctor is trying to save the fourth marriage at the moment."

Adrian smiled at Basil and encouraged the next patient to start his introduction. Theodore Whitfield was a forty-year-old single father whose wife had been murdered when four assailants broke into their house. He spoke in a quiet voice, and his fiddling hands in his lap was a testament to the anxiety that he inherited together with the sole custody of his five-year-old daughter.

Next up was Eliza Hanson, a twenty-two-year-old artist that was brutally attacked in her studio by her ex-boyfriend. A light scarf covered an angry scar that stretched from one side of her neck to the other. Her light blue eyes contrasted against her porcelain skin and black hair. Adrian found herself paying close attention to Shae's reaction to the beautiful young woman, which turned out to be a simple nod and a bright smile. When Shae caught Adrian watching her, she shrugged as if to prove her innocence.

"Thanks, Eliza. Andie, you're up," Adrian said.

Andie was completely oblivious. She was staring at Jax, who was leaning back against the futon with her eyes closed. Judging by the look in her eye, she liked what she saw.

"Andie?"

Shae cleared her throat and poked Jax in the side with her elbow.

"Just fucking shoot me. What do you want, Shae?" Jax exploded.

Shae had suspected that Jax spewing hate at her would leave the young Andie jarred. It certainly had the desired effect—Andie's eyes darted across the room and rested on Adrian, who encouraged her to introduce herself to the group.

"Hi, everyone. I'm Andie."

She seemed nervous when Jax finally opened her eyes and peered at her.

"I have been seeing Dr. Ramsey for a few months now and she's just helping me work through a few things."

Jax frowned deeply and let out an irritated sigh.

"Yes, Einstein. The question is why."

Andie was flabbergasted and again her gaze landed on Adrian, visibly sending out an SOS.

"Jax, calm down. Let's try and keep things respectful, shall we? There's no pressure on anyone to share anything that they are not comfortable sharing at this point. You will have enough time to get to know each other in these sessions, at your own pace," Adrian said.

"Shae, why don't you go next?"

Pulling her fingers through her hair, Shae stretched her legs out in front of her and crossed her ankles. She repeatedly ran the tip of her thumb across her right eyebrow, a nervous habit that Adrian found endearing.

"Why don't I ever feel this uncomfortable when I have twenty sets of eyes on me in the classroom?"

Jax rolled her eyes and imitated stabbing herself in the neck.

"Perhaps because you don't have to spill your guts to those twenty students," Jax offered.

Adrian's patience was running thin, but before she could reprimand Jax, Shae winked at her as if to say she would handle Jax. She turned to face Jax then.

"I was attacked by a deranged student some time ago. He held me hostage in the back of my classroom, after which he shot himself. I was trapped in that room covered with his blood and brains for four hours before the janitor found me."

Adrian smiled at her proudly. She was always impressed by Shae's bravery. She spoke now in a steady voice and relayed the facts of that horrible incident as if it had happened to someone else. It was always rewarding when her patients' hard work paid off. Shae was the perfect example of what could be achieved by a shift of focus.

"That's fucking hard-core shit right there," Jax said and whistled.

"What I'm trying to say, Jax, is that my students know all the gruesome details. It happened on their playground, so to speak. I guess talking about it in this setting is more nerve-wracking because I'm among strangers."

Adrian leaned closer to Shae and touched her knee lightly.

"The idea is that over time, you won't feel like you're among strangers here."

CHAPTER TWELVE

"I see the hickey healed quite well," Easton said as she kissed Avril on the cheek.

"I see you're still being a meddling asshole," Avril replied.

Adrian was standing at the stove preparing a sauce for the roast. Ally didn't comprehend the meaning of a small get-together. Dinner was always a lavish affair and only a three-course meal would do for her family. This usually resulted in some delegation from Ally's side, and tonight it was Adrian's turn to assist.

"I see you're both still twelve years old," Adrian said as she lifted the spoon to her mouth for a taste.

Avril wrapped her arms around Adrian from behind and licked her neck, something she had started doing in their younger years when she had realised that Adrian found nothing more disgusting than other people's spit on her skin. Squealing, Adrian tried to escape her grip. In the process, she spilled sauce all over the stove.

"Adrian, it can really be fun. Especially if the licking is done by a woman other than your sister. You should give it a try sometime, now that you're unattached," Easton said.

"God, you're so disgusting, Easton! Mom should have tied her tubes after she had me," Avril said as she finally released Adrian and wiped down the stovetop.

Blowing Avril an air-kiss, Easton winked at Adrian as she took a seat at the kitchen nook.

"Easton, the fact that you can't quite choose between men and women doesn't mean the rest of us experience the same difficulty," Avril said.

Easton grabbed an apple from the fruit bowl that Ally still kept filled to the brim especially for her. Easton never just ate, she devoured. In most ways, it was as if she was stuck in her teens. The majority of her meals were still her mother's leftovers. She still spent at least three nights a week on the couch in her parents' house, and she still loved annoying her sisters. Avril winced as Easton groaned in a provocative manner and sucked on the juices escaping her apple. Avril's face was scrunched up as if she had stepped in something nasty.

"Why choose? They both have such valid benefits," Easton said.

"Spare me the filthy details of your perverted sex life, Easton," Avril said as she took a seat at the opposite end of the nook.

"No, please indulge us," Adrian said.

Lately, Adrian had reminisced about her younger years, more specifically a time in her life when she came very close to exploring what had been her growing fascination with dating both sexes. She figured that a combination of finally divorcing Frederick and the arrival of Shae had brought on the little private trips down memory lane she had been indulging in. Avril was now staring at Adrian.

"Really, Adrian? What the fuck?"

"Avril, just relax. It's not contagious," Easton said.

Licking her lips, she took aim, closed one eye, and tossed the core across the room and directly into the dustbin. She celebrated her success by mimicking a roaring crowd and performing a fist pump, but Avril and Adrian were unmoved.

"Such dreary people you are."

Avril drummed her fingers on the counter while Adrian gestured for Easton to start talking. After a while, she did.

"No stubble. You can make out with a woman all night and not have a rash the next morning."

Avril slammed her head against the counter in dramatic fashion.

"Stubble? Really? That seems like a terrible reason to act against your nature," Avril said.

"Against my nature? Who decided that sleeping with men exclusively was in my nature? Just stop interrupting now so I can get to the good stuff."

Avril stood up, headed to the fridge, and started preparing a green salad, but Easton had Adrian's undivided attention, the sauce-making abandoned and long forgotten.

"Breasts. Breasts are probably the main reason I can't swear off women. Sometimes it's just nicer to have that soft landing instead of a hairy chest."

"Adrian, please ask her to stop," Avril begged.

"Be strong, Avril. Maybe she'll eventually get to the part where her need to date women goes beyond the lust."

Avril started slicing tomatoes and cucumber for the salad while Easton carried on with her lesson.

"You don't ever have to guide a woman toward your G-spot—ever. I don't know if it's because we know our own bodies, but it's just like women instinctively know how and where to touch you."

Shaking her head, Avril rinsed the lettuce.

"This is bordering on harassment. I don't want to listen to this."

Easton winked at Adrian and went in for the kill.

"Oral sex. Holy fucking shit. Men tend to lap at our vaginas like they're trying to keep up with a melting ice cream cone. It's messy, and I prefer not having a bruised clit the morning after. With a woman, it's just slow and sensual. Trust me when I say that men can't compare with women when it comes to cunnilingus."

Avril slammed the fridge door.

"That's it. I'll be outside. Adrian, finish this salad."

They both watched as Avril stormed past them, chucking the dishrag in Adrian's direction. Shrugging, Easton leaned on her elbows and smiled at Adrian.

"I knew that would send her over the edge. At least now you have carte blanche. Ask me anything you want to know."

"What makes you think I want to know anything?" Adrian mumbled.

The knowing smile on Easton's face prompted Adrian to work on the salad. She felt like she was under a microscope and needed a distraction. Following her across the kitchen, Easton leaned her back against the counter and folded her arms across her chest. When she spoke, her voice was softer than before.

"Look, Adrian, it's not a crime to be inquisitive. I actually figured that you had climbed the fence a few times. Were you not interested in that Shelly girl at varsity?"

Adrian blushed deeply and turned away from Easton to rinse the lettuce a second time.

"If you rinse that lettuce one more time it will be cleaner than Avril's conscience."

Adrian chuckled at that.

"Fuck. Do you think she ever colours outside the lines?" Easton asked.

"No. I don't think she does."

Adrian rummaged through the fridge and finally found the feta cheese. She tossed a few pieces into the salad bowl and when she looked up, Easton was still studying her closely. Sometimes, Adrian figured that Easton would have been a better psychologist than her. She had a cunning sixth sense, and she also happened to be very easy to talk to.

"I was never brave enough. I suppose having a lesbian patient kind of rekindled some of those feelings I had been warring with at some point. That's all."

"Does this patient have a name?" Easton asked.

"She sure does, but that is confidential and you know it."

Easton nodded slowly, encouraging her sister to continue. "Do you see her often?"

"I see her once a week for a private session, and then she participates in a group session every other week. So, some weeks I see her once and other weeks I see her twice, only because she attends the group session."

Easton smiled and shook her head.

"What?" Adrian asked.

"I just find it peculiar that you felt the need to explain that to death. She's a patient, right? So, why do you need to justify seeing her twice? You don't have to explain anything to me."

Adrian turned away from her again, this time to search the fridge for salad dressing and possibly an excuse for her reaction to a simple question like the one that Easton had just asked. She found the dressing, but not a satisfactory explanation for her strange behaviour. Adrian's eyes darted around the kitchen, making sure that her audience consisted of Easton only.

"She's rather fascinating," Adrian said.

"What is fascinating about her? The fact that she dates women?" Easton asked.

Biting down on her lip, Adrian drizzled some dressing over the salad. If she was being completely honest, she could probably list a few things without giving it much thought. She wasn't about to share that little titbit with her sister.

"No, it's not that. She's just different from anyone I've ever met."

"What makes her different?" Easton insisted.

Adrian sighed as she slipped the salad into the fridge.

"*Is* she really different from other people? Or does she make you *feel* different than other people?"

For weeks, she had been aware of the connection she felt with Shae. The fact that she was intrigued by her was undeniable, but she had been so focused on being professional that she hadn't realised that it was more than intrigue. Mentally dressing her patient using items from her own cupboard was not intrigue. Enjoying the fact that Shae's perfume lingered in her consulting room long after she left was not intrigue. It dawned on her now—it was attraction. Forbidden attraction.

"You're absolutely right! That's all it is. I'm not attracted to *her*. I'm attracted to how she makes me *feel*."

Easton lifted both brows and held her palms in the air.

"Whoa. You didn't mention the fact that you're attracted to her."

"No, I didn't want to admit that to myself. I mean, that would be so dangerous, but now that I understand it better, it takes the power out of it, right?" Adrian reasoned.

"Just back up a bit. You're physically attracted to her?"

"I thought so, but you just enlightened me! I clearly just enjoyed the fact that she pays so much attention to me. I simply liked being flirted with, the constant compliments and chivalry. It's just so flattering after being stuck in a loveless marriage." Adrian wiped her brow and let out a sigh of relief. "God, I feel so much better now."

Adrian felt certain that she would have less of an emotional battle now fighting what she had thought was attraction. Finally, Shae would just be another patient.

Closing her eyes, Easton pinched the bridge of her nose between her thumb and forefinger. When she opened her eyes, she crossed her arms and whistled softly.

"Adrian, sometimes I wonder how you can be so successful in your career. You have no self-awareness, girl."

"What do you mean?"

Easton took her by the shoulders and looked into her eyes.

"Adrian, you have a problem."

Norman entered the kitchen and kissed both girls on the cheek. The moment Norman turned his back on them, Adrian mimicked sealing her lips. Easton returned the gesture, pretending to chuck the invisible key over her shoulder. Adrian thanked her wordlessly with a smile that didn't reach her eyes. Being attracted to a patient was not simply frowned upon in her profession, it was a cardinal sin.

Adrian was withdrawn for the remainder of the evening. Once they had finished their dessert and all the dishes had been stacked in the dishwasher, she joined her father in his study. Norman was busy building a three-dimensional model of the Brooklyn Bridge. She remembered admiring him as a little girl, thinking that her Daddy was the cleverest man in the world. At the time, she hadn't realised that the modelling sets came with detailed instructions. She had been under the impression that he had built all those structures blindly.

"Hi, baby girl. Would you hand me that magnifier, please?"

"I can't believe you still build these, Dad."

Using the magnifier, Norman was able to position the first spoke of the bridge perfectly. He held his thumb in place, waiting for the glue to settle.

"It takes longer these days. My eyes are not as good as they used to be. How are things going at the practice?"

Adrian sat on the edge of Norman's desk and crossed her arms over her chest. Her practice. That's what she needed to focus on. Easton seemed convinced that Adrian was dangerously close to crossing a line.

"Things are going really well. I started a little support group, well, it's actually just a group session with some of my PTSD patients. They don't know that it's a support group yet, but they will find that it can be."

Norman looked up from his desk and flashed her a brilliant smile.

"That's my girl. I love that you help so many people."

"I try my best, Daddy. It's really important to me. You know, through the years, that practice has been my oasis. Living through some trauma in my marriage, surviving the divorce. I always found a refuge in my job. It defines me."

"I am so proud of you, my girl. Your patients are lucky to have you."

"I'm lucky to have them too," Adrian said.

She believed this to be true. Lately, she felt extremely lucky to have a certain obnoxious, dangerously flirtatious blond patient around. Tonight, she had been reminded why she had to remain very cautious. Whether whatever she felt toward Shae was attraction or not, what she knew for certain was that it certainly wasn't worth risking her career for.

Wasn't it?

CHAPTER THIRTEEN

Closing the lid of her laptop, Adrian pulled her fingers through her hair. She had overslept this morning and had rushed out of the house with her hair still wet. The result was slightly wavy locks tumbling across her shoulders and into her face instead of the tight bun she normally preferred. She had spent the majority of the morning catching up on paperwork, until the smell of Ella's scones lured her out of her office.

She paused in the doorway. Shae was leaning across Ella's desk, her palms flat on the surface and her jean-clad bottom on display. Peering over her glasses, Ella fumbled with her phone. Following Shae's instructions, she finally managed to open an image of a wrinkled baby boy. Ella chuckled as Shae raved over her newborn grandson. Adrian couldn't help but laugh aloud at Shae's high-pitched cooing.

"I'm so sorry to interrupt, but Ella's scones are calling my name."

"Hi, Doc. Have you seen this cutie pie?"

Adrian cocked her brow at Shae in passing on her way to the kitchen.

"I have. Can I get you some scones? That's if you still need me now that you've discovered the ultimate form of therapy," Adrian said.

"The ultimate form of therapy?" Shae asked.

"Yes. Looking at images of newborn babies are probably the most natural source of dopamine," Adrian said as she disappeared into the kitchen.

She returned with a tray of scones and a pot of tea. She wasn't the least bit surprised when Shae took the tray from her and carried it back to the consulting room. There was that chivalry she had mentioned to Easton a few days ago. When Adrian closed the door behind them, she intended to shut out all thoughts about her highly inappropriate feelings toward Shae as well. She was fighting the good fight. The first words out of Shae's mouth dismantled her entire resolve.

"Talk about dopamine…did I tell you that I went on a date with Maddison?"

Adrian busied herself with buttering the scones and preparing the tea in an effort to avoid locking eyes with Shae.

"Maddison? Jax's cousin?" Shae offered.

"Yes, I assumed that you were referring to Jax's cousin. Sugar?" Shae was on a roll.

"Talk about sugar…did I tell you how sweet Maddison is?"

Adrian was in no mood for this nonsense. It was time for Shae to take things a little more seriously and that meant less chitchat and more boundaries. Boundaries? Who was she kidding? Could she even mention boundaries when she had disregarded her own?

"Cut it out, Shae."

Her tone seemed to catch Shae by surprise. She accepted the cup of tea from Adrian with a look of concern on her face. Wordlessly, she nibbled on the scone, all the while studying Adrian closely. She finally dusted crumbs from her chest and cleared her throat.

"So, do you want to tell me what that was all about?"

Poking at the teabag in her cup, Adrian considered reminding Shae who the patient was in the room. She figured that she had created this monster by allowing their relationship to slip into friendly territory. She still wasn't sure how and when that had happened. It was such a delicate situation, though. She didn't want to disclose too much information to Shae.

"Shae, our conversations should be structured around your treatment plan. You don't need to share the intimate details of your personal life with me unless it aids your healing process."

Leaning back in the recliner, Shae twirled a lock of hair around her forefinger and sipped on her tea.

"You don't like Maddison. Why is that?"

"Did you even hear a word that I said?" Adrian asked.

"Tell me. Why don't you like her?" Shae insisted.

Adrian traced the rim of the cup with her index finger and convinced herself that she would find a way to steer this conversation in a more professional direction.

"No, Shae. You tell me. Why do you like her?"

"Is that a trick question, Dr. Ramsey?"

"Stop answering my questions with more questions. Why do you like Maddison?"

Shae rested her elbow on the armrest of the recliner and swirled her tea around in the cup. The one thing Adrian appreciated was the fact that Shae was always willing to indulge her. That's how they managed to make this much progress in a relatively short while.

"I guess I like Maddison because she distracts me. It's nice to have dinner with someone who doesn't care to dissect me."

Adrian took a moment to think about what Maddison offered Shae. She had to admit that what Shae had said made complete sense to her. Everywhere Shae turned, she was faced with people who probably considered her a victim. Maddison didn't know the gory details; to her, Shae was just a beautiful woman with crazy sex appeal.

"It must be quite refreshing," Adrian said.

"That's exactly what it is! It's so refreshing. Maddison doesn't know anything about me. What makes it that much more appealing is the fact that I can choose what I want to share with her. She will only ever know what I want her to know."

Adrian couldn't help but feel a little cheated. If she was being completely honest, she would have loved the opportunity to get to know Shae outside of therapy. She figured that they could have become great friends. She loved her sense of humour, and after seeing her around others in the group session, she realised that Shae was very compassionate. Unfortunately, her purpose in Shae's life was to help her deal with those less pleasant things—the things Maddison didn't have to know.

"I get that. I can imagine that you need that kind of escape."

"I'm glad that you understand. I promise that I won't share anything that will make you uncomfortable," Shae said.

"So, how did you find the group session?" Adrian attempted to change the subject.

They discussed the group session for a while and Adrian encouraged her to try her best to form connections with the other patients. Since the majority of them suffered from PTSD, Shae would be in good company. The purpose was to find comfort in each other and offer support where it was needed. Adrian assured Shae that if she utilised the opportunities that group therapy had to offer, she would reap considerable benefits.

"I wanted to thank you for helping me out with Jax. For some reason, she likes you."

Chuckling, Shae slumped in the recliner, slipping into her customary position, her right ankle resting on her left knee.

"Is it really that far-fetched? The idea that I am likable?"

"Not at all. It's just not in Jax's nature to like someone so quickly," Adrian explained.

"Is it in yours?" Shae asked.

Adrian shot her a warning look, but she took the bait nonetheless.

"Not really. I tend to gather loads of information before I invest in anyone. Perhaps you should follow my example?"

Adrian would have to work harder at erecting new boundaries. Dropping hints about her dislike of Maddison was no way to go about it. What she should have been doing was to focus on the next step in Shae's treatment plan. During the CPT sessions, Adrian had identified that Shae harboured some feelings of guilt. Shae was yet to incorporate and integrate those feelings into an active part of her healing, and Adrian was hoping that the group sessions might speed this part of the process along. All of her PTSD patients had experienced similar emotions and perhaps Shae would connect with one of them.

"I'll take that to heart, Doc. By the way, I did my homework like a good girl."

"I had no doubt that you would. So, you considered all the pros and cons of doing some research on Devon?"

"Well, I've started doing that. I have been trying to find out what I am hoping to achieve by it. It turns out being honest with myself is not always that easy," Shae said.

Adrian nodded knowingly.

"So, I approached it from another angle. I painted myself two scenarios. In the first scenario, I find that Devon really was as disturbed as we like to believe he was. He was out of control, and what he did was random and inevitable. In that scenario, I was faceless and simply in the wrong place at the wrong time."

Shae smiled at her when she gathered her unruly hair, twisted it around her wrist, and draped it across her shoulder. Adrian gestured for her to carry on talking.

"Have I told you that your hair looks gorgeous today?" Shae digressed.

"No, you haven't, because I'm your therapist and we have boundaries. Do carry on."

Flashing Adrian a crooked smile, Shae continued.

"So, then I considered how that scenario would make me feel. I guess I would feel like it could have happened to anyone. I will probably feel a little less angry."

"Tell me about the second scenario," Adrian said.

"In the second scenario, Devon was in fact just evil. He chose me for very specific reasons—perhaps I resemble his mother or someone he hates. That will make me feel infuriated and wronged."

Shae dusted some residual crumbs from her chest and shifted in the recliner.

"When I look at both scenarios, I have to admit that I don't think the possible reward outweighs the risk. What do you think, Adrian?"

Finally leaning forward, Adrian clasped her hands between her thighs and looked at Shae through narrowed eyes.

"I think that you're on the right track, Shae. They say that advice is something you ask for when you have the answers but need the courage to make the decisions. I happen to think you have the answers as well as the courage to make the tough decisions. I have such faith in you."

Blushing slightly, Shae bent at the waist and performed a bow.

"Thank you, Dr. Ramsey. That is quite touching."

"It's not as comfortable on the receiving end of the compliments, is it, Shae?"

Adrian decided that a bit of a blush looked good on Shae. She was always amazed by how seamlessly Shae could move from stern to playful. They could be discussing the most serious matter one moment only for Shae to say something completely hilarious the next. No session ever passed without laughter, and Adrian found herself looking forward to her time with Shae.

"I really love your hair like this, so wild," Shae said.

There was a scuffle outside the door, and the next moment Jax stood in the middle of the room. Her cheeks were stained and her neck blotchy, a sure sign that she was distressed. Her shoulders slumped, and for once she didn't say a word. Shae was up in a second, her hand on Jax's shoulder.

"Jax, what happened? Are you okay?"

In an uncharacteristic show of weakness, Jax wrapped her arms around Shae's waist and crumpled in her arms. Shae rocked her gently and gave Adrian a sad smile—probably apologising for overstepping another boundary, which seemed to be the topic of discussion for the day. Adrian nodded quietly and stepped aside to give them a moment alone. She fetched Jax's file from the cabinet and poured her a cup of tea, which she accepted once Shae managed to calm her down to the point where she took a seat.

"Have some tea, Jax," Adrian said.

Adrian could tell that Shae was still unsure about whether she should hang around or leave.

"Shae, why don't you stay for a while if that's all right with Jax?" Jax nodded, so Adrian continued, "Jax, do you want to tell us what upset you?"

Sniffing, Jax sipped on her tea and wiped the back of her hand across her cheeks. Shae pulled some Kleenex from the box on the coffee table and offered them to Jax, who accepted and blew her nose loudly. When it was clear that she was ignoring Adrian, she touched Jax's trembling knee lightly.

"Jax?"

"Jesus, Ramsey, give me a fucking chance to catch my breath."

"Jax, you need to stop treating Dr. Ramsey like this. She's not the enemy. Now, please tell us what's wrong," Shae said.

"I'll tell you what's wrong. My monster of a dickhead father is sending me to Willowmore!"

Adrian winced and started picking at her cuticles. Jax had been a tough nut to crack and she had tried to approach her from various angles. She had tried to be extra attentive and caring, which Jax simply didn't trust. She had tried keeping her advice to a minimum and just serving as a sounding board—which Jax hated even more. She decided to try a more relaxed approach now.

"Wow, Jax. That really sucks. What brought this on?" Adrian asked.

"It sucks? It fucking sucks? That's your professional opinion?"

"No, it's my personal opinion. I know how much you hate government schools. I can only really offer you my professional opinion if you stop attacking me and allow me to do an assessment of the situation."

"I didn't ask for your personal opinion. My father's cash buys you those fucking designer suits and ridiculously expensive stationery. I suggest you fucking earn it."

"Jax, just stop!" Shae shouted.

Caught off-guard, Jax's jaw dropped to the floor and she glared at Shae, who held her hands up in the air.

"That's enough. Take a look around you. Everyone in this room is rooting for you—everyone but you. Do you deserve to be heard? Understood? Valued? Most certainly, but you're making it impossible. I hate to break it to you, but your father is not standing in the way of your happiness. You are," Shae said.

It was clear to Adrian that Jax was battling to hold her composure, but the fact that she showed any restraint was refreshing. Shae wasn't quite done.

"Why don't you give this a real shot? What's the worst that can happen?"

Jax's chest heaved with anger and Adrian feared the worst, but Shae was unrelenting.

"Show up—in time and in peace—and do everything that Dr. Ramsey asks of you for six sessions in a row. If there is no improvement, walk away and tell the world that she failed you, but don't sabotage her like this. It's a dick move, Jax, and you are not a dick."

Adrian had to take charge of this and quickly. How dare Shae interfere like this? What she was doing was dangerous and reckless.

"Ladies, I would like to remind you both that my name is stencilled on that door over there. That's not because your father paid for it, Jax. It's because I happen to be really good at what I do. Now, Jax, I would love to help you, but my patience is wearing a little thin."

Both Jax and Shae were gobsmacked as Adrian had never taken a tone like that. For the moment, it shocked both women into silence. Jax turned to Shae, who was suddenly sitting up straight with wide eyes. Taking a deep breath, Adrian made a show of pulling her "ridiculously expensive" pen and a business card from her blazer pocket. She scribbled on the card and offered it to Jax.

"That is to remind you of your appointment. You don't get to burst into my office whenever it suits you anymore. If you need me before next Wednesday, you can call my receptionist and I will get in contact with you."

Wordlessly, Jax slipped the card into the pocket of her jeans. Adrian couldn't let her leave thinking that she was angry with her. She gripped her shoulder and looked into her eyes.

"Jax, I hope to see you next Wednesday. Please take care of yourself in the meantime."

Jax nodded slightly and turned to Shae.

"Six sessions. That's it."

When Jax slammed the office door behind her, Shae dared to offer Adrian a nervous smile.

"Don't, Shae. I know you probably don't realise it, but you quite possibly just set that girl up to fail. You gave her the opportunity to tap out. You had no right to do that!"

Shae looked at her watch and jumped up.

"Would you look at that? Our time's up," she said.

Adrian was fuming, but at a complete loss for words. She watched as Shae wrapped a scone up in some Kleenex and slipped it into her pocket.

"I'll take this to go."

Adrian opened her mouth to speak, but still had no words.

"Adrian, I didn't think it possible, but you are even more alluring when you are angry."

CHAPTER FOURTEEN

"Am I early, or are they all late?"

Shae collapsed on the futon and clutched a scatter cushion to her chest. Arranging some snacks on a tray, Adrian barely looked up to acknowledge her arrival. She was still irritated with Shae after she ran interference with Jax. Desperate to get some kind of reaction from Adrian, Shae chucked the scatter cushion in her direction. She chuckled when Adrian turned just in time to catch it.

"Let's kiss and make up, Adrian. I hate this."

Adrian chucked the scatter cushion back at her and added lemon to the pitcher of Kola Tonic and lemonade.

"The fact that you made that for me despite being upset with me tells me that there is hope," Shae said as she pointed to the pitcher.

"You were out of line, Shae."

"I know that, but can you honestly say that the outcome was less than desirable?" Shae argued.

Adrian paused and shot her a look of indignation.

"Are you kidding me? You managed to buy me an impossible deadline while encouraging Jax to give up on treatment."

"That's not how I see it, Doc."

"Shocking," Adrian mumbled.

"The way I see it, I bought you six weeks of her undivided attention and devotion. I have no doubt that you'll get through to her."

Adrian took her frustrations out on the cling wrap as she ripped and pulled frantically at the end. Since Shae walked out of her room last week she had been brewing on this. She was just overwhelmed by all of her mixed emotions. On the one hand, she had to deal with what was now an undeniable growing attraction to a patient. On the other hand, she felt like she was losing control of the situation with Jax, which she blamed Shae for. It was convenient, because it gave her an excuse to be angry at her. She felt her skin tingling when Shae rested her hands on her shoulders.

"Here, let me do that."

Biting down on her bottom lip, she closed her eyes for a moment, handed Shae the roll of cling wrap, and poured herself some juice.

"I am sorry, Adrian. I promise you that this will work out. Trust me."

Adrian simply stared at Shae while she calmly rolled out the cling wrap and effortlessly covered the bowls. She doubted that a caterer could have done a better job. She added patience to the ever-growing list of positive attributes of Shae McPherson. A list of attributes she needed to ignore if she wanted to keep her practice and her pristine reputation.

"I hope you're right, Shae. I really hope you're right."

"I have an idea, but I don't know if we'll have enough time to discuss it before everyone else gets here. Can I see you after the session?" Shae asked.

Adrian found it increasingly more difficult to spend any time alone with Shae, and this setting would be even more of a challenge. Somehow, she felt less in control in the safety of her home, but she couldn't exactly tell Shae that. Before she had an opportunity to dream up an excuse why she couldn't see Shae afterward, the other patients started arriving.

Jax seemed preoccupied, but at least she wasn't foaming at the mouth. She also decided to remove her earphones for the entire duration of the session. Adrian suggested that they start the session by listing goals that they hoped to achieve through therapy. She was reminded of the uniqueness of each patient's individual journey when their goals ranged from surviving a single day without an episode of anxiety, to being restored to competent caretaker of a needy toddler. The reason she had grouped these patients together was because she felt that despite their varying journeys, they all had certain things in common. The purpose of this session was to highlight the similarities.

"Jax, how about you? Are you hoping to achieve something specific in these sessions?" Adrian asked.

Jax simply shook her head and shrugged. Adrian decided not to push her too much because she was actually making eye contact with everyone in the room. Shae had other plans, though.

"Are you sure, Jax? A gorgeous woman once told me that we always have expectations, even if we aren't aware of what they are," Shae said.

Blushing as she remembered the first conversation she ever had with Shae, Adrian jumped up and refilled her glass. She reminded everyone that they were welcome to help themselves to something to drink any time during the session. Meanwhile, Shae and Jax were participating in one of their stare-offs.

"I don't think a goal and an expectation is the same thing," Jax said.

"I think there's a direct link between your goals and your expectations," Shae replied.

"This is not Willowmore, Shae, but please do explain," Jax insisted.

Shae glanced in Adrian's direction, asking for permission to engage with Jax. Adrian nodded ever so slightly. She couldn't exactly ask one of her patients not to engage in a group setting. Shae was very unpredictable, but Adrian was going to have to trust her.

"I think an expectation can be the destination, while your goals can be pit stops on the journey. For instance, if my expectation is to walk away from the group sessions with a restored sense of worth, my goals will have to be centred around that."

Not for the first time, Adrian was deeply impressed by Shae's intuition. Without knowing much about Jax or her history, Shae had instinctively identified the root of the young girl's problems.

She was amazed by the way that Shae was able to connect with people on such a deep level without much effort and in a very short space of time.

"My goals will probably have to include things like examining how I see and value myself, assessing how others see and value me, and finding ways to bridge the gap between my reality and what is perceived by others."

Nodding and smiling sarcastically, Jax slowly started clapping her hands.

"Wow, Shae. The good doctor is certainly rubbing off on you. Perhaps not in the way you would like, but you do sound like her," Jax said.

Adrian silently hoped that her patients didn't take to heart the ridiculous insinuations about Shae's intentions with her. She knew that Shae had hit a nerve, though, and she could only hope that Jax would go home and give it some thought. Jax could definitely benefit from introspection about her self-worth and Adrian had suggested it to her before, but perhaps a second opinion would serve as validation.

"Dr. Ramsey, my expectations are very simple. I expect to be pried open like Pandora's box. My goals are slightly more complicated, so if it's quite all right with you I will try and figure that part out as we go along."

"That's a deal, Jax. There will be no prying. I promise to keep that for our one-on-one sessions," Adrian said and winked. "Now that you've set your goals for these sessions, I would like for you to talk a little bit about goals you've already achieved. These can be goals that you achieved outside of therapy as well, anything that you found challenging and are proud of mastering."

Andie started off by telling the group about the first goal she had set for herself when she had started seeing Dr. Ramsey. It was relatively simple: she only wanted the courage to finally sell the house where her mother had committed suicide. She had been consumed by guilt, thinking that she would be abandoning her mother by walking away from the house she'd grown up in.

"Dr. Ramsey worked with me on separating the memory of my mother from the house where she took her last breath. It was by no means a small feat, and knowing that I am able to let go of that house gives me hope. It feels like I can do anything now."

She actually earned a half-smile from Jax, something that Adrian had never seen. Basil was up next. He spoke about how his experience in the military had impacted his life and how difficult it had been admitting to his wife that he needed help.

"Military men are a different breed. We are from the generation of men who were brought up to believe that real men don't cry. Exposing your weakness is worse than dying. I had to bite the bullet in order to even have a chance of saving my marriage."

Eliza nervously tugged at the scarf around her neck when Adrian indicated that she was next. She seemed embarrassed when she finally told the rest of the group what her biggest challenge had been.

"I should have just gone first! My biggest challenge suddenly seems so insignificant compared to what you both have had to face," Eliza said.

"No challenge is ever insignificant, Eliza. It's a relative concept. The goal or challenge might be different for everyone, but the emotions it evokes are probably the same for everyone," Adrian said.

Up until the attack by her ex-boyfriend, Eliza's art had been her refuge and she had earned a living by selling her paintings and teaching art classes. For quite some time after the attack, she hadn't been able to pick up her brushes and she had given up on her teaching as well.

"Needless to say, that had a huge impact on my finances, but what was even more devastating was the toll that my absence from art took on my psyche. It felt like my ex-boyfriend had ripped out my soul and left behind a shell of the woman I had once been. Art was what defined me, and I hated that he had taken that from me as well."

Blushing, Eliza clasped her hands together in her lap.

"It's so silly, but the biggest challenge for me was to start painting again. I can still remember the first time I mixed some paint on my palette. I was trying to re-create the colour of this ugly slash across my throat. It almost felt like I could transfer the scar from my neck to the canvas and finally be rid of it."

Shae seemed engrossed. "Did you?" she asked.

"Excuse me?" Eliza replied.

"Did you match the colour?"

Eliza seemed perplexed by Shae's question. Frowning, she glanced at Adrian as if to ask her where she found this nutcase. Adrian gave her an encouraging smile.

"I did, actually. I matched it perfectly, and my first post-attack painting sold within two hours of being exhibited."

"That must have been such a great feeling. Was that a catalyst for your healing process?"

"Jesus, Shae, just take her number," Jax interrupted.

Adrian reminded all of her patients that interaction among the group was highly recommended. She admitted to herself that she was also getting slightly uncomfortable with Shae's fascination with Eliza, but for completely inappropriate reasons.

"It actually did so much for my healing process, Shae. It gave me hope and that was what I needed the most at the time."

Shae nodded in understanding.

"I know what you mean. Before the attack, I used to host an event for the students. I bought a Wendy hut and erected it on the school premises. Every Friday, the students would gather in the hut, which they named the Zen Den, to play board games, pool, and darts."

Shae shifted in her seat and started cracking her knuckles.

"The first few months following the attack was the worst for me. I couldn't spend time in that hut, surrounded by loud teenagers, some with sneakers and hoodies resembling that of my attacker. Eventually, I started missing the kids and I realised that if I sacrificed something I loved doing, I was still stuck in that storeroom in the back of my class, held hostage by a deranged boy."

There was a beat of silence as Shae took a deep breath and offered her captive audience a weak smile.

"So, I showed up at the Zen Den one Friday with a thumping heart, clenched fists, and a stomach in knots. I only stayed for a short while, but I did it. I kept showing up every Friday, and eventually I was able to enjoy my time with the kids again. For me, it certainly set things in motion. I read a whole bunch of books written by survivors of violent attacks, and a few months later I agreed to see Dr. Ramsey."

Adrian found herself winking at Shae and quickly turned her attention to Theodore, who was yet to say a word. She convinced herself that her reaction to Shae was no different than her reaction to any of her other patients. Was it?

Theodore explained how his entire life had seemed like it consisted of one challenge after another since his wife's passing. To him, the accomplishments were served in small daily dosages. Every day that he managed to get up in the morning, dress and feed his daughter, drop her off at preschool, and tuck her in at night was a victory.

Adrian was always taken aback by the intensity of Theodore's pain. When she had started treating him, she couldn't help but be a little envious of his deceased wife. To be the object of affection that ran quite that deeply was a privilege that had eluded Adrian. After more than a year, Theodore didn't seem an iota less devastated by his wife's departure.

"It takes every ounce of strength that I have, but I do it. Every day that I manage to take care of Lilly gives me just enough strength to do it for one more day."

Adrian snapped her fingers and pointed to Theodore with wide eyes.

"That is exactly what I was hoping to achieve today. Thank you so much, Theodore. We don't ever have to gather enough courage to make it through a week, a month, or a year. We only need to get through one day at a time. Whether you believe it or not, getting through one day will give you exactly the amount of courage you may need to get through just one more day."

There was a collective sigh, and Adrian spent some time explaining to her patients what she had in mind for the next few sessions. Moments later, they loaded their plates with snacks and chatted among each other. The atmosphere was considerably lighter as the topics of discussion shifted to the mundane and ordinary. For a while, none of them were damaged souls, they were just people discussing the latest outrage surrounding President Trump and the effect of the global recession. Adrian was surprised to see Andie talking to Jax, her cheeks aflame.

"I know, right? Brave move," Shae whispered in her ear.

The shiver that travelled down Adrian's spine finally escaped through her toes, and by the time she turned to Shae, she felt her cheeks must have resembled that of Andie's. The smirk on Shae's face told Adrian that the blush hadn't gone unnoticed.

"I'm very curious to see where that could lead. God knows Jax needs a few good friends," Adrian said as she bit into a cocktail sausage roll.

"That's the downside of having proper cleavage," Shae said.

She stared at the cleft between Adrian's breasts where a few flakes of pastry had come to rest. Adrian's immediate response was to make sure that her other patients were not privy to Shae's flirting. Once she confirmed that they were all engaged in conversation and not paying her any attention, she dipped the tip of her finger into her mouth, dabbed at the flakes, and flicked them in Shae's direction.

"You just can't help yourself, can you, Shae?"

"Guilty as charged, Doc. Now, please stop distracting me. I wanted to chat to you about Jax."

Grateful for the diversion, Adrian sipped on her juice while Shae glanced in Jax's direction to make sure she was not within earshot. Andie seemed to have her undivided attention for the moment, so Shae tugged on Adrian's elbow, leading her to a futon at the back of the room. Perching on the edge of her seat, Shae stretched her legs out in front of her and slipped her joined palms between her thighs.

"Are you actually nervous, Shae McPherson?"

"Would it make you more accommodating if I said that I was?" Shae asked.

"What are you up to, Shae? Just spit it out."

Leaning back on the futon, Shae shifted so her body was facing Adrian, who had her arms crossed over her chest.

"Why do you feel the need to protect yourself in my presence, Dr. Ramsey?"

"Why do you insist on psychoanalysing me, Shae?"

"Because you're such an easy study, Doctor. So, can you stop flirting with me so I can discuss a serious matter with you?"

Adrian swiped her hand through the air, indicating that Shae had the floor.

"Now, please just stay calm. This is just an idea and if you really hate it, I won't do it."

"My disapproval has never stopped you before, but please carry on."

"Would you be comfortable with Jax spending some time with my kids at the Zen Den? I mean, you can come and personally vet the kids if you don't trust my judgment. I just think that she could use some friends. You said so yourself earlier."

Adrian was amused by the grovelling. Shae had clearly learned her lesson when it came to overstepping the boundaries with Jax and her treatment. Technically, Adrian couldn't stop Shae from inviting Jax anywhere, and she was touched by her courtesy. It was no surprise to her that Shae was invested in Jax's wellbeing. She had come to realise that when Shae cared, she cared deeply. Naturally, as a therapist, Adrian was worried about Jax and the challenge she was facing of adapting in a new environment. Perhaps Shae could alleviate some of that anxiety.

"Don't make me regret this, Shae."

"The only thing you'll regret is not trusting me sooner, Adrian."

"I would like to observe one of the sessions, though."

"The only way I'm going to allow that is if you immediately stop calling them sessions. Come by this Friday. Obviously, we can't tell Jax that you're there to observe her. We'll have to think of something," Shae said.

Adrian couldn't agree more, but Jax was no fool. She wasn't sure that Jax wouldn't see right through any façade. That kid's intuition had caught Adrian off-guard so many times before.

"Maybe she'll think that you're stalking me because you find me so completely irresistible," Shae teased.

"The fact that you find that believable tells me you're not in touch with reality, Shae. Sometimes, I worry about you."

Shae chuckled loudly. "Oh, Dr. Ramsey, I don't know how long you will be able to fight your desires, but I do admire your courage."

Shae frowned when Adrian suddenly shook her head and rolled her eyes. Staring across the room, Adrian had gone from playful to almost hostile in three seconds flat.

"Do you admire my courage as much as Maddison admires your backside?"

Shae turned around to find Maddison leaning in the doorway with a wicked smile on her face. Offering her a small wave, Shae made a show of leaning into Adrian's personal space.

"Even more."

CHAPTER FIFTEEN

Drumming her fingers on the steering wheel, Shae stared at the neatly trimmed hedges surrounding a quaint little house. Apart from needing a paint job, the house seemed well maintained. In her mind, she had pictured the house that Devon Nelson had grown up in as a dilapidated shack, mirroring the mental state of the boy himself.

She took a deep breath and finally exited her car. No amount of pep talks or encouraging mantras could have prepared her for what she saw when Hillary Nelson opened that front door. For a few seconds, Shae was staring into the same blue eyes that had haunted her on many a sleepless night.

"I'm so sorry, dear. I'm afraid that boy was the spitting image of his mother."

Digging her nails into her palms, Shae tried to control her breathing. It had been a while since her last panic attack, but the onset of the needles and pins in her hands meant that it was imminent. Shae felt her throat constricting and her eyes darted around as she searched for something to ground her in the present. She flinched when Hillary gripped her by the shoulder.

"I'm going to lead you to that bench right over there, darling. Just breathe."

Shae was moments away from blacking out completely and she desperately needed some air. She felt a warm hand on her back as her legs gave out mere seconds before her buttocks hit the bench. The darkness behind her eyelids was quickly followed up with a wave of nausea.

"That's okay, darling. Just take deep breaths and the nausea will pass. I would run inside to get you a glass of water, but I find that being alone when these attacks hit is much worse than being nauseated."

Shae's entire scalp tingled and her fingers started curling up as every cell in her body was deprived of oxygen. She could feel her heart hammering, the fierce thrumming echoing behind her eyes and in her ears.

"Okay, you simply have to start breathing. Deep breaths. Come on, breathe with me."

Holding Shae's momentarily deformed hands in her own, Hillary inhaled deeply. She squeezed Shae's hands gently to encourage her to follow her example.

"Come on, dear. Let's do this together before your hands get worse. I know how painful it is to pry open those fingers when they really start curling up."

Shae tried to focus on Hillary's calming voice, but her mind wouldn't let her forget for a second that this same woman had given birth to the boy that had tortured her for hours. Desperate for release, Shae conjured up the image of Adrian admonishing her for being so foolish. Adrian certainly wouldn't think this wise. She should have told Adrian that she was planning this visit today, but here she was hyperventilating in the front yard of Devon Nelson's mother.

"Miss McPherson, if you don't get this under control I'll have to drive you to the emergency room. That in itself could be disastrous since I'm half-blind."

Shae focused on her breathing while silently reasoning with herself. Devon was long gone, and she was no longer trapped in that pool of blood in the back of her classroom. Slowly, the sounds in the background made their way through the throbbing in her ears. A flock of birds were perched on a bird feeder nearby, softly chirping. In the far distance a dog was barking and she focused on the sound of cars passing on the main road behind the house.

"That's better, my girlie. You're doing just fine."

Hillary stroked Shae's fingers and kept talking in an effort to distract her. After a few minutes, Shae's breathing stabilised but her cramped fingers were still rigid. The muscles in her throat were finally relaxed enough to allow her to speak.

"I'm so sorry, Mrs. Nelson."

"Don't you apologise, dear. Just take your time. Would you be okay if I slip away for a second to get you a glass of water?"

Wincing as she tried to flex her fingers, she simply nodded. Moments later, Hillary returned with a tender smile and a tall glass of water. Seeing Shae's cramped hands lying motionless in her lap, Hillary held the glass to Shae's lips.

"We need to get those fingers straightened out," Hillary said.

"I'm not looking forward to that. Thanks, Mrs. Nelson."

"I find that it's much like ripping off a plaster. You have to be quick about it," Hillary replied.

Half an hour later, Shae was seated in a cosy living room clutching a cup of sweet tea with her right hand and slowly flexing the fingers of her left. Across from her, Hillary looked more relaxed now that a trip to the emergency room was off the cards. Shae suspected that there was more than a dash of whiskey in her tea because she could feel her shoulder muscles relaxing.

"Thank you for taking care of me. I haven't had an attack that severe in quite some time," Shae said.

"You are quite welcome, young lady. Thank goodness I have some experience in that department. How are your fingers now?"

"They'll be stiff for a few hours, but they're already feeling much better. Do you also suffer from panic attacks?"

Seemingly hesitant to answer, Hillary started picking at her cuticles. When she finally made eye contact with Shae, she seemed at least ten years older and her shoulders hunched.

"My Devon was afflicted with many forms of anxiety from a very young age. He suffered his first panic attack when he was five years old."

For such a long time, Shae had imagined being in that very chair, facing that very woman, in that very house. In her mind, she'd had many conversations with Devon's mother. She'd had a long list of questions that she needed answered. Now, looking Hillary in the eye, she was at a loss for words.

"I can't begin to imagine what it must be like for you, my dear. I've hoped that I would be afforded the opportunity to lay eyes on you, and here you are. Suddenly, I don't know what to say," Hillary said.

For the first time, Shae imagined the suffering this woman must have endured. Strangely, she was comforted by what she now realised was a shared burden to a certain extent.

"I know what you mean, Mrs. Nelson. I felt so prepared driving over here, and all it took to make me come undone was one look at you. I'm sure you hear this all the time, but he looked just like you."

"He sure did. I don't expect you to understand, but that boy was my whole life. You know, it was always just the two of us. His father was never involved in his life. In fact, he never met his father."

This was all news to Shae. At the time of the attack, very little information was available. Shae had never wanted to know more about the boy until now. She finally felt ready to learn the more intimate details of who Devon had been. Perhaps getting to know the person behind the violence and cruelty would assuage the anger that Shae still felt.

"Mrs. Nelson, for the first year after the attack, I was sure that I could deal with the trauma by myself. I immersed myself in self-help books and tried all kinds of different treatment options, but a few months ago, Mr. Foster, the school principal, insisted that I meet with a therapist."

Straightening her dress, Hillary simply nodded, encouraging Shae to carry on.

"I was reluctant at first, but I figured that if my job depended on it I had no real choice in the matter. My therapist has been working with me on a few techniques, and I have to admit that some of them brought me relief and offered me skills that I find tremendously helpful."

Hillary offered a weak smile.

"I don't know if this makes any sense, but it feels like I will only truly be able to find some peace if I can find some meaning. It's so easy to call it a senseless attack, but that hasn't been enough for me. I know that the only person who would really have been able to answer my one burning question was Devon."

"You want to know why he did it," Hillary said.

Shae drained the cup that suddenly felt like lead in her hand and returned it to the tray in the middle of the rickety old coffee table. Shaking her head, Hillary pointed to the mantelpiece with an arthritic index finger.

"Right over there, I keep the last picture that I had taken of my Devon. I've laid it down flat on the surface so the two of you wouldn't have to stare at each other. From time to time, I sit right in this chair and talk to that picture like a crazy old bat."

Shifting in her chair, Hillary softly cleared her throat.

"I've asked him many a question, but never why. The truth is, Devon wouldn't even know the answer to that question. His diseased mind only ever held questions, never answers. He was diagnosed with schizophrenia at the age of sixteen."

Shae started wringing her hands in her lap but quickly stopped when her fingers painfully reminded her that she had been deprived of oxygen for quite some time. If Hillary sensed her discomfort, she didn't mention it. Something told Shae that this woman needed to tell her Devon's story as much as she needed to hear it.

"The process of diagnosing an illness such as schizophrenia is just the naming of a beast you've cohabited with for years. Suddenly, Devon's moods had a name. There were complicated terms that I couldn't pronounce, a prognosis I never understood, and boxes and boxes of medicine I put all of my faith in. What lacked, was reason."

Hillary let out a long breath before she continued.

"No doctor could tell me why Devon was afflicted by this monstrous disease, why he was withdrawn, emotionally distant, and at times so far removed from reality. Nobody told me why my son's skin crawled when I bestowed him with affection. The doctor never did explain to me why my son was so self-destructive and irrational."

Shae had very limited information on this illness, and she made a mental note to pick Adrian's brain later on. Some of the things that Devon had shouted at her in the back of that room had left her assuming that he was an addict and that the attack was fuelled by desperation. He had banged the gun against his temple repeatedly, asking her where his pills were. She now realised that he could have been referring to his prescription meds.

"Mrs. Nelson, I had no idea. Devon seemed disorientated, and in so many ways his behaviour matched that of a drug abuser. I assumed that he was battling some kind of addiction."

"He suffered from episodes of grand delusion and was often pestered by hallucinations. His reactions would definitely have mirrored that of an addict, Miss McPherson. I have no doubt that my entire family thought me a liar for always denying the fact that he was a user."

Shae felt so sad for this woman, who had probably lost all of her family and friends for something that was out of her control.

"Please, call me Shae."

Leaning forward in her chair, Hillary placed her hand on top of Shae's knee and clucked.

"I wish we had met under different circumstances, Shae. You seem like a lovely person, and it pains me to know that flesh of my flesh caused you so much misery."

"Mrs. Nelson, healing is a process and not an event. Coming to see you is just a part of that process and the intention was never to lay blame at your door. Just from what I've learned in the last few minutes, I don't doubt that you couldn't have prevented my misery."

Hillary insisted that Shae have another cup of tea—without the whiskey this time around. She spoke about Devon and his last weeks. It became clear to Shae that Devon's mental state had deteriorated in those last few days and that he had no longer been rooted in reality when he had stepped into her classroom. Hillary had found his meds stashed in a pillowcase under his mattress months later when she cleaned out his room. Devon had been completely unhinged and off his meds by the time the attack had occurred. By the time Shae was ready to leave, Hillary seemed almost sad at her departure.

Shae felt overwhelmed as she waved at the forlorn figure in the driveway. Mindlessly, she drove around for over an hour. The intended purpose was to clear her head, but in reality, her mind felt saturated with so many conflicting emotions. She didn't know how to even start breaking down all of the information she had gained by that single visit.

Her journey ended when she parked her car in Adrian's driveway and knocked on the front door.

CHAPTER SIXTEEN

"Shae?"

Adrian's heart skipped a beat when she opened the door and saw a very distraught Shae with slumped shoulders and bewildered eyes. Without giving it a second thought, she pulled Shae across the threshold and into the warmth of her foyer.

"Talk to me. What happened?"

Shae seemed to be searching her mind for the right words, but she came up empty. Adrian led her to the lounge and sat her down on the couch. Her empty coffee cup and the stack of reports that she had been working on minutes earlier occupied the majority of the coffee table. She swiped it all aside so she could position herself across from Shae. Sitting down carefully, she leaned forward and took Shae's hands in her own, squeezing lightly.

"Oh, God, please don't do that!" Shae exclaimed.

Assuming that she had crossed a boundary, Adrian self-consciously wrapped her hands across her upper arms and leaned back.

"Sorry, Adrian. Look at my hands," Shae said softly.

She held them out to Adrian, palms facing up. Her thumbs were still wedged between her middle and ring fingers. Cupping both of Shae's hands softly now, Adrian inspected her fingers. Gently, she tested the flexibility and shook her head when Shae winced at every touch.

"You hyperventilated. Shae, you need to flex your fingers, even if it's very painful. Has this happened before?"

Shae nodded as Adrian started rubbing her warm hands across two cramped ones.

"Heat might help a little bit, but you need to flatten out these hands. Rest them on your thighs for me," Adrian said.

"The worst is over, Adrian. I can move them now."

"Okay, well, don't allow your thumbs to curl up like that. Just open your fingers and rest your palms on your thighs."

Shae obeyed and let out a long breath. Resting her hands on Shae's knees, Adrian silently questioned Shae with deeply concerned eyes. Shae told her about the visit she had paid Mrs. Nelson and the initial horror of looking into her kind but startlingly familiar eyes. Ten minutes later, Adrian had taken a seat next to a slightly calmer Shae.

"You should have told me that you were planning to do that, Shae."

"I know. I didn't want to be dissuaded, Adrian. I know it probably doesn't make sense to you, but I needed to do this. The PET and CPT that we've been applying in treatment really works wonders, but there was always just something in the way."

Nodding slowly, Adrian absentmindedly drew her fingers over her scalp and through her hair.

"Like a blockage?" she asked.

"Yes, that's exactly what it was. Even with all the other forms of treatment I attempted on my own. It all alleviated my symptoms, but only ever up to a certain point. Driving away from Mrs. Nelson, I could feel that tension releasing. It washed over me in waves of emotion. On the drive over here, I felt saddened, relieved, rejuvenated, exhausted, proud, and exhilarated, all almost simultaneously."

Flexing her fingers, Shae rhythmically balled her hands into fists for short periods before opening her palms and wiggling her tight fingers.

"That was an extremely intense panic attack, but would you believe me if I said that I instinctively know that it was my last one?"

Adrian stared at her for a few silent moments.

"I would," Adrian finally replied.

"Really?"

"Yes, really. Shae, you seem to forget sometimes that I'm a qualified therapist. I recognise a breakthrough when I see one. I've seen a few," Adrian said.

Knowing that Shae needed to decompress after what she had just been through, Adrian had to find a way to get Shae to talk more about her experience. She excused herself and encouraged Shae to just sit back and relax for a few minutes.

In the kitchen, she worked quickly. She buttered a few croissants, arranged an assortment of cold meats that she had bought from a German bakery on a plate, and sliced some fresh cheese. She filled a ceramic bowl with a homemade balsamic onion marmalade.

"What's all this?"

She jumped at the sound of Shae's voice. When she turned around, she found Shae leaning against the doorjamb with her hands in her pockets, looking as lovely as the spread she had just prepared. That was her cue—if she was comparing Shae to something she wanted to taste, she had to get rid of her as soon as possible. She would let her decompress and then make up some lunch meeting she had to attend.

"I thought you could use something to eat. You need to keep your blood sugar levels up, you know. I mean, it's what any responsible doctor would do, right?"

The lopsided grin on Shae's face confirmed her worst suspicions: she had been caught staring at Shae like she was a snack and not her patient. Better get to that meeting as soon as possible then.

"I wouldn't think that blood sugar levels form part of your expertise, Doc. I don't mind you making up creative little excuses to get me to decompress, though. Besides, this spread looks awesome."

So, the smile had nothing to do with Adrian's slip of professionalism. Shae simply saw through her façade designed to trick her into decompression. Adrian sighed with relief.

"I'll be polite and not mention that you totally just mentally licked your lips while checking me out."

Shae slowly approached from the doorway, hands still in her pockets and that silly smile now spreading wider. Adrian was certain that Shae could hear the thundering of her heart as she leaned closer, eyes locked on Adrian's. Shae slipped her right hand out of her pocket and reached for the plate containing their lunch feast. Her fingers brushed lightly across Adrian's arm and Adrian wasn't able to hide her reaction since Shae's eyes were still locked on hers.

"Don't flatter yourself, Miss McPherson."

It came out as a whisper, and Adrian performed a mental eye roll. What was this? High school?

"I'll just get this for you while you pretend to get us something to drink simply so you can gather yourself," Shae replied and strutted off to the sunroom.

"Get a grip," Adrian admonished herself while preparing a pot of coffee.

By the time she reached the sunroom, Shae was halfway through her croissant and clearly enjoying the unexpected lunch.

"If the noises you're making are anything to go by, that marmalade is everything the lady at the deli promised it would be."

"Did she promise you that the earth would move? Because it did," Shae said through bites of bliss.

Adrian poured herself a cup of coffee and sampled various slices of cold meat, all covered in the revered marmalade. She caught Shae staring at her when she recovered a smidgen of marmalade in the corner of her mouth with the tip of her tongue. Time to move this session along.

"Well, if I'm ever making it to that meeting, we should get started."

"Who is your meeting with?" Shae asked.

Adrian had no doubt that Shae was onto her.

"It's just a colleague. Now, tell me more about your meeting with Mrs. Nelson."

Shae licked some marmalade off her thumb and washed her last bite down with sweet coffee.

"Where are you meeting?" Shae continued her interrogation.

Adrian dumped her croissant back on her plate and wiped her fingers on a napkin.

"Shae, please. Give me a break. Can we do this?"

Shae held her hands in the air and smiled sincerely.

"Okay, Adrian. Let's do it."

Shae spent the next half hour digging into her feelings and answering all of Adrian's questions, which were all designed to break down into minute details the experience of meeting the mother of her attacker. Adrian softened when Shae explained how the panic attack had unfolded and how efficient Mrs. Nelson had been in calming her down.

"It turns out Devon was diagnosed with schizophrenia when he was only sixteen."

"Oh, Shae, that's terrible."

"I know, right? Is that common? Being diagnosed at such a young age?" Shae asked.

At that point, the session had turned into something more personal. Shae didn't seem like she was talking to a therapist and Adrian didn't feel like she was attending to a patient. It wasn't decompression anymore. Adrian was genuinely interested in what Shae had discovered on her visit. Dangerous, but what was she supposed to do? It would be rude to chuck Shae out. Both women had kicked off their shoes and Shae clutched a scatter cushion to her chest. Adrian turned sideways and draped her arm across the back of the futon.

"I certainly wouldn't say that it's common. Unfortunately, some of the symptoms can easily be mistaken for normal teenage behaviour. It's not uncommon for teenagers to become isolated as they start valuing their privacy. As I'm sure you know, some teenagers reach a point where they feel like they can't relate to their parents anymore and they kind of shut themselves in their rooms from time to time."

Shae nodded in agreement, drawing circles on the cushion with her index finger.

"Most teenagers also go through a phase where they don't want their parents' affection, especially in public. There's no doubt that they all get irrational occasionally. The fact that Devon was diagnosed so early is probably a testament to a very attentive mother."

"I think it's safe to say that she was a good mother to that boy. From what I gather, she worked her hands to the bone to afford him the professional help that he needed. She was a receptionist and had to do part-time work to add to her income. I imagine that it can be expensive looking after a child with that kind of mental disability," Shae said.

"Did she mention anything about his father?"

"No, she simply said that he wasn't part of Devon's life. I suppose that fact didn't exactly help the situation."

Adrian picked at the fluff on the throw draped across the futon.

"I don't think having a more involved father would really make much of a difference, Shae. Devon's illness wasn't sparked by abandonment, it's more of a chemical imbalance most of the time. Generally, if a patient remains on medication and is monitored closely, they can function pretty well."

Shae flipped the cushion around and turned sideways on the futon to face Adrian.

"Mrs. Nelson found a stash of pills months after the incident. Devon had been hiding his meds for quite a while, so by the time he attacked me, he had been completely unstable."

"That certainly explains a lot. Are you saying that he wasn't a drug addict? I remember you mentioning that had been an assumption you made at the time," Adrian said.

"No, I was wrong. His poor mother mentioned that she had to defend him against her own family, who had all been under the impression that Devon was an addict. I feel so sorry for that woman. She had literally no support structure to lean on while dealing with an angry and unstable young man."

Adrian poured herself another cup of coffee while Shae devoured another croissant. Adrian was always inspired by the amount of passion Shae applied to every single thing she did, whether it was flirting with her therapist or eating a croissant. She hardly noticed when a blob of marmalade landed on her white T-shirt.

"That's going to leave a stain," Adrian said and pointed to Shae's chest.

"Some things are worth the trouble, Doc. Can you hand me one of those napkins?"

Adrian handed her a clean paper towel and tried her utmost not to gawk at Shae's chest as she tended to the stain on the long-sleeved T-shirt that clung to her like a second layer of skin. Had she not been focused on Shae's bosom, she wouldn't have noticed a clearly sensitive nipple standing to attention due to some vigorous rubbing. But she had noticed. Shae had noticed too, but she didn't seem embarrassed at all.

"I'm really glad you were home, Adrian."

"Me too."

Dumping the paper towel on the table, Shae rested her hands on her hips and winked at Adrian.

"I better leave before you actually pretend to get ready for your fake meeting."

Adrian advised Shae that although she truly believed Shae had had a breakthrough, it didn't mean that she could abandon her treatment plan. They would monitor her progress for the next few months while considering a shift in direction with her treatment.

"Thanks for everything, Adrian. If you weren't so wildly attracted to me, I would have given you a heartfelt hug. We can't risk you brushing up against my sensitive nipples, now can we?"

CHAPTER SEVENTEEN

Laughter filled the room as Adrian's patients gathered around the snacks table at the close of another group session. Seeing these people connect on such a deep level and form meaningful friendships with each other filled Adrian with a sense of pride. When she had started the group session just over four months ago, she had been optimistic, but she certainly hadn't expected this.

The connection between Jax and Andie was undeniable. Jax had miraculously made some headway in her sessions with Adrian as well. Adrian wouldn't admit it, but Shae's suggestion of a six-session truce worked wonders and the change in Jax's attitude was remarkable to say the least. Adrian was certain that Andie's attention had everything to do with the blush on Jax's cheeks and the pep in her step.

Theodore and Basil also seemed to have found a few common interests and were currently discussing the joys of fly-fishing. Adrian's heart skipped a beat when she glanced across the room and saw Shae laughing with Eliza. Adrian's growing attraction to Shae had not faded in the six months of treating her as a patient. She had spoken to Easton on various occasions about the matter, believing that voicing the truth, albeit using hypothetical situations and no names, would take the power out of it. If the unease settling under her skin every time Shae clutched Eliza's arm in a fit of laughter was any indication, her theory didn't work.

"That's just wonderful," Adrian mumbled to herself.

"Adrian, your garden is just bursting with colour. How you manage a garden this size beats me," Theodore said.

She hadn't even noticed that the conversation between Theodore and Basil had dried up.

"Thanks, Theodore. I guess gardening is my therapy. I have help, though. My dad's gardener comes by once a month."

"Summer is around the corner and by then once a month won't be enough. I don't mind helping out. Just let me know if you ever need a hand," Theodore offered with a sincere smile.

"I'm not too bad with a shovel myself, Doc," Shae interrupted.

Shae had the uncanny ability to appear out of thin air. Just seconds ago she had been deep in conversation with Eliza, clearly enjoying her company. Now, here she was winking at Adrian and stealing a cheese puff from her plate. Adrian wondered if she was so overly familiar with everyone else she knew.

"Thanks, guys. I'm sure I'll be fine. Are you hungry, Shae?"

"Nope, everything just tastes better off your plate," Shae replied.

Theodore excused himself promptly, said his goodbyes to the rest of the patients, and rushed to his car. Shae had accompanied Adrian to see him off—uninvited, of course. Adrian turned around as his car disappeared around the corner and found Shae leaning against her own car in the driveway, arms crossed over her chest.

"What?"

"That look on your face…what's that all about?" Adrian asked.

"What look?" Shae asked, shrugging her shoulders.

"I can tell that you're dying to say something. I can also tell that I won't like it," Adrian said.

At that moment, Eliza and Basil strolled down the driveway. They both thanked Adrian for a wonderful session and then Eliza turned to Shae. She gave her a hug and swiftly rubbed her hand over Shae's upper arm.

"Thanks for the chat earlier, Shae. I think I might take you up on the offer. Can we discuss it over coffee sometime this week?" Eliza asked.

"Sure thing. I'll call you later. Take care, Eliza."

Adrian offered Eliza a strained smile and rushed back to the sunroom, reminding herself all the way that she had no reason to care about what Shae McPherson planned to do with Eliza, or any other woman for that matter. Not much later, Jax and Andie excused themselves, explaining that they had arranged to meet up with some friends for a movie. In the meantime, Shae had made herself comfortable on the futon and showed no signs of leaving anytime soon.

"Do you live here now, Shae?" Jax asked sarcastically.

"No, Jax. I'm old school. We can't live in sin. My mother would never approve," Shae said.

Adrian had no desire to chitchat with Shae and found it difficult to hide her irritation. Jax declined Adrian's offer to walk them out, punched Shae in the shoulder—her way of showing affection—and left the two women in awkward silence. Adrian took one look at Shae and wordlessly started cleaning up, stacking up the dirty plates and arranging the leftover snacks on one tray. When all the dishes were stowed away and the bar counter wiped down, she sat down on the futon opposite Shae, who was staring at her intensely.

"No more distractions, then?" Shae asked.

The fact that Adrian's arms were crossed over her chest and her foot was bouncing up and down warned Shae to approach with caution. The bouncing suddenly stopped.

"Jax makes a valid point. You're quite familiar, Shae."

"Would you like for me to leave?" Shae asked quietly, probably knowing the answer to the question.

"What are your intentions with Eliza?" Adrian asked, convincing herself that she was simply acting in the best interest of her patients.

Shae cocked a brow and crushed a scatter cushion against her chest.

"What are yours with Theodore?" Shae countered.

Adrian burst out laughing, but Shae did not look amused.

"Are you kidding me, Shae? You know you're completely out of line, right?"

"It's never stopped me before, Adrian. That guy is flirting with you and you're just pretending that you don't notice."

Adrian could feel the frustration building inside of her and she commenced the bouncing, glaring at Shae with a clenched jaw.

"For the record, I don't agree with you. Theodore is simply being friendly, and you might have noticed that I didn't take him up on his offer."

"So Theodore is simply being friendly, but I am being familiar?" Shae asked.

"Let's assume you are not wrong, which you clearly are. Let's assume he is being flirtatious, which he is not. Why is it okay for you to flirt with me, but not for him?" Adrian asked.

Shae obviously didn't have an acceptable answer, so she counter-attacked.

"Why do you have such strong feelings about my interaction with Eliza?"

"I think it's inappropriate, Shae. She's not ready for a relationship. She's my patient, so I trust that I have a little more insight than you."

Rolling her eyes, Shae chucked the scatter cushion aside and threw her hands in the air.

"Adrian, I don't know why you assume that I want to fuck every female I come across. Do you honestly think that I'm that shallow? I am really starting to take offense."

Shae seemed really insulted and Adrian almost regretted saying anything, but flashes of that tender hug between Eliza and Shae left her feeling irritated all over again.

"Despite not owing you any kind of explanation, I will indulge you simply so that you can sit here and overanalyse your behaviour once I leave. I know that Eliza had been battling to make ends meet, so I asked her to consider offering my students some art classes in her spare time."

Adrian felt like she was shrinking into the futon as she leaned back and rested both of her open palms across her eyes. She hoped that by the time she opened her eyes, she would have forgotten the wounded look on Shae's face from minutes before.

"I have no desire to have a romantic relationship with her, but I do think that this project could be mutually beneficial. She needs the cash and I think my students can slowly ease her back into teaching since they will have very low expectations."

Adrian prayed that the futon would just swallow her alive. She had no idea how she would defend her immature and irrational behaviour. The more Shae talked, the worse Adrian felt.

"I also happen to think that art is one of the most therapeutic activities that I can expose my students to. Some of them really need the outlet, Adrian."

"Shae, just stop."

Shae gave her a crooked smile when she finally looked at her again.

"Have I made you feel every bit as terrible as you should?" Shae asked.

Adrian nodded meekly.

"Good. Now, can we talk about Theodore?" Shae asked.

"No, Shae. We can't. There is nothing to talk about and you know it. It's unethical to discuss my patients with each other. Quite frankly, you say that you feel insulted by me for assuming that you want to sleep with every woman you meet. Don't you think I feel insulted? Do you honestly believe that I would be that unprofessional? That I would cross the line with a patient?"

Slouching farther down the futon, Shae rested her right ankle on her left knee while slipping her hands under her thighs. The wounded look was now replaced by a daring one and Adrian could feel her skin tingling under Shae's scrutiny.

"What's it going to take, Adrian?"

"I have no idea what you're talking about, Shae," Adrian lied.

"I'll just pretend that I believe you and I'll even go as far as changing the subject. How do you think Jax is doing?" Shae asked.

Adrian suddenly felt completely drained. These group sessions often left her feeling exhausted, and the constant bickering with Shae and the conscious effort it took to keep a professional distance from her didn't help the situation. Kicking her high heels off, she put her feet up, wedging a scatter cushion between her knees.

"The same professional ethics that you questioned earlier prevents me from discussing my patients with you."

"I hate your ethics," Shae mumbled.

"Even if it keeps me from throwing myself at Theodore?" Adrian mocked.

Following Adrian's example, Shae kicked her boots off and propped a pillow under her head as she lay down. Adrian couldn't help but wonder if she would allow any of her other patients to get this cosy at her house.

"I don't think he's your type, Doc. I do know that you're his type, though."

"How would you know what my type is?" Adrian took the bait, knowing that she would beat herself up later for not ending this conversation and sending Shae home.

Shae crossed her hands over her stomach and stared at the ceiling.

"I just can't see you with a laid-back fisherman who only wears camo jackets and hiking boots. The guy has a moustache, Adrian. That's so gross."

"How do you know that I'm his type?" Adrian asked.

"You're everyone's type, Adrian."

Adrian wondered if she was Shae's type, but there was no way of ever finding out without jeopardising her professionalism. Shae suddenly turned on her side to face Adrian.

"Indulge me, please. What is your type, Adrian?"

Adrian spent a few quiet moments, trying to picture the perfect man. Frederick had short, dark hair, which she liked until she had been rapped across the fingers for pulling her fingers through his hair in a moment of passion. He didn't like for his hair to be touched. He had strong but perfectly manicured hands, the first thing that had attracted her to him. Not long after they got married, she had experienced the strength of those hands as they settled around her wrists every time that they argued. She pictured Frederick's green eyes for a moment. She had always found green eyes so alluring, but to be penetrated by his emerald gaze had often left her feeling petrified.

"Adrian?" Shae interrupted her thoughts.

"I don't have a type anymore. Shae, I'm exhausted and you're not even pretending to respect those boundaries I keep talking about. Can we call it a day?"

"Sure, I have to go anyway. Maddison is probably waiting for me."

Slipping her legs off the futon, Adrian pulled on the pins that had been holding her hair in the standard bun on top of her head. As she released it, a subtle shake sent her dark hair spilling across her shoulders.

"I'm sorry Shae. I don't mean to be rude."

Shae had been busy putting on her boots before Adrian had let her hair down. She was now staring at Adrian with a shoe in her hand and a strange look on her face.

"No problem, Doc."

She quickly slipped on her other shoe and stood to leave.

"Please, don't ever wear your hair down like that for our one-on-one sessions, Adrian. Let's not forget that I am not bound by ethics, and I am not entirely sure I can respect yours if you're looking like that."

CHAPTER EIGHTEEN

Adrian dumped yet another shirt on her bed. She had spent the last forty-five minutes obsessing about her outfit, and she was swiftly running out of time. She had not been able to attend one of the Zen Den meetings since Shae had asked her to assess whether Jax would fit in with the crowd.

The truth was that Adrian had come up with excuse upon excuse not to venture into such risky territory. It was one thing having Shae in her house for group sessions, but it was completely different allowing Shae to pull her into *her* personal space. Pointing out that she was completely onto her, Shae informed her that Jax would be joining the group regardless of her therapist being too chickenshit to even check them out.

Adrian had planned to apply the same tactics when Shae had asked her to assess the situation with Eliza, but when Eliza had asked her personally to attend the first get-together, she could hardly decline. Tonight was all about her doing her job and supporting a patient, so she had no business tearing through her cupboard, mixing and matching outfits like she was getting ready for a date. Yet, here she was creating a mountain of abandoned clothing on her bed. She had to meet Eliza and Shae at the school in half an hour and all she had committed to was a pair of snug Levi jeans.

"Oh, fuck it."

She grabbed whatever was next on the "maybe" pile, put it on hastily, slipped her feet into her most comfortable loafers, and headed out the door. She was quite adept at applying her makeup while driving and tonight that skill would come in handy. By the time she reached the main entrance of Willowmore, she was as ready as she would be. She dragged her fingers through her hair—she had opted to let her hair down since it was a Friday evening that would ordinarily be spent on her couch with a glass of wine and a good book. Finally, she spritzed some perfume on her wrists and let out a deep breath as she flipped down her visor to study her reflection in the mirror.

Her heart dropped to her feet when there was a rap on her window. Shae's broad smile did nothing to calm her racing heart.

"Adrian, I distinctly remember asking you never to wear your hair down like that."

"Well, good evening, Shae. I am well. Thanks for asking," Adrian said as she exited her car.

"Do you not remember us having that conversation?" Shae continued.

"Actually, you asked me not to wear it down in a one-on-one session, which this is not. Besides, I don't really care what you think. It's Friday and I belong in sweats on my couch."

Shae made no secret of how impressed she was with Adrian's outfit. The shirt she ended up wearing was a simple black satin collared shirt with small pearl buttons. The neckline plunged low in the front and the hem at the back swooped well below her waist. Shae's eyes were locked on Adrian's chest, and she would be lying if she said it wasn't flattering.

"Am I too casual for the occasion?" Adrian asked, tugging at her shirt.

"Quite the opposite. You're too classy for this joint and I am dying to have a long conversation about that shirt, but I see that Eliza just arrived," Shae replied.

They crossed the parking lot and greeted Eliza. Moments later, Adrian and Eliza followed Shae down cemented pathways and past abandoned classrooms and offices. The school grounds were deathly quiet, and their footsteps bounced off the walls. Shae finally led them down a staircase at the end of a row of classrooms, across a netball field, and past the tuck shop. Adrian could tell when they were getting close to the den as laughter and high-pitched cheering sliced through the silence. Adrian watched Eliza closely and was relieved to see her finally looking a little more relaxed.

"Ladies, brace yourselves. These kids are smack in the middle of a darts championship and they are competing for a cash prize that buys them a monthly supply of pizza. They will be loud."

Shae finally opened the door and there was a loud shriek as the bunch of rowdy teenagers saw her. They all started talking at the same time and it took Shae quite a while to calm them down enough so that she could introduce her visitors.

"Guys, you'll notice that I, too, brought along two friends tonight. This is Dr. Ramsey and Miss Hanson."

The kids mumbled a collective greeting and some of the boys started whispering behind their cupped hands, no doubt commenting on the physicality of their two beautiful visitors. Shae pointed at some of them and lifted a brow as if in warning. That earned her a few nervous chuckles and a headshake or two. Before long, the championship commenced and all of the children were focused on the dartboard in the front of the den.

"Hi, Doctor A!" Jax shouted from the front.

Adrian offered her a friendly smile and waved enthusiastically.

"How is Jax doing here, Shae?"

"She does really well. Let me tell you, the other kids adore her! She shows up every single Friday and she's always the last one to leave," Shae said.

Similar to a proud parent, she pointed out some of the close friends that Jax had made and gave them some background information on all of them. It was very evident that Shae knew all of her students on a personal level. While Eliza and Shae discussed the art programmes that the school offered, Adrian took in their surroundings.

The den resembled the inside of a game arcade and Adrian had no trouble understanding why these teenagers loved the space. One of the walls was covered in graffiti and she wasn't surprised to hear Shae tell Eliza that the students had painted it themselves. It seemed like something Shae would have encouraged. Even the pool table in the corner of the den seemed more like an art project than a pool table. The felt was covered in math equations, lines of poetry, Shakespeare quotes, and graphs in various colours and fonts. Clearly Shae's students were very creative.

Eliza pointed to the hopscotch rectangles on the floor.

"I love this little touch," Eliza said.

"I painted that the day we moved the pool table into the den. The idea is that the children don't forget to do some old-school playing. I don't want them to forget how much fun there is in simplicity. We end every single Friday night with a game of hopscotch. That's my only rule."

Had it not been for her ears, Adrian's smile would have stretched all around her face. She couldn't believe what Shae had managed to build here for these kids. She had created a space that not only encouraged play and relaxation, it enforced it. There was no way you could feel anything but delighted in this room. It was cheery and light and inspiring.

"I absolutely love that idea," Adrian said.

"I have to say that my favourite part about this place is that wall. How often do you think these kids get handed a tin of spray paint and the freedom to create whatever they want with it? It's so liberating. It's actually kind of brilliant," Eliza said.

There was a small pang of disappointment deep in her belly when Adrian saw Shae winking at Eliza. She reminded herself why she was there. Her only task at hand was to assess whether Eliza was ready to interact with these children. She excused herself and wandered closer to the commotion at the dartboard. She took her time studying all of the students and their behaviour. There was very little that one could tell on the surface in such a short while. She was more interested in assessing Eliza's behaviour around the kids. She seemed at ease when Shae was with her, but every time that Shae's attention was focused on someone else, she seemed to slightly crawl back into her shell. Adrian felt that this could be expected as Eliza had pretty much been living as a hermit for quite some time now.

Finally, the darts game came to an end and the victory was celebrated with some homemade macaroni and cheese that Shae had organised for them. As could be expected from teenagers, they wolfed down their dinner in no time. After dinner, the kids formed little groups. Some groups played card games while others gathered around the pool table. Some of the others approached Eliza and Shae who were chatting away in a corner. Adrian would have loved to see what Eliza would be like without Shae being present. As if on cue, Jax linked her arm through Shae's and pulled her aside for some private conversation.

"I could kiss that girl," Adrian mumbled to herself.

At first, Eliza seemed highly uncomfortable, searching the crowd to find Shae. Jax was hogging her attention and Eliza had no choice but to live through the discomfort. Soon, she relaxed as a few students kept her engaged. Adrian had no idea what they were talking about, but she assumed it was art since Eliza's face relaxed completely and she started gesturing wildly. Adrian had only ever seen Eliza that excited about her art.

"How is she doing?"

Shae had appeared out of nowhere yet again, leaning against the pool table with her arms crossed over her chest.

"I'd say she's doing quite well. She was nervous for a moment, but I think she recovered quickly," Adrian said.

"That's great. So, what do you think of this place?"

Adrian looked around the den as if to give it a final once-over. When she finally turned her attention to Shae, she was moved by the look of anticipation on her face. She couldn't help but to give Shae her brightest smile.

"I fucking love it," she said.

Shae held her open palm against her heart in sincere appreciation.

"That is all the validation I've ever needed in one foul sentence. I can't even begin to tell you how much it means to have you here tonight," Shae said.

An hour later, the den was all cleared up and following the game of hopscotch, all the students started leaving. Adrian organised the dirty dishes and loaded the leftovers in Shae's car that was parked just behind the den. When she closed the boot of the car, she saw Shae giving Eliza a long hug. Turning around, she leaned against the back of Shae's car and closed her eyes. Before she could start a stern conversation with herself about ethics, she was interrupted by Jax clearing her throat less than subtly.

"Doctor A, can I walk you to your car?"

"Hi, Jax. That would be wonderful. Let me say goodbye to Shae quickly."

Wrapping her arms around her own waist, she approached Shae slowly. Part of her really wanted to interrupt what she felt was the longest fucking hug in human history, while another more mature part of her wanted to be professional and respectful and wait for them to say their goodbyes.

"Hi, Doc. I have something I want to show you quickly."

Shae beckoned Jax closer and asked her to walk Eliza to her car. After thanking Adrian for her support, Eliza followed Jax, who had also said her goodbyes, to the parking lot. Dusk was in full swing and the sky was painted in hues of pink that surely could never be re-created on any artist's palette.

"Adrian, I want to show you this cool project I'm working on. Can you spare a few minutes?"

"Yes, sure I can."

Shae led her around the den, back to the row of classrooms that they had passed on their way in earlier tonight. She unlocked the door of the room closest to the den and switched on the light. When Adrian followed her inside and saw the sliding gate at the back of the room, she paused in the doorway. Realising that Adrian had stopped following, Shae turned around to find a very pale Adrian frozen on the spot.

"Adrian, are you okay? What's wrong?"

"Shae, I'm sorry, but I have to go."

"Adrian, don't be silly. Tell me what's wrong."

Adrian's eyes were locked on the sliding gate leading to Shae's storeroom and suddenly Shae understood what her hesitance was all about. Sliding her hands into her pockets, she approached Adrian slowly, with a tender smile.

"It's been repainted, retiled, and cleaned with every chemical Fiona could lay her hands on, Adrian."

Adrian was torn. Every single part of her being was begging her to put space between herself and the spot where Shae's life had almost ended. At the same time, every part of her being wanted to close every last bit of distance between herself and the woman who survived the brutal attack that happened in that very room. She simply stared at Shae, motionless.

"Come on. Give me your hand, Adrian."

Adrian's heart started hammering in her chest when Shae's fingers closed around hers and she anticipated crossing the boundary leading from the classroom to the storeroom. Instinctively, she knew that another boundary would be crossed entirely outside of this setting, and she found herself terrified at both crossings.

"Shae, please don't make me do it. I just can't do it," Adrian begged.

Reluctantly, Adrian let go of Shae's hand and left the room, mentally banishing the image of the sliding gate that served as the entrance to what very nearly became the temporary tomb of the most beautiful person she had ever had the privilege of knowing.

Shae locked up her classroom and walked Adrian back past the den and in the direction of her car.

"I don't want you walking back here by yourself. Get your car and you can drop me off in the parking lot out front," Adrian suggested.

Minutes later, Shae parked right next to Adrian's car. Adrian mistook Shae's disappointment for anger, and she didn't want to part ways like that.

"Tell me about the project."

Shae turned to Adrian with a small, sad smile on her face. Sighing, she leaned back in her seat and pulled her hands through her hair. Adrian had never seen Shae this deflated, and it just about broke her heart.

"Shae, please tell me about it."

"It's just an awareness initiative that I'd like to get off the ground," Shae said.

After more prompting from Adrian, Shae finally spoke about the initiative in more detail. The idea was to get all the teachers at Willowmore involved. Teachers would be trained by professional therapists to identify the signs of various mental disorders ranging from depression to schizophrenia. They would arrange monthly presentations to students on a wide variety of subjects including eating disorders, drug abuse, and self-destructive behaviour such as cutting. Every month, they would get a different motivational speaker, generally a survivor of the related disorder, to address the students.

"What you would have seen in that room is just a vision board for now. It's just Fiona and me brainstorming. That's all."

Shaking her head, Adrian reached for Shae's hand despite her better judgment. Tonight, she was simply too tired to fight that good fight.

"The work you do here at Willowmore is invaluable, Shae. I don't need to see that room to be reminded of your purpose. I hope you'll understand that I need to *not* see that room to be reminded of mine."

Without another word, Adrian got into her car and drove off.

CHAPTER NINETEEN

"It's not getting any better, Easton. I am actually considering referring my patient to another therapist."

Easton had been a sounding board to Adrian over the past few months. She was easy to talk to and she didn't have a judgmental hair on her head. Adrian's constant effort keeping her feelings hidden from everyone else, including Shae, was taking its toll. The internal struggle she faced every single day was driving her insane.

"Adrian, does she still need therapy?" Easton asked.

Adrian was tending to a bonsai that Theodore had recently gifted her with, something she had lied to Shae about when questioned in their individual session a week ago. She simply didn't have the strength to argue with Shae, which is exactly what would have happened if Shae had known that Theodore had pitched for his one-on-one session with a box of chocolates and the most beautiful bonsai Adrian had ever seen.

Now, clutching the phone to her ear, she paused midair, twirling the pruning scissors around her index finger.

"In your professional opinion, does she still require a therapist?" Easton repeated.

"No, she doesn't," Adrian finally replied.

She dropped into her office chair and clutched the scissors in her palm.

"Fuck, Easton. What am I doing?"

Suddenly, Adrian realised that not only had she been keeping certain truths from her family and patients, she had also been lying to herself. For the last few months, she had convinced herself that Shae had needed just one more session. If she was being brutally honest with herself, she had to admit that Shae's treatment plan had stopped making sense at least two months ago. She no longer experienced those intense panic attacks and she was well equipped to deal with her anxiety when it did flare up, which was very seldom. She didn't suffer from insomnia anymore and she even spoke to her attacker's mother from time to time.

Adrian had convinced herself that she had kept Shae around because of her contribution in the group sessions. All of her patients had benefited from Shae's presence and Jax had found a true friend in her. She had also played a crucial role in Andie's recovery when she recently started helping her with some renovations around her house, transforming it from the house her mother had committed suicide in to a house that Andie could learn to love again instead of selling. It was undeniable. Shae had been a godsend to all of them.

Easton had a way of slicing away all the excuses and laying bare the cold hard truth. There it was. Sitting in her lap uncomfortably, like a burning ember. Shae wasn't her patient. She hadn't been for quite some time.

"Adrian, just calm down. Do you honestly think that this woman doesn't know that she doesn't need to be there? I'm pretty sure that she goes to her sessions for the exact same reason you want her to. You haven't done any harm, sis."

"This is highly unprofessional, Easton. I can lose my license!"

"No, you can't! You haven't crossed a line here, at least not physically. Yet."

"Easton, you are not really helping at the moment. I have to go. I have a session with the object of my hugely fucking inappropriate affection."

"When did you get this dramatic? Just relax, Adrian. These things have a way of working themselves out."

"I don't know exactly what that would look like, but I also don't have the luxury of pondering over it now. I'll talk to you later."

"Please do me a favour. Stop thinking of all the reasons you should punish yourself for feeling like this and spend just a little bit of time thinking about the reasons that you deserve feeling like this."

Adrian flicked the scissors across her desk and shoved the bonsai out of her sight.

"You think I deserve feeling tortured? Conflicted? Alien?"

"Avril better look out. You just might dethrone her and live happily ever after wearing the crown of Drama Queen," Easton replied.

"I have to go, Dr. Phil. Don't worry. Avril's throne is safe. I will get over this eventually," Adrian said.

When she looked up, Shae was leaning against the doorway. She was wearing a pair of beige chinos and a black dress shirt with the top three buttons undone and the sleeves rolled up to expose her forearms. You could tell by Shae's bulging veins that it was a warmer day. Adrian had recently discovered—among so many other things—that she found the popping vein thing quite sexy.

"You'll get over what?" Shae asked.

"The last time I checked, I employed a receptionist. Why is she not receiving you?"

"I told her not to get up since I know my way around here so well. You'll get over what?" Shae repeated as she closed the door behind her.

"Please come in and have a seat, Shae."

"I am in and I will sit, right after you tell me what you need to get over," Shae insisted.

"It's a personal matter, which is why you should have waited in reception until I was ready to see you," Adrian said.

Shae plonked herself down on the recliner and blew out a long breath, all the while studying Adrian closely. She poured herself a drink from the still ever-present pitcher of Kola Tonic and lemonade and drank half of it down in four seconds flat.

"How unfair? I discuss all of my personal matters with you, Adrian."

"Yes, that's because I am the therapist and you are my patient. Now, let's get to it. How are you doing Shae?"

They needlessly discussed Shae's progress; there simply wasn't much to report these days. Shae slept like a baby and the panic attacks were nonexistent. Shae had been keeping herself busy with various projects at school. She was always busy thinking of ways to enlighten her students, like offering them art lessons from Eliza. Eliza of the longest hug in the history of humankind.

"So, Eliza has been booked for four lessons so far. Don't you think that's wonderful?"

"I'm not surprised. The students seemed really taken with her last Friday," Adrian replied.

"What's not to like? She is such a sweetheart, and I think the kids will find her extremely approachable," Shae said.

"Just tell your boys to keep their hands to themselves, please. The last thing Eliza needs right now is some hormonal young man overstepping a boundary, like calling her a sweetheart."

"You think I'm overstepping a boundary by calling her a sweetheart?" Shae asked.

"Shae, you wouldn't know what a boundary was if it hit you in the ass."

Shae's phone started buzzing and a deep frown creased her forehead when she glanced at the display. She rolled her eyes and dumped her phone on the coffee table, swearing under her breath. Adrian could sense that her mood had shifted, and when she saw Shae reaching for the box of chocolates that had caught her eye on the coffee table, she winced inwardly.

"My favourite. You shouldn't have, Doc."

Shae removed the lid of the box and peered inside. Theodore's handwritten note was exactly where Adrian had left it. Shae almost choked on the truffle that she had slipped into her mouth seconds before. For a minute, Adrian was sure that Shae would spit it out, but instead she swallowed with some difficulty and held the note in the air.

"What the fuck, Adrian?"

"Shae, I helped him out with his daughter. He was simply showing his appreciation."

"By buying you the most expensive chocolates he could find? Why are you doing him favours?" Shae continued, her cheeks aflame.

"It wasn't a favour. I am a therapist, Shae. I assessed his daughter and wrote a report for her school. It's my job."

"Is his daughter your fucking patient?" Shae just about shouted.

"Lower your voice, Shae. No, she is not my patient, because she doesn't need therapy."

Adrian was slowly but surely losing her temper. Who did Shae think she was? She was way out of line, and if she didn't take a step back Adrian would have to ask her to leave. Shae chucked the box aside and read the note again, as if she needed to. Clenching her jaw, she folded the note into a tiny square and slipped it back into the box.

"If she's not your patient it's a favour. This guy is infatuated with you and why you refuse to admit that is just fucking beyond me. It's none of my business, though," Shae said and drank the rest of her Kola Tonic and lemonade.

"Really? You're most definitely acting like it's your business," Adrian said. She was getting angrier by the second and when Shae's phone buzzed again and Maddison's name appeared on the display, she lost it.

"Can you please get rid of her before I do it?" Adrian mumbled through clenched teeth.

Shae gave her a daring look, not believing for a second that Adrian would go that far. Her eyes widened when Adrian snatched up the phone. Giving herself a few seconds to figure out what she would actually say to Maddison, she simply held Shae's phone to her ear.

"Baby, please. I don't care if you're in love with someone else. I won't get attached. Let's just have some more fun," Maddison begged.

Turning her back on Shae, Adrian cleared her throat and finally spoke up.

"Hi, Maddison. Shae is in the middle of a session right now. Can you please call her back in forty-five minutes?"

"Oh, shit. No problem, Dr. Ramsey. Is she okay?" Maddison replied.

"Yes, she's fine and dandy. Call her back. Bye, Maddison."

When Adrian turned to Shae, her jaw was almost on the floor. She was clearly deeply angered by Adrian's behaviour but couldn't seem to find the right words. There was no need, because Adrian wasn't done. She stormed back to her recliner and dropped Shae's phone in her lap.

"Your fucking lapdog will call you later. You need to get back in line, Miss McPherson, or you can walk out that door. You're being obnoxious and I'm so frustrated with you right now."

Jumping up, Shae paced the room with her hands on her hips, huffing and puffing all the while. When she crossed the room to stand in front of Adrian it was clear that her self-control was teetering on the edge. She balled her fists and leaned into Adrian's personal space.

"You want to talk about boundaries? Theodore is fighting the urge to cross a boundary with you every time he sees you."

"Stop being so dramatic, Shae!"

"Stop being so oblivious, Adrian!"

Shae's phone started buzzing again as Maddison sent her another text.

"My God, you can have any woman you want and you pick this needy fucking airhead!"

At that final outburst of Adrian's, Shae closed the distance between them and gripped the back of Adrian's head as she pulled her in for a searing kiss. In that very instant, the world stopped turning for Adrian. Her mind was blank, and she realised that she was either about to have a seizure, or a deeply desired kiss that just might topple her world off its axes. When their lips collided, Shae wasted no time slipping her tongue into Adrian's mouth.

For a moment, Adrian was completely overwhelmed. All she could smell, taste and feel was Shae McPherson. When Adrian heard Ella's chair scraping on the floor tiles just outside her door, the world came rushing back and she pulled away from Shae, panting. There, in the middle of her office, stood Shae, her patient, with slightly bruised lips and shivering hands on her hips.

"I think a boundary just hit me in the ass," Shae said.

Adrian had no words. Her mouth hadn't started working yet because her lips were still buzzing beautifully and her tongue was tingling with the taste of Shae McPherson.

"I won't let the door do the same," Shae said as she left Adrian's office.

Adrian was rooted to the spot for quite some time after Shae had left. When she could feel her legs again, she rushed to her desk, grabbed her keys, and swept through reception, briefly explaining to Ella that she would be out for the rest of the day.

CHAPTER TWENTY

"Mom, can you please tell Avril that chicken is a vegetable?"

Easton winked at Avril and ducked just in time to dodge the carrot that she had launched at her from across the table.

"Easton, that's disgusting. Avril, just have a small piece. At least it's free range," Adrian suggested.

Avril's vegetarianism was a constant topic of discussion at the dinner table, and nothing gave Easton more pleasure than to give her crap about it. Ally always tried preparing a special meal for Avril, but Easton hardly ever allowed her to eat it in peace.

"Thanks so much for that, Adrian. It's most definitely more acceptable to let a chicken roam around the coop before you slash its throat," Avril replied.

"She makes a valid point, Adrian. Now, can you please hand me that scrumptious piece of free-spirited dead chicken?" Easton said.

"Easton, don't be an asshole. Avi, how are the boys?" Adrian asked, hoping to steer the conversation into calmer territories.

"They're loud, messy, and unruly. Yeah, I guess they're doing great, Adrian. So, are you ready to tell me what the earlier whispering was all about?"

Just when Adrian was about to pretend she had no idea what Avril was talking about, the two boys stormed into the kitchen and each started pulling on one of their mother's arms. They also both started talking at the same time in their high-pitched voices and Adrian had never loved them more. The distraction was welcome, but Avril was not going to give up that easily.

"I will be back, and I won't develop amnesia in the time that it will take me to give these monsters a bath and return to this kitchen."

"I have no idea what you're talking about, but I do think it would be quite awesome if you could forget that you're a vegetarian," Adrian joked.

Moments later, the boys were in various stages of undress on their way to the bathroom, Easton was packing the dishwasher, and Ally and Norman were playing Scrabble in the living room. Resting her chin in her right palm, Adrian sat staring into her coffee cup. She jumped when Easton chucked a dishrag at her.

"We have about ten minutes before Avril starts interrogating you. So, spill."

Earlier, Adrian had started telling Easton about the glorious disaster that was her personal life after Shae had kissed the crap out of her, but they were indeed interrupted by Avril. Adrian moved her cup around in circles in an effort to dissolve the excess sugar at the bottom. Finally, she took the last sip and pushed the cup aside.

"She kissed me."

There was a beat of silence as Easton absorbed the information.

"What the actual fuck?" Easton said.

"Easton, keep it down! You're doing that shout-whisper thing that you always do."

"What is shout-whispering? She kissed you?"

"Shout-whispering is when you convince yourself that you're whispering, but in reality the damn neighbours can hear you. Yes, she kissed me."

Easton covered her mouth with both of her hands and unsuccessfully suppressed a squeal, which earned her an eye roll from Adrian. It was strange for Adrian to see Easton this excited about anything that didn't involve food.

"How?"

"What do you mean how? How do you kiss someone, Easton? Thanks for making this easy, asshole."

Easton let out a sigh, trying to gather herself. Finally, she held her hands in the air.

"Okay, you're right. I'm going to sit here in silence while you tell me exactly, and I do mean in filthy detail, what happened."

After taking a deep breath, Adrian gave Easton the shortened version of what she now referred to as "the kiss." She explained that one minute she was arguing with Shae and the next minute they were locking lips. She could feel a blush creeping up her neck and her ears were on fire. This was partly because she was confessing to her sister, but also because reliving "the kiss" left her feeling hot in some places—her neck and ears were the least of her problems.

Easton nodded from time to time and managed to only squeal one more time. Ending with the part where Shae disappeared from her office before she could even respond, Adrian let out a long breath and dropped her chin to her chest. Silently, she waited for Easton to either condemn her or let her off the hook.

"I think you're going to lose your license and go to hell," Easton said.

"Thanks, Easton, for letting me down easy."

Easton grabbed a banana from the fruit bowl and started peeling it while Adrian banged her head on the counter in exaggeration.

"Okay, Cersei Lannister. Calm down and look at me."

"Cersei?" Adrian asked.

"It was the first overly dramatic woman that popped into my head, but now that you're paying attention, listen to me," Easton said.

Adrian looked at her wristwatch, reminding her that Avril would be done any second.

"You have two choices here. You can stop seeing her as a patient—actually, you don't have a choice about that unless you want to be homeless and eat scabs off the plasters at the back of the state hospital," Easton said.

"Are we really blood relatives?" Adrian asked, frowning.

"As I was saying, you have to stop seeing this woman who shall not be named as a patient. Right now. Then, keeping your job, you can choose either to start seeing her as a potential romantic interest—which is what I would suggest if the goofy look on your face when you talk about her kissing is anything to go by—or you can tell her to get lost because you're too much of a pussy to actually go for what you want."

Shaking her head, Adrian looked at her watch again.

"Would you look at that? Time's up. Great talk."

"Adrian, I mean it. You should take some time and think about what you want, but also about what you deserve. Yes, the circumstances are far from ideal, but not everything in life that is a gift comes in a neatly wrapped little package."

Easton squeezed Adrian's shoulder lightly.

"For years, you've been accommodating everyone around you, making decisions based on what others would be comfortable with. That didn't really end too well for you, sis."

Adrian nodded in agreement.

"You don't have to tell anyone about this if you're not ready. Take it slowly and see where it goes with her. If it turns out that she's someone that will be part of your life for more than one roll in the hay, you can start telling people. If not, make sure it's a brilliant roll in the hay, tell me all about it, and then forget about her. Nobody has to know."

Adrian started banging her head against the counter again, making Easton chuckle.

"Don't overcomplicate things, Dr. Ramsey. Stop analysing and start feeling. I promise it won't kill you. Or her for that matter. You do have to ask her to fire your ass as soon as possible, and no more making out at the practice."

Avril suddenly leapt around the corner and slammed her palm down in front of Adrian.

"I knew it! You kissed that lesbo patient!"

"Avril, for goodness' sake, please keep your voice down. I did *not* kiss her."

"You didn't kiss her back?" Easton asked with a deep frown on her forehead and her hands on her hips.

"What do you mean?" Adrian asked.

"Did you kiss her back?"

"I don't think you could call it that," Adrian replied, now blushing profusely.

"Did you have your tongue in her mouth at any point?" Avril asked.

Easton gave Adrian a look that encouraged her to answer Avril's question.

"Yes," Adrian mumbled.

When Adrian dropped her head to start banging again, Avril grabbed her by the shoulders and gave her a stern look.

"Stop this shit, now. Adrian, please grow up and stop being so foolish. Just fuck her and get it out of your system," Avril said.

Adrian and Easton just stared at each other in shock. Avril had never made a secret of her disdain toward bisexuality, something she shared with Frederick. Adrian shrugged as if to say she had no idea what had happened to Avril. Easton folded her arms across her chest and peered at Avril.

"Did you bump your head in the bathroom? I thought you hated bisexual women," Easton asked.

"Hate is such a strong word, Easton. Besides, Adrian is almost forty years old and she is just not very approachable. She needs all the help she can get."

Adrian's jaw fell to the floor and she dropped her shoulders in defeat. "Why wasn't I given up for adoption?"

Avril kissed the top of Adrian's head and shoved Easton off her stool.

"Don't worry, sis, I ask myself the same question all the time," Avril replied.

The rest of the night went like every other family night. The boys fell asleep on the couch, curled up against their mother, who was constantly on her phone. Adrian made a mental note to find out what that was all about. She figured the hickey from a few weeks ago and the sudden constant activity on her phone could possibly be connected. Adrian was simply too distracted to get to the bottom of it right now. She was plagued by inappropriate thoughts about a certain perky-breasted, charismatic, blond bombshell with a flirty streak.

She had no idea what she was going to do about said bombshell. Both Easton and Avril made it sound so easy, but she didn't see one of them uprooting their entire life on a whim. She also had images of handing over the keys to her practice to some military, scolding judge. Would it be the judge, or would they send the police? Her divorce hadn't even been this consuming. She understood exactly why her marriage had to end. It had simply been a matter of finding the courage to do it. To walk away.

With this stupid attraction to Shae, on some level she didn't completely understand why it had to end, which was probably why the courage to walk away was evading her. Sighing loudly, she looked at her feet.

"Just walk away, already, you damn traitors."

CHAPTER TWENTY-ONE

It turned out that shaking off the nonsense with Shae was much harder to do than she had anticipated. She had spent the entire weekend in agony, plagued by the memory of Shae's tongue inside her mouth, her strong grip at the back of her head as she held her firmly in place for the duration of that gloriously mind-blowing kiss.

Adrian was nowhere closer to knowing what she would do about this mess when she walked into her office on Monday morning. Ella took one look at her and offered to shuffle around her appointments so that she would be free for the first few hours.

"Thanks, Ella. I'll appreciate that."

Adrian threw herself into paperwork immediately, hoping that the admin duties would occupy her mind and keep thoughts of Shae at bay. When there was a light knock on her door, she assumed that Ella was unable to reschedule her nine o'clock appointment.

Her tongue got stuck to the palate of her mouth as the door opened and Shae stood in front of her. By the time she was able to form words, Shae was sitting across from her desk.

"You don't have an appointment, Shae."

"Neither do you, it seems," Shae replied.

Adrian closed the lid of her laptop and folded her hands on top of it, staring at Shae and hoping that someone would intervene or even just interrupt this meeting. Why did Jax only storm into sessions when it was inconvenient? When it was clear that the universe had turned her back on her, Adrian took a deep breath and then the words just started pouring out.

"No, you don't get to walk into my office wearing that look on your face."

"What look?" Shae asked.

"That one! The almost-apologetic-but-oh-so-proud look."

"I just—" Shae started explaining before Adrian interrupted.

"No. Today you sit and you listen. You do not talk."

Shae simply nodded and sat back.

"What you did was extremely reckless, Shae. What if I didn't kiss you back?"

"But you did," Shae mumbled, ignoring Adrian's instructions.

"No talking, Shae. If I didn't kiss you back it would have been harassment. Actually, taking into consideration the intensity of that kiss, it would have bordered on assault."

"Well, thank you, Adrian."

"That was not a compliment, Shae. Don't be cute right now. I'm so mad at you. You made a real mess of things. You're forcing my hand to do something I'm not ready to do. I can't see you as a patient anymore, Shae, and I'm not ready. I'm not ready not to see you."

It felt good finally voicing the truth out loud, and Adrian paused for a second to enjoy the release.

"Then don't," Shae said.

"What?"

"Don't see me as a patient. Have dinner with me," Shae continued.

"You're unbelievable. You turn me inside out, just ruining my professional reputation, and when it all finally goes to shit you ask me out to dinner?"

"Would lunch be more appropriate?" Shae joked.

"You're just incorrigible," Adrian said.

Shae smiled sweetly and just stared at Adrian for a while. Then she folded her hands in her lap and leaned forward.

"Look, Adrian, we can sit here and list all of my annoying qualities or we can admit that this attraction is building."

"You are my patient. I am also straight," Adrian reminded her.

"You're fired, and you kissed me. Quite passionately in fact."

"What? You can't fire me!" Adrian said in exasperation.

"Sure I can, and I just did. You are fired, Adrian."

"I don't accept that, Shae. This is just ridiculous."

"No, Adrian. What you're reluctant to accept is how you feel about me. Now, just tell me this: do I need to see a therapist twice a week?"

Adrian glared at her with a clenched jaw. "What exactly are you implying?"

"Adrian, just give me your professional opinion. Do I need to see a therapist?"

"I really don't appreciate being accused of abusing my position to see you as often as I like," Adrian spat out.

"Adrian, stop. I'm not accusing you of anything. I'm asking you if I need to see someone so that you can refer me to someone that you trust."

Adrian folded her hands over her chest. "This is insane. I can't believe that you're doing this to me."

Shae started biting the inside of her cheek but didn't say a word and the silence was becoming uncomfortable to Adrian.

"Do you feel like you still need to see someone?" Adrian finally asked.

"No. I haven't felt like I needed to see someone for months now. The panic attacks have diminished to an extent where I don't consider myself as suffering from them anymore. The only nightmares I have are the ones where you push me away without even giving this the shot that it so clearly deserves."

"Did you practice your lines before you came to see me today?" Adrian asked.

"Honestly? I only practiced the one line: You're fired. I really wanted to do my Donald Trump impersonation, but you didn't seem ready for it," Shae said.

Adrian let out a long sigh and pulled her hands through her hair. Her anger was mounting again, and Shae clearly realised that it was probably wise to suggest a change of scenery.

"Just have one cup of coffee with me down the road. There's a quaint little coffee shop that I've been meaning to check out."

What Adrian really wanted to tell her was to leave so she could try and figure out what she was going to do about the messy situation that she had created, but she found herself agreeing to meet Shae at the coffee shop in ten minutes.

Ella gave her a strange smile when she told her that she would be out for half an hour tops. She decided to walk to the coffee shop to clear her mind, but when she spotted Shae in the back at a secluded booth, her heart hammered so wildly that she unconsciously placed a hand on her chest to make it stop.

"I didn't think you would actually show up," Shae said as Adrian slipped into the booth across from her.

"It's probably not wise, but I figured I already shattered my pristine reputation by allowing you to ambush me in my office."

Shae chuckled as she beckoned the waiter closer so they could place an order. She ordered a bottomless coffee and a slice of chocolate cake while Adrian ordered only an espresso.

"Shae, you won't be needing a bottomless coffee, because I don't plan to stay for long."

"You also didn't plan on kissing me, but you sure did a great job of that," Shae replied.

"I did not kiss you. You ambushed me," Adrian said.

"Ambush is such a harsh word, Adrian."

Draining her espresso in one big swallow, Adrian wiped her palm across her lips.

"You know what else is a harsh word, Shae? Expulsion. I could lose my license to practice the only profession that I am qualified for. Does that not matter to you?"

"You can't lose your license because I kissed you, Adrian."

Looking around to make sure that she didn't have an audience, Adrian leaned across the table.

"I could lose my license for kissing you back, Shae. What you did was completely reckless and selfish and it infuriates me that you don't even realise it."

Stirring two spoons of sugar into her coffee, Shae sighed loudly. Livid, Adrian leaned back against the upholstery of the booth, folding her arms across her chest.

"Adrian, I am sorry that I can't give you what you want. I refuse to apologise for that kiss, but before you stab me with that spoon, just let me finish."

"Unbelievable. You have five minutes before I walk out of here, Shae. You better come up with something better than 'sorry, I'm not sorry.' I am running out of patience with you."

Abandoning the piping coffee, Shae linked her fingers together and ran her right thumb around the left one in slow circles. Knowing Shae quite well, Adrian knew that Shae understood that Adrian would walk away from her if she didn't soon offer something that resembled an apology.

"Adrian, I care about you enough never to be anything but honest with you. If I apologised for what I did, it would not be sincere, because I don't regret what happened. I do wish that I approached it a little calmer. Perhaps talking to you about how I feel was a better option."

Adrian raised both her eyebrows and held her hands in the air. "You think?"

"It was just such a heated moment and you were frustrating the shit out of me. You were talking about the fact that I could have any woman I fancied, and in that split second I wanted to make you understand how wrong you were," Shae tried to explain.

"So, you didn't use your vocabulary like the educated, intelligent woman that you are," Adrian replied.

"No, Adrian. I used my tongue, like the arrogant and fiercely determined hot-blooded lesbian I also happen to be. I am not saying that it was the better decision, but it's a little too late for using my words."

Adrian glanced at her wristwatch, and when the waiter passed their booth she ordered another espresso.

"Are you sure you should have another one? That stuff is making you slightly aggressive." Shae risked a little humorous jab.

"What is making me aggressive is the fact that you're wasting my time. Now, what is the purpose of me sitting here with you instead of working?"

Her espresso arrived and Shae's eyes widened as Adrian knocked it back in one big swallow again. Thank goodness Shae didn't twist her arm for a dinner instead—she was imagining downing shots of tequila in the same manner. At least tequila would have relaxed her somewhat, while the coffee was certainly having the opposite effect.

"Fine. You're off the hook, Dr. Ramsey. Thank you for your excellent service."

Rolling her eyes, Adrian grabbed the bill from the waiter and asked him to give them a minute. She stared out the window for the longest time, watching all the people outside going about their business with their lives seemingly firmly on track and in control of their destinies. Was this it? Was this her final opportunity to restore sanity and tranquillity to her life? Could she be like those passing by the little coffee shop? Heading along without a care in the world not knowing the inexplicable exhilaration of being wanted by Shae McPherson?

She had no doubt that she had reached a crossroads. The one path was paved with comfort and security, two things she had always needed in her life. The other was paved with uncertainty and fear, but also endless possibility and excitement. When she finally looked back at Shae, who was pale and clutching her hands together, she realised for the first time that there was a distinct possibility that Shae was secretly every bit as petrified as she was. Her resistance slowly crumbling, she leaned across the table and rested her hand on Shae's.

"I'm off the hook? I've never been this far from off the hook. I am wrapped around the hook. I don't know where the hook ends and my butt starts. You made a mess of things, Shae."

Shae nodded in agreement.

"What do we do?" Shae asked in a small voice that Adrian had never heard before.

"We pay this bill so that this kid can disappear. Then I go to work and you go wherever you need to go until we can discuss this over dinner," Adrian said.

She waved at the waiter who practically sprinted to their booth, swiped Adrian's credit card, and forced a smile. Adrian had no clue what his problem was, but she was just as eager to get out of here as he was to get rid of them. If she was not mistaken, she had just invited Shae to dinner. No, she was not mistaken. Shae was beaming at her across the table.

"Shae, please don't do that."

"What am I doing?" Shae asked innocently.

"You're grinning like a Cheshire Cat and I can just tell that you're dangerously hopeful."

"I was born dangerously hopeful, Adrian. It's a handicap. If it will make you feel better, I will work hard at becoming bitter and resentful. Now, can I walk you back to your office?"

Both women were quiet on their stroll back to Adrian's office, Adrian because she clearly couldn't trust herself around Shae, and Shae probably because she didn't want to say anything that could possibly make Adrian change her mind about dinner.

"Are we having this dinner that should not be accompanied by any hope in my fragile heart tonight?" Shae asked when they finally reached the office.

"We can. I suggest we have it in public. I'm not risking another attack from you," Adrian replied.

Leaning against Adrian's car that was parked in the driveway, Shae crossed her arms over her chest and let out a breath.

"I know this romantic little Italian restaurant close to your place."

"Great. We should probably avoid it at all costs," Adrian said.

"I also know this totally gross Greek diner close to my place," Shae offered.

"That's the one. Send me the address and I'll meet you there at seven," Adrian said.

Smiling, Shae slipped Adrian's pen from her lapel. She wrote the address on the back of a receipt she dug from her pocket and slid the pen painfully slowly between Adrian's breasts.

"Leave *now*," Adrian whispered.

At that moment, Theodore pulled into the driveway with his khaki 4x4 and parked right behind Adrian's car. Wearing an overly confident smirk on her face, Shae slipped onto the bonnet of Adrian's Mercedes and extended her hand to Theodore. Adrian had to admit that Theodore seemed less than pleased to see Shae, but she had no intention of fuelling that fire.

Reluctantly, he took Shae's hand in greeting. Adrian figured that he was probably trying to determine why Shae was practically draped across the bonnet of her car as if it was the most natural thing on earth. It looked like a scene out of *Grease*, and she was almost expecting Shae to burst into a verse of "Hopelessly Devoted To You."

"Hi, Theo. What's up?" Shae said.

Adrian pictured Shae with a slicked cowlick across her forehead and her collar upturned, and she mentally started humming "You're The One That I Want." The next words out of Shae's mouth brought her crashing back to reality.

"Thanks for the coffee, Adrian. I can't wait to see you tonight."

By the time she had gathered herself, Shae had slipped off her car and was happily making her way back to the coffee shop where she had left her own car earlier, whistling all the way. Theodore stared after her, and when he turned his gaze to Adrian he looked like a wounded animal. She had a good mind to phone Shae and cancel this silly dinner, but who was she kidding. She was looking forward to it. Besides, Theodore had no right to act like this. She had gone from being a single divorcée with no love interest to speak of to being the object of the highly inappropriate and misplaced desire of two of her patients, one of whom she had kissed.

"Shall we get started then?" Adrian said as she led Theodore inside.

"Do we have a group session tonight?" Theodore asked.

"No, we don't, Theodore. Are you ready to start?"

"I was just confused when Shae said that she would see you tonight. I thought maybe you rescheduled it."

She would have to chat to Shae about pissing on her like she was her territory all in an effort to get under Theodore's skin, which she clearly managed to do. She had no intention of being anyone's possession ever again. In fact, she wasn't even sure what she intended to be to Shae. Either way, that kind of behaviour actually scared the crap out of her, and she would certainly tell Shae that. Perhaps right after she admitted to herself, and only to herself, how damn good it felt to be marked by Shae.

"Dr. Ramsey?"

"Sorry, Theodore. No, I didn't reschedule it. We should start now."

CHAPTER TWENTY-TWO

"Holy shit. You actually kissed the shrink?"

What was meant to be a drink before her dinner with Adrian had now turned into a full-blown interrogation by Fiona. Shae didn't mind. It kept her mind busy with something other than questioning her outfit, something she had been doing for the last two hours.

"I did. Now, do you think these skinny jeans make my ass look big?"

"Why the fuck would you do that? What if she slapped you?" Fiona asked.

In the bottom of her glass, Fiona chased a lemon pip around with her straw. She had kicked off her high heels and was now leaving damp footprints on the floor as she followed Shae to her room. It always amused Shae how Fiona could pass judgment her way for every transgression, completely disregarding her own, which were generally more fundamental than a kiss behind closed doors.

"She did slap me...with her tongue. Should I rather wear slacks?"

"You are so fucking scandalous. She is bound by some code or governing body or some shit, Shae."

Shae decided to go with the skinny jeans. She slipped on a green flannel shirt, rolling the sleeves up around her forearms. Her hair was still semi-wet, but already too dry to tame into something smooth, so she applied a generous amount of mousse and simply pulled her fingers through it a few times, scrunching here and there.

"Are you going for the just-fucked look?" Fiona asked.

"No, I am running out of time because you're being overly dramatic. You once had a threesome with twin brothers the night of their wedding, yet you are harassing me about one kiss," Shae said.

Fiona paused with her hands on her hips. "I'll have you know that they were not twins and it was the night before their wedding."

"Oh, pardon me. That makes it much better, Fi."

Fiona coughed violently as the elusive pip made its way up the straw and to the back of her throat at high speed. Banging on her back, Shae encouraged her to take deep breaths.

"Don't worry, Shae. I've had much bigger things down my throat and I lived to tell the tale."

"You are so gross, Fiona. Now, I invited you over for a drink because I thought you might have some useful advice for tonight."

Collapsing onto Shae's bed, Fiona nuzzled her pillow and stretched her arms and legs wide.

"I need a bed this size," Fiona said.

"To accommodate your sordid sexual appetite?" Shae asked.

"I'm just saying that it gets crowded, buddy. So, you want my advice?"

"I should have emphasised, *useful* advice."

Linking her hands behind her head, Fiona seemed to search the ceiling for some deep and meaningful truths that she could bestow upon her friend. After a while she turned on her side, cuddling Shae's second pillow and looking very serious.

"Whatever you do, don't order curry. I once shat my pants on a first date."

"That is so insightful, and I feel much more prepared now. Thanks, Fi."

"You are so very welcome, Shae."

Fiona spent the next few minutes digging in Shae's drawers and paging through the books on her nightstand. Very little remained sacred when Fiona was your best friend, but it was a small price to pay for her loyalty that could be likened to that of a service dog. Finally, she kissed Shae's cheek, told her not to come back pregnant, and drove off.

Shae quickly sent Adrian a text with the address for the Greek diner and took a final look in the mirror. Pouting, she winked at herself and spritzed her wrists with her favourite perfume before heading to the restaurant. She arrived at Basil's first and chose a table on the sidewalk, hoping it would be public enough for Adrian. She ordered a Coke and studied the menu while she waited.

"You were right. It's quite gross."

When Shae looked up, Adrian was scanning the restaurant with a wrinkled nose. She wore tight jeans, a royal blue off-the-shoulder top, and black heels. Her black hair fell down her shoulders in shiny, soft layers, and Shae couldn't help staring at her.

"Is this public enough for you, Adrian?" Shae asked as a crowd of rowdy teenagers walked past their table.

"It should do. Don't they have Kola Tonic and lemonade?" Adrian asked, pointing at Shae's drink.

"Trust me, you should keep your orders very simple. The owner doesn't speak English too well. You also shouldn't order anything that can't be served in its original packaging," Shae suggested.

Standing up, she pulled a chair out for Adrian, who peered at her before taking a seat.

"You're confusing this dinner with a date, Shae."

"Because I pulled out your chair for you? It's a good thing I didn't buy that bunch of flowers then."

"Don't be cute. This is not a date," Adrian said.

"Yet here you are letting me know that I'm cute. I'm really glad that you showed up for our non-date, which you certainly dressed up for. I appreciate the show of collarbones."

Shae suspected that Adrian was attempting to hide her blush behind the sticky menu but couldn't touch the greasy surface of the battered old menu for too long. She dumped it on the table and wiped her hands on her jeans. Shae smirked at her from across the rickety table.

"I knew you would regret your decision."

"Right. I know the concept of regretting your decisions is a completely foreign concept to you, Shae."

"I've always found it such a futile process. It doesn't serve my hopeful heart, Adrian."

When Basil stormed past their table in a rage, swearing at one of the cowering waiters, Adrian carefully put her hand up, hoping to draw the attention of anyone that could offer her a beverage. Basil peered at her through bloodshot eyes, not even attempting to hide his irritation.

"Hi, can I please have a glass of your house red?"

"What?" Basil barked.

"Can I please have a glass of red wine?" Adrian repeated.

"Krasi?"

Drawing Basil's attention, Shae ran her finger down the menu until she reached the beverages. She pointed at the red wine that one could order per glass. Basil shook his head and stormed off, leaving them both unsure about whether a glass of wine would be sent their way.

"I'm not sure if you should hope that Basil will send it or not. Did I not tell you to order something that could be served in its original packaging?"

"Well, I won't be able to get through this stone-cold sober, Shae."

Shae touched her heart as if wounded.

"That will certainly leave a mark. Most women don't consider dinner with me to be their Everest," Shae said.

"I was actually referring to the food. I have a bit of a sensitive stomach, and if the menu is this greasy, I can only imagine what the food will be like," Adrian explained.

Basil delivered foul-smelling wine in a glass adorned with his dirty fingerprints. He gave Adrian an even dirtier look before he disappeared into the kitchen. Adrian closed her eyes and took a deep breath before risking a sip.

"That is by far the worst thing I've ever tasted."

"You know who has the best selection of red wine in town? Lorenzo's Kitchen. You know, the Italian restaurant I suggested," Shae said with a chuckle.

"Yes, I know that, Shae. Is there something safe to order as a main here?"

"I only ever order the pastitsio. It's not too unappetising. Otherwise, you should stick to desserts," Shae said.

Adrian decided to go with Shae's suggestion and ordered the pastitsio. She admitted that it wasn't entirely unpleasant, but Adrian seemed relieved when it was finished. She rewarded herself with baklava for being brave enough to finish her wine as well. They were yet to have a serious conversation by the time their table had been cleared.

"I was thinking Wednesdays and Fridays," Shae said out of the blue.

"Excuse me?"

"You said it yourself, Adrian. You are not ready to stop seeing me. So, see me. Wednesdays and Fridays."

Ordering an espresso from a waiter with a tear-streaked face no doubt caused by the temperamental Basil, Adrian steepled her hands together and wordlessly studied Shae for a while. Chin propped on her right palm, Shae spun the damp coaster that she had slipped out from under her Coke around in slow circles, eyes locked on Adrian.

"I have dinner with my family on Wednesdays," Adrian said.

"I'll accept Tuesdays and Fridays as well."

Driving over here, Adrian probably had no intention of setting up recurring dinner dates. Shae bet that she would have been quite happy just surviving this one. Yet Shae had the feeling that Adrian was about to commit to two nights per week of exposing herself to what would undoubtedly include in-depth conversations about a variety of topics that she could no longer declare inappropriate based on their professional relationship.

"Shae, I feel like I have to just lay out all my cards on the table. I don't know what I have to offer you. I'm thirty-seven years old, divorced, and still recovering from an abusive relationship. For all I know this infatuation is simply a symptom or a side effect."

"Infatuation you call it. I like it," Shae said proudly.

"Shae, please just take me seriously for a second."

"Adrian Ramsey, I've been taking you seriously since the day I walked into your office expecting a fat bald guy to poke around my psyche and found a dazzling, heart-stopping, beautiful woman carefully peeling away the layers instead."

Adrian didn't say a word.

"If you decide to pursue this, and God knows I hope that you do, I will give you all the time and space that you may need. I can do that. What I can't do is deny how I feel."

Shae could tell that Adrian finally realised that the ball was now left in her court and that simply sitting there and staring at Shae would not be helpful to anyone. She was relieved when Adrian finally spoke.

"I have some things I need to work through, Shae. I know what I am feeling right now, but clearly I can't be trusted anymore. Who knows what I might get up to tomorrow or a week from now?"

Shae could tell that Adrian was rattled and overwhelmed and she felt responsible, but not horrible, about the fact.

"Adrian, don't be too hard on yourself. We don't like to admit it, but when it comes to attraction we have about as much control over it as we have over the seasons. It's a force of nature."

"You reckon?"

"I'm a teacher, Adrian. I know a few things, and one day I will tell you everything I know about the four known forces of nature."

"There also happens to be a few things we can control, and we should have a serious conversation about our expectations at some point."

"Adrian, I hope that time is not right now because I find it really difficult having a serious conversation with you when you have a blotch of syrup and chopped nuts on your chin."

Adrian wiped her fingers across her chin and seemed surprised to actually find a blob of sticky baklava residue there. Shaking her head, she ripped a cleansing wipe from a packet in her handbag and dabbed at her chin. She rolled the wipe into a tiny ball and chucked it at Shae, who caught it just before it made contact with her face.

"How long were you going to let me sit here with nuts on my chin?"

"Well, that depended on whether you agreed to see me again," Shae replied without missing a beat.

"Shae, how about you let me know when you are ready to take things seriously?" Adrian said as she stood, dropped some cash on the table, and stormed out of Basil's.

Swearing under her breath, Shae signalled for the waiter to collect the payment so she could chase after Adrian. When she finally caught up with her, Adrian was leaning her forehead against her steering wheel, eyes closed.

Filled with trepidation, Shae softly knocked on her window. For long moments, there was no movement inside the car. When Adrian finally looked at her, Shae witnessed a vulnerability in her eyes that she had never seen before. She walked around the car and pulled on the door handle until Adrian unlocked her car. Adrian faced forward, refusing to look at Shae for quite some time.

"Adrian, one thing you should know by now is that I won't go away if you ignore me. Please look at me."

"I don't want to, Shae."

"Why not?"

"I just don't."

Turning sideways, Shae gripped the headrest of Adrian's seat with one hand and slipped a lock of shiny black hair behind Adrian's ear with the other. Adrian closed her eyes when Shae slowly dragged her index finger down her arm.

"It seems like you forgot all about my excellent diversion techniques, Doctor. I divert attention from my inadequacies and I try to make light of things that have the potential to shake my foundation. You, Adrian Ramsey, shake me to my core."

Adrian finally turned to look at her, leaning her cheek against the headrest and trapping Shae's hand in the process. Turning her hand to lightly cup Adrian's cheek, she winked at her and smiled. She was relieved when Adrian melted into her touch, closing her eyes again.

"Shae, have I mentioned that I am still recovering from an abusive relationship that most certainly left some emotional scarring. I don't even know who I am in a relationship anymore, much less how to be in a relationship with a woman."

The entire monologue was delivered with her eyes closed and her cheek tucked into Shae's palm.

"It's pretty much the same as being with a man, except for the fact that the sex lasts longer than five minutes and generally both parties experience an orgasm," Shae replied.

Finally opening her eyes, Adrian chuckled and brought Shae's hand to her lap, interlocking their fingers.

"Sorry, I don't know if the untimely jokes will ever really end. I'll work on it."

"The truth is that I really don't want you to change a thing. I just want you to take this seriously and talk to me about your expectations, Shae."

Shae brought their linked fingers to her lips and softly kissed Adrian's knuckles.

"It really wouldn't be fair for me to have any expectations, Adrian. All I want is for you to stop fighting what you're feeling for once. I just want you to give this a chance and see where it goes. You're as attracted to me as I am to you. That's undeniable."

Adrian let out a deep breath and lightly squeezed Shae's fingers.

"What if there's nothing beyond this crazy attraction, Shae? What if my infatuation with you really happens to be a side effect of divorce?"

"Do we ever pursue a relationship based on more than that? What do we really know at the onset of a romantic relationship? It's never stopped any of us before. Don't overthink this," Shae said.

Biting down on her lower lip, Adrian faced forward again, staring at a young couple that strolled past her car blissfully unaware of the world around them. Shae knew that she was probably picturing walking down this stretch of road with Shae. Wondering if she would feel comfortable holding Shae's hand in public and whether Shae would take offense if she wasn't. Adrian probably hadn't spent much time thinking about lesbian relationships and how they differ from heterosexual ones. Up until now, she had no reason to.

"Will you be patient with me?" Adrian asked and confirmed Shae's suspicions.

"Adrian, I have been exposed to your tight suits and low-cut shirts for more than six months. I have seen collarbone, cleavage, and calves in mini dresses. I think I've already proved that I can be very patient."

As the couple that Adrian had been watching disappeared around the corner, Shae willed Adrian to start imagining what life could be like if she relinquished control and just allowed this force to wash her away. Shae wanted her to stop struggling against the current of her attraction to Shae before she slowly disappeared beneath the surface. In the ideal world, Adrian would head toward the shore where Shae was waiting with arms outstretched, hoping to show Adrian around on this island she had never explored before.

"Come over on Tuesday. You don't have to commit to anything more than that," Shae said.

Adrian nodded in agreement.

"Tuesday it is."

CHAPTER TWENTY-THREE

When the doorbell sounded, Shae paused midway through applying a layer of crumbs to the chicken breasts. She glanced at the clock on the kitchen wall; Adrian was way too early. The chicken needed quite some time in the oven, and she hadn't even started on the salad. She also would have loved to smell slightly better by the time Adrian arrived.

She quickly covered the final piece of breast in crumbs before sliding the pan into the oven. Wiping her hands on a dishrag, she chucked it aside and pushed her hair out of her face. When she opened the front door and saw Maddison standing there, she was equal parts relieved and surprised.

"Maddison?"

"That's me. What's that on your face?"

Shae wiped some crumbs off her cheek.

"Come in. I might be terrible company, though, because I'm running a bit late. What can I do for you?"

Maddison dropped her bag on the couch as she made her way to the kitchen. When she saw the mess in the kitchen, she paused in the doorway with her hands on her hips and whistled.

"Did something explode?"

"No, I just had a small issue with the flour. I also had a minor disagreement with the blender, but that's okay. I abandoned the dessert altogether. Chicken looks good though, right?" Shae asked as she pointed to the chicken in the oven.

Maddison peered through the glass and nodded slightly.

"Not too bad. Who's the lucky lady?"

Shae and Adrian hadn't discussed the details yet, but Shae also had some experience in what she liked to call "The beautiful and maddening awakening of the bi-curious." It was a slow and excruciating experience for most, and she had no intention of rushing Adrian into grand revelations about their pre-relationship. That's essentially what this was—a test drive of sorts. Besides, Adrian was just plain scary when it came to Maddison.

"What do you mean?" Shae asked.

"Well, you're not playing Martha-fucking-Stewart all by yourself. Clearly, you're cooking for a date."

"Martha Stewart?" Shae asked.

She wasn't comfortable with lying, and she most certainly wasn't comfortable with telling the truth in this instance. She rushed to the dishwasher and started packing away all the dirty dishes like her life depended on it. She scrubbed down every surface in the kitchen and mopped the floor, all under the watchful eye of a very curious Maddison.

"You never did say what I owe the pleasure to," Shae finally said.

"Jax forgot her textbook here last night. She asked me to pick it up on my way to her."

"Is she sure about that? I'll have to take a look around," Shae said.

Glad for the distraction, Shae stormed off to the living room in search of the missing textbook. She overturned all the scatter cushions and looked under every magazine. Maddison made herself comfortable on the couch while Shae continued the search. Finally, she saw the dog-eared textbook peeking out from underneath the couch. Facing the couch, she bent over and slid the tattered textbook into view.

When she turned around clutching the textbook, Adrian was staring at Maddison, who was staring at Shae's ass.

"Adrian! I didn't hear the bell."

Adrian was yet to make eye contact with her. Maddison was now smiling broadly at a clearly irritated Adrian and Shae was frozen in her spot. This wasn't exactly how she wanted their first proper dinner date to start. Suddenly, Adrian dropped her keys in the bowl by the front door and slowly made her way to Shae. When she reached her, she lifted Shae's chin slightly, dusted off the patch of crumbs still stuck to the right side of her face, and kissed her deeply.

"You look adorable in that apron, by the way."

She turned to Maddison then.

"Hi, Maddison. How are you doing?"

"Great. I'm great. Just popped around for a quick visit," Maddison said.

"She just came to fetch Jax's textbook," Shae said and held the book in the air as if she needed to prove it.

Winking at Maddison, Adrian playfully slapped Shae's bottom and headed to the kitchen. Completely shocked into silence by Adrian's unusual behaviour, Shae just kept clutching the textbook. By the time Adrian returned with a glass of wine, Shae quickly dumped the book in Maddison's lap and excused herself to check on the chicken.

"So, Adrian. What can you tell me?"

Since Shae had an open-plan kitchen, she could observe from a safe distance. Maddison clearly was in no rush to leave as she spread her arms across the back of the couch. Adrian was not intimidated easily and took a seat right next to her. Leaning her head back against the headrest, she crossed her legs as she kicked off her heels. She let out a long sigh and closed her eyes, balancing the stem of the wineglass on her thigh.

"I can tell you that I had a long-ass day and I am so looking forward to spending tonight with Shae. I mean, you saw what her ass looks like in those jeans, right?"

"I did. Indeed. You should see what it looks like without those jeans," Maddison said.

Chuckling, Adrian finally opened her eyes and turned to Maddison.

"Oh, darling. I plan to. Right now, the only thing standing between me and those ass cheeks is you. So, why don't you take that textbook to Jax and enjoy your evening?"

There was the slightest crack in Maddison's façade of confidence as she winked at Adrian and stood up. Shae reentered the room just in time to witness the fakest smile she had ever seen on Adrian's face.

"Shae, you're just in time to see Maddison off. She was just leaving," Adrian said, still wearing the fake smile.

Maddison kissed Shae on the cheek and waved the textbook around.

"I'm off to deliver some news to Jax. And this textbook, of course."

Shae finally let out a sigh as Maddison's car turned the corner minutes later. Shae had built such a strong bond with Jax, and the thought of Maddison ruining the trust between them by telling her that Shae was romantically involved with Adrian sickened her. She just knew that there was no changing Maddison's mind. Adrian offered her a sad smile from across the room and her heart just melted.

"I'm sorry, Shae. There were probably better ways of communicating the fact that you're off-limits than an unnecessary public display of affection."

"No, it's fine. Her mission has always been to get under your skin, and I suspect it will only get worse now that she knows about us."

"I don't know what got into me," Adrian said and cradled her head in her hands for a moment.

"Jax will come around. She always does. Besides, I love that you did that," Shae said.

Adrian looked up at her, standing there in her stained apron and messy hair and her heart dangling from her sleeve.

"That's not healthy, Shae. Marking one's partner like a dog should be entirely unattractive. We haven't even discussed exclusivity, which I clearly hope will be our arrangement since I somehow turned into a hormonal teenager."

Shae untied the apron behind her back and chucked it aside as she sat down next to Adrian. She stuck her nose under her own armpit and pulled a face. Turning sideways so she could look at Shae, Adrian draped her right arm across the back of the couch. With her free hand, she slipped a lock of hair behind Shae's ear.

"You smell like butter, but it's not entirely unpleasant."

"Who doesn't love butter, right? I'm going to jump in the shower quickly," Shae said.

"I'll be right here," Adrian said and returned to her wine.

After what indeed turned out to be a quick shower, Shae made her appearance. Her hair cascaded down her shoulders in big waves and her hooded sweatshirt clung to her breasts and to a spot on her lower back that wasn't dried off properly. The pair of jeans she had decided to wear relaxed around her hips like only a pair of well-worn jeans could. She had socks on her feet but hadn't bothered with shoes.

"Sorry, Adrian. Nothing about this night actually worked out the way I planned it."

"Come sit here and tell me what you had planned," Adrian suggested.

She held her glass of wine out to Shae and patted the couch next to her. Shae accepted the offered wine and took a small sip.

"Not a wine drinker, hey?" Adrian asked.

"Not particularly. What gave it away?"

"That beautifully open face of yours. You must be terrible at poker."

Shae slipped into the kitchen quickly, checked on the food, and retrieved a beer from the fridge before taking her spot next to Adrian. Hesitantly, she leaned into Adrian's personal space. When she was fairly certain that Adrian welcomed the intrusion, she started a trail of soft kisses down her neck, stopping just short of her collarbone. When she leaned back, Adrian's eyes were closed, and from her flaring nostrils it was clear that she was trying to control her breathing.

"Hi, there," Shae said when Adrian finally opened her eyes and took a huge gulp of wine.

"Hi, yourself."

"I can't believe you're sitting here on my couch."

Adrian cocked a perfectly trimmed brow.

"Trust me. Nobody is more shocked by that than me," Adrian replied.

"I know. Are you terribly disturbed by all of this?"

Adrian placed her now-empty glass on the coffee table and crossed her arms over her chest as she rubbed her cheek against the velvety couch.

"I love this serious side of you. Can I be completely honest with you?" Adrian asked.

"I would certainly hope so," Shae said.

"I am disturbed by the fact that I'm *not* disturbed by all of this. Before tonight, I was apprehensive and appropriately terrified of what I feel for you and the impact that it will have on my life. Then, I walked into your house, saw you in that cute little apron with crumbs all over your face and hair clinging to your sweaty forehead, and it was like a switch flipped."

Shae started tugging at the label on her beer bottle, eyes locked on Adrian still.

"I can't pretend that I know how this is going to end for us, Shae. I also don't have the first clue about the practicalities of dating a woman, but I do know that I am ready to figure it out with you."

Shae smiled broadly at Adrian's confession. Rolling her eyes, Adrian gripped the strings of Shae's sweatshirt and pulled on them until Shae's mouth was close enough to kiss. Pulling the hood over Shae's hair, Adrian softly cupped her face and kissed her. The kiss was soft and sweet at first, but when Shae pulled Adrian into her lap things escalated quickly. Straddling Shae's lap, Adrian pulled her hands through Shae's wet hair and deepened the kiss. Suddenly, she groaned softly.

"Shae, I think we should have some dinner."

"We probably should. You want to slip off my lap?"

"Not really, but I think it's for the best. I am not sure my legs will work right away though," Adrian said.

Resting her forehead against Shae's, she gave her a final kiss and fell back against the couch, covering her eyes with her forearm.

"We can eat outside so you can cool off, Doc."

"That'll be great," Adrian said.

She followed Shae to the kitchen and watched her drizzling a balsamic reduction over a beautiful salad and nibbling on some cucumber.

"Anything I can do to help?"

"You can grab that bottle of wine and another beer and follow me outside," Shae said as she gripped the salad bowl, some utensils, and paper napkins.

Adrian followed her to the enclosed patio that led off the living room. In the middle of the space was a beautiful, handcrafted oak table and two benches. The centrepiece of the table was a vintage candleholder with three long white candles. After another trip to the kitchen to fetch the chicken and vegetables, Shae arranged the bowls and cutlery on the table. She smiled when she noticed that Adrian had set some placemats next to each other.

"Is that okay?" Adrian asked.

"It's perfect. I think we should dish up before the food gets cold."

Shae refilled Adrian's wineglass and opened another beer for herself before dishing up. She held a plate out to Adrian, who was watching her from across the table.

"Would you like to dish up, or can I do it for you?" Shae asked.

"I'll do it, thanks."

Twenty minutes later, their plates were empty and shoved to the side. The conversation between them had been flowing easily all night, and Shae was surprised by how natural it felt having Adrian in her house.

"What would you be doing right now if I wasn't here?" Adrian asked.

"The same thing I'm doing right now—picturing you on my couch flipping through the channels to find us a romantic movie," Shae said.

Resting her hand on Shae's thigh, Adrian squeezed lightly and smiled.

"You're so full of crap. I mean it. What is a normal Tuesday like for you?" Adrian asked.

"I have dinner, mostly pizza and beer. If I don't have papers to mark or assignments to assess, I go upstairs to play with my models."

Adrian squeezed her thigh a little harder.

"Those better not be the kind of models that I would have to chase out of your house."

"No, I think you might actually approve of these models," Shae said and covered Adrian's hand with her own.

"Show me."

"Really?"

"Yes, I want to see what you keep yourself busy with. Show me."

"I have to warn you that it's really quite boring. I've never used it as a pickup line. Imagine that. 'Hi, I'm Shae and I build 3-D models.' That would never have gotten me laid."

Adrian took another sip of wine.

"I don't know about that. I think I might have been just slightly intrigued."

"You're such a liar, Adrian. You would have been on the other side of the bar chatting up some sophisticated buff guy."

Adrian linked her fingers through Shae's, getting braver by the minute. Shae attributed Adrian's sudden confidence to the calming effect of the red wine.

"Not the younger version of me. The varsity version of me would be very intrigued by a beautiful, hazel-eyed woman with a body like yours."

"I hate to generalise, but that is such a bi-curious thing. Every single straight woman that I've ever dated claimed to have been on the verge of lesbianism at varsity. Where were all of you when *I* was at varsity?"

Shifting away from Shae slightly, Adrian swung her right leg across the bench so that she was sitting sideways, facing Shae. She leaned her elbow on the table and draped her hair across one shoulder.

"We should probably chat about how many straight women you've dated. In fact, let's just discuss how many women you've dated."

Shifting closer, Shae also turned sideways, resting one foot on each side of the bench. She then lifted Adrian's legs and draped them across her own thighs. Wrapping her arms around Adrian's waist, she pulled her closer and rested her hands on Adrian's hips.

"We should do nothing of the sort. We should talk about Varsity Adrian and her fake interest in women."

"Varsity Adrian loved women and the way they made her feel, but she also met Frederick soon after. That man hated anyone that was different from him—bisexual people, gay people, religious people, and obese people."

Shae was surprised to hear Adrian talk about her ex-husband. She had mentioned very little about him in the past, always changing the subject when Shae started digging too much. Adrian took another sip of wine and twirled a strand of Shae's hair around her index finger.

"The fact is that you've roused Varsity Adrian from a deep slumber. She's been in hibernation for so long that we are now faced with a potential disaster."

Shae turned her face into Adrian's hand and kissed the inside of her palm.

"What potential disaster?" Shae asked.

"Well, we have to figure out if either one of us even likes her," Adrian replied.

Shae had no doubt that she would like just about any version of Adrian that existed. She could only hope that Adrian would embrace her awakening with the same enthusiasm.

"As far as I can tell, all the different versions of you look great in tight jeans, so we should be just fine," Shae said.

CHAPTER TWENTY-FOUR

Easton was sprawled out on Adrian's couch, scrolling through pictures on Instagram. They had just finished dinner and the conversation had all but dried up. Both parties were content just staring at the displays of their cell phones. When Adrian suddenly giggled, Easton sat up abruptly.

"Who are you talking to?" Easton asked.

"Just a friend. Who are you stalking on Instagram?" Adrian countered.

"You don't have any friends, Anne of Green Gables. Now, spill."

Sending off a quick text to Shae, Adrian focused her attention on Easton, who was staring at her so intensely that Adrian had to disarm her with a scatter cushion. When Adrian finally lost the scatter cushion battle, she surrendered and accepted her fate: she had to tell Easton about her pre-relationship with Shae. Shae insisted on calling it that, and she found it quite amusing.

"I would like to start off this conversation by objecting to your comment about me not having any friends," Adrian said.

"I would like to ask you to bite me. Now, please can we get to the part where you admit that you're finally screwing the patient?"

"That is hugely offensive and also inaccurate. If you're going to stick your nose in my business, you will have to stop calling her The Patient like she has leprosy," Adrian warned.

"Well, you refuse to tell me who she is. Are you fucking her?" Easton asked.

"No. You are so rude, Easton."

Easton chucked another scatter cushion in Adrian's direction.

"I'd much rather be rude than a prude. Now, are you telling me, or am I going to overpower you and read your texts? Or are you sexting?" Easton asked, wiggling her eyebrows.

"We're in a pre-relationship," Adrian finally admitted.

"You're such a nerd. Did you think of that ridiculous term?"

"I did not. I quite like the term, actually. It defines exactly what we are doing. We're assessing whether we have enough to build a relationship on. Don't you think that's wise?"

Rolling her eyes, Easton disappeared to the kitchen and returned shortly with two glasses of wine and a bag of chips. She handed Adrian a glass and took up her seat on the couch again.

"You're not sharing the chips with me?" Adrian asked.

"I'll share when you share. Have you slept with her?"

"No, I haven't. Please can I have some?" Adrian begged.

"Have you been to second base?"

Adrian really wanted some chips. Knowing that Lay's Salt and Vinegar was Adrian's favourite snack, Easton had opted for exactly that. She had two options here: she could sit here and salivate while watching Easton eat, or she could share some slightly intimate details with Easton for a portion of chips.

"Not entirely. Easton, don't be so mean."

"These are really awesome. Maybe I should make myself a nice dip," Easton said.

"Fine. We made out on her couch, in her car, on her patio, in my sunroom, and exactly where you're sitting right now."

Stuffing a handful of chips in her mouth, Easton lifted herself off the couch slightly and inspected the upholstery.

"What are you expecting to find?" Adrian asked.

She grabbed the bag of chips, capitalising when she realised that Easton was distracted.

"The Patient's bodily fluids."

"We made out a few times, Easton. That's it. It's like I explained earlier, we're trying to find a basis for a relationship. These things take time."

Frowning, Easton grabbed back the bag of chips.

"Is it a fucking business transaction? It seems like The Patient might just be as neurotic as you."

"Her name is Shae. It's only been two weeks, Easton. Do you realise that this is all completely new to me? My marriage was like sailing across the ocean. At the worst of times, I found myself cowering in a corner, the sinking of our boat imminent. At the best of times, I was in the eye of the storm, comforted by a false sense of security."

Easton had stopped stuffing her face and was now completely engaged in the conversation. It was the first serious conversation Adrian had attempted to have with her sister regarding her failed marriage.

"Now it feels like I've reached that sweet spot, Easton. Just beyond the choppy part, where you still can't see the bottom of the ocean but you're so tempted to leap over the edge and find out what it feels like to be enveloped by this force of nature."

Adrian's voice was low and quiet now and she was conflicted. Easton dumped the bag of chips next to the couch and turned to her sister. Squeezing Adrian's knee softly, she nodded at Adrian, encouraging her to continue.

"I'm hovering at the edge, dipping my toes into the water. I have to tell you, Easton, I love how it feels. I have to keep reminding myself that the ocean is a dangerous place. When I look at Shae, I forget all about the creatures lurking just beneath the surface."

Sipping on her wine, Easton shook her head. Finally, she took Adrian's hand in her own.

"Adrian, that's the beauty of it. You don't have to go over the edge alone. I don't have much information to go on here and I certainly need to meet The Patient before I can be sure, but for the first time I think there is someone waiting right behind you to take the plunge with you."

Adrian smiled and touched her glass to that of Easton's. "I certainly hope that you are right."

"The fact is that you don't really have much of an option here, sis. When you strip away the fear of getting hurt, the insecurities that you inherit from a messy relationship and the uncertainty of a new adventure like this, the only thing that is left is possibility."

Adrian tipped her glass to the side, coating the surface with a thin layer of merlot. She lifted it upright again, watching the thin layers retreat until they disappeared completely, restoring the liquid to its original equilibrium. For that first little while after her divorce, it seemed like her life would finally reach the same equilibrium. Then Shae walked into her life with her blond curls and big, hazel, soulful eyes and completely unravelled her. It was a strange process, getting used to her newfound freedom. Suddenly, nothing prevented her from telling Shae how irresistible she looked in tight jeans and those ridiculous collared shirts. No longer did she have to pretend that she didn't notice how unbelievably hot Shae looked when her hair was all windswept after a day on the golf course.

Slowly, she was starting to feel more comfortable in Varsity Adrian's skin. Varsity Adrian didn't hesitate to tell Shae about the butterflies that took flight in her stomach every time she saw her. What she hadn't told Shae in so many words yet was that Varsity Adrian was ready for so much more than kissing and fondling. Varsity Adrian was confident, but not slutty.

"Earth to Adrian," Easton said.

"Sorry, Easton. I was a mile away. You mentioned possibility. I hear you. The truth is there is also a possibility that I might get burned quite badly. I haven't even told anyone yet, but technically I am not allowed to enter into a relationship with her for two years after she stops being a patient of mine."

"How the hell do you plan to get around that?" Easton asked.

"I'm not sure yet, but I am playing around with a few ideas. Maybe I'll refer my patients to someone else and start teaching again," Adrian said.

"Well, the fact that you're even considering giving up your practice just shows me how serious this is and how deeply you're feeling for her. Adrian, you survived a marriage with Frederick— trust me, you will survive anything that comes your way. The point is that you have to take that leap. Love is something that only ever works if you're all in. For the moment, you have to let go of the fear and focus on the thrill."

Taking another sip of wine, Adrian shook her head and whistled softly.

"And how absolutely fucking thrilling this is I can't even begin to tell you. I don't know if Shae is an exceptional kisser or if kissing a woman is just generally more exciting, but it's mind-blowing. It's probably a combination."

"We should be certain. I could take her for a ride and let you know if she is that exceptional," Easton said with a wry smile on her face.

"You realise that I will break your kneecaps, right?"

Easton resumed her attack on the bag of chips while interrogating Adrian. At least she was now sharing the chips with Adrian, who was finding the release of chatting about her relationship with Shae refreshing. They laughed and talked for hours, and by the time Easton was ready to go home, Adrian was desperate to see Shae.

She walked Easton to her car and sent her off with a heartfelt hug.

"Thanks for the chat, Easton. I didn't realise how badly I needed it."

"You are welcome, Anne of Green Gables. I think you actually might have found a friend worth keeping. Have a good night."

After walking Easton to her car, Adrian brewed a pot of strong coffee, a terrible idea right before bed, but it wasn't like she would be getting much sleep. Easton was right. She had no choice but to take the leap. Realising that certainly wouldn't prevent her from tossing and turning all night. She poured herself a cup of coffee and curled up on the couch. The texts from Shae had dried up a few hours ago when Shae went out for drinks with Fiona. She was fighting the urge to send her a quick message to say good night when her phone buzzed.

Hey, Doc. Are you sleeping yet?

Adrian smiled and quickly typed a response.

Not even close. How was date night with Fiona?

Sipping on her coffee, she kept a close eye on the display of her cell phone. Just when Adrian assumed that Shae had fallen asleep, her display lit up.

Not nearly as exciting as date night with Varsity Adrian! Missed you tonight.

"This woman," Adrian said out loud, smiling in the semidarkness.

She jumped when the phone started ringing in her hand. Adrian felt giddy when Shae's voice filled her ears.

"I am way too lazy to type right now," Shae said.

"Thank goodness for that. It's really good to hear your voice," Adrian replied.

"Is it really?"

Sipping on her coffee, Adrian shifted into a sitting position on the couch. The surprise in Shae's voice made her feel so guilty. She pictured Shae treading water, waiting patiently for her to finally make her way overboard. Since that kiss in her office a few weeks ago, Adrian hadn't even come close to letting herself go. She knew that Shae was a very attentive woman and that she was probably fully aware of Adrian's hesitation.

"Yes, it is. The fact that you're so shocked by that revelation just means that I'm doing a lousy job of letting you know how I feel," Adrian said.

There was a soft chuckle before Shae cleared her throat. "You're not doing a lousy job. It's just very nice to know that you appreciate the call. Is your sister still there?"

"No, she left a while ago. I love this Demi Moore thing you're doing with your voice. Really works for me."

"I'd love to say that I can keep it up for you, but I'm afraid it's just a side effect of trying to have a conversation in a crowded pub."

"That's too bad."

They chatted for a while longer, and Adrian could tell that Shae was battling not to fall asleep when she took slightly longer to reply, and she started to make a little less sense when she finally did. She smiled when Shae unsuccessfully tried to stifle a yawn.

"Go to bed, Shae. In the morning, we can talk about stormy seas, life jackets, and taking the plunge."

Shae took even longer to reply, and Adrian could swear she heard a soft snore as Shae startled awake.

"No idea what that means. Sweet dreams, Adrian."

CHAPTER TWENTY-FIVE

After months of grappling with her feelings for Shae, weighing up the risk of jeopardising her career and the reward of opening her heart to Shae, Adrian was finally starting to feel more anchored. Although she still had to figure out exactly what her professional life would look like, she felt more relaxed than she had in months.

Adrian sliced her apple into quarters, added a handful of fat red grapes to the small plate, and slowly made her way to the sunroom clenching the latest *Psychologies* magazine under her arm. Dropping the magazine on the futon, she sipped on the fresh orange juice that she had pressed earlier.

Right after the divorce, she had no idea what to do with her Saturday mornings. Initially, she would catch up on paperwork or find some maintenance tasks around the house that needed to be done. Soon, she ran out of DIY projects and office admin and was left with a big chunk of idle time on her hands. Slowly but surely, she had relaxed into some of the rituals that she had enjoyed before she got married.

One of those rituals was a quiet breakfast. Flipping open her magazine, she popped a grape into her mouth. Engrossed in an article about life coaching, she didn't even notice Shae approaching from outside the sunroom.

"Never have I envied a grape like this before," Shae said.

Startled, Adrian let out a loud yelp and knocked over her orange juice. Dabbing at the mess on the table with a paper napkin, Adrian coughed loudly in an effort to dislodge the grape that had slipped down her throat.

"I can totally perform the Heimlich manoeuvre on you while you're wearing this little."

Taking a big swallow of orange juice to soothe her throat, Adrian chucked the soggy paper napkin at Shae.

"You're such a stalker. Why not just make use of my front door?"

"I gave up after ten minutes of knocking. Are you sure you don't need that Heimlich manoeuvre after all?" Shae asked.

"I'm perfectly fine, but I certainly wouldn't mind feeling your arms around me," Adrian replied as she jumped into Shae's embrace.

Wrapping her arms around Shae's back, she pulled her closer and let out a contented sigh as Shae nuzzled her exposed neck. She loved the way Shae's hands always wandered in these embraces, almost always ending up cupping and squeezing her ass. She rewarded Shae with a smouldering kiss that left her slightly out of breath.

"Good morning, Doctor."

Before Adrian could even reply, Shae's phone started ringing.

"You are killing me. I literally just walked in. I said I would call you later," Shae said.

"So stop making out and let me know if we have a date!" Jax said.

Adrian had returned to her spot on the futon and was now nibbling on a slice of apple. She could hear Jax's voice from where she was sitting.

"I will call you back, Booger."

Shae ended the call before Jax could protest any further. She took a seat next to Adrian and stole a slice of apple from her plate.

"Booger?" Adrian asked.

"What's wrong with Booger?" Shae asked as she took a huge bite of the apple.

"That was Jax. You call her Booger? Why?"

"You don't think it's fitting? I came up with it all by myself. She's like a booger. You're often not even aware of her, but she is sitting there, just waiting for the opportune moment to humiliate you. She loves that name."

Shae wiped some apple juice from her lips with the back of her hand before she popped a few grapes into her mouth.

"All this time I've been waiting in suspense for you to gift me with a pet name. Thank goodness you never did. You suck at it," Adrian said.

"I was thinking of calling you Fig," Shae replied without missing a beat.

"What?"

"Yes. Figs are the only fruit that I find as beautiful on the inside as they are on the outside," Shae explained.

"Figs are also plump," Adrian pointed out.

"Did you know that a fig is actually an inverted flower? When you split it open, what you are looking at is actually the flower blooming on the inside of the flesh," Shae said.

Leaning back against the futon, Adrian shifted and rested her feet in Shae's lap. She popped another grape into her mouth and groaned as the sweet juice burst into her mouth.

"Did you know that figs are plump?"

"You're not plump. If it makes you feel better, I'll call you Figlet."

"That's not a word," Adrian said.

"It can be."

Adrian groaned as Shae hit a sensitive spot while massaging her feet. It had been almost a natural process, the shifting of their relationship into more intimate territory. After all, Shae had been pushing the boundaries when their relationship had been one of a purely professional nature. The fact that the two women had seen each other a few times per week for the last six months had certainly contributed to their easy rapport and familiar comfort.

"So, what's up with Jax?" Adrian asked.

"She wants me to go to the movies with them, but I already have plans. I am going to the Pride parade."

Shae squirmed as Adrian dug her toes into her side.

"Oh yeah? All by yourself? Stag?"

"Absolutely," Shae replied.

"You're really not going to ask me to come with you?" Adrian asked.

"I don't think so. It's not going to be your scene."

"Hey! Let me be the judge of that. I've grown to like the autonomy that came with the divorce, and if you don't mind, I'd like to keep it."

"You're absolutely right. So, you think you can handle your first Pride parade, Doctor? While I do agree that you can make your own decisions, you should at least be informed of what you can expect."

Adrian tapped her foot against Shae's thigh, encouraging her to continue with the massaging.

"I'm going to humour you, Miss McPherson. What would I be letting myself in for?"

"There will be lots of glitter, cheap makeup, hairy armpits peeking out from under slinky dresses, tutus and tiaras, two hundred different versions of 'It's Raining Men,' and portable toilets."

Adrian nodded slowly. "Fascinating."

"There will also be priests clutching their bibles and bombarding you with quotes from Leviticus," Shae continued.

Adrian frowned.

"Even if you decide to keep the public displays of affection to a bare minimum, you will be guilty by association. If you're not for them, you're against them, remember."

Adrian had never been particularly religious, but she would be lying if she said that the thought of a priest bashing her simply because she was attending a parade didn't intimidate her. At the same time, she had to admit that she was intrigued. There was also the fact that she had planned on spending the day with Shae. Hairy armpits on display and portable toilets hadn't been part of her plans, but she could probably survive it.

"Let me take a quick shower."

Smiling, Shae leaned over and planted a kiss on Adrian's cheek.

"That's my Figlet. I will be right over here fantasising about your naked perfection. I will also call Jax to let her down easy," Shae said.

Less than half an hour later, Adrian was on her way to her first Pride parade. She was wearing a pair of tight Levi's, a flannel shirt that she left unbuttoned over a tight black tank top, and a pair of comfortable sneakers. The comfortable shoes had been a recommendation from Shae. Adrian had no idea why Shae had collapsed into a fit of laughter when she saw her, but she mentioned something about her shirt being very fitting for the occasion. She had no idea what that meant, but she loved this shirt and she refused to take it off.

Shae had not been overexaggerating. The first thing Adrian saw when Shae parked the car some distance away from the entrance to the park was a hulk of man stuffed into a pink tutu. Apart from the tutu and fishnet stockings, the only other thing he was wearing was a bow tie and black boots. The glitter on his hairy chest almost made him sparkle in the bright sunlight. He winked at Adrian from underneath thick, fake lashes.

"Are you ready for this?" Shae asked as they made their way to the entrance.

"Ready as I'll ever be," Adrian said. Slipping her sunglasses onto her head, she held her hand out to Shae. "Have I told you that you look like a million dollars today?" Adrian asked.

Adrian was not wrong. Shae was wearing a snug pair of chino shorts that showed off her well-toned legs. The loose-fitting vest exposed shapely tanned shoulders and Adrian had trouble not staring at the cleavage on display where the vest dipped in the front.

"You have not," Shae said as she wrapped Adrian's hand in her own.

"Well, you do. That vest is killing me."

Shae brought their joined hands to her mouth to place a soft kiss on Adrian's. For the next hour they browsed through the stalls and snacked on corn dogs and ice cream. The march was about to start when Adrian heard the familiar swearing.

"As I live and fucking breathe," Jax said.

Jax and Andie were manning a stall where one could buy LGBTQI-plus-themed novelties. Jax took one look at Adrian and turned her attention to Shae. Pointing her thumb at Adrian, she snorted. "Did you make her wear that?"

"I did not. Our lovely Adrian loves her autonomy and makes her own decisions," Shae replied, winking at Adrian.

"Flannel? What the fuck? We value the support, Doc, but that's overkill," Jax said.

"What is wrong with the two of you?" Adrian asked, tugging on her shirt again.

Shoving Jax in the shoulder, Andie leaned across and smiled at Adrian.

"I think it's a beautiful shirt, Dr. Ramsey."

"Thank you, Andie. I happen to think so too. You know you're welcome to call me Adrian, right?"

Jax planted a kiss on her cheek and chuckled when a blush crept up Andie's neck instantly.

"This one is way too conservative. Isn't it so fucking super refreshing?" Jax said.

"Super refreshing, indeed," Adrian said.

The floats were lined up for the march and Jax pulled on Andie's hand. "Well, we're off. You old ladies are welcome to join us. If not, please buy some shit from my dad. That's him over there," Jax said, pointing over her shoulder.

Before Adrian or Shae could even reply, Jax started dragging Andie to a nearby float.

"Jacqueline, your next shift starts in two hours! Have fun, girls!"

The first thought Adrian had was that this man looked nothing like Hitler or Stalin. He certainly had a military look about him—perfectly ironed shirt and not a hair out of place. He also had kind, soft blue eyes that lit up when he smiled.

"Mr. Wesley, what a pleasure to meet you, sir. My name is Shae McPherson. I'm a friend of Jax's."

Adrian watched as Jax's father shook Shae's outstretched hand and then offered her own.

"Hi, Mr. Wesley. I am Adrian Ramsey, Jax's therapist. It's so nice to finally meet you."

Mr. Wesley sure had a good grip on him. Adrian almost croaked out loud when he squeezed her hand in greeting.

"Ah, Dr. Ramsey, the pleasure is mine. Please take a look around. My friend does wonderful work in the LGBTQI community. He's a counsellor and runs a halfway house for abandoned teens. We help out at his stall every year," Mr. Wesley said.

"We'd love to check it out," Adrian said and led the way.

Adrian browsed through the stall while Mr. Wesley gave her some background on the foundation that his friend had established in honour of his son that had committed suicide some years ago. The boy had struggled with his sexuality despite the fact that his parents were supportive. Unfortunately, teenagers were not as accommodating, and he had suffered abuse from various bullies in his high school.

Adrian and Shae were still completely engaged in conversation with Mr. Wesley when Jax and Andie returned from the march. The stall got quite busy, and the foursome said their goodbyes to Mr. Wesley before they headed off for a quick lunch. Jax and Andie wandered off to have a stroll around the grounds, Adrian suspected for a make-out session. Her suspicions were confirmed when the girls finally made their appearance, looking quite flustered.

"Can you two OGs please give us a lift back home?" Jax asked.

"Sure thing, *Jacqueline*," Shae said, winking at Jax.

CHAPTER TWENTY-SIX

Jax and Andie had been quiet all the way home, Adrian noticed. Shae pulled up in Andie's driveway and smiled as Jax gave her a quick peck on the cheek.

"Bye, Booger. Are you sure that your dad is picking you up here later?"

"No, Shae. We're eloping," Jax said.

Respecting her boundaries with Adrian, Jax simply squeezed her shoulder and thanked her for a lovely day. Andie did the same, and soon they rushed into the house, no doubt in a hurry to make the most of their time together before Mr. Wesley would fetch Jax.

"Finally, I have you all to myself," Shae said as she leaned across for a quick kiss.

"I thought this moment would never come," Adrian said.

"So, how was your first Pride parade, Figlet?"

Adrian chuckled in the semidarkness and rested her hand on Shae's thigh.

"God, I hope that name doesn't stick. I would say that it was interesting. Did you have a good time?"

"I did. I quite like Mr. Wesley. I think Jax might have misled us a little bit about him."

"I think so too," Adrian said. She turned sideways so that she could look at Shae. "Anyway, enough about everyone else. Right now, it's just you and me." Shae nodded with a huge smile on her face. "And that damn vest," Adrian said as she slid her hand a bit higher on Shae's thigh.

Shae's breath seemed to catch when Adrian's fingers brushed lightly against her inner thigh. She could feel Shae stiffening immediately, and the knowledge that she had that effect on this woman was intoxicating.

"I've wanted to slip my hand under it all day."

Adrian softly dragged her index finger across the seam between Shae's legs, emboldened by the fact that Shae couldn't turn her gaze away from the road. She felt her blood rush to her ears when Shae spread her legs ever so slightly, allowing Adrian more access.

"I think you better drive a bit faster," Adrian said.

Clearing her throat, Shae rested her hand on Adrian's, sliding it back and forth against the seam as she groaned softly. Shifting around in her seat, Adrian bit down on her bottom lip. Her heart was hammering in her chest and she barely noticed the cars speeding past them. All she was aware of was the subtle rocking against her hand.

Moments later, Shae parked her car and released the clasp of the safety belt in one swift motion. She leaned across and pulled Adrian into her lap. Somehow, Adrian managed to straddle her in the cramped space and their tongues met in a clash of hunger. Shae's one hand gripped the back of Adrian's neck, pulling her closer. The other hand cupped Adrian's breast, paying special attention to a hardened nipple. Trapping Shae's lip between her teeth, Adrian unbuttoned her chinos and ran her fingers across the silky garment that clung to Shae's wet centre. When Shae arched her back, Adrian's ass pushed against the steering wheel and a loud horn sounded.

"Sorry," Shae mumbled before Adrian covered her mouth with her own again.

Shaking her head, Adrian slipped both hands under Shae's vest and brushed her thumbs across her nipples. Leaving a trail of wet kisses down Shae's neck, she slipped a hand between her own legs, taking it upon herself to unbutton her jeans. She desperately wanted to feel Shae's hands on her. She battled freeing her belt in the restricted space, and when she gave it a hard pull it suddenly gave way and she hit her elbow against Shae's window. Adrian suddenly sat up and swiped her hair from her eyes.

"What are we doing?"

Staring at her lap, Shae sucked on her lower lip. "I know. Sorry, Adrian. I just got a little carried away."

"No, I mean what are we still doing in this car? Follow me," Adrian said as she slipped back to the passenger side and hastily exited the car.

Shae took a moment to button her chinos and search for her vest, but Adrian knocked on the window to hurry her along. "Leave that off."

"If you insist," Shae said as she followed Adrian.

Adrian fumbled with the lock of her front door as if she hadn't opened it millions of times before. Her hands were shaking and she could hear the blood rushing in her ears. Had she planned on having sex with Shae at some point? Certainly. Had she planned to do it today? Hell no, but here she was leading Shae inside and quite possibly up to her room.

"Adrian, hang on just one second," Shae said as she gripped Adrian's elbow.

When Adrian turned around, Shae was smiling sweetly.

"We don't have to do this, Adrian. You can take all the time that you need. I'm not going anywhere."

Leaning against the front door for a moment, Adrian crossed her arms over her chest and let out a long breath, studying Shae closely. She loved the little line through Shae's left brow where the hair refused to cover an old scar. She also loved the way the tip of her nose turned up ever so slightly and the way the left side of her mouth didn't quite cooperate with the right side when she smiled. Every smile was lopsided and utterly beautiful. She happened to like the beauty spot positioned right at the apex of Shae's perfect cleavage.

Wordlessly, she turned and managed to finally unlock the front door, beckoning Shae inside. She dumped her bag on the floor and her keys on the couch. Slipping off her sneakers and the infamous flannel shirt that had grabbed everyone's attention, she padded to the kitchen. Shae followed her cautiously. Adrian handed her a beer and poured herself a glass of wine.

"Let's take this upstairs," Adrian said.

She turned off the lights in the kitchen and headed upstairs. Realising that Shae was not behind her, she paused halfway up the staircase.

"Adrian, just give me a minute."

Shae was glued to the spot at the bottom of the staircase with a bewildered look on her face. Adrian's heart fell to the floor. She had been trying to work through her own feelings for so long that she never took a minute to consider the fact that Shae might not be ready for this.

"I think it's only fair that I be honest with you, Adrian. I've been quite determined not to rush you into anything physical, but the fact is that I am not certain that I can control myself in the confined space of your bedroom with a bottle of wine and that fucking tight tank top you're wearing."

Grinning from ear to ear, Adrian descended the stairs. She hooked her index finger through one of the loops of Shae's chino shorts and pulled her so close that she could feel Shae's breath on her lips.

"Now would be a really good time to follow me," Adrian said.

This time, Shae didn't hesitate. She followed Adrian all the way into her room, which represented everything that Adrian was: organised and elegant. The sleigh bed was covered in a simple white quilt with a band of delicately embroidered flowers along the bottom with matching scatter cushions propped up against the headboard. The only items that could be found on the two bedside tables were two reading lamps, and the rest of the room was just as uncluttered.

"This is where you help me out, Shae. We both know that I have no clue what I'm doing."

"Really? When you had your fingers between my legs earlier it certainly felt like you knew what you were doing," Shae said.

"You weren't paying attention to me then. You were focused on not crashing your car," Adrian replied.

Placing her beer on the dresser, Shae took Adrian's hands in her own as they sat down at the bottom of the bed. Adrian's heart was beating dangerously fast and she felt light-headed.

"Hey, look at me," Shae said as she laid two butterfly kisses on Adrian's knuckles.

Adrian finally looked up with wide eyes and a nervously clenched jaw.

"I've been paying attention to you since the day I walked into your office expecting an overweight bald guy in that chair. The last thing I ever expected was to find this intriguing goddess of a woman instead. You might not know this, but you completely unnerve me."

"I do?" Adrian asked.

"You do. It's not just because you are exquisitely beautiful and completely out of my league. It's because of how you make me feel."

This earned a little smile from Adrian, despite the nerves.

"I haven't been this excited about anything in my life. When you looked at me by the staircase earlier, you made me feel so beautiful. You make me feel so wanted and that's something I haven't felt in such a long time," Shae continued.

Adrian ran her hands all the way up Shae's arms and finally lay a soft palm against her cheek.

"You do happen to be both of those things, Shae. You are beautiful. You are wanted. You also happen to be strong, intuitive, compassionate, and inspiring. For tonight, I'd like to focus on the first two things, though."

Leaning closer, Adrian started a trail of soft kisses down Shae's neck and across her shoulder. Tugging at the hem of the tank top, she slowly lifted it over Shae's head and chucked it aside. Shae returned the favour and Adrian's top joined what was becoming a heap of their clothing.

"Holy shit. I'd love to come up with something sophisticated to say, but that's all I have."

Adrian chuckled at that and slowly closed the distance between them. She rested a finger under Shae's chin and lifted it ever so slightly. The kiss started softly and slowly. Adrian simply wanted to distract Shae while she wrapped her arms around her back and undid her bra. By the time Shae's bra hit the floor, though, Adrian was engrossed in the most passionate kiss they had ever shared.

She kicked the bra aside and ran her hands up Shae's neck and buried her fingers in the curls she loved so much. Shae pushed her tongue into Adrian's mouth and groaned softly when Adrian sucked on it lightly. She undid Adrian's bra and quickly got rid of the garment, cupping a perky breast in her right hand.

"Fuck," Adrian whispered into Shae's mouth as she felt Shae's fingers closing around her nipple.

"Is that a suggestion or an order?" Shae asked as she carefully pushed Adrian into a horizontal position.

Adrian scooted up to the top of the bed while Shae hovered above her, supporting her weight with her arms. Needing to feel Shae against her flesh, Adrian gripped Shae's hips and pulled her down and straight into another scorcher of a kiss. Their legs intertwined and Adrian felt an overwhelming rush as Shae's thigh connected with her throbbing centre.

"Shae, take my jeans off. Now."

Shae kissed her way down Adrian's torso and finally slipped her jeans off as instructed. She didn't wait for another instruction to take her own chinos off, and seconds later Adrian gripped the headboard as their wet centres connected for the first time. She bit down on her lower lip as Shae paid special attention to her breasts, sucking on one nipple and twisting the other lightly between her thumb and index finger.

"I'm running out of time, Shae. Please touch me."

"I am touching you," Shae said as if she didn't understand what Adrian had meant.

Letting go of the headboard, Adrian covered Shae's right hand that was doing crushingly beautiful things to her nipple and guided it to her swollen clit. Adrian didn't let go of Shae's hand, pushing her fingers slowly down the peak of her clit into her wet folds. She arched her back and gripped the headboard harder with her free hand.

"Let me take it from here," Shae said as she wrapped her lips around the abandoned nipple, sucking lightly as Adrian's hand joined the other one on the headboard.

"Please, Shae. Make it stop."

"Make what stop?" Shae whispered as she ran her tongue around Adrian's hard nipple.

"Throbbing. It almost hurts."

Shae slipped her fingers in and out of Adrian slowly, running her tongue down Adrian's cleavage. She pushed the tip of her tongue into Adrian's navel and gripped her hip with one hand as she arched her back again. Letting go of the headboard, Adrian took hold of Shae's shoulders and slammed her nails into the soft flesh as Shae increased the speed of the thrusting between her legs.

She screamed out the minute Shae's tongue slid over her painful clit, the motion matching the rhythmic thrust of her fingers. It took only seconds for her body to crash into the biggest orgasm she'd ever had, and she all but lost her hearing for as long as it took for her arms and legs to stop convulsing. The first sound she heard again was Shae's ragged breathing.

Shae had collapsed on top of her with her head on Adrian's chest and her arms wrapped around Adrian's own like a vine. Their legs were also still entwined, and Adrian could feel a lovely wet presence against her thigh. Adrian was still catching her breath and wasn't able to speak, but she disentangled one arm and snaked it around Shae's waist, resting her hand on a firm buttock. The other hand she ran through Shae's matted hair until they both fell asleep.

CHAPTER TWENTY-SEVEN

Adrian stirred slightly as the first rays of sunshine danced across her bedroom floor. Her eyes remained closed as she wrestled with her consciousness, desperate to keep the dream alive. She groaned softly as Shae's index finger drew an invisible line down her spine. It was only when Shae chuckled that Adrian realised she was in fact not dreaming, and almost immediately her brain flooded with memories of the night before, flashes of Shae on top of her and, more importantly, inside of her.

She felt the heat running up her neck and spreading across her cheeks as a tingling sensation settled between her legs. She could feel Shae's tight nipples on her back as she gathered Adrian's hair in her fingers, sliding it across her shoulder to expose her neck. Shae placed the softest of kisses just under her ear and slowly worked her way down Adrian's neck and spine. She squealed when Shae bit into the flesh of her buttocks and quickly rolled on top of her. Now that their positions were switched, Adrian saw Shae for the first time that morning.

"Good morning, Miss McPherson."

"Indeed, Dr. Ramsey. You seem a little flushed. Was it something I said?"

Shae wrapped her arms around Adrian's back and quickly rolled her onto her back again.

"Months of dissecting your psyche and not once did I realise that you had these control issues. Not that I mind the view from the bottom, but I wouldn't mind experiencing it from the top for once," Adrian said.

"Would you now?" Shae asked as she placed another kiss in the hollow cleft under Adrian's collarbone.

"I certainly would. What exactly are you doing down here?" Adrian asked and lightly pinched Shae's thigh that was slowly rocking against her centre.

Shae ran her hand through Adrian's hair and softly pulled on the fine strands at the base of her neck, tilting her head backward so she could suck on her neck. She was careful not to leave any marks, which could not be said of Adrian, who was digging her nails into Shae's back.

"I distinctly remember you promising me last night that this morning would be my turn," Adrian complained.

"Did I say that?" Shae paused, hovering above Adrian still.

"You did."

"Well, you'll have to be patient, Doctor. I have to meet Fiona in half an hour."

Adrian pouted, and that earned her a quick kiss.

"I certainly can't meet her smelling like this, either, so I have to head home for a quick shower."

"You're just going to leave me here with all of these thoughts?" Adrian asked, cupping Shae's breasts in her hands.

Shae rolled off Adrian, and seconds later the two women lay facing each other. For a long while, no words were spoken as they studied each other closely. Adrian placed her palm against Shae's cheek and smiled sweetly.

"Before you rush off this morning, I want to tell you that last night was absolutely amazing," Adrian said softly, blushing profusely. "My body did things that I didn't know it could, and I'm hoping that I won't run into any of my neighbours because I think there were times that I couldn't contain what I was feeling." Shae did a fist pump as if celebrating a personal victory. "I've imagined you making love to me before, but nothing could have prepared me for the kind of intensity I felt last night. I want you to know that I have no regrets this morning."

Shae laid her hand on top of Adrian's and kissed the inside of her palm.

"Thanks for saying that. It was a real concern for me. In my mind, there was a distinct possibility that you could wake up this morning and cringe at the memory of last night. That was a risk I was willing to take, but nothing makes me happier than knowing you have no regrets."

Shifting closer to Shae, Adrian pushed her onto her back and rested her head on her chest. Adrian let out a long, contented sigh as Shae pulled her fingers through her hair with one hand and rested the other on her hip.

"Adrian, I want you to take your time with this. Let all of this sink in and figure out anything you may need to before you even think about reciprocating. Being with a woman for the first time can be overwhelming and very daunting. Don't underestimate it. There's no rush."

Lifting her head, Adrian rested her chin on her hand between Shae's breasts so she could look into her eyes. She touched Shae's bottom lip with the tip of her index finger and ran it all the way down her neck and across her nipple.

"You're such a thoughtful, beautiful soul. Trust me, I don't just want to reciprocate because it seems like the polite thing to do. I want you just as much as you want me. I will take you up on the offer, though, because I would certainly be lying if I said that I wasn't overwhelmed. I am, but in the best possible way."

Slipping a lock of hair behind Adrian's ear, Shae leaned forward and kissed the tip of her nose lightly.

"Waking up with you was every bit as magical as I expected it to be, Adrian, but your hospitality needs some work. By this time, I thought I would have been offered a cup of coffee in return for the multiple orgasms I provided."

"Apologies. One cup of coffee coming up. In fact, that thing you did with your middle finger and thumb earned you a rusk as well," Adrian said.

Rolling away from Shae, she stood and slipped into a silk robe that left very little to the imagination. By the time Adrian returned with a strong cup of coffee and a muesli rusk, Shae was dressed in the same chinos and vest that she had worn to the Pride parade the day before.

"Muesli? I imagine if I added my index finger into the mix, it could have earned me at least a honey and almond rusk," Shae joked.

"I would imagine so," Adrian replied.

They had their coffee out on the patio, and after a long and passionate goodbye, Shae drove off. Adrian spent at least an hour just staring off into the distance, trying to make sense of what was happening between her and Shae McPherson. Her daydreaming was interrupted by the loud ringing of her phone.

"I need to come over."

"Well, good morning to you too, Avril. I am doing exceptionally well. Thanks for asking," Adrian replied.

"I'll see you in ten minutes," Avril said and disconnected the call.

Frowning, Adrian stared at the phone in her hand for a few seconds. If Avril was really coming over, it must be something serious. She jumped into the shower quickly, and by the time she was dressed, she heard Avril park in the driveway. Taking a quick glance in the mirror, she slipped her feet into her slippers and opened the front door. Within seconds Avril was in her arms and sobbing. Adrian was used to comforting Easton, who was more emotional, but she hadn't had her arms around Avril since the second grade. She held her for a while and quietly led her inside.

"Avi, what's wrong, girl?"

"Just life. It fucking sucks donkey dick," Avril replied.

"Okay, sailor, have a seat. Can I offer you a cup of coffee?"

"You can offer me a fucking lobotomy," Avril said, sniffing.

"Sure. Would you like a cup of coffee before I scrub in?" Adrian asked.

She busied herself with preparing another pot of coffee and arranging a few snacks on a plate. Avril didn't say another word until they were both seated and nibbling on some spring rolls. Finally, Adrian wiped her mouth with the back of her hand and focused her attention on Avril.

"Maybe a lobotomy would be easier after all," Adrian said.

"I slept with him," Avril said.

Chewing on the inside of her lip, Adrian stared at her sister through narrowed slits.

"Avril, you're going to have to be more specific."

"Leonard. I slept with him last night."

Adrian was trained not to react visibly to anything shocking, but this was Avril, and Leonard was her cowardly ex-husband. The same man that had left Avril with two newborn babies and a broken heart. Why on earth would she give that man the time of day?

"I am going to assume you mean the sperm donor of your children and not some other random Leonard I know nothing about."

"Adrian, please don't make this harder than it has to be."

"I have questions, Avril."

"So, ask your questions, but please don't be all judgmental and self-righteous."

"Since when do you have contact with him?" Adrian started her long list of questions.

"I've always had contact with him, Adrian. We share two boys."

"Well, that part is debatable since he's never changed a diaper or wiped a snotty nose."

Noticing Avril's immediate irritation, Adrian held her hands in the air.

"But since I am not going to be judgmental and self-righteous, I will not mention any more ways that he's been absent in their lives. Do tell me how you went from having contact with him to swopping bodily fluids with him."

"I could ask you exactly the same question, Adrian."

Blushing profusely, Adrian stuffed another spring roll into her mouth.

"I don't know what you are talking about, Avi. Was it the first time you slept with him since your divorce?" Adrian deflected.

"Was it the first time you slept with her since you got fired?" Avril asked.

Adrian knew that there was simply no way that Avril was going to let this go. She had two options here. She could lie to her sister, or she could own the fact that she had finally been intimate with Shae. Neither option came without consequences, but she realised that lying about their intimacy would feel like she was betraying Shae.

"Yes, it was," Adrian confessed.

"But I kissed you on that mouth earlier," Avril said, grimacing.

"Oh, don't be gross, Avril. Besides, my mouth is still virginally clean since I haven't had the opportunity to go down on her."

Covering her ears with her hands, Avril kicked her feet and shook her head like a child throwing a tantrum.

"Stop being so dramatic, Avril. Are we talking about you banging your ex-husband or not?"

Sighing heavily, Avril rolled her eyes and slipped her feet onto Adrian's lap. Resting her hands on Avril's legs, Adrian shifted into a more comfortable position.

"Adrian, what are we going to do? Mom and Dad are going to be furious with us."

"*Us?* What have I done?" Adrian asked.

"Come on, Adrian. Do you really think they are going to give you a pat on the back for becoming a lesbian all of a sudden?"

"Avril, one doesn't *become* a lesbian. I've been attracted to women for a long time," Adrian said.

"No, we're not talking about you. Tell me what to do about my mess," Avril said.

For the next hour Avril explained to Adrian how Leonard had steadily been building a relationship with her. The two had been communicating via email and social media for almost two years. Initially, it had started with Leonard asking for pictures of the boys or arranging with Avril to pick up gifts for them. Eventually, they had agreed to meet once a month at a neutral location to catch up so that Avril could keep him updated on whatever was happening with the boys. Apparently, last night was the first time that one of their monthly visits had ended between the sheets of a hotel bed.

"Let me get this straight. Leonard didn't leave you for another woman?"

"No, he was just overwhelmed when the boys were born. He wasn't ready to be a father to one child at the time, not to mention twins," Avril said.

"So, he went to work and just never fucking returned?" Adrian asked, outraged.

"Calm down, Adrian. Nobody said that he didn't make a huge mistake—he did. He fucked up and he knows that. All I'm saying is that he's not the same man anymore."

"How is he not the same man, Avril?"

Avril sat up straight and stared at Adrian.

"Really, Adrian? You're going to ask me that question? How are you not the same woman that devoted herself completely to a man several years ago? In fact, how are you not the same woman that had sexual relations with men exclusively up until a few hours ago?"

Adrian could explain to Avril how she had always considered herself to be bisexual, but what would be the point? The fact was that she wasn't the same woman that she had been before she met Shae. She hated to admit it, but Avril was right. It was entirely possible that Leonard had evolved since their divorce. Did she like the fact that her sister was comparing her sexual awakening to Leonard's realisation that he had been a coward? Not really.

"Look, Avril. I don't think me not acting on my desire to be with a woman until very recently is the same as abandoning your wife and newborn twins. Having said that, the only person that can define what your relationship should look like, is you."

"That's easy for you to say, Adrian. You know exactly how everyone feels about Leonard."

"How do you feel about Leonard?" Adrian asked.

"I am still trying to figure that part out for myself. What I do know is that I don't want to hide our connection anymore," Avril said.

"So, how did you leave things this morning?" Adrian asked.

"I left before he woke up and we haven't spoken since. I was hoping to get some clarity by speaking to you."

Adrian rubbed her hands on her knees and turned to Avril, taking her hands into her own. Never before had she seen Avril so confused and despondent. She squeezed her hands lightly and offered her a reassuring smile.

"Sis, I don't have all the answers, but I think it all comes down to one thing. If it's your conscious choice to give Leonard another chance, you should do exactly that. It would be wise to have a serious discussion about your mutual expectations and to lay down boundaries with the boys."

Avril looked like she might actually vomit.

"I'll support whatever decision you make, Avril. You deserve to be happy, and if your happiness is with Leonard, we will accept it. I'll talk to Mom and Dad if you want me to."

Adrian was surprised when Avril actually wrapped her arms around her and hugged her. When she pulled away from her, she had tears in her eyes. Adrian knew how difficult it must have been for Avril to take her into her confidence and she felt honoured.

"I suppose I'll have to make peace with your muff-diving urges as well."

"I think it might help if you stopped being so graphic about it," Adrian suggested.

CHAPTER TWENTY-EIGHT

"Dr. Ramsey?"

Adrian was turned toward the window, staring at nothing in particular. She heard Ella's impatient throat-clearing from behind her and swivelled her chair around to find her receptionist standing in the doorway with her hands on her hips.

"Sorry, Ella. What can I help you with?" Adrian said as she rested her hands on her desk.

"Are you feeling okay, Doctor?"

"Yes. Yes, I am feeling perfectly fine. Thanks, Ella. Now what can I do for you?"

"I just wanted to remind you about the conference tomorrow. I confirmed your attendance this morning. Lately, you've been a little distracted," Ella said.

Ella slipped her glasses off her nose, letting them dangle from a chain around her neck. The blush creeping up Adrian's neck probably didn't escape Ella. She had known Adrian for many years, undoubtedly long enough to notice that something was up.

"Thanks, Ella. I promise I won't forget. Sorry, I just have a lot on my mind at the moment."

"Dr. Ramsey, can I speak frankly for a minute?"

Adrian smiled at the sweet old lady that had become like a grandmother to her over the years.

"Always, Ella."

Ella shuffled closer to the desk and finally pulled out the chair across from Adrian. Lowering herself into the chair, she sighed as she finally managed to find a comfortable position.

"At my age, dear, we settle for some comfort. For years, I have been watching you settled into your marriage and willing you to start shuffling around for a comfortable spot. Deep down, I also knew that there would be no comfortable spot to be found."

Adrian reached for Ella's hand across the desk. She was deeply touched by Ella's emotional display, something she didn't see often. Ella was always very affectionate to her, but she never mentioned anything about her personal life like this.

"May I just say that it's been heartwarming to watch you find that sweet spot where your bum cheeks fit into the upholstery like a hand into a glove."

Adrian had to chuckle at that, and she softly squeezed Ella's hand.

"Shae McPherson is a fine young woman, Dr. Ramsey. Yes, she's a woman, but she also happens to be the one person who not only offers you comfort, but makes you stare off into the distance with a big old grin on that beautiful face of yours."

Ella kissed the top of Adrian's hand before she leaned back in the chair and folded her arms across her chest.

"My dear, I don't know what's going on in that pretty little head of yours, but I certainly hope that the same courage that helped you out of that poisonous marriage will help you to accept this thing with Shae for what it is—a blessing."

"Ella, she certainly feels like a blessing to me. Thank you so much for taking the time to chat to me this morning. Knowing that you approve of our relationship gives me hope that others will find their way to acceptance as well."

"Dr. Ramsey, do you think I care what other people think of my ratty old recliner at home? The one with the big stain on the armrest and the chunk of upholstery missing in the back? I don't. You know what I care about? I care about the fact that when I finally get to sit back in that chair with my feet up at the end of every day, I feel like I'm right where I'm supposed to be. Home."

The process of getting out of the chair across from Adrian seemed painful as Ella slowly rose out of it. She leaned across the desk and squeezed Adrian's cheek affectionately before she made her way back to reception, humming.

Adrian spent a few minutes just thinking about everything that Ella had said. Ella had spoken about finding the courage to accept Shae into her life, but she'd already done that. In her own way she had already started dealing with her feelings and where they might lead. Shae had taken the first step in their physical relationship and introduced her to the wonderful world of multiple orgasms and deep fulfilment. If she was being honest, she was definitely nervous about reversing the roles. She had been constantly fantasising about all kinds of beautifully exhilarating things she wanted to do to Shae, but if she had the courage to finally take that step was still to be discovered.

Inspired and emboldened by Ella's pep talk, she picked up the phone on her desk and dialled Shae's number.

"This is a lovely surprise. Hi, Doc," Shae answered after two short rings.

"You certainly are not stained, and as far as I could tell you didn't even have a chunk of upholstery missing, either. No, you are not only comfortable. You are luxurious and stylish and you look so damn good in my living room," Adrian said, twirling the cable of her phone around her index finger.

"Um…thanks, I guess?" Shae said.

"Sitting on you was the best decision I ever made, Shae. Would you like to come over for dinner tonight?"

"With that strange but arousing intro, how could I possibly refuse?"

"Great. Come over whenever you're ready," Adrian said.

"Sounds good. I'm assisting Fiona with hockey training after school today. I will probably finish up around five?" Shae said.

"Works for me. Are you in class right now? It didn't even occur to me that you can't just take my calls whenever you please."

"I stepped out quickly. Good thing I did too because I have to clear my mind quickly of the image of you sitting on me. I'll see you later, beautiful."

Instead of staring out the window, Adrian spent the rest of her morning typing up reports and filing since she had no appointments. She had started referring her current patients to other therapists, preparing to take a hiatus to figure out next steps for her career. She also managed to run through her notes for the presentation that she had to deliver at the conference the following day. On her drive home, she mentally ran through the contents of her fridge. She wanted tonight to be really special, and she was having a hard time figuring out what the perfect meal would be.

By the time Shae rang the doorbell, she was positively anxious and wearing out the carpet in the foyer with all the pacing. She managed another quick glance in the mirror in the hallway before she opened the front door.

"I have nothing," Shae said. She covered her mouth with her right hand, shaking her head.

"That's okay. I have a good bottle of wine and ice-cold beer," Adrian said and pecked Shae on the cheek as she pulled her inside.

"No, Adrian. I mean, I'm completely speechless. You look so beautiful. You caught me off-guard for a second."

The hem of Adrian's tight black cocktail dress didn't quite reach her knees. The silky garment hugged her breasts and wrapped around her neck like a choker and across her shoulders in a cross on her back. The exposed flesh on her sides and back appeared to be as smooth as the silk itself. Shae's eyes roamed down her legs and rested on her naked feet, the nails of her toes painted bright red.

"You're a bit early. I haven't had time to put on some shoes."

"Please don't," Shae said as she wrapped her arms around Adrian.

"Don't be silly. I have the perfect heels for this dress!" Adrian said.

"I can just picture you coming home from work and kicking off those perfect heels. Since I am totally underdressed tonight, I insist that you leave them off."

Shae was wearing her favourite Levi's and a white chiffon double-breasted blouse with a very low neckline. Her exposed sun-kissed forearms contrasted with the white sleeves that only covered three-quarters of her arms. Her bouncy curls were draped across her right shoulder, reaching the first button of the blouse and the apex of her cleavage.

"Oh, I beg to differ. You look gorgeous, Miss McPherson. If you let me have a peek under that blouse, I might leave off the heels."

Adrian leaned back in the embrace and hooked her index finger behind the first button and pulled on it slightly, peeking down Shae's shirt.

"Varsity Adrian seems to be a boob chick then," Shae said.

"I need this shirt in my life. When do we start sharing clothes?" Adrian asked.

"Are you going to let me come inside any time soon, Doc?"

"Not before I do this," Adrian said.

Slipping her hands into Shae's hair, she pulled her into a deep kiss that left Shae breathless and Adrian trembling. Adrian silently wondered if she would ever get used to the physical jolt that travelled down her spine whenever their lips connected. Adrian's nerves were still frayed, and she was hoping a few glasses of wine would remedy the situation.

Shae whistled softly as she watched Adrian lead her inside. The living room's lights were dimmed and the coffee table was set for an intimate dinner for two. In the centre of the table was an ice bucket filled with beer. A bottle of red wine was breathing next to the ice bucket, and close by, steam was rising off a large, cheesy pizza. Two fluffy pillows were positioned in front of the coffee table.

"I wanted to treat you to a special dinner tonight, and I wracked my brain trying to figure out what I should cook. Then I realised that you would appreciate some pizza and cold beer more than a huge meal."

"This is perfect. You are perfect," Shae said.

"Have a seat, then. How was your day?"

They spent the next hour just catching up, discussing the mundane details of the hockey training that had kept Shae busy after school and the upcoming conference that Adrian had been preparing for. Slowly, with the help of two glasses of wine, Adrian relaxed.

"There she is," Shae said as Adrian clutched her stomach laughing at one of Shae's inappropriate jokes.

"What's that supposed to mean?" Adrian asked.

"Well, you've been visibly distressed since I walked in that door, Adrian. I don't know what's weighing on your mind, but I often find the best way to deal with a busy mind is to get outside of it."

Adrian shifted closer to Shae and tugged a stray curl behind her ear.

"I am certainly not distressed, but you do tend to unnerve me with those big hazel eyes and crooked smile."

"Good. Can we take a walk outside? I think I was in the sun for too long today."

Hand in hand, they took a slow stroll through the garden. It was a clear, cool night and the breeze was a welcome relief. Shae's entire face lit up when she saw the maze, and she tugged on Adrian's hand excitedly.

"I've never been in a maze before."

"I can assure you that it's completely overrated. It does serve as a wonderful hiding place when you need distance from a raging, abusive husband, though," Adrian said.

Adrian suddenly paused, squeezing Shae's hand. She looked around the garden and her eyes rested on the deck chair next to the pond in her favourite corner of the garden. She pulled Shae in that direction.

"Would you mind terribly if we gave the maze a skip tonight?"

"Knowing that you ever had to seek refuge there tainted the idea for me. You should get rid of it," Shae said.

Adrian turned around and into Shae's arms where she remained for a long while. They didn't speak when Adrian made herself comfortable on the reclining deck chair. She shifted onto her side and patted the space in front of her, inviting Shae to lie down.

"Let's just stay here for a second," she said.

Kicking off her shoes, Shae lowered herself into the spot Adrian had created for her. It was a snug fit and Adrian was delighted when the only comfortable arrangement turned out to be a cuddle. She wondered if Shae could feel her heart banging as she lay her head down on Adrian's chest. She snaked a hand down the back of Shae's jeans and cupped her ass possessively.

"I've wanted to smack this behind since the first time you tested my patience in therapy."

Shae chuckled softly and hooked her leg around Adrian's, settling in even more comfortably.

"At other times, I wanted to just give it a gentle squeeze, but without losing my license."

"That must have been quite the predicament. You're so lucky that I assaulted you with my lips then," Shae replied.

"Luckiest day of my life, actually," Adrian said after a while.

They lay locked in that tight embrace for a long time as Adrian stared up at the stars, trying to find the courage to finally make some of her fantasies come to life. Shae's eyes were closed and her right hand rested on Adrian's hip. Adrian wasn't entirely certain that Shae was even awake when she started running her index finger up her leg, across her hip and to her breast. Shae moaned softly when Adrian rolled her nipple between her fingers, but her eyes remained shut.

"Keep them closed," Adrian whispered.

Reaching down, she unbuttoned Shae's blouse slowly. The fact that Shae couldn't see her allowed her to explore more freely. She took her time. She could feel Shae's hand tightening on her thigh, but she obeyed the order, keeping her eyes shut. When the final button gave way, Adrian slipped the sleeve off her one arm, exposing her one breast and her toned stomach.

"Turn around," Adrian ordered again, shifting just enough to allow Shae to turn on her side, facing away from her.

Before Shae lay down, Adrian slipped the other sleeve of the blouse off and chucked the garment aside. Now spooning Shae from behind, Adrian moved Shae's hair aside and started a trail of kisses down her neck and across her shoulder, hands roaming. She finally found the clasp of Shae's bra, and moments later the bra was cast aside as well. Shae groaned as Adrian worked her hard nipples while sucking on a sensitive spot in her neck. She writhed around under Adrian's touch.

"Don't rock this chair too much now. We might end up on the ground," Adrian said as she flicked her tongue inside Shae's ear swiftly.

"You're killing me here," Shae said.

Adrian hooked a leg around Shae's hip, opened the button of her jeans, and slowly pulled down the zip. Shae's breath caught as Adrian's fingers brushed across her centre. She wrapped her arm around the back of Adrian's head and anchored her fingers in Adrian's hair.

"Take it off," Shae whispered urgently, tugging on her jeans with the other hand.

Adrian slipped Shae's jeans down her legs, slipping her own leg between Shae's to create a wedge. She rubbed her index finger down Shae's clit and smiled when she felt Shae's underwear dampen with desire. Shae turned her head to the side and bit down on the inside of Adrian's arm. Adrian pushed her middle finger through the folds of Shae's underwear, through moist lips, and against a very swollen clit. She could feel her own wetness pooling between her legs, and suddenly she pulled Shae's panties aside and plunged two fingers deep into her. Shae responded by thrusting her hips and biting down even harder on her arm. Adrian reached for her chin and turned her face toward her.

"Stop that, darling. You'll leave a mark."

Shae gripped Adrian's hand on her cheek and pulled it down, willing her to continue the thrusting between her legs.

"Perhaps we should take this inside. I'd like to have the freedom of laying both my hands on you," Adrian said.

"No time," Shae responded and shoved Adrian's fingers back inside of her.

"We should keep that mouth of yours busy before it takes a chunk out of my arm then," Adrian said as she claimed Shae's mouth in a kiss, surprisingly satisfying despite the awkward angle.

Increasing the rhythm between Shae's legs, Adrian finally claimed every part of Shae's body as she crashed into a thunderous orgasm that very nearly toppled a deck chair that was never meant to carry the weight of two writhing bodies.

"Varsity Adrian just graduated," Shae whispered.

CHAPTER TWENTY-NINE

"So, guess who called last night?"

After spending the majority of her Saturday in Adrian's bed, Shae had built up quite an appetite. Just minutes ago, she had finished off a side order of chicken wings and currently she was working on her fourth slice of pizza. Licking the tomato base off her fingers, she looked up to find Fiona staring at her.

"Excuse me? I was slightly distracted by the sticky sauce on your cheeks and the melted cheese on your chin," Fiona said.

"It was only four wings," Shae countered. "Anyway, guess who called."

Drumming her fingers on the table, Fiona beckoned the waiter to their table.

"Hi, could you please send over a Fanta for me and an ambulance for my glutton of a friend?"

Ignoring Fiona, Shae doused another slice of pizza in balsamic vinegar before stuffing it into her mouth.

"My mom. She called last night. She wants to come visit," Shae said.

"Is she sick? Are you? My God, that's why you're devouring all of this junk! You don't care if it clogs up your arteries anymore. How much time do you have left?" Fiona asked.

"That's not even remotely funny, you evil person. She just said that she wants to come through for a few days. Do you think I should introduce her to Adrian?"

Fiona slapped the table so hard that the balsamic vinegar almost fell over.

"Absolutely fucking not. I haven't even been introduced to the lover that inspired gluttony on this scale. I will cut you, Shae."

Finally, Shae pushed her plate aside and wiped her mouth with the paper napkin. Washing the cheesy bite of pizza down with a mouthful of Coke, she pointed at the remaining two slices of pizza and rolled her eyes dramatically.

"You should totally take that home and let it make love to your mouth later tonight. It will change your life."

"You're so twisted. Now, please can we talk about the fact that you considered introducing Absent Audrey to your girlfriend before me?"

"I'll tell you what. I will arrange a dinner party when she's here and you can both be introduced at the same time," Shae said.

They chatted for a while longer before Shae finally headed home with a full tummy and a dinner party to plan. She hadn't seen her mother in over six months and the thought of introducing her to Adrian and Fiona was terrifying, but she didn't know how to avoid doing that without offending anyone. She had made her peace with the fact that her mother was eccentric and distant, but she had no idea how Fiona and Adrian would react to Audrey.

Either way, Audrey was on her way and Shae had pretty much committed to a dinner party with Fiona. Opening her front door, she chucked her keys onto the counter and collapsed on the couch. Switching on her television, she flipped through the channels unseeingly. It suddenly dawned on her that perhaps Adrian wouldn't be ready to meet her mother. She would have to do some fishing first.

It had been only six weeks since that first kiss that she had been certain would either earn her a slap or a restraining order. Instead, that kiss had earned her the opportunity to connect with the heart and soul of the most beautiful woman she had ever laid eyes on.

She had been on a constant high since the moment she had crossed that line. She hadn't expected Adrian to open up to her in the way that she had, particularly not in the relatively short period that they had been seeing each other.

Shae smiled when Adrian's name flashed across the display on her phone.

"I thought you had work to do, Dr. Ramsey."

"I just said that so you would leave. I needed my bed to myself. You hog the sheets."

"I was only trying to cover up my breasts so you would stop assaulting my poor sensitive nipples," Shae said.

"That's funny. I don't remember you complaining too much. Maybe a little moaning, but certainly no complaining. How was your lunch with Fiona?"

"It was interesting. She threatened to cut me and she ordered me an ambulance."

"What? Why?" Adrian replied.

"Long story. Did you do any actual work after I left?"

"I had really good intentions, but Easton showed up with donuts and lots of questions," Adrian said.

"Questions about what?" Shae asked as she settled on the crime channel and dumped the remote control on the couch beside her.

"Mostly about your sexual prowess. I hope you'll understand that I had to lie to her, Shae. I'm just not taking the risk of her trying to bag you."

"And to think I've worked on my reputation for so long," Shae said.

She watched as Detective Summer Benton questioned a dodgy-looking guy in her attempt to solve a murder within the first forty-eight hours. It was her favourite show on the crime channel, but lately nothing held her attention the way Adrian did.

"Avril's boys' birthday is coming up and we're having a little get-together at my parents' house on Saturday. If you're not busy and you'd like some cake you're welcome to join us, but only if you really want to. No pressure," Adrian said.

Wiping her hand across her brow, Shae smiled as she realised that she no longer had to run the risk of overstepping a boundary by asking Adrian to meet her mother. It seemed that she would be meeting Adrian's family first.

"I do happen to like cake. Will there be a big crowd?"

Shae still avoided crowds of strangers as far as she possibly could, despite the fact that she hadn't experienced a panic attack in such a long time.

"No, it will just be my parents, my two sisters, and the boys. You don't have to commit right now, darling. If you feel up to it, just let me know on Saturday."

Adrian wasn't typically someone who liked using terms of endearment, but Shae's heart skipped a beat every time she did. They only came in tender moments and when Adrian felt protective of her—and it was never the generic "babe" or "baby." It was always "darling."

"Wild horses couldn't drag me away from birthday cake, or you. So, count me in," Shae said.

"Guess who called me today?"

"Meddling Maddison?" Adrian took a wild guess.

"Really? No, Adrian. My mother called me today, for the first time in months. She's coming to visit next week."

"That's awesome, Shae! Are you excited?"

Shae had certainly discussed her mother with Adrian in her therapy sessions, but she didn't know if any amount of chatting could prepare people for the wonder of Audrey. Was she excited to see her mother? She had learned through the years not to expect too much from the woman, but she was always secretly hoping for a deeper connection with her.

"I am not rolling out the red carpet, but I am filling the fridge with her favourite snacks, if that makes sense?"

"It makes total sense. Do I get to meet her this time?" Adrian asked.

"Would you really like to?"

"Why would I not want to meet the woman that gave birth to a creature that turned my entire life upside down?" Adrian joked.

"Well, I learned from the best. My mom can certainly teach you a thing or two about creating havoc. I am going to have a small dinner party. Fiona mentioned that she will cut me if Audrey meets you before she does. I don't really want to find out if she was joking, so let's invite her along?"

Some weird cop with a bow tie was now driving around the precinct on a bicycle while Summer interrogated another witness.

Shae flipped through the channels and suddenly a skinny, polished youngster doodled on a notepad while calling on the dead. Rolling her eyes, Shae switched off the television and dumped the remote control on the coffee table.

None of her old hobbies seemed to excite her anymore, and she blamed Adrian for distracting her with those dazzling blue eyes. Lately, she was consumed by the need to know everything there was to know about Adrian Ramsey, professional psychologist and extraordinary lover.

"Absolutely. What happens if they both hate me?" Adrian asked.

"Impossible. Besides, I have never particularly cared what Audrey thought about any of my girlfriends. If you consider the fact that she loved Miranda, who turned out to be every bit as dependable as her, it becomes clear that Audrey shouldn't get a vote."

Shae frowned as the doorbell sounded. She wasn't expecting any company. Reluctantly, she slipped off the couch and padded to the door. Her jaw dropped when she opened the door.

"Miranda?"

"Yeah, I know we don't talk about your ex-girlfriend very often, but I know who she is," Adrian said.

"Adrian, I think I'll have to call you back. I have an unannounced visitor to get rid of quickly," Shae said.

"Is everything okay, Shae? You sound weird."

"It's Miranda. The unannounced guest is Miranda."

"Holy shit," Adrian said after a long silence.

"You can say that again. I'll have to go, Adrian. We'll chat later."

Stepping inside, Miranda made herself comfortable on the couch that Shae had been occupying a few minutes earlier. Still in shock, Shae didn't quite know whether to offer her a drink or ask her for some kind of explanation for disappearing into thin air almost two years ago.

"How are you doing, Mac?" Miranda asked with a tentative smile on her face.

"Well, Miranda, quite a bit of time passed since your slightly abrupt exit. So, I don't know if you have the time or if I have the patience to get into it. What exactly are you doing here?"

Crossing her arms over her chest, Shae took a seat across from Miranda and put her feet up on the coffee table. Miranda's foot started bobbing up and down as she nervously chewed on her lower lip. She didn't make eye contact with Shae, choosing to glance around the room instead. It was probably in an effort to spot something that had remained the same since her departure.

"I was in the neighbourhood, so I thought I'd check in on you. You look good, Shae."

"You were in the neighbourhood? I find that extremely hard to believe. Did Audrey put you up to this?" Shae accused.

It had been a shot in the dark, but the guilty look on Miranda's face confirmed it. Running her hands through her hair in exasperation, Shae swore under her breath. One thing Shae could always count on was that once Audrey did show up, she always came with some kind of baggage.

"Audrey has nothing to do with it. I wanted to see you and I happen to know where to find you. So, you didn't sell the house?"

"Why would I sell the house? I'm not the one who wanted to get away so badly. Is there a purpose to this visit, Miranda?"

"Like I said, I simply wanted to see you. How have you been, Shae?"

Shae let out a sigh and started picking at her cuticles.

"Do you and Audrey always travel together? Or is this the exception?"

"I honestly don't know what you are talking about, Mac. I speak to Audrey from time to time, but that has always been the case. We share a close bond. You've always known that."

"If you think that Audrey has the capability to form a bond with anyone, perhaps you don't know her as well as you think you do. Call me crazy, but somehow I don't think receiving a call from Audrey and you showing up on my doorstep less than an hour later is a big coincidence."

Miranda switched her crossed legs and tugged at the hem of her jeans.

"Mac, I didn't expect you to welcome me with open arms, but I certainly also didn't expect this kind of hostility either. I come in peace," Miranda said.

"I'm curious, Miranda. What exactly did you expect to find—a cowering mess crying in the corner of my room? Or did Audrey perhaps let on that I was doing exceptionally well? Is that why you are sitting on my couch right now?"

Miranda peered at her through narrow slits.

"That's right. The woman you left behind that night, drowning in fear and barely able to tie her fucking shoelaces doesn't live here anymore. I am not sure what you are looking for, but I am quite sure that I can't give it to you," Shae said.

Shifting to the edge of the couch, Shae leaned her elbows on her knees and wrapped her right hand over her left forearm.

"Now, I don't mean to be rude, but I was in the middle of a conversation with my girlfriend before you stopped by. I'd love to call her back now."

"Mac, I am sorry if I unsettled you by showing up out of the blue. I didn't mean to do that."

"Really, Miranda? You seem to have a way of doing exactly that. You up and leave out of the blue and you show up in the exact same manner. While it was most definitely unsettling when you left like a fucking thief in the dark, you showing up here tonight was far from unsettling, more of an inconvenience."

Uncrossing her legs, Miranda splayed her fingers out on her thighs and studied her perfectly manicured nails for some time. Shae was reminded of her ex-girlfriend's inability to face any confrontation head-on.

"While I can understand the fact that you harbour some feelings of anger, I fail to see how this kind of behaviour makes anything better," Miranda said without making eye contact.

"That's where you are wrong, Miranda. I don't harbour any feelings toward you at all. In fact, I wish you really well, but please don't underestimate the accuracy of my bullshit detector. This little visit has Audrey's signature all over it. Now, you can either be honest with me for once, or you can walk out that door—for old time's sake."

Miranda nodded slowly and stood. She kept her eyes on her feet as she made her way to the door. Shae didn't bother to follow her. She simply leaned against the back of the couch and watched her leave. With her hand on the handle of the front door, Miranda turned around.

"She has cancer, Mac. She's not planning on telling you, but I figured you should know."

CHAPTER THIRTY

Adrian drummed her fingers on the armrest of the sofa while staring at the clock on the wall. It had been twenty long minutes since Shae ended their call to attend to her visitor. Miranda Ball had been a blurry figure in Shae's past up until a few moments ago… well, as far as Adrian was concerned. Shae's ex-girlfriend barely came up in therapy sessions, and the reasonable, professional part of Adrian assumed that she had nothing to worry about. Surely if Shae still had feelings for the woman, her name would have come up more often?

Sighing loudly, she picked up her phone and dialled her sister's number.

"Hey, Nympho. Did you finally come up for air?"

"Hi, Easton. I have a huge problem and I need your advice."

"No worries, sis. I have the number of a lady that leads a support group for people with sex addictions. I can hook you up," Easton replied.

"Didn't you date a woman heading such a support group at some point?" Adrian asked, frowning.

"I did. Let's just say she does not practice what she preaches. She broke me."

"I did not want to know that. Anyway, Miranda is back," Adrian said.

"You are kidding me! I love that show. Which channel?" Easton replied.

"Don't be daft, Easton. Miranda is Shae's ex-girlfriend and she showed up unexpectedly tonight."

There was a slight pause on the other end.

"That is unreal, Adrian."

"I know, right?"

"I had no idea that people named their children Miranda in real life. Fascinating," Easton said.

Rolling her eyes, Adrian questioned herself on why she always turned to Easton for advice. Granted, Easton usually ended up giving her great advice, but the relentless teasing was a given. Right now, Adrian didn't have the patience for it. Shae was probably getting reacquainted with Miranda while Easton was joking around.

"Easton, please. I'm going crazy here."

"Adrian, have you spoken to Shae since this fictional *Sex and the City* character showed up?"

"No, we were talking on the phone when she arrived. She promised to call me back once she got rid of her. It's been twenty minutes."

"Okay, I just think that you should give her time to do exactly what she promised she would. You can't start acting like a lunatic when you have no information. You'll probably find that Shae had nothing to say to her. Has she ever given you reason to believe that she was still into her?"

Running her index finger across her chin repeatedly, Adrian was quiet for a moment.

"I love her, Easton. I don't know why I haven't told her that, but now Miranda is probably reminding her that she does too. I have to get over there right now."

There was an audible gasp from Easton.

"What? No! That is the exact opposite of what I told you to do. I really hope your patients are slightly better at following advice than their therapist. I suck at this sisterly advice business."

"No, you're great. I have to go. Thanks, Easton."

Adrian disconnected the call and quickly slipped on her shoes before she headed to her car. Various scenarios played out in her mind on the drive to Shae's house, all of which left her feeling queasy. What normally was a ten-minute drive felt like a two-hour journey, and by the time she parked in Shae's driveway, she was firmly gripped by a state of panic.

She switched off the engine and flipped down the visor to look at herself in the mirror.

"A little lip gloss wouldn't have hurt, Adrian," she mumbled to herself before exiting the car and heading to the front door. "Miranda is probably wearing lip gloss. And perfume."

Shae's car was the only one in the driveway, but Miranda could have used an Uber. She must have been quite confident that Shae would welcome her visit. Was that the case? Did Miranda have reason to be confident, or did she walk away disillusioned tonight?

Squeezing the back of her neck where all the tension had gathered, Adrian rang the bell.

"I got the fucking message, Miranda!"

Adrian winced as Shae flung open the door, looking conflicted.

"Bad timing?" Adrian mumbled.

Shae closed her eyes and pulled Adrian into her arms. They stood wrapped in a tight embrace for a while before Adrian gently extracted herself from Shae's trembling arms.

"Let's go inside," Adrian suggested.

None of the scenarios she had played out in her mind on her way over here prepared her for what she actually found. Shae seemed completely shaken and Adrian had no idea how to comfort her—or if she was even supposed to try. Perhaps it had been a selfish act on her behalf to rush over here before Shae had even had a moment to process her feelings.

"Actually, I forgot the chicken in the oven," Adrian lied as she paused in the doorway.

Shae wrapped her right hand around Adrian's cheek and kissed her softly.

"Adrian, you're a terrible liar, but a super talented kisser. I'll keep you. Now, please can we go inside?"

Adrian was relieved not to find any evidence of Miranda, not even a whiff of her perfume or a wineglass stained with her perfect lip gloss. She was saddened by the slump she could see in Shae's shoulders though. She had clearly been affected by Miranda's appearance tonight and Adrian didn't know how to feel about that. She decided to let Shae do the talking because she didn't like opening her mouth when she had no idea what would tumble out of it.

"I'm sorry for not calling you back, Adrian. I just needed a few minutes on my own."

Holding her breath, Adrian nodded slowly as she took a seat opposite Shae. Still not trusting her ability to form sentences that would not cause any long-term damage, she offered Shae a tiny smile. Shae responded with a shake of her head. Then she rubbed her palm across her face repeatedly and leaned against the back of the couch with her eyes closed. This was not going well.

"Did I tell you that Miranda is close to my mother?"

No, this was not going well at all.

"No, I don't think you did. Has she always been close to Audrey?"

Shae slipped her hands under her thighs and rested her right ankle on her left knee. Adrian recognised this pose. Shae had the habit of sitting on her hands when she felt powerless or nervous. Adrian had the urge to reach across the coffee table and pull those hands into her lap, but she wrapped her arms across her chest instead.

"Well, as close as anyone can get to Audrey. I told my mother about you, you know?"

"All good things I hope?" Adrian joked.

"Great things, actually. Anyway, Miranda likes being needed, but she also doesn't have bucket-loads of patience. So while she loved the fact that I needed her for even my basic needs after the attack, she quickly grew impatient when I couldn't bring myself to be intimate with her."

Adrian took a deep breath and linked her hands in her lap, needing something to hold on to.

"Shae, can you please look at me?"

Shae opened her eyes, but her hands remained under her thighs.

"Miranda never expected me to cope without her, and I think she was taken aback when Audrey told her that I'm doing well. When she showed up here tonight, I figured she wanted to remind me how much I needed her."

Adrian started chewing on the inside of her cheek.

"Did she get what she came for?" Adrian asked softly.

Shae finally leaned forward and took Adrian's hands in her own.

"I thought that I would secretly enjoy the fact that you are jealous, but the truth is that I don't ever want you to doubt what I feel for you. Not even for a second. Seeing you in agony like this is not flattering at all. It's disappointing, because I should have told you that I am deeply in love with you a long time ago," Shae said.

Adrian had heard those words from people before, more than once. Never had she felt them reverberating through her bones and settling in her heart like this before. Knowing that she had inspired something so deep and pure in this beautiful woman across from her left her speechless. When Shae had walked into her consulting room almost a year ago, she slowly started imagining what it would feel like loving this special creature. It dawned on her now that she had not anticipated what if would feel like *being* loved by Shae McPherson. She had no words to describe the feeling.

"I'm not going to lie, when I heard that Miranda was on your doorstep tonight, I felt disorientated. I sat in my living room imagining all kinds of terrible things, slowly driving myself insane. So, I called Easton and she suggested that I calm down and wait for you to get back to me."

Adrian slipped a lock of Shae's hair behind her ear and rubbed her thumb across Shae's bottom lip.

"I told her that I couldn't do that, Shae. I realised tonight that I can never lose you, not without a fight. I came over here to tell you that I love you so much more than I ever thought possible, and I don't want to spend a moment of the future wondering if you realise it."

Shae smiled that crooked smile that had become the highlight of Adrian's existence on a daily basis. Carefully, she straddled Adrian and slipped her hands into her hair, pulling it back until Adrian's neck was exposed and the back of her head was resting against the couch. Her lips found all the sensitive spots on Adrian's exposed flesh.

"I realised it a long time ago, Adrian. It's lovely to hear it anyway."

Adrian gripped Shae's hips and pulled her closer until she could feel their breasts touching. She slipped her hands into the back of Shae's shirt, running her nails across her back, eliciting a low groan from Shae.

"Can you kiss me now, please?" Adrian begged.

The kiss was long and deep and when it stopped, Shae rested her forehead against Adrian's, catching her breath.

"I am going to tell you something now and I need you to remember that you are my girlfriend and not my therapist. Can you do that, Adrian?"

Adrian gently created some space between them to look at Shae.

"I haven't been your therapist since you kissed me the first time. Tell me."

"Miranda came here to tell me that Audrey has cancer," Shae said.

"What? Is it serious? What kind of cancer?" Adrian asked.

"Well, if I hadn't been intent on pissing Miranda off so badly, I might have known a little bit more. She just said that Audrey isn't planning to tell me."

Shae kissed Adrian once more on her forehead before she slipped off her lap. Kicking off her shoes, Adrian followed her to the kitchen and made herself comfortable at the breakfast nook while Shae prepared two cups of coffee.

"I'm really sorry to hear about your mother, darling. I think you should call Miranda and get more information."

Shae looked at her with lifted brows.

"Is that your professional opinion, Doc?"

"No, it's not. You asked me to wear my girlfriend hat. Professionally speaking, I would have to consider all parties involved—Audrey and Miranda. As your girlfriend, I don't care about their feelings. I just care about you."

Handing Adrian a steaming cup of coffee, Shae sat down next to her and stared into her coffee as she let out a long sigh.

"I've always had a very strange relationship with my mother and we might not share a typical mother-daughter bond, but this is still hard for me. I'd be lying if I said that I'm not petrified, which is confusing for me. Audrey has always been in and out of my life. She's definitely more of a variable than a constant."

Sipping on her coffee, Adrian reached for Shae's hand and squeezed it lightly.

"All relationships are unique. It's no different between mothers and daughters. A tight emotional bond is not a prerequisite for unconditional love, Shae. The truth of the matter is that where there is love, there is always the potential for loss."

Shae nodded quietly.

"You seem confused by the fact that you're afraid of losing Audrey. You'll figure that part out. But before you even start thinking about that, you need to get the facts from her. I know it will be hard, but try to relax until you can speak to her about this."

Clearly battling to fight back the tears now, Shae remained focused on the contents of her coffee cup. Seeing Shae this vulnerable and scared left Adrian feeling helpless. This was different from not being able to change the fate of a patient. This was not being able to assure her lover that everything was going to be fine.

"When does she get here, darling?"

"I have to pick her up at the airport on Tuesday," Shae said.

"You let me know what I can do for you, okay?" Adrian said as she stood and kissed the top of Shae's head.

Remaining seated, Shae leaned into Adrian, burying her face in the folds of her sweater and wrapping her arms around her waist.

"You can just keep smelling good and rocking up at my house with your hair all messy and your heart on your sleeve," Shae mumbled.

When Shae finally stood up and made eye contact with her, Adrian cupped her face in her hands.

"Finally, I get to look at those beautiful hazel eyes that always kept dipping to my cleavage when I was bound by all those pesky rules and regulations."

That earned her a smile at least.

"I don't know what happens in the near future for you, Shae, but I do know that I will be right here smelling good and wearing my heart on my sleeve. I might even try with the messy hair."

Still smiling, Shae wrapped a lock of said messy hair around her index finger and lightly pulled on it until Adrian was close enough for a slow, tantalising kiss.

"Let's go to bed, Figlet."

CHAPTER THIRTY-ONE

Shae hated airports. The general idea of what an airport represented was not the problem. In some ways it was the only place where people completely let their guard down. At the airport, you witnessed the saddest of goodbyes and the happiest reunions. There was always a buzz of raw emotion in the air.

It also always involved lots and lots of people. Shae hadn't had a panic attack in such a long time that the idea of having one now almost paralysed her. Would she still know how to breathe through it? Adrian had offered to accompany her this afternoon, but she figured that she could use some time alone with Audrey. So, here she was, sitting in her car with clenched fists and a stiff jaw.

"I can do this."

She made a mental note of the parking spot since she had a habit of losing her car in huge parking lots. Slipping on her earphones, she scrolled through the albums on her iPhone. Jack Johnson should do the trick. She turned the volume up high and made her way to arrivals, focusing on the music and her breathing instead of the people around her.

She made it safely to the waiting area and found a spot right in the front where Audrey could find her easily. A short buzz interrupted the music: a text from Adrian.

How are you doing, my darling?

With a goofy smile on her face, Shae started typing a reply.

Banana pancakes are keeping me calm xx

The reply came almost immediately.

My little emotional eater. Save some room for dinner with your mother.

Shae was completely unaware of her surroundings as she typed.

Not actual banana pancakes—the Jack Johnson song. Love you xx

When she felt a hand on her shoulder, all the blood rushed to her feet and her stomach did a backflip. For a moment, her senses stopped working and she stared at her mother's moving lips without hearing a sound.

"Shae? What's wrong, baby?"

Still unable to respond, Shae clutched her phone in her one hand and ran the other one through her hair, clutching the curls at the back of her neck. Audrey dumped her luggage and sat down next to Shae, wrapping her arm around her shoulders and squeezing lightly.

"Come on, Shae. Don't embarrass your mother now. I thought you were cured by the handsy doctor."

Apparently, anger was another method of escaping the grip of a panic attack. Suddenly Shae's hands were steady and her lungs filled with air as she stood and picked up her mother's luggage.

"Hi, Audrey. I'm glad to see you too."

"Don't be so sensitive, Shae. You were staring at me with unseeing eyes. It freaks me out."

"You know what freaks me out, Audrey? People sneaking up on me. Let's get out of here before I send you back on the first available flight."

That made Audrey chuckle. It was always the strangest and most unexpected things that made her laugh. She chatted about her flight and the interesting young man that had the pleasure of being seated next to her on the plane. She had attempted to read his palm but shockingly was not restrained with cuffs. She wondered why he had avoided her at baggage claim, but she was certain it had something to do with the fact that all of his chakras were blocked.

"Speaking of which, your throat chakra is also blocked, Shae. You need to check that out."

"Mom, my throat chakra is perfectly fine. Get in the car so we can work on dinner, please."

"You should really just consider why it's blocked, baby. It is usually indicative of a battle with self-expression and an inability to communicate your inner conversations."

Rolling her eyes, Shae held the door for Audrey so she could get into the front seat.

"You don't want to hear me express my inner conversation right now. Can we please just go?"

"Where is the perverted doctor, honey?"

At that, Shae forced her into the car and slammed the door. She could hear Audrey laughing, and she reminded herself that this too shall pass…even if it would pass like a kidney stone. She had just survived the airport. Surely she could survive a few days with her mother. Audrey spent the entire drive home chatting about the yoga retreat she had visited a few weeks ago. She had met yet another charming young man that she would probably spend some quality time with in the future—between the sheets, no doubt.

Once they arrived at Shae's house, Shae stored away Audrey's luggage and started preparing their dinner. Her mother loved nothing more than to watch people work, so she predictably poured herself some wine and made herself comfortable at the breakfast nook and offered unwelcome advice as Shae prepared the steaks and put together a quick salad. Audrey didn't wait long to get right to business.

"So, you're really banging the doctor?"

"You've always been very subtle. Adrian is no longer my therapist," Shae replied as she handed Audrey a plate and set two places at the dining room table.

"Well, do I get to meet her at some point?" Audrey asked.

"That depends on how you behave yourself. At the moment, it's not looking good."

"Oh, come on, baby. Don't take yourself so seriously. How are you planning to keep me entertained for a week?" Audrey asked as she sliced into her steak.

"I have to work, Mom. I'm planning a little dinner party for the weekend if you're up for it."

"I say let's do it. Why don't you invite Miranda? You know she's back in town?" Audrey asked.

Audrey's audacity still shocked Shae from time to time. Dumping her cutlery on the table, Shae wiped her mouth with a paper napkin and pushed her chair back. She folded her arms across her chest and stared at Audrey.

"I've learned from a very young age not to rely on you, Audrey. I've managed to cope with your intermittent appearances and I've accepted the fact that you don't know how to be supportive. This is just slightly ridiculous."

"Honey, that's getting a little old. What exactly do you find ridiculous? The fact that I suggested we all catch up over a meal?"

Shaking her head, Shae stalked off and dumped her untouched food in the bin. She spun around and started clearing the table around Audrey as well.

"I have no desire sharing a meal with Miranda or catching up with her for that matter. I certainly can't prevent you from spending time with her, but I will appreciate it if you don't share any details of my private life with her," Shae said.

"You know it's really not a healthy approach. All the people we meet in life serve a specific purpose and not acknowledging who Miranda is to you is detrimental to your spiritual growth."

"I am not in the mood for the mumbo-jumbo nonsense, Audrey. Miranda is a chapter in my past that was closed quite some time ago. You're absolutely right, by the way. She did serve a purpose in my life. She made me realise that I deserve so much more than she had to offer."

Audrey made a satisfactory noise as she pulled her last piece of steak through the salad dressing.

"This steak is perfectly seasoned and so tender."

Shae paused in front of the kitchen sink and turned to her mother.

"Do you actually listen to a word that I say?"

"Yes, I do. You said that Miranda wasn't good enough for you. I don't agree."

"That's not what I said at all, but I don't see the point of arguing about this. I honestly don't want to spend every single minute we have together fighting. Can we please try to get along?" Shae asked.

Smiling, Audrey neatly placed her fork and knife across her plate and held her empty wineglass in the air for a refill. Shae obliged, filling the glass to the top before fetching herself a beer from the fridge. Rinsing Audrey's plate quickly, she stuffed it into the washer and wiped down every surface in the kitchen except for the floor and the ceiling.

"God, you always do that. Please can you stop cleaning?" Audrey asked.

"Are you going to stop trying to get under my skin?" Shae asked in return.

"You make it so easy, baby. Just come and sit with your mother. I might be dying, you know!"

Shae's jaw dropped to the floor. Since Miranda had told her that Audrey was sick, Shae had imagined dragging the information out of Audrey. She certainly never imagined that Audrey would volunteer the information. Shocked into silence, she joined her mother at the dinner table again. Both women just sat staring into their drinks for a few minutes.

"Well, I guess Miranda doesn't know you as well as she thinks she does. She figured that you weren't planning to tell me about the diagnosis. Your bedside manner is utterly despicable, by the way," Shae said and sipped on her beer.

"She's right. I didn't plan to tell you, but you know your mother. I am just as shocked as you are by the things I say sometimes."

"Is it breast cancer? What are your treatment options?"

"Yes, I not only inherited your grandmother's knack for raising well-balanced children, but also the breast cancer gene. Let's hope the chemo goes better than the kid-raising exercise," Audrey said and winked.

"Let's hope so. When do you start the first round of chemo?" Shae asked, rubbing her thumb across the label on her beer bottle until it started peeling off.

"I'm having these babies cut off and then following it up with one round of chemo. I might actually sell the implants online. Do you think there's a market for that kind of thing?"

Shae just stared at her mother. She had always considered Audrey to be a strong and resilient woman. Audrey had been a single child whose mother had been distant and constantly angry, and as a result she had learned not to need anyone's approval. While she tended to crave attention, she was completely capable of coping with life's adversities on her own. Shae did not, however, imagine her mother treating her cancer diagnoses with the same indifference she did everything else.

"Are you sure it's absolutely necessary to go through with a mastectomy?"

"It's probably not necessary, but I'm doing it and that's that. I can't live with the constant uncertainty, wondering when it will come back to finish me off. I don't need these," Audrey said, squeezing her breasts.

"What was the suggested treatment plan from the oncologist, Mom? You can't just remove both breasts because you're scared."

"I'm not removing them because I am scared. I am doing it because I am annoyed."

"Annoyed? You're annoyed with your cancer?" Shae asked.

"Yes, it's very inconvenient, baby. I was planning a trip to Bali next month, and now I have to recover from the stupid treatment first. No, I couldn't live like that, going bald slowly, vomiting three times a day, no sex drive. Count me out."

Shae finally peeled off the entire label and chucked it aside.

"I think it's a little extreme, but I'm pretty sure you don't care what I think. I'll take some time off to come and help out when you go for treatment. You'll be exhausted most of the time, and I'd like to know that you're eating," Shae offered.

Sipping on her wine, Audrey reached across the table for Shae's hand. She slowly ran her fingers across Shae's and rubbed her thumb across Shae's nails. Uncomfortable with the sudden show of affection, Shae coughed dryly and extracted her hand from Audrey's. There was a flicker of pain in Audrey's eyes and Shae regretted her actions immediately.

"You have my hands, you know," Audrey said.

"I do. Would you like more wine?"

"You also have my habit of avoiding physical contact, but that's on me," Audrey continued.

"So no to the wine?" Shae asked.

"No, I don't think I'll have more tonight, baby. Thanks for dinner. Apart from the fact that you practically cleared the table while I was still eating, it was very pleasant."

Realising just how rude she had been, Shae blushed profusely.

"The battle with self-expression is an obstacle for me too, Shae. I don't always know how to express what I feel for you and it's no secret that I won't earn any awards for mother of the decade, but every time I see you there's an explosion of pride that starts in my chest and settles in my toes. I look at you and I want to nudge the person next to me to tell them that I did that," Audrey said and pointed at Shae. "I did steal my mother's car that one year to go to some Woodstock-like event and I may or may not have transported vast amounts of weed, but on the back seat of my mother's car, at that very same festival, I did something magical. I'll be damned if I don't take at least some of the credit for it."

Touched by Audrey's rare outpouring of emotion, Shae stood and wrapped her arms around her mother. She was comforted by the familiar smell of her hair and not even a little bit surprised when she noticed a piece of string with some feathers dangling from it.

"What's this?" Shae asked, tugging on it.

"I went to this ceremony called the Great Feather Dance and for the life of me I can't get it out," Audrey said.

"The Great Feather Dance? I'm almost too scared to ask."

"It's actually such a lovely ceremony, Shae. It's basically just a bunch of like-minded people in beautiful outfits dancing in a circle, chanting and singing. It can be a very powerful experience."

"I don't see the point, Mom."

"The point is to show the creator how grateful you are to be alive, Shae."

Nodding slowly, Shae finally smiled at her mother.

"I am that—grateful that you are alive. I'd be even more grateful if you could keep the mumbo jumbo to a minimum when you meet Adrian."

Rubbing her hands together excitedly, Audrey winked at Shae before she headed to bed.

CHAPTER THIRTY-TWO

Shae added the final touches to the pot of curry and covered it with the lid before she turned her attention to the rice. She added a dash of coconut milk and allowed the rice to simmer for another few minutes. She had fried some papadum earlier and was about to whip up some salsa when Audrey made her first appearance.

"Oh, so you are in fact alive and well," Shae said as Audrey made herself comfortable at the breakfast nook.

"I scheduled an extra yoga session this afternoon that ran a little late. Sorry, sweetie. Can I give you a hand?" Audrey offered half-heartedly.

"No need. I'm just going to slap together some salsa and we'll be good to go. How was yoga?"

"I don't have the stamina that I used to, but I still enjoy working out. Luckily, I had good company. I ran into Miranda."

Shaking her head, Shae slipped a chunk of tomato into her mouth, working on the salsa. She could feel Audrey watching her closely, no doubt hoping for some kind of reaction to the news that she had spent the afternoon with Miranda.

"That's great, Mom. Do you want to chop this onion for me?"

"That seems like unnecessary punishment, don't you think?" Audrey asked.

"I figured with your lack of sensitivity it wouldn't be a problem, or do you mean to tell me that the only thing about you that is sensitive is your eyes?"

Audrey rolled her eyes dramatically as she topped up her wineglass. Reluctantly, she started peeling the onions for the salsa. For a while, they worked alongside each other in silence, Shae dicing the cucumber into the tiniest of squares and Audrey making quick work of the onions as well. Wiping her hands on a dish towel, Shae pointed at Audrey's wine.

"Starting a little early, wouldn't you say?"

"I figured I might need some extra courage meeting your shrink. Thought the wine might help," Audrey said.

"Well, technically she's not my shrink, Mom. You are also meeting Fiona, remember. I'd rather you be sober for the occasion if you don't mind. Besides, they are probably only going to show up two hours from now."

Once Shae was satisfied with her pot of chicken curry and its accompaniments, she treated herself to a long, relaxing bath while Audrey made some calls to her friends back home. Shae didn't spend too much time wondering what to wear. She opted for her trusted old Levi's, a V-neck T-shirt, and an oversized black cardigan. If she was going to panic about Adrian and Fiona meeting her mother, she was certainly going to do it in comfort.

She found Audrey paging through a copy of *Curve Magazine*, looking engrossed in the latest article about trendy sex toys. Her mother was one of a kind indeed. Realising Shae was watching her intently, she shrugged and chucked the magazine aside.

"Just keeping an open mind and all," Audrey said.

"Now that is something you never lacked, Audrey."

There was a quick knock on the front door before Fiona appeared, clutching a bottle of wine to her chest. Her smile stretched just about from ear to ear and Shae was reminded of her childlike excitement, one of the qualities that Shae loved most about Fiona. She accepted the wine and pulled Fiona across the threshold.

"You look like a million bucks. Thank goodness I know you're firmly rooted on the other side of the fence and won't be charming my girlfriend."

"Well, said girlfriend was as firmly rooted on my side of that fence not too long ago," Fiona said.

"Not too firmly, actually. Anyway, meet my mother, Audrey."

Fiona held her hand out to Audrey, who stared at it for a few seconds before pulling Fiona into a very tight hug that she clearly had not expected. Not really much of a hugger, Fiona's wide eyes pleaded for Shae's help, but Audrey was onto her.

"No, don't be looking at my daughter with those Bambi eyes, dear. Now, let's get cracking on that bottle of wine while we discuss Shae's indiscretion with the doctor lady," Audrey said as she whisked Fiona off to the kitchen.

Winking at Shae across her shoulder, Fiona wrapped her arm around Audrey's waist and giggled.

"I'm going to like her, Shae. I can tell."

"I bet you can," Shae said and glanced at her wristwatch.

The next hour was spent by Audrey recalling every single embarrassing story there was to tell about Shae to a rapt audience of one. Adrian was yet to make her appearance and Shae was getting antsier by the minute. By 6:30 p.m. Shae was ready to start serving dinner. Fiona helped her carry the food to the patio and by the time the table was set, Adrian knocked on the front door.

"I am so sorry I'm late, darling," Adrian said.

"I tried calling, but your phone is off," Shae said as Adrian stepped inside the house and into her arms.

Adrian was shaking and Shae couldn't see her car in the driveway. She kissed Shae swiftly and held her phone in the air to display a cracked screen and scuffed back cover.

"I think it might be broken," Adrian said.

"Adrian, how did you get here? What happened?"

"Ella ordered me an Uber. Long story. Let's not keep your guests any longer, though. We can talk about all of this a little bit later."

Shae stepped outside and looked around as if she would find some kind of explanation lurking in the dark. Sighing loudly, Adrian beckoned her inside and slipped her phone in the back pocket of her jeans.

"I had an emergency with a patient tonight. Things got out of hand and I had to admit him to the hospital."

"Is it someone I know? What happened to your phone though?" Shae asked.

"I can't discuss this with you, Shae. You know that. I managed to get one of my colleagues to sign him up as a patient, so it shouldn't be a problem," Adrian explained.

Just as Shae started protesting, her phone started vibrating in her pocket.

"Hi, Ella. Yes, she just arrived here a few minutes ago."

Adrian stared at her feet while Ella relayed the events of the afternoon to Shae. Bound by the same ethics as Adrian, Ella told Shae as much as she could but kept the details vague. She said that just when she had headed out, a patient had showed up at the office and insisted to see Adrian. He had seemed a little agitated and Ella had been reluctant to let him in. Adrian had offered to talk to him for a few minutes and assured Ella that she would be fine. Unbeknownst to Adrian, Ella had ducked into the back office just to be sure that Adrian was safe. Not very long into the session, Ella heard a commotion coming from Adrian's office and then a loud thud as something crashed against the wall.

When she finally stormed into the office, she found the patient bleeding profusely, confessing his love for Adrian, who was desperately trying to dial the ambulance from her desk phone. Ella then summoned the ambulance and drove Adrian to the hospital, where Adrian had insisted on helping to admit her patient. She hadn't been able to get hold of Adrian since she ordered her the rideshare, and she had been worried sick.

"Thank goodness you stuck around the office, Ella. Adrian is fine. She's shaken up, but I will look after her. I will certainly let her know that you called."

Disconnecting the call, Shae swore under her breath and took Adrian in her arms again. They stood wrapped in that embrace for a while before Adrian extracted herself.

Shae met her eyes before speaking. "I am too fucking thankful to have you here right now to talk about that prick. Listen, Adrian, I would totally understand if you didn't feel up to this tonight."

Cupping Shae's face in her trembling hands, Adrian kissed her on the tip of her nose. "Are you kidding? I wouldn't want to be anywhere else right now. We really shouldn't keep them waiting any longer though."

"It was Theodore, right? And he chucked your phone against the wall, didn't he?" Shae asked as they made their way to the patio.

Wrapping her arm around Shae's waist, Adrian shook her head. "Not discussing my patients with you, Shae. Can we please forget about all of it for now?"

"But you said he's not your patient anymore," Shae argued.

"Who's not her patient anymore?" Audrey asked.

Audrey was dragging a piece of bread through the curry sauce on her plate, and judging from the fact that half of her plate looked wiped clean, it wasn't the first time, either. Shae shot her a reprimanding look.

"Mom, this is Adrian Ramsey. Adrian, this is my nosy mother, Audrey."

Adrian extended an unsteady hand and offered Audrey a brave smile.

"I am so pleased to meet you, Mrs. McPherson."

"Oh, God, no. I didn't take that deplorable man's name. It's just Audrey, sweet cheeks. If you keep losing patients at this rate, you'll be unemployed soon."

Adrian seemed puzzled.

"Did you not lose Shae as a patient recently as well? What about this guy—did you make advances at him too?" Audrey continued.

"Mom!"

"I'm just kidding, my angels. I'm sorry, Dr. Ramsey. My sense of humour takes a bit of getting used to," Audrey explained.

Shae turned to Fiona, who was picking the onions out of her salsa.

"That precious creature is Fiona."

Fiona drizzled some balsamic vinegar over the heap of onions and shoved a spoonful into her mouth.

"She's every bit as weird as she seems right now. I apologise," Shae said.

Wincing, Fiona shook Adrian's hand before loading another spoonful of onions into her mouth.

"It's good to finally meet you, Dr. Ramsey."

"Please, call me Adrian. It's nice to meet you too."

An hour later, Shae had devoured a generous helping of curry while Adrian had mostly pushed her food around on her plate, no doubt having lost her appetite after the drama with Theodore. Sure, Adrian hadn't named him, but Shae had no doubt that he had been the attacker. Fiona and Audrey then challenged Shae and Adrian to a round of 30 Seconds, which turned out to be quite entertaining. Audrey kept breaking the rules, hiding the more challenging cards when nobody paid attention and shouting out all the answers that she knew, regardless of who was asking the questions. Fiona had tried her utmost to turn it into a drinking game, but even Audrey was reluctant to lose control in front of Adrian.

Undoubtedly, a lot of fun was had by all, and judging by the way both Audrey and Fiona teased Adrian, they really liked her. Shae was grateful that both her mother and her friend had made an effort to make Adrian feel welcome. Fiona constantly topped up Adrian's wine and Audrey patted her hand in sympathy every time they had a terrible round.

"Next weekend we swop team members, sweetie. Doctor A can be on my team," Audrey suggested to Shae as they started packing up the board game.

"I would love that," Adrian said, winking at Shae.

Fiona had scheduled a hockey practice session for the next morning and couldn't leave too late. Knowing her way around Shae's kitchen, she brewed a strong pot of coffee and raided the pantry for snacks. Returning with a pot of coffee and some biscotti, she kissed the top of Shae's head.

"Thanks for dinner, buddy. It was the best curry I've had this year," Fiona said.

"You are so very welcome, Fi. This coffee smells divine."

"Those biscuits are the only thing in your pantry that hasn't expired. Your shopping skills are atrocious. Adrian, do you like food shopping?" Fiona asked.

"I actually love food shopping. I happen to have an entire shelf in my pantry just for snacks," Adrian said.

"We should totally have game night at your place next weekend then," Fiona said.

"Just invite yourself, why don't you?" Shae exclaimed.

"You don't mind, do you, Doctor A?" Audrey asked.

"Not at all. In fact, it's a date."

CHAPTER THIRTY-THREE

"I'm so glad you agreed to stay," Shae said.

"As much as I didn't want to have a sleepover the first night I met your mother, I also don't really want to be alone tonight," Adrian said.

And she didn't. The incident with Theodore certainly could have been much more dangerous, and the last thing she wanted to do was be at home alone ruminating on all the things that could have happened. Wearing one of Shae's long-sleeved T-shirts only, Adrian tugged at the pin that was holding her hair in a tight bun on her head. Shaking her head, she sighed as her hair finally came crashing down in dark waves. Closing her eyes, she pulled her fingers through her hair and scratched at her scalp.

"Get in here, Aphrodite," Shae said as she lifted the covers.

"I feel more like Hephaestus tonight," Adrian said and slipped in beside Shae.

"Hephaestus is a god, not a goddess. Did you know that Aphrodite's appearance was known to change? She took on the appearance of whatever signified the personification of perfection in the eyes of the beholder," Shae said.

Adrian shifted closer to Shae, resting her head on her shoulder and draping her leg across Shae's.

"I'm your Aphrodite?"

"Must be, because you're just perfect," Shae mumbled, kissing Adrian's forehead.

Adrian suddenly rolled on top of Shae and slowly traced the line of her brows with the tip of her finger.

"Nobody is perfect, but I do believe people can be perfect for each other. I am slowly discovering all of the ways that we are perfect together. You always know exactly what I want. It's almost like you are programmed to detect my needs."

"Is that so?" Shae asked as she ran her hands up and down Adrian's back.

"When I arrived here tonight, I wanted to feel safe, not judged. I know that you saw this thing coming and you easily could have reminded me tonight that you had warned me. Instead, you chose to comfort me."

Shae drew small circles on Adrian's lower back with her finger.

"What would be the purpose of pointing out that I was right? I would rather be wrong in this case, Adrian. If I stop to think about what could have happened to you in your office tonight, my blood runs cold."

Sighing, Adrian rested her head on Shae's chest.

"Shae, I am referring my patients to other therapists, and not all of them will take it well."

"What? Why are you doing that?" Shae asked.

"Ethically, I can't have a relationship with you for two years after you stop being my patient. Now, please understand that it's not up for discussion and I don't have the strength to get into it tonight," Adrian said.

Shae was quiet for a few minutes.

"For a moment I wanted to apologise for uprooting your life, but then I just realised that we can't be sorry, Adrian. This thing between us is too real," Shae finally said.

"I couldn't agree more. I really want to forget about today's trauma and focus on the fact that I'm here with you."

Shae slipped her hands under Adrian's shirt and slowly ran them up her sides, her thumbs brushing the sides of Adrian's breasts. She smiled when Adrian's nipples reacted under the thin shirt.

"I am actually having some trouble focusing on anything apart from the fact that you are not wearing very much in the way of clothing," Shae said as she lifted her leg slightly, pushing her thigh against Adrian's centre.

"Well, what's a girl to do? I didn't pack an overnight bag this time," Adrian said.

"What you are packing is a pair of A-class boobs and the most inviting thighs this side of the hemisphere," Shae said and tugged the T-shirt over Adrian's head.

She wrapped her hands around Adrian's breasts that were now exposed, squeezing gently. Moaning, Adrian shifted into a sitting position, straddling Shae. She pinned Shae's hands above her head and shifted slightly, lowering her breast to Shae's waiting mouth. Just as Shae's mouth closed around her nipple, she yelped.

"Oh, shit. Your mother is just down the hall!"

"Should I lock her in the garage instead?" Shae suggested.

"This is too weird, Shae. We should put on some more clothes and just cuddle."

"We could do that. Or you could lie back and hook this perfectly toned leg over my shoulder while I go down on you," Shae said.

Biting down on her lower lip, Adrian groaned softly. "You're so bad."

"Really? If I'm not mistaken you told me, just a few days ago, that I was so good at this. Audrey is probably fast asleep anyway."

"You don't know that, Shae. Go check quickly."

Shae chuckled. "Sure, Adrian. I'll just knock on her door and ask her if the coast is clear for us to make sweet love."

Sitting up, Shae slowly pushed Adrian onto her back, covering her body with her own and wedging her thighs apart with her knee. Adrian groaned softly as Shae ran her fingertips across the sensitive skin on the inside of her thigh. Shae then replaced her fingertips with the tip of her tongue, and soon Adrian was guiding Shae lower and lower.

"Have I told you that I never particularly liked oral sex?" Adrian whispered.

"That's probably because I wasn't always the one going to work between these killer legs. Now, can you please bite down on the inside of your arm so we don't wake Audrey?"

Shaking her head, Adrian closed her eyes and slipped her leg across Shae's shoulder.

"I do not need to bite down on…Oh wow!"

Adrian turned her head so she could drown out the majority of her moaning as Shae flicked her tongue across her clit and followed it up with an excruciatingly slow lick right down the middle of her swollen lips. Slipping her hands under Adrian's buttocks, she pulled her closer and cupped her breasts. Flicking her thumb across one hard nipple, Shae raked her teeth across Adrian's clit as she arched her back. At that moment, Shae slipped two fingers deep into Adrian, and after a few moments of thrashing, Adrian finally relaxed.

"Fuck, this is going to leave a mark," Adrian said and winced as she rubbed her hand across the indentations her teeth had left on the inside of her arm.

"Yes, you might want to wear long sleeves for a while, Doc," Shae said.

"Proud, are you? Do you mind if I hold you now, Miss Vixen?" Adrian asked as she crept into Shae's arms for a cuddle.

"I thought you'd never ask," Shae said and turned on her side as Adrian spooned her from behind.

Adrian wrapped her arms around Shae and rested her chin on her shoulder. Shae let out a contented sigh and covered Adrian's hand that was resting on her belly. Just as soon as she was certain Shae was close to falling asleep, Adrian started a trail of soft kisses down Shae's neck, across her shoulder, down her arm, and back up again. She licked the sensitive spot on Shae's neck, which elicited a soft groan from Shae. Adrian added some teeth to the equation, nibbling lightly as Shae started pushing her buttocks into her groin.

"Did you really think that I would go to sleep before returning the favour?" Adrian asked very close to her ear.

Shae gripped Adrian's hand that was now travelling up her side and sped up the process by covering her own breast with Adrian's hand, squeezing hard. She gasped as Adrian wedged her hand between her thighs and plunged her fingers into Shae from behind. Clenching Adrian's hand between her thighs, Shae rode Adrian's fingers and quickly plummeted into orgasm. Adrian kissed her shoulder as she slowly withdrew her fingers.

"I'll admit that I had no idea I could climax that quickly. You're going to ruin my reputation if you carry on like that," Shae said between breaths.

"Sorry, my darling, but there was no time for foreplay. Audrey will probably be doing a bathroom trip any minute now."

"No, trust me. That was not a complaint."

A few minutes later, Adrian could tell that Shae had fallen asleep when her breathing deepened and her grip on Adrian's hand loosened. Adrian propped herself up on her elbow and spent some time watching Shae in the moonlight that was painting slivers of sparkly dust across the bed. Shae was a somewhat restless sleeper, and from time to time her long lashes fluttered and her brow rippled. One minute her lips were pursed and the next minute they were relaxed and almost smiling. Pulling the covers up to Shae's chin, Adrian kissed her cheek.

"How on earth I fell so completely and helplessly in love with you is beyond me," Adrian whispered before she lay down and reclaimed her space behind Shae, wrapping her arms around her closely.

For hours, Adrian stared around the room, identifying shapes that the trees just outside the window reflected across the floor, the cupboards, and the ceiling. She tried to read the names on the spines of the books arranged on the bookshelf across the room. Finally, she gave up. She carefully lifted the sheets and slipped out, heading to the kitchen for some comfort.

She tiptoed past Audrey's room and into the kitchen. Opening the fridge slowly, she spent a few seconds studying the contents, hoping to identify something that would offer the needed solace. She jumped when Audrey suddenly spoke behind her.

"Fancy meeting you here."

"Are you also battling to sleep?" Adrian asked.

She was grateful for the fact that she hadn't switched on the kitchen light; perhaps Audrey would not see the blush on her cheeks in the semidarkness. If Audrey had been awake all this time, chances were she had a pretty good idea of what Adrian and Shae had been up to a few hours ago. Self-consciously, she crossed her arms to hide the scar that she had probably inflicted on herself.

"I've always been a bit of an insomniac. You won't find the answers to your questions in that fridge, sweetness."

Closing the fridge, Adrian filled a glass with water and leaned against the counter. Audrey was sitting at the kitchen nook with a glass of wine, a cigarette dangling from the corner of her mouth.

"What's on your mind, Doctor?"

Adrian drank down the entire glass of water before she spoke.

"I had to watch a patient cut his wrists today, right there in front of me in my consulting room. He took a blade, looked me in the eye, and slashed his wrists."

Audrey's brows shot up in horror as she quietly sipped on her wine.

"For months I treated this man, and I was honestly under the impression that I was helping him."

"What makes you think that you didn't?" Audrey asked.

"Did you miss the part where my patient took a blade to his wrists?" Adrian replied.

Audrey slipped the cigarette between her fingers and tapped the ash into a brimming ashtray. "Good point. You can't save them all."

"I suppose not," Adrian said.

She refilled the glass and took a seat next to Audrey. For a few quiet moments she ran her index finger around the glass, catching droplets that were making their way down the glass. She could feel Audrey studying her and when she looked up she pointed to the cigarette.

"I could use a drag of that cigarette right about now," Adrian said.

"Far be it from me to refuse such a simple wish," Audrey replied as she handed Adrian what was left of the cigarette and lit another for herself.

The first lungful of smoke was always all that Adrian needed—she hardly ever finished a cigarette. She forced the smoke out of her nostrils and her eyes followed its path across the kitchen until it disappeared altogether. Audrey was poking around in her ash with a matchstick, deep in thought.

"You managed to save my daughter, though, from herself. She can be her own worst enemy. I haven't actually thanked you for that, have I?"

"Shae did all of the hard work. She pitched for every single session and she was always willing to cooperate with me no matter what I suggested for her treatment plan."

Audrey nodded quietly. "Shae is the bravest person I've ever met, and despite the harrowing experience she had, she remains a generous, kind, and hugely inspiring person. That is just her nature, and I certainly can't take the credit for any of that."

Adrian laid her hand on Audrey's for a moment. "I think you should, though. You birthed this amazingly beautiful and giving creature, and you can take at least half the credit for that, Audrey."

"You know, when they handed her to me, wrapped in a little blanket, I panicked. I realised that I had no idea what this kid needed and the concept of figuring it out was so very daunting. I tried, though, but it doesn't mean that I was ever any good at it. When she was just a baby, I thought she needed to be burped when she actually had colic and needed medicine."

Audrey shook her head and took another sip of wine.

"When she was a toddler, I thought she needed a hiding when all she actually needed was attention. Not surprisingly, when she was a teenager, I thought she needed a cool best friend when all she needed was the constant comfort of a dependable mother."

Adrian squeezed Audrey's hand lightly.

"To this day I don't ever know what she needs, Adrian. God knows I never, ever stopped trying to figure it out, and perhaps somewhere along the line I got it right sometimes. So, thank you. I think I will take some of that credit after all."

Adrian offered her a sincere smile and kissed the top of her hand before she stood.

"Between the two of us, we will always know what she needs, Audrey. We're a tag team now."

CHAPTER THIRTY-FOUR

There was a beehive of activity at the Ramsey family home. Ally and Norman had insisted to host the boys' birthday party and all hands were on deck to prepare for the celebration. Adrian had arrived earlier to help with the décor and food but was already exhausted just watching them all buzz around the house. Avril had been complaining all morning. She had decided on Spider-Man as a theme, and for weeks she had hunted down every single Spider-Man decoration she could find. She had found cups, paper plates, serviettes, balloons, cupcakes, and a wide variety of toys in keeping with the theme. She had even bought a tin of magic that promised to create spiderwebs on the walls if she shook twice and sprayed.

Two days before the party, the boys informed her that they wanted a Teenage Mutant Ninja Turtles party instead. Avril spent two days trying to convince her sons that a man that could climb walls with his bare hands was way cooler than a turtle with a bandanna. Both boys were still on the fence about it but agreed to the Spider-Man theme for now.

"Mom, do you have candles for the cake? Avril gets this fancy cake, but they don't even give her candles? Where is she anyway?"

"In the pantry, Easton," Ally replied.

"What is she doing in the pantry?" Easton asked.

"The candles. The candles are in the pantry. The last time I saw Avril she was going through her closet like she was heading out on her first date."

Adrian whistled through her teeth when Avril appeared in the doorway, wearing tight black jeans, a low-cut red silk blouse, and black boots. Gone was the trusted old ponytail; her hair cascaded down her shoulders in soft waves today. Easton paused midway through arranging five candles on top of the cake.

"Holy crap. You washed your hair!"

"I always wash my hair, asshole. I just let it down a bit today," Avril said and flipped her sister the bird. "And you're doing this wrong. How can you place a candle on Spider-Man's crotch? It looks like a huge boner," Avril said and took the remaining candles from Easton.

"That was the plan, Avril. You're such a drag."

"No, dear. I think your sister is right. That looks odd," Ally said and plucked the candle off Spider-Man's crotch.

"Where is Dad? He would totally love the placement of my candles," Easton said.

"No candles on his crotch, Easton," Norman said as he appeared in the kitchen with four overflowing gift bags.

Kissing his cheek, Adrian took the bags from him and added them to the collection in the corner of the living room. She collapsed on the couch while Norman helped Ally to arrange helium-filled balloons all around the room. The two of them had been chasing each other around the house all morning, and Easton had accused them of indulging in the punch. Adrian suspected that she was right.

"Norman...No!" Ally shrieked as Norman untied one of the balloons, inhaling the helium.

There was a loud knock on the front door and Avril stormed out of the kitchen as if it were on fire.

"I'll get it," Avril said.

Adrian heard the front door opening, some whispering, and then a long stretch of silence. She was distracted by her helium-vaping father, who clearly also picked up on the awkward commotion at the front door.

"What's that all about?" Norman asked in the voice of a chipmunk.

Ally burst into laughter, clutching her stomach and crossing her legs in what Adrian assumed was an effort not to wet her pants. Laughing uncontrollably was a huge risk if you were sixty years old and had given birth three times in your lifetime. When Avril cleared her throat loudly, Norman's jaw dropped to the floor and the colour drained from Ally's face.

"Remember Leonard? He's back. Let's talk about it in three weeks when the colour has returned to Mom's cheeks," Avril said.

"Hi, Ally. Norman. You both look great," Leonard said as he nervously shifted his weight from the one foot to the other.

Norman ran his hands through his hair and Ally's mouth opened and closed like a fish on dry land. Probably sensing that something was not quite right, Easton emerged from the kitchen with a dish towel draped across her shoulder and a smear of blue icing on her chin.

"Jesus!" Easton said.

"No, he just goes by Leonard now, Easton. Can we please just calm down?"

At that moment, the boys stormed in through the kitchen, chasing each other around the table in the dining room and swerving between adult legs in the living room. It must have been the absolute silence that made them suddenly pause.

"Hi, Uncle Leonard. Mommy, when can we cut the cake?" Jayden asked.

"Hi, boys. Happy birthday! These are for you," Leonard said as he handed Jayden and Jonah matching gift bags.

"How nice of you, *Uncle* Leonard," Easton said, placing just a tad of emphasis on the "uncle."

Norman and Ally were yet to move from their spot in the living room. Easton and Avril were competing in a stare-down and Leonard chose to focus all his attention on the boys—the only two people in the room who didn't hate him intensely.

"Did you know about this?" Easton directed the question at Adrian.

"The blue patch of icing on your chin? No, I guess we are all discovering it together," Adrian said.

Leonard offered Adrian a small wave. Smiling sweetly, Adrian held her hand out to Leonard and pulled him into a hug.

"Hi, Leonard. It's good to see you."

"Really, Adrian? Is it, really?" Easton asked.

"Easton, please try to remember that we were not raised in a barn and we have two impressionable little rascals around. It happens to be their day, and nobody here gets to mess with that. Are we clear?" Adrian said and looked around the room to make sure everyone received the message.

Easton stormed off into the kitchen and out the back door while Avril looked apologetic. Norman was tugging at his beard while Ally was staring at the ceiling. Jayden and Jonah followed Easton outside, each with the fourth cupcake for the day since nobody paid much attention to what they were doing. When there was a loud knock on the door, Adrian held her hands up in the air.

"I don't know how, but all of you are going to get your shit together. I am going to let my guest in, and by the time I get back you will act like normal people."

Shaking her head, she sighed and headed to the front door, where Shae stood clutching two gift bags, looking like she was about to vomit. Adrian stepped outside for a second and closed the door behind her.

"Hey, gorgeous. How are you feeling?" Adrian asked.

"Hi, yourself. I haven't been around this many strangers in a while, so I guess I'm a little overwhelmed."

"That's okay. You let me know whenever you need to get some air and I'll get you out of there in no time. Are you ready, my darling?"

"As ready as I'll be," Shae said and followed Adrian inside.

In the meantime, Easton had returned and was now deep in conversation with Avril in hushed tones. Just looking at their body language, Adrian could tell that very little was being accomplished in the way of calling a truce. Ally was trying to convince Norman to keep quiet, and every time he spoke, she stuck the end of another balloon in his mouth, deflating it and blowing the helium into his mouth. Leonard looked like a cat on a hot tin roof.

Slipping her fingers through Shae's, Adrian cleared her throat in the hopes of getting the attention of her family. Easton just pushed her chest out farther and poked Avril in the chest with her index finger repeatedly as she tried to make a point. Snippets of the conversation was now loud enough for everyone to hear.

"No, Avril. You are not thinking clearly. Did you bump your fucking head?" Easton poked Avril in the side of the head.

"Easton, you stop this shit right now," Adrian said and grabbed her by the shoulders and turned her around.

"No, Adrian. Easton is right. This is a terrible idea," Norman said in his chipmunk voice.

There was a beat of silence as the entire crowd turned to Norman, frowning. Adrian was now fuming and had run out of patience.

"Dad, I have to say that I'm finding it hard to take anything you say seriously right now. What the hell is wrong with you all?" Adrian asked.

Ally held her hand over Norman's mouth when he started protesting. Easton and Avril both started talking at the same time again, their voices even at first but picking up in volume within a few seconds. Shae and Leonard had drifted to the back of the room, slipped through the kitchen, and found a bench in the backyard. In desperate need of some air and space from her erratic family, Adrian followed them.

"What are you in for?" Shae asked Leonard as if they were meeting in prison.

"Abandoning the feisty one with two newborn babies," replied Leonard.

Shae nodded quietly.

"You?" asked Leonard.

"Corrupting the brainy one with the killer boobs."

Leonard nodded in return.

The rest of the Ramsey clan remained in the living room for a while, and when they finally ventured outside, Norman's voice had returned to normal and everyone else seemed focused on getting through the rest of the day without further outbursts. Easton still shot Leonard nasty looks from across the yard every time one of the boys jumped up on his lap, but Adrian tried to distract her with the cooking of the meat.

"How are you doing?" Adrian asked as soon as she found a minute to check on Shae.

"I am getting to know Leonard really well in the castaway corner. Nice lad."

"Sorry about that. Avril caught everyone off-guard today and I had to do some damage control. I was hoping that you'd only get to know the crazy side of my family after I've completely won you over with my sparkling personality and my physical flexibility."

"Oh, but you have," Shae said and winked at Adrian.

Handing Norman her apron and a pair of tongs she had been using to flip the meat, Easton wiped her hands on her jeans.

"Hi, I'm Easton. I know you have no reason to believe me, but I'm normally the sane one around here."

Shae smiled and shook Easton's outstretched hand.

"Hi, Easton. I'll give you the benefit of the doubt. Do you need help at the grill?"

"I wouldn't mind some help. Let me get us some drinks and we can discuss my sister's sudden awakening as an adulterous lesbian."

"Sounds good," Shae said.

Easton returned with two beers and they joined Norman at the grill, where Adrian formally introduced Shae to everyone.

"Now that you are all well-behaved and calm, this is Shae McPherson."

Shae went around the grill and shook hands with Norman, Ally, and Avril. Leonard and the boys had formed a triangle in the backyard and were kicking a soccer ball to each other.

"Welcome, Shae. Sorry about earlier. I hope what they say about first impressions aren't true," Ally said and patted Shae on the back.

"Thanks, Mrs. Ramsey. No harm done."

"Please, call me Ally. Mrs. Ramsey is Norman's mother. You'll have to excuse us for a second. Norman and I will be right back with some finger foods," Ally said as she pulled Norman by the sleeve and they quickly disappeared into the house.

Adrian watched as Easton kept an eye on the scene in the backyard. Avril ran quickly to intercept the ball on its way to Leonard. The boys squealed loudly as their mother joined the game and caused amok. Easton shook her head and swore under her breath.

"Easton, this is strange for all of us. Please just promise me that you'll try. This has always been a safe zone, and let's keep it that way. We've both needed the comfort of acceptance between these four walls. It's Avril's turn now."

"Yes, Adrian. I know that, but this is different. She's making a mistake," Easton said.

"We don't know that. What we do know is that if you're right, Avril needs to know that we have her back," Adrian said.

"I know that you're right, just let me hate what she's doing for a few days, okay?"

CHAPTER THIRTY-FIVE

"I'll see you next week, baby," Audrey said and ruffled Shae's hair before she gave her one final hug.

Audrey had ended up extending what would have been a week visit to a three-week visit, and for the first time Shae was sad to see her go. They had spent a lot of time together the past three weeks, and Audrey had even discussed her treatment options with Shae. Together, they had decided that Audrey would give the chemo a shot before she committed to a mastectomy.

Shae had insisted that Audrey arrange to undergo the treatment sessions in Johannesburg so that she could look after her mother. The purpose of Audrey's trip today was to go home and make arrangements for her stay that was planned for the following week.

"Please don't bore Adrian to death in the meantime. I would like to have her around when I come back."

"I'll see what I can do." Shae kissed her mother's cheek before she made her way to the boarding gate.

She waved at Audrey until she couldn't see her anymore before she found her car in the crowded parking lot. She had declined Adrian's offer of accompanying her to the airport, offering to meet her at the Ramsey residence instead. Both Audrey and Shae had been to the Ramseys' for dinner a few times since the twins' birthday, and Shae found Easton and Avril very entertaining. Norman and Ally had been quiet and seemed preoccupied all the time, but they were welcoming.

"Just in time," Easton said as Shae finally made her appearance.

"In time for what?" Shae asked as she gave Adrian a peck on her cheek.

"To settle this argument. Adrian reckons that Lagertha Lothbrok can't be considered bisexual now that she is sleeping with Astrid," Easton explained.

"Personally, I don't think every straight woman who's had a roll in the hay with another woman should be labelled bisexual either. Women in prison aren't all lesbians. Gay for the stay, as they say," Shae said.

"Thank you, darling," Adrian said and pulled Shae down on the couch with her.

"I disagree. The fact that she is able to sleep with Astrid proves that she is fluid," argued Avril.

"I don't know about that, hey. I could probably tolerate sleeping with a man, but it doesn't mean that I would enjoy it," Shae said.

"How about you, Adrian? Do you enjoy sleeping with men?" Avril asked, wiggling her eyebrows suggestively.

Handing Shae a beer, Easton shook her head and shrugged as if to admit that she had no idea how Avril's mind worked. Adrian looked at Shae apologetically and chucked the lid of a beer bottle at Avril.

"If I hadn't married Frederick, I would have enjoyed the company of both men and women much earlier, which is exactly why I am bisexual. Lagertha has only ever been seen with one woman, the exception to the rule for her," Adrian explained.

"Why are we discussing Lagertha Lothbrok's sexual preferences?" Shae asked.

"Avril seems to think that bisexuality is a trend. Like mullets," Easton said.

"No. Mullets are a fucking abomination. All I am saying is that I don't understand the concept of bisexuality, and the fact that producers are writing bisexual storylines into every other TV series is liberating to some, but it's not educational. We still don't understand it," Avril said.

"What don't you understand?" Adrian asked and rolled her eyes in exasperation.

"If you enjoy sex with both genders, how do you commit to one?"

"Are you kidding me, Avril? You enjoy sex with various men, so how do you commit to having sex with only one of them?" Easton asked.

Adrian leaned forward and slapped her palm against that of Easton. "Preach it!"

"Hey, don't gang up on her now. I think bisexuality is quite complicated. I know some lesbians feel quite insecure dating bisexual women," Shae said.

Adrian stared at Shae with a deep frown on her forehead.

"Well, at least the dating pool is as vast as the ocean for you people. You have it so easy," Avril said.

"You couldn't be more wrong, actually. You are only physically and emotionally attracted to men. That's easy. Your physical needs and emotional needs are all met by one gender. For someone that identifies as bisexual, the challenge is to meet someone that you find both physically and emotionally attractive," Adrian said.

Avril looked at Shae as if to ask if she was just as confused by Adrian's explanation.

"I find men physically attractive, but I battle to connect with them on an emotional level. When I met Shae, I realised that I was able to connect with her deeply on both a physical and emotional level. For me, I can only be truly happy with one person, if I can connect on both levels."

Easton nodded in agreement. "I am the other kind of bisexual. I find both genders mutually attractive on a physical and emotional level."

"Avi's right. You have it so easy," Adrian said finally, pointing to Easton.

Everyone turned to Adrian and started laughing then. Norman and Ally burst through the front door at that moment, returning from the golf course.

"Hi, ladies. It's certainly more cheerful in here than on the course," Norman said and handed out hugs all around.

"Your dad is just a bad loser. I should let him win again soon," Ally said and collapsed on the couch next to Easton.

Easton crept into her mother's lap and instinctively, Ally started playing with her hair. While Norman stowed away their golf clubs, Ally regaled the ladies with a detailed account of her victorious golf adventure. Avril ordered some pizzas for dinner and gave the twins a quick bath. By the time she reappeared with two squeaky-clean boys, Easton was half-asleep on Ally's lap. Desperate for a moment alone with Adrian, Shae was delighted when she suggested a quick stroll around the garden. Adrian stopped and pointed at a tattered platform in a tree a few metres from her childhood bedroom window.

"Right up in that tree is where I had my first kiss," Adrian said, clutching Shae's hand to her chest.

"Who was the lucky boy?" Shae asked.

"Danny Foster. We were eleven years old."

"Who initiated the kiss?"

"I did," Adrian said proudly.

"Did you break his heart?"

"I think I did, actually. I ended up dating his cousin the same year," Adrian said, laughing.

Shae paused under the tree and pulled Adrian into her arms. She linked her hands behind Adrian's back as a serious look flashed across her face.

"Are you going to break my heart too, Dr. Ramsey?"

Adrian smiled and pulled Shae closer, rubbing the tip of her nose against Shae's.

"I hope that what I'm seeing in your eyes right now has nothing to do with that silly discussion we all had earlier. I don't subscribe to the weekly bisexual newsletter and I don't know much about society's opinion. None of that matters to me. What I do know is that every single part of me loves you deeply."

Shae finally managed a small smile.

"My body certainly responds well to yours if the almost constant throb between my legs is anything to go by. More importantly, my heart skips a beat when you walk into a room and my soul soars when I think about my future with you."

Adrian slid her hands into Shae's hair and closed the gap between them, kissing her softly. She groaned as Shae deepened the kiss and cupped her ass possessively.

"Now if Danny Foster had kissed me like that, I wouldn't have needed to date his cousin."

"Danny Foster is probably still crying himself to sleep about the one that got away," Shae said and kissed Adrian's forehead before they headed inside.

They met the pizza delivery guy on the front porch, and by the time they stepped into the kitchen with steaming hot pizza the Ramsey clan was ready for dinner. Norman was bouncing Jonah and Jayden on his knees, pretending to drop them to the floor every now and then, which resulted in bouts of uncontrolled laughter from the boys. Easton and Avril sipped on glasses of sangria. They were at least engaging in their usual banter again, which Adrian told Shae was a sign that Avril had forgiven her sister for her outburst when her rekindled relationship with Leonard was revealed.

"Dinner is served, my lovelies," Adrian said and slid the pizza boxes to the coffee table in the living room.

Leonard knocked on the door three times before he entered cautiously. His eyes searched the room frantically until he found Avril's encouraging smile. Shaking her head, Easton beckoned him inside.

"God, don't be such a drama queen and come in, Leonard," Easton said.

"Uncle Leonard!" the boys echoed and rushed to him.

"Avril, honestly, how long are you going to keep them in the dark?" Easton whispered.

"Easton, I swear you're bipolar. Just the other day you were crucifying me for seeing Leonard, now you want me to tell the boys who he is?"

Shae had to agree. Easton's question caught her off-guard too.

"Don't make it weird, Avi. Just do it."

Shae hid a chuckle as she watched Leonard standing around awkwardly after greeting both boys briefly, not sure how he should approach Avril in the presence of an audience. Rolling her eyes, Easton slid three slices of pizza onto her plate and took a huge bite of the first slice.

"Can we please arrange a coming-out party soon? Adrian can come out as a bisexual maniac and Leonard can come out as the boys' progenitor and maybe we can then just go back to the seminormal state that we all existed in before this *Twilight Zone* shit started?" Easton said.

Her entire family just stared at her for a while.

"I really didn't know that you had that word in your vocabulary, sis," Adrian said.

"Maniac?" Easton asked.

"No. Progenitor. Colour me impressed. Also, I didn't know it was humanly possible to say all of those words around a mouthful of pizza."

This time the chuckle escaped Shae's mouth as she winked at Adrian, whose sense of humour was on point.

"I agree with Easton. I have a plan," Norman said.

"You do?" Ally asked.

"I do. I am starting a project soon that I will need help with. Leonard, you will be here with your tool belt on next Saturday and every Saturday after that until our project has been completed. This time around you will undergo an introduction programme."

Leonard was white as a sheet and Easton's hand was frozen in front of her mouth with cheese dangling off the side of her pizza. Adrian seemed amused until Norman turned to Shae.

"Shae, you will join us, but I didn't want to make the tool belt comment in fear of being accused of stereotyping. I call this programme 'how to love a Ramsey daughter right before I break your knees,' and I hope you both graduate with flying colours."

Adrian no longer had the smug look on her face and Shae's eyes widened under arched brows. Dumping her pizza on her plate, Easton started slow-clapping and smiled at Adrian and Avril, who both seemed petrified.

"Let's eat," Norman said with a twinkle in his eye.

CHAPTER THIRTY-SIX

"Adrian, please tell me your dad was joking earlier."

"I don't think that he was. I don't know who was more shocked, you or Leonard. Now, tell me. Do you have a tool belt, Shae?"

Shae gave her a stern look before she collapsed on the couch. Adrian was delighted that Shae felt so comfortable in her home, which was no wonder since they spent the majority of their time together at Adrian's house. Smiling sweetly, Adrian took a seat on the opposite side of the couch.

"I might actually have one," Shae said.

"For once, I would like to see if I can spend time with you on my couch without ripping your clothes off. So, you need to distract me from fantasising about you wearing nothing but a tool belt right now," Adrian said.

Leaning forward, Shae gripped Adrian's feet and tugged them into her lap. Staring off into the distance, she started rubbing them.

"Remember back when you were still undecided on whether to stop fighting this wild attraction for your alluring patient?"

"Vaguely," Adrian said.

"I told you that I would teach you everything I know about the four forces of nature. How about that science lesson?" Shae suggested.

"I bet that would kill the mood instantly. I was never any good at science. Go for it," Adrian said.

Shae smiled at her in a way that said that the challenge had been accepted. She held her thumb in the air.

"Number one: gravity. Gravity is the force that attracts two bodies to each other." Shae pulled Adrian to her side of the couch. "It's what caused me to gravitate toward you despite your Hippocratic oath and your supposed straightness."

"Complete myth. Therapists take no oaths," Adrian corrected her.

"Really? Why is that?"

"Perhaps because it's much less of an exact science. It's more volatile than any other science. We don't have a set of rules that tells us how to diagnose and treat. Yes, any mental illness or condition is diagnosed by identifying a set of characteristics, but we're also faced with patients who can be fickle and even deceitful. What we can achieve is determined by the information we receive."

Shae nodded slowly while running her fingers up and down Adrian's arms.

"How is that, Doc?"

"Well, if a medical doctor needs to check your pulse, he simply needs to place his index finger on a pulse point," Adrian said and rested her finger on the side of Shae's throat. "The wonderful thing about the human body is the fact that it doesn't possess the ability to be untruthful. The body doesn't lie. I can tell that your pulse is elevated right now and you can deny it with your mouth all you want, but you can't influence my assessment."

"Oh, I deny nothing, Adrian."

Shae pulled Adrian closer, and Adrian didn't mind it one bit.

"The same goes for fever. There are very distinct markers in place. A medical doctor can't possibly misdiagnose a fever," Adrian continued.

"Anyway, as I was saying before I was so delightfully interrupted, gravity causes objects to have weight. The formula for weight is mass times gravity," Shae said.

"Do you know what that sounds like? If you have four pencils and I have seven apples, how many pancakes will fit on the roof? Purple, because aliens don't wear hats," Adrian said.

Shae frowned deeply. "What?"

"Exactly!" Adrian exclaimed.

"I can tell that I'm losing you, so I'll summarise what I know about the forces of nature before you strain something," Shae said.

"The key is to keep it relevant, Shae."

Shae nodded, smiling.

"Gravity is a fundamental force that attracts two bodies to each other. That's the simple part. The second force of nature is electromagnetic force. This is a force that acts between charged particles. It holds atoms together in molecules. You know what my favourite part about electromagnetic force is?" Shae rubbed her hands across Adrian's thighs. "It creates friction. It's what pulls iron to a magnet." Adrian cocked a brow and arranged her arms around Shae's neck loosely as Shae continued, "The third force of nature is called weak force. While other forces hold things together, this force allows things to fall apart."

"Why do things need to fall apart?" Adrian whispered in Shae's ear, finding it harder to concentrate by the minute.

"Don't worry, Figlet. Falling apart can be beautiful. Weak force is the main driver behind radioactive decay, which allows stars to release excess energy in the form of heat that causes the stars to shine." The word "heat" was whispered against Adrian's skin as Shae sucked lightly on her neck. Adrian had visions of her good intentions of not undressing Shae on her couch flying right out the window. "Why do I get the feeling that you're battling to pay attention, Dr. Ramsey?"

"It's probably because of the friction," Adrian mumbled, climbing into Shae's lap now.

"Hang in there. I saved the best for last. Strong force is probably the most complicated force of nature. It's stronger than gravity," Shae said and kissed Adrian's chin. "It's stronger than electromagnetic force," she said and kissed the tip of Adrian's nose. "It's stronger than weak force," she continued as she kissed Adrian's lips. "However, it has the shortest range. Particles must be extremely close before the effect of this force can be felt."

Adrian threw back her head and chuckled loudly. "You are totally making this up!"

"You can check my facts on Google later. I kid you not, but please stop interrupting me, because I'm getting to the crucial part," Shae begged. "Molecules are the cornerstone of existence, but in essence they are nothing more than atoms that are bound together. The nucleus of an atom contains protons, which are positively charged. Because all protons carry positive charge, they feel the force of repulsion instead of attraction."

Adrian tucked a lock of hair behind Shae's ear. "Can I just object to the word 'repulsion'?"

"No, you can't, Adrian. It's science. They are not drawn to each other and won't be able to stick together—not on their own, at least. That's why strong nuclear force exists. It's created by the continuous exchange of mesons or particles between the protons."

Adrian was enthralled. "Carry on."

"The force of exchanging these particles creates an invisible band of energy keeping the atoms together despite the protons being positively charged," Shae said.

"So, they send these mesons right back to each other?" Adrian asked.

"Exactly. Like a game of ping-pong. The force only exists for as long as the exchange is active. So, for this to work, protons need to be and stay very close to each other," Shae said and pulled Adrian even closer. "If the nucleons can't get close enough, the strong force is too weak to make them stick together."

Adrian closed the distance between them, kissing Shae deeply and slowly.

"Other competing forces can influence the particles to move away from each other," Shae continued. Adrian leaned back slightly and cupped Shae's face in her hands. "For the strongest force of nature to work, the particles must cross the barrier of electrostatic repulsion," Shae said.

"Shae, this particle might have needed to cross a few barriers, but repulsion was never one of them," Adrian replied. "Also, I don't think this lesson was very successful in the distraction department. The persistent throbbing between my legs has escalated from discernible to unbearable."

Shae smiled proudly. "Are you saying that you need a recap on the friction part of my lesson?"

"Shae, I am saying that I have mastered the theory of friction and would like to move on to the practical part if you wouldn't mind."

"I do prefer the practical part myself and would gladly demonstrate if you would be so kind as to follow me upstairs, Dr. Ramsey."

Adrian followed Shae upstairs, switching off lights as they went. With every stair that they ascended together, her heart felt fuller, and by the time they reached her bedroom she was barely able to control her emotions. Their lovemaking was intense and slow and every touch had the same purpose: to instil in each other the unwavering truth of their connection. They were not only attracted to each other on a physical level, but they were bound by the strongest force of nature, by the invisible band of energy that came into existence when Adrian had accepted her fate.

Lying in Shae's arms, physically spent and emotionally raw, Adrian rested her hand on Shae's heart.

"Are you still awake?" she asked softly.

Shae mumbled in response, drawing small circles on Adrian's bare back.

"This force, the one that drew me to you, is stronger than anything I ever imagined. I don't know much about science, but I do know that nothing can change how I feel about you. Loving you is by far the bravest stupid thing I've ever done."

"Are you saying that you need me to keep up the lessons, Adrian?"

"I am saying that I was always meant to love you, but if all of your lessons end the way this one did tonight, please do sign me up."

Shae was quiet for a long time before she rolled onto her side and pulled Adrian close so that her back rested snugly against Shae. She ran her fingertips slowly up and down Adrian's arm, hip, and thigh until her entire body was covered in goose bumps. Adrian groaned softly.

"Strong force," she whispered before she fell asleep.

CHAPTER THIRTY-SEVEN

Shae and Leonard spent the following Saturday in the backyard with Norman. First, they demolished what was left of the old tree house. Well, Leonard had demolished it. Norman's method of teaching was somewhat different from what Shae had been used to. He never really broke down the lesson plan. He relied on symbolism and the old double entendre. Shae had pitched for the first lesson hoping to put her tool belt to good use, but Norman made it clear that Leonard had to rip the old structure out of the tree, reminding him that the boards had been exposed to the elements for so long that they no longer had anything to offer and wouldn't withstand any pressure.

Judging by the look of despondence on Leonard's face, Shae knew that he understood that he wouldn't be able to simply pick up with Avril where they had left off. So, Shae and Norman sat in camping chairs sipping on iced teas that Ally had delivered while Leonard battled with the rickety platform. Norman kept a close eye on Leonard while reminding Shae that the crucial part about building anything was to envision the end product.

"That boy thinks I will give him some new board to build a platform once he manages to get rid of the old ones," Norman chuckled.

"You don't plan to?" Shae asked.

"Oh, I will...eventually. First, you both need to do some homework. I can only buy new material once you've convinced me that you have a clear vision of what this tree house will look like. You need to let me know exactly what you will need to build the perfect tree house."

Shae nodded and sipped on her iced tea. Norman shook his head as Leonard slipped from the tree and skinned his knee against the rough bark.

"That was bound to happen. You've skinned a few knees in your life as well, haven't you Shae?"

"I sure have, Norman."

It was Norman's turn to nod and sip on his iced tea. Swearing under his breath, Leonard climbed back into the tree.

"Don't you have a ladder that he can use?" Shae asked.

"I sure do. I guess he needs to learn to ask for help. There is a chest of tools in this life, Shae. Leonard needs to learn to open it and get what he needs to get the job done. If you're not ready to be a father but your wife happens to give life to twins, you find the right tools. You ask for help. You admit that you're scared."

Norman didn't take his eyes off Leonard.

"You can also run away, take a few years to realise you've made the biggest mistake of your life, and beg for another chance. It's harder work, though, and it's not always guaranteed to be easier the second time around. Also, you have to rip out some pretty rotten boards and skin your knees," Norman said and chuckled again. "Do you think Leonard understands that you are not really learning how to build a tree house, Shae?"

"I think he does, but I guess we can't be sure," Shae said.

Norman shouted some instructions from the comfort of his camping chair but still didn't offer much help.

"Shae, when you met Adrian she was on the mend. She was also vulnerable and ill-equipped to resist your advances."

Oh, how quickly the tables turned. One minute ago they were both laughing at Leonard, and now Shae was blushing profusely and shifting around uncomfortably in her seat.

"Let's be clear about one thing. I really don't care whether my Adrian spends her time with a man or a woman. Shae, just be worthy of that girl."

Leonard was now dangling from a branch, swinging his hammer around in an attempt to scare off the wasp Shae had seen buzzing around earlier. Norman seemed to be enjoying the scene.

"Norman, I don't know if I am worthy of Adrian, but I know that I want to be," Shae answered honestly.

"That's a great start. Now there's no use sitting around waiting for Leonard to drop out of that tree like a ripe avocado. I believe Adrian is planning a nice dinner for you and your mother. Why don't you head out there?" Norman suggested.

"Thanks, Norman."

"Don't forget your homework, kid."

"Vision and planning. I'm on it," Shae said before she waved at Leonard and headed to her car.

Adrian had offered to pick Audrey up from the airport that morning while Shae attended what she now called Romancing the Ramseys 101. Audrey was scheduled to start with her chemotherapy sessions that Monday, a fact that had Shae on edge and feeling anxious for the first time in months. Shae watched as Audrey moved around Adrian's kitchen like it was her own. Audrey had her hands wrapped around a cup of tea when Shae entered the kitchen.

"Did Adrian run out of booze?" Shae asked and hugged her mother from behind.

"No, I figured the next cocktail I have should be my chemo cocktail."

"You're such a ray of sunshine, Mother."

Adrian stepped into the kitchen, wearing an apron and her hair in a messy bun on her head. She smiled brightly when she saw Shae.

"Hi, darling. I brought your mother to my humble abode for a visit. I didn't expect to see you so soon. Did you fake a tummy ache?"

"I did not," Shae said and wrapped her arms around Adrian.

"Was it painful?" Adrian asked.

"Not for me, but Leonard was bleeding by the time I left. He may also break an arm, and a wasp sting seemed imminent."

"I hope you're joking." Adrian gave Shae a quick peck on her lips and tended to the vegetables.

"Afraid not. Also, we have homework to do, but that can wait for later. Did Audrey behave herself?"

Winking at Audrey, Adrian added some butter to a pot filled with green beans. Shae could smell baked potatoes and her stomach started growling loudly.

"Perfectly. We went grocery shopping."

"Yes, we all know what your pantry looks like, sweetie. So, Adrian helped me to get a few things together for next week."

"Audrey, I told you I'll take some time off to be with you. You don't need to cook for yourself," Shae said and sat down next to her mother.

"Who said anything about cooking? We just bought some ready-made meals that I can stick in the microwave. Apparently the first round of chemo won't spoil my appetite yet. I might even get to keep my lovely locks until the second round."

Images of a bald and pale Audrey flashed through Shae's mind in that instant and she felt sick to her stomach. Clearing her throat, she excused herself and fled to the sunroom where she collapsed on the sofa, clutching a scatter cushion to her chest. She took a few deep breaths and closed her eyes. By the time she became aware of a warm hand on her shoulder, she was calm.

"Are you okay, my darling?" Adrian asked softly.

"I just needed a moment. Please don't tell me you left the cooking in Audrey's hands."

"She insisted. Apparently, she's making space cake for dessert," Adrian said.

"Sadly, I don't think she's joking," Shae said and pulled Adrian onto her lap.

"No, I saw her taking a chocolate cake mix out of my pantry. I think we are safe."

Adrian wrapped her arms around Shae's neck and kissed the sensitive spot under her ear. Shae sighed and pulled her closer, digging the pins from her bun so she could let down her hair. Then she arranged Adrian's smooth black hair around her face.

"Want to help me with my homework?" Shae asked.

"I can give it a shot," Adrian said.

"So, if you imagine our relationship as a tree house, what are we building it with?"

Seemingly impressed with the question, Adrian made herself comfortable in Shae's arms. With her cheek resting on Shae's chest, she slipped her hand under Shae's shirt and started rubbing her belly. Combing her fingers through Adrian's hair, Shae leaned back against the sofa and listened to Audrey's banging in the kitchen not far away.

"The cornerstone of a healthy relationship is love, something we have in abundance as far as I am concerned. I think a lot of people think that love is the Alpha and Omega when it comes to relationships, and that's just not true."

Shae groaned softly as Adrian tickled a sensitive spot just left of her navel.

"You know that Patty Smyth song 'Sometimes Love Just Ain't Enough'? It's very true. So while love is the cornerstone, I would say that trust is a crucial part of any relationship," Adrian continued.

Shae closed her eyes and started humming the tune of the song.

"Trust is so much more than believing you'll stay true to me," Adrian said. "If I trust you implicitly, it means that I know that I am safe with you. Not just my heart, but also my body and my soul."

"So do you? Do you trust me, Adrian?"

Adrian shifted on Shae's lap so she could look into her eyes.

"I trusted you enough to take my entire life and turn it upside down, my love. Do you trust me?" Adrian asked in return.

"I do. So is that it? Love and trust?" Shae asked as she kissed Adrian on her forehead.

"Not quite. What about respect? I happen to think respect is the most overlooked of all the qualities you might want in a relationship. In my mind, respect is not just how you speak to me. It's allowing me enough space to be my authentic self, to reach my own goals, and to set my own boundaries."

Shae nodded slowly as she rubbed her thumb across Adrian's knuckles.

"I was trapped in my marriage. I felt like I was lost and stuck inside that maze my husband had built in the backyard, because I wasn't free to live my truth in any aspect of my life. I had no more goals because his goals automatically became mine. There were no boundaries to speak of since he owned me, and I had no clue who I was anymore."

"That sounds terrifying, Adrian."

"It really was, but it taught me how crucial respect is. I have that with you—the freedom to just be myself."

Shae cupped Adrian's face and leaned in close enough to feel Adrian's breath on her lips.

"Passion," Adrian whispered before she parted Shae's lips with her tongue.

Groaning, Shae sucked Adrian's tongue into her mouth and slipped her fingers into her hair, massaging her scalp. When Shae deepened the kiss, Adrian leaned back slightly and smiled.

"We don't have to make an argument for passion. We have that in spades. So much so that you risked being thrown out on your pretty ass when you assaulted my mouth with your gorgeous lips that day in my office. Somewhere in between that kiss and the extremely informative science lesson the other day, you have taken my body to heights of pleasure it has never known before."

Shae smiled proudly as she pulled Adrian against her chest and ran her fingers through Adrian's hair. Adrian tapped her finger against Shae's chest, matching the rhythm of Shae's heartbeat.

"You know my mother could still sneak some pot into that cake mix, right?"

"She would never. Would she?" Adrian asked.

"My dearest Figlet, I have stopped trying to predict what that woman will do quite some time ago, but I still expect the worst."

Sighing deeply, Adrian slipped off Shae's lap and kissed her one more time.

"I am pretty sure we'll have the most beautiful tree house, Shae. Thanks for being willing to set my father's mind at ease."

"You are most welcome, Adrian."

CHAPTER THIRTY-EIGHT

Over the next few weeks, Shae and Leonard had showed up religiously for their lessons with Norman, and the tree house looked promising. The syllabus consisted of firstly laying the foundation and sketching out the detailed plans for a great tree house and relationship. The planned outcome for lesson two was to emphasise the importance of constantly checking in to ensure that they were sticking to the plan and on schedule to achieve the desired result. The desired result was what Norman phrased as a safe tree house for his grandchildren and a fulfilling relationship for his daughters. Failure to stick to the plan would result in broken arms for his two grandsons—and broken kneecaps for Shae and Leonard.

Lesson number two was brought home to Shae and Leonard when Norman sat by and watched them miss a crucial step in setting up the floorboards, which led to a platform that didn't fit into the tree. Norman had advised them to look more closely at the plan—but only after three hours of watching them cry and sweat as they laboriously put together a platform that they ultimately would have to take apart again to make it fit.

Part three of the syllabus was dedicated to aesthetics. Shae and Leonard showed up bright and early with decorations they had worked on in their own time. Shae and Adrian had decorated letters made of wood that spelled out both boys' names, and Leonard had built two model planes that would dangle from the roof. All the boards still had to be painted as well, and when they arrived at the Ramsey house there was an array of supplies under the tree.

"Welcome to your last lesson of the first course," Norman said as greeting.

Battling to hide their dismay, both Shae and Leonard stopped what they were doing and stared at Norman. They had been through the wringer the last few weeks and neither had escaped without injury. Leonard had had a small accident with the staple gun, and Shae had so many wood splinters under her skin that Adrian had started calling her Pinocchio.

"The first course?" Leonard asked with a deep frown on his forehead.

Shae must have looked like a deer in headlights, and Norman couldn't stop from chuckling at them both.

"Did you honestly think it only takes three lessons? Let me tell you a secret. I have been loving Ally for over forty years and I haven't graduated yet. Now get going, ladies," Norman said and winked at Leonard.

Shae playfully punched Leonard in the shoulder before she started looking through the supplies that Norman had arranged under the tree for them. She collected a can of paint, some brushes, and a roller, while Leonard focused on sealing the roof before he could attach his model planes. He struggled with the sealant for quite some time before Norman decided to assist. He fiddled with the silicone gun but soon realised that the tube of silicone was rock-hard.

"I'll have to return these," Norman said and started checking the other tubes. "Shae, would you mind getting me the receipt quickly? It's in my wallet," Norman said, pointing to his camping chair's side pocket.

Balancing her wet paintbrush on the can, Shae quickly rushed to the camping chair, pulled Norman's wallet out of the side pocket, and flipped it open. She pulled at what she figured was the receipt in question and handed it to Norman. On her way back to stash the billfold where she had found it, she discovered a glossy photograph on the ground that must have slipped from Norman's wallet. All colour drained from her face when she turned it over.

Staring back at her was the icy blue eyes of Devon Nelson. Granted, it was a younger version of the Devon Nelson that Shae had had the misfortune of meeting, but those eyes were unmistakably Devon's. If she had any doubts, the scar on his chin confirmed his identity. She was frozen to the spot as she wiped her thumb across the photograph. Despite not expecting to see his face, Shae wasn't panicked as much as she was utterly confused. Picking up the picture, she opened Norman's wallet to put it back inside. In the front card slot, she found three other pictures, similar in size, of very young versions of Adrian, Avril, and Easton.

"Jesus. That's just not possible," Shae whispered to herself when she finally made the connection.

She slipped all the pictures back into the wallet, excused herself, and rushed inside the house. She made it to the bathroom just in time as she spilled the contents of her stomach into the basin. All of her blood rushed to her ears, and she could feel sweat beading on her forehead. For long moments she just stood hunched over the basin. When she realised that an intense panic attack was imminent, she rinsed her mouth and took a deep breath.

"Shae, are you okay, my girl?" Ally asked as Shae rushed past her through the front door.

"Oh, Mrs. Ramsey. I am so sorry. It must be something I ate. Can you please apologise to Mr. Ramsey for me?"

"Dear, I don't think you're quite okay to drive. Let me just take you home," Ally offered with wide eyes.

"No, please. I'll be just fine. Thanks."

Shae was out of the door before Ally could say anything else. When she parked her car in her own driveway fifteen minutes later, Shae realised that she had no memory of driving. All she knew was that she needed to be alone in the safety of her room.

She said a silent prayer when she discovered that Audrey was still fast asleep on the couch. She had received the final chemo session of her first course of treatment the day before and as a result had spent the majority of the day resting. Shae covered her mother with the blanket that was draped across the back of the couch before she headed to her room where she collapsed on her bed.

She stared at the ceiling, wondering how it was possible for her to feel both empty and as if something was going to explode from her chest at the same time. She kept hoping that she was mistaken, but she had a sinking feeling that she wasn't. What frustrated her the most was that she had no idea where to turn.

"Don't you ever lock a fucking door?"

Shae jumped up, clutching her heart.

"Fiona, what the fuck?"

Shae fell back onto her bed, trying to catch her breath. She could feel the surface of the bed dipping as Fiona made herself comfortable next to her.

"Your mother looks like shit, babe," Fiona said.

"Fiona, she just finished her treatment."

"True. So, what is your excuse because you don't look much better."

"Have I told you that you are the most sensitive soul I know?" Shae said.

"You actually neglected to do so. What's up, Shae? Don't let me drag this out of you. I had a very long night with a very fit young man."

Covering her eyes with her hands, Shae rolled onto her side. "If I tell you, will you promise to spare me the disgusting details of your *sexperience* last night?"

"Deal."

Fiona tugged at Shae's hands to uncover her eyes, turning onto her side to face her. Shae let out a deep sigh and clutched her best friend's hands, resting them on the bed between them. For a few moments, they just stared at each other. When Fiona started pulling funny faces, Shae finally started talking.

"Fi, Adrian betrayed me in the worst way possible."

"What? Did she cheat on you?"

"No, it's even worse, Fiona. It was all a huge fucking setup."

"Shae, I'm going to need you to use all of your words. No more cryptic clues. Start at the beginning and keep going until you can tell from the look on my beautiful face that you are making sense."

Shae rolled onto her back simply because she wasn't certain that she could get it all out if Fiona kept looking at her with concern masked as comedy. Running her hands through her hair, she let out a deep breath and rested her hands on her roiling stomach.

"Norman asked me to retrieve a receipt from his wallet today. He needed to return some stuff he bought for the tree-house project. So I did, but then I found a picture that had slipped out accidently."

Feeling bile at the back of her throat, Shae closed her eyes for a second.

"It was a picture of Devon Nelson. He keeps a picture of Devon inside his wallet—right next to the pictures of all of his daughters. I am such a fucking fool, Fiona. Adrian knew that it was her brother that had attacked me. She never should have been my therapist."

Fiona now sat up in shock.

"What the actual fuck? Her brother very nearly kills you, tortures you for hours, and just about ruins your life, and she tries to clean up his fucking mess by becoming your therapist? I wouldn't be surprised if she is in cahoots with Mr. Foster. She probably convinced him to send you to her."

Shae's entire body turned ice cold when she realised that Fiona could be onto something. Mr. Foster did insist that she went to see Doctor Adrian Ramsey specifically. He made it a fucking condition of her continued employment. She swallowed softly in the hopes of not puking on her bed.

"All this time she fucking knew. She knew exactly what had happened and she made me tell her everything in detail so many times. She put me through the trauma of reliving that nightmare so she could feel less guilty about what her brother had done?"

Shae was growing angrier by the second, and Fiona seemed dumbstruck for once.

"She had the nerve to fucking accuse me of crossing a line with her. She preached to me about her so-called fucking professionalism and pristine reputation while she was lying to me! Why the fuck didn't she tell me the truth when she realised that I had fallen in love with her?"

Shaking her head, Fiona clasped her hand over her mouth.

"Did she think that I would be fine with dating the sister of the boy that caused me so much pain and misery? How do I look at her and not see Devon now, Fiona? She absolutely ruined it."

Fiona jumped up and started pacing the room, but she was still speechless.

"She clearly wasn't planning on telling me the truth at any point. That entire family kept this disgustingly disturbing secret from me all this time. How could they do that?" Shae shouted.

Taking her hand, Fiona sat down next to her.

"Shae, calm down. Audrey is sleeping and you need to gather your thoughts before you tell her what you discovered today. Have you spoken to anyone else about this?"

"No, I said I wasn't feeling well and just left. I don't think Norman saw me stashing the picture back into his wallet, so I doubt he even knows that their secret is out. I mean, I had no idea what to say. It just felt like a panic attack was unavoidable, so I left as quickly as I could."

In a rare show of affection, Fiona stroked Shae's shoulder as tears welled up in Shae's eyes. She had been trying so hard not to cry, because it felt like she wouldn't be able to control herself once the first crack appeared. With every passing moment, Shae's heart felt heavier and breathing became harder, but she understood now that what she was feeling wasn't the onset of a panic attack. It was utter and total devastation. It was the realisation that her life was coming apart at the seams.

When the first sob escaped, Fiona took her in her arms and gently rocked her while Shae's entire body shook with the grief of losing what she considered to be the love of her life. She had felt betrayed before, but nothing had ever left her feeling so lost and broken. She had no idea how she was going to survive this. She had survived a brutal attack and intense torture session by a very disturbed young man, frozen in shock and covered in blood and brain tissue. She had survived growing up without much comfort and support from her mother and being abandoned in her hour of need by Miranda.

The soul-crushing disappointment Shae felt knowing that Adrian had betrayed her and lied to her was worse than anything she had to live through simply because she loved her so deeply. She had trusted Adrian completely, something she had never done before. By the time she stopped crying, Fiona had tucked her into bed, promising to take care of Audrey.

"I'll tell her you came down with a stomach bug. Take some time and I will be here in the morning to check on you," Fiona said as she kissed Shae's cheek.

Shae wanted to argue, but she just had no capacity. It felt like every ounce of energy had drained from her body and her head was throbbing. She closed her eyes and begged for sleep to come and make it all disappear—if only for a while.

CHAPTER THIRTY-NINE

Adrian parked her car in front of the office and simply sat hunched across the steering wheel for a few moments. She had not slept a wink, but she couldn't postpone; she had to see her last few patients to do the referrals. Ella had cleared her schedule for the last three days—three days she had spent in despair. Less than a week ago, she had been cooking some soup that she was planning to take over to Audrey when she received a very cryptic message from Shae.

Every moment since had been agonising. She was so confused, and her mind just couldn't make sense of anything anymore. Shae had asked her never to contact her again, with no explanation. Adrian had begged her for a meeting so they could clear up what obviously had to be the biggest misunderstanding of the century. All of her text messages were left unanswered and all of her calls ignored. Short of showing up at Shae's door unannounced, she had tried everything, including talking to Fiona and Audrey. Fiona had disconnected the call after calling her a fucking piece of work. Audrey simply hadn't answered her calls or messages.

She leaned her head back so she could apply some eye drops before she finally made her way inside. Ella hadn't asked too many questions when Adrian had called in sick, but she sure made up for that this morning.

"My goodness, Dr. Ramsey. How are you? Are you feeling better? Was it the flu? Can I get you anything?"

"Hi, Ella. I am getting there. Thanks for taking charge in my absence. Could you hold any calls for me, please? Let's just get through the appointments today."

"Whatever you need, Dr. Ramsey. I'll make some tea."

Rushing to her office, Adrian closed the door and leaned her forehead against it for a few seconds. She had no idea how she would get through the day, or any of the ones to come. After crying for days on end, she had finally reached the stage where she was just feeling numb. Her body felt like lead, and it had taken Herculean efforts to get out of the bed this morning, brush her teeth, dry her hair, get dressed, and generally carry on like the world hadn't dropped from its axis.

She had actively been avoiding her family as she simply couldn't answer any of their many questions. She also couldn't deal with the sympathetic looks, the long hugs, and the knowing smiles. She just wanted to be alone so she could be as miserable as she wanted to be. She had stopped trying to make sense of it. If she was going to get through this, she had to start accepting that she would never have the answers.

She managed to keep it together for two consultations before she cracked up. Her third patient for the day was Jax, who had showed up on time and wearing a bright smile. Since she had been seeing Andie and working on improving communication with her father, there had been sightings of a few smiles and even a chuckle at one point.

"Hey, Doctor A."

"Hi, Jax. Please come and have a seat. It's good to see you," Adrian said.

"Is it though? You look less than enthusiastic this afternoon. Are you ill? Fuck, is it contagious? I can't afford to catch what you have because Andie is taking me out tonight," Jax rambled.

Adrian smiled weakly and sat down across from Jax, who was still fond of lying across the recliner instead of sitting down like a normal human being.

"Fuck, you gave it to Shae as well, hey? That would explain why she is ignoring my calls. She hasn't been at school all week, but according to Mr. Foster she will be back at school today so I'll catch up with her at the Zen Den tonight. Do you think I can go to the den even if I skipped school today?"

All day the pain and frustration kept snowballing, and in that one moment it all just exploded from Adrian. It started with one sob, but very quickly Adrian's entire body was shaking. Jax obviously had no clue how to handle the situation but figured some kind of physical touch was required. She shifted closer to Adrian and placed a hand on her knee.

"Doctor A, are you okay?"

Hiding behind her hands, Adrian simply shook her head and tried gaining control of the sobs that were racking through her.

"Should I get someone? Or something? Water? Yes, I'll get you some H2O and you'll feel fucking amazing," Jax said and jumped up.

She poured Adrian a glass of water from the pitcher on the table.

"Please, Dr. Ramsey, take this."

The fact that Jax was addressing her as Dr. Ramsey, like every patient should, conveyed to Adrian just how stressed and desperate Jax was. Wiping her eyes, Adrian took a deep breath and accepted the glass of water from a pale-looking Jax. It was several minutes before she was able to finally talk.

"Shae decided that she doesn't want to see me again."

"What the fuck do you mean she doesn't want to see you again? Why?" Jax asked.

"Jax, I really don't know. She didn't say."

"She didn't say? Was she fucking probed by an alien? Is she on smack?" Jax continued her rant.

Adrian simply shrugged and sipped on the cold water.

"I will fucking body slam her if she doesn't pull herself together. What happened?"

"Jax, I really have no idea. She sent me a text on Saturday, and I haven't heard from her since then."

Jax jumped up, resting her hands on her hips.

"That is such fucking bullshit. Maybe someone texted from her phone because this does not make any sense."

Adrian brushed her fingers through her hair and cleared the smudges under her eyes. She felt horrible for the breakdown, but she really needed to take some more time off.

"Jax, I am so sorry you had to see that. It's highly unprofessional, and in all honesty I should have taken another day off. Would you mind terribly if I head home and catch up with you tomorrow instead?" Adrian asked.

"You are sorry? Shae. Shae is the one that will be sorry when I see her," Jax threatened.

"Jax, please don't discuss any of this with Shae. I shouldn't have said anything to you today. I am sorry about that. Now, please will you excuse me?"

"Yes, please don't explain, Doctor A. If Andie dumped me via text, I would be in bed with a bottle of tequila and a cheap slut. We can reschedule whenever you feel ready," Jax offered.

Adrian didn't have the energy to drive home, plus she had a pounding headache. She cancelled her last appointment, sent Ella home, and lay down on her couch to close her eyes for a few minutes. Sheer exhaustion overtook her, and a few minutes quickly turned into a few hours. When she woke up with a very dry mouth, her office was dark. She sat up slowly, rolling her neck from one side to the other.

When she switched on the desk lamp, she peeked at her wristwatch. She was shocked to discover that it was well past nine. Fifteen minutes later, Adrian was heading home when a sudden, unexpected burst of anger ripped through her. She took the next turn, and before she knew it she found herself in front of the Zen Den. There was no sign of movement, but Shae's car was parked in front of the den.

She hadn't planned on coming here, much less what she would say to Shae, so when she saw Shae exit the den, her heart skipped a beat and she felt like she might faint. Shae froze as soon as she caught sight of Adrian. She clutched her chest and closed her eyes, and for a moment Adrian felt guilty for possibly scaring her into a panic attack. Then that flash of anger resurfaced.

"So you are in fact alive and well. The one thing I didn't take you for was a coward, but I was clearly mistaken," Adrian said.

"Really? You have some fucking nerve, Adrian Ramsey. What do you want? You are trespassing."

"I want the truth," Adrian said.

Locking the door of the den, Shae shook her head and stormed past Adrian without even looking at her.

"The truth? How fucking dare you ask me that? The truth?"

"I deserve the truth, Shae."

Shae spun around, stalked up to Adrian, and paused with her nose inches from that of Adrian.

"So did I!" Shae shouted so loudly that Adrian's ears started ringing.

Adrian had never seen Shae this angry, and it was truly frightening. She clutched her chest and took a step backward, more confused than ever.

"I don't know what you mean."

Throwing her hands in the air, Shae continued screaming. "Save it, Adrian. I saw it. I saw the fucking picture in Norman's wallet. Now leave before I have you arrested."

Shae slammed her car door and sped off without even looking back. Adrian was frozen to the spot, her mouth agape. She felt so many things all at once: anger, confusion, disappointment. Shae actually might hate her. She was almost convinced of it after looking into hard eyes that held contempt for her.

Her mind reeling, she drove to her parents' house in turmoil. Upon arrival, she stormed inside, right past her mother and father who had been having tea in the lounge.

"Adrian?" Ally called out after her.

She found her father's wallet on the kitchen nook and opened it. In the front slot, a gap-toothed Easton smiled at her. Frowning, she pulled the picture out and discovered a few more. Right at the back she found a picture she hadn't seen before. Could this be the picture that Shae had been referring to?

"Adrian, what on earth is wrong?" Ally asked when Adrian stormed back to the lounge.

Adrian ignored her mother and handed Norman the picture.

"Dad, who is this?"

Norman suddenly looked like he had seen a ghost and Ally closed her eyes before leaning back against the couch, seemingly swearing under her breath.

"Who is it?" Adrian insisted despite the fact that Norman looked like he was about to vomit.

Clearing his throat, Norman shifted uncomfortably in his seat until Ally took his hand in hers and nodded quietly for him to speak.

"Adrian, do you mind having a seat?" Norman said.

"I do. I do mind having a seat. Who is that?" Adrian asked, pointing at the picture in his hand.

Norman was quiet for another few moments before he let out a deep breath.

"It's my son," Norman said softly.

Adrian couldn't comprehend the words that were coming out of her father's mouth. There was a ringing in her ears, so she simply stood there staring at him. She was vaguely aware of a shuffling on the staircase, and she winced when she heard a loud thud. Easton and Avril had been carrying a heavy box downstairs. Both of them had lost their grip when they heard Norman's confession.

"Adrian, please sit down."

Slowly but surely, the ringing in Adrian's ears dimmed. Her legs felt weak and she was entirely certain that collapsing was a distinct possibility. Easton had her hands on her ears and it was her turn to look like she might vomit.

"Your son? Your son?" Easton kept asking.

Avril stood at the bottom of the staircase looking equally wounded and shocked. She cleared her throat after what seemed like an eternity. "Dad, do you mind explaining?"

"While you're at it, please explain to me why Shae broke up with me after finding that picture," Adrian added.

Norman dropped his chin to his chest and sighed again, shaking his head. Ally shifted closer to him, rubbing his back in slow comforting circles. While Norman was clearly trying to work up the courage to confess to a well-kept secret, Ally seemed nothing but supportive, a fact that confused and angered Adrian even more.

"Adrian, my son is Devon Nelson."

Adrian finally took that seat that Ally had suggested earlier because her legs would no longer carry her. She rested her head in her hands and images of Shae's face distorted in anger flashed behind her closed eyelids. Her heart sank into her shoes when she finally realised it. She had lost Shae forever. Shae probably didn't even realise that Norman had been keeping this secret from his own children as well. For a long time, Adrian felt like she was in a huge bubble. She was vaguely aware of voices but couldn't tell what they said.

Her father had a son. The man she loved the most in this world had fathered the beast that had almost killed Shae. They had been betrayed—all of them. Well, everyone except her mother, apparently, which also made no sense.

"How could you do that to us?" Avril said, staring at her father.

"He's younger than me, right? Well, he was?" Easton asked.

Norman simply nodded.

"It was a mistake I made only once, and I confessed my infidelity to your mother shortly after it happened. I only very recently discovered that Devon was born from my transgression," Norman explained.

"How noble of you, Dad. Confessing your adultery," Easton said sarcastically.

"His mother sent me that picture a while ago. She said that Shae had paid her a visit. Something about that visit must have wanted her to share the truth with me," Norman continued.

"Too bad you didn't feel like sharing your truth with your family, Father," Avril said.

Ally jumped up and threw her hands in the air, rolling her eyes.

"Now, listen to me, girls. You don't get to judge your father for something that happened a long time ago. Something he owned and confessed to me—the only one he had to admit anything to at the time. It was no one else's business but ours."

Adrian was still slumped on the couch and not making eye contact with anyone, especially with her mother, who continued, "After I gave birth to Easton, I suffered from postnatal depression. I was a mess, and both physically and emotionally unavailable to your father. He was lonely and overwhelmed and found some much-needed comfort from someone else. He didn't know that a child had been conceived."

Easton and Avril were both staring at their feet.

"We both made mistakes and we both made amends," Ally concluded.

Slowly, Adrian stood and walked to the door. Before she left, she turned around and faced Norman.

"It's a pity, Dad, that I ended up paying for your mistake."

Norman didn't say a word, but he stood and approached Adrian.

"No, don't get up, Dad. It's over for me. I lost the love of my life because of you."

CHAPTER FORTY

Shae watched as Fiona made quick work of a double cheeseburger, washed it down with a beer, and celebrated with a loud burp. They were sitting at their favourite booth at Plunge after a round of golf.

"How on earth did you fit that last bite into your mouth?" Shae asked.

"I have had huge things in my mouth, my friend," Fiona said proudly and winked.

Shae herself still had no appetite and the round of golf hadn't been optional. Fiona had appeared on her doorstep looking extremely threatening that morning. The golf itself had been relaxing and it took Shae's mind off things for a while. It had been three weeks since she last spoke to Adrian—if that final text message counted as talking. Shae thought that she would start feeling better as time went by, but the reality was that she still felt every bit as hollow and lost.

"Do you ever wonder why you are still single? I don't."

"It's one of life's great mysteries, Shae. Who wouldn't want a piece of this on the daily?" Fiona asked, rubbing her hand down her boobs suggestively.

"I can't believe they allow you to teach impressionable kids," Shae said.

"They allow Teacher Fiona to teach. They don't know Slutty Fiona. I am a great teacher, and you know it. Anyway, Slutty Fiona has a hot date tonight with a willing bearded submissive, so I have to go and prepare my weapons of mass seduction."

Closing her eyes, Shae pinched the bridge of her nose and winced at the unwelcome images of Dominatrix Fiona wielding a whip.

"Leave now."

"See you later, Shae. Don't wallow. It's unattractive," Fiona whispered before she kissed Shae's cheek.

She sent Fiona off with a small wave before she settled the account. She was almost out the door when she realised that she had left her newspaper at the booth, so she turned around and rushed back.

"Shae?"

She looked up when she heard a familiar voice.

"Easton. Hi," Shae said.

She hadn't planned on seeing any of the Ramseys again, and she was caught off-guard. She'd never seen Easton around Plunge since it wasn't exactly in the Ramsey neighbourhood. Easton wiped her hands on a napkin that the cute redhead accompanying her handed to her.

"It's good to see you, Shae."

Shae could think of a few comebacks, but none of them were very kind. The nerve of the Ramsey family was quite something. For months they had been withholding the truth from her. Easton even went so far as cultivating a real friendship with her.

"What brings you to my neighbourhood?" was the kindest thing Shae could come up with.

"I'm crashing with Janice until things at home are a bit less awkward. It's been a strange couple of weeks since Adrian's shocking discovery. As you can imagine, we are all still trying to process it," Easton said.

Shocking discovery? Shae was fuming now and could only practice so much self-restraint.

"It must have been quite shocking. I am fairly certain she thought that I would never find out," Shae said.

Frowning, Easton dumped the crumpled napkin on her plate.

"It's a real shame, Easton. She could have told me the truth a long time ago."

Easton swore out loud when the penny finally dropped. She clasped her hand over her mouth, shaking her head.

"Shae, can you please sit down for just a second."

"No, thanks."

Shae stormed outside, clutching the newspaper under her arm as her feet kicked up dust in the parking lot. She chucked the newspaper in the back of the car and slammed her door as hard as she could. She let out a frustrated cry as she banged her arms on the steering wheel, not caring that the sound of her car hooter drew some attention. She clenched her jaw when Easton knocked on her window.

"Easton, please. Just leave me alone."

"She didn't know, Shae. None of us did. Well, my mother did, which strangely makes it worse for us."

Shae was thankful that she had been sitting because her entire body went numb. She could feel her lungs deflating, and it felt like someone was tugging her stomach through her throat.

"She would never have agreed to be your therapist if she had known that she was related to the monster who did those things to you, Shae. Adrian is in a world of pain right now, and she doesn't deserve it."

Defeated, Shae rested her head against the steering wheel and closed her eyes. Of course Adrian would never do that. Adrian was honourable, painstakingly honest, and she valued her integrity immensely.

"Shae, for what it's worth, I truly detest the fact that I am related to anyone that caused you harm. I hate the fact that we're all losing you because of a once-off, random, meaningless roll in the hay. Straight people suck, dude."

Easton stuck her hand through the window and squeezed Shae's slumping shoulder. Shae let out a deep breath and clutched Easton's fingers for a few seconds.

"Thanks, Easton. I'll see you around, okay?"

Shae watched Easton walk away with her hands in her pockets and drooping shoulders. She was touched by Easton's display of emotion, and it broke her heart knowing that Adrian was in the same kind of pain, just amplified. Shae had messed up. Badly.

As she drove away, she thought about the conversation she had had with Adrian about the building blocks for a happy relationship. Adrian had spoken so beautifully about trust and what it meant to her, that she trusted Shae enough to take her own life and turn it upside down for her. She had said that because she trusted Shae, she felt safe with her. Well, it was safe to say that now all of their lives were turned upside down and nobody felt safe.

Adrian had been through so much in her marriage which she was courageous enough to end. Now, the very first time she risks trusting someone again, she gets burned. There was no way Shae could make it up to her, but at the very least she wanted to apologise. Adrian deserved that.

Despite it being a Saturday, Shae found Adrian's car parked in front of the practice. Shae banged the knocker several times and had almost given up when Adrian finally opened the door. The shock that registered on Adrian's face was fleeting, quickly replaced with what Shae could only describe as agony.

* * *

Adrian squinted into the bright sunlight that assaulted her when she opened the door, trying to discern who stood before her. It didn't take long for her to recognize the all too familiar shape of Shae's silhouetted body. Her heart leapt and then fell, and the throbbing behind her temples intensified. She grabbed her head with both hands.

"Adrian, are you okay?" Shae asked.

"It's the light. I have a migraine," Adrian said and quickly pulled Shae inside so she could shut the door.

"What are you doing here?" Shae asked.

"I could ask you the same thing, actually."

Adrian paused on the way to her office, clutching her head again. She leaned against the wall with her eyes shut and her palm flat against her stomach.

"Adrian, you shouldn't be here."

"Well, neither should you. Shae, I honestly can't do this right now. I was about to go home for a nap."

"You're not driving like that. You can barely stand up straight. Get your things together so I can take you home."

Adrian attempted to shake her head but regretted the motion instantly as a sharp pain shot through her eyes and straight to the back of her head. This was no time to be stubborn, so she retrieved her laptop and briefcase and quietly closed the office. She allowed Shae to guide her into the passenger seat of Shae's car.

She kept her eyes shut for the entirety of the drive and had just drifted off when Shae's phone started ringing. The audio automatically switched to her stereo.

"Shae, you're a real piece of shit, you know."

"Yes, Jax. I know. However, I don't have time to get into it right now. Chat later," Shae said and disconnected the call.

"Sorry about that," Shae said when she realised that the call had woken Adrian up.

Concentrating on her breathing in an effort not to vomit in Shae's car, Adrian simply nodded slowly. Short minutes later, Shae brought the car to a stop and Adrian took a deep breath. She was not looking forward to getting out; every little movement jarred a fresh bout of nausea and painful jabs through her skull.

"Leave your stuff in the car. I'll get it once I have you inside."

Finally opening her eyes, Adrian tugged on the door handle and shifted her weight so she could get out. Another bout of nausea washed over her, and she closed her eyes for another few seconds. She felt a warm hand on her own.

"Adrian, let me get you inside. Do you think you can stand?"

She summoned all of her strength and stood on wobbly legs, but before she knew it Shae had her arm around her waist.

"Put your arm around my shoulder. I've got you."

Slowly they made their way to the front door, but the moment Shae slipped her key into the lock, Adrian lost the battle. Hastily she looked around for something that could hold the content of her stomach but found nothing. She aimed for the flower bed leading up to her front door but missed with a mile as she started retching.

"That's okay." Shae's lie was not very convincing.

Adrian knew that Shae had a very sensitive stomach and was close to hurling herself. She didn't have time to apologise as Shae picked her off her knees and guided her inside. She took her straight to the bathroom so she could rinse out her mouth, which was a gradual process since every movement made her feel worse.

After what felt like an eternity, Adrian was finally tucked into bed wearing her comfiest sweats and an oversized T-shirt. Shae rested a cold cloth on Adrian's forehead for a while and then draped it across her eyes, which brought almost instant relief.

"Keep that right there. I put your laptop in the study, but please don't work tonight."

Adrian nodded quietly and turned on her side. When the cloth slipped off her eyes, Shae repositioned it, tucking her hair behind her ear.

"There's some water right over here and some painkillers for when your stomach settles. Do you need a bucket before I go?"

Suddenly the worst prospect on earth was being alone, and the mere thought of Shae leaving left Adrian feeling anxious. She didn't care if it was selfish, but she needed Shae to stay with her tonight. She had no doubt that being with her was the last thing Shae wanted. She probably couldn't look at her without thinking about the fact that the same blood that used to course through Devon Nelson's veins also ran through hers. She would let Shae go forever…but she would do that tomorrow. For now, she just really needed to be close to her.

"Don't go," Adrian whispered.

For a beat or two there was absolute silence, and she feared the worst—that Shae couldn't even grant her appeal for reprieve for one night.

"Please, Shae. Just one night."

Shae's lips touched her temple softly.

"I had no intention of leaving. I was going to hide in your living room until you felt better. Now, please get some rest."

CHAPTER FORTY-ONE

Only a dull throb at the back of her head remained when Adrian woke up the following morning. She carefully opened her eyes and rolled her neck from side to side. Her breath caught in her throat. Right next to her, Shae was sleeping peacefully. Her hands, palms stuck together, were tucked under her left cheek and her jaw was slack.

The shorts that she had clearly borrowed from Adrian had ridden up high to expose the scar on her thigh, the scar from a wound that was inflicted to her by Adrian's own flesh and blood. The thought made her stomach turn, so she pulled the covers up around Shae, who started stirring immediately.

"Good morning," Adrian whispered.

Her heart skipped a beat when Shae opened her eyes and offered her a lazy smile.

"Colour looks good on your cheeks. How are you feeling?" Shae asked.

"A little fragile but very grateful. Thanks for staying with me last night."

"You're quite welcome. Can you handle a cup of coffee, or would you rather have some tea?"

"Perhaps tea is the safer option, but I'll make some," Adrian said and sat up slowly.

It felt like her brain had stayed behind on the pillow, so she quickly lay back down, brushing her palm across her forehead.

"Seems a little ambitious. Don't worry about it. I can find my way around your kitchen. Don't move," Shae said as she got up.

She returned moments later with a cup of tea for Adrian and a strong coffee for herself. Climbing back under the covers and leaning back against the headboard, she sipped on her coffee and let out a satisfied groan.

"I miss this coffee fiercely."

"I am wounded," Adrian said as she sat up much slower this time, holding her head in her hands.

"Why?" Shae asked as she slipped a pillow behind Adrian's back.

"You miss the coffee?" Adrian asked.

"Among other things," Shae said, a smile tugging at the corners of her mouth.

Adrian sighed as the sweet tea soothed her scratchy throat. It burned a hole in her empty stomach but still felt good. Running a hand through her hair, she leaned her head back and turned to face Shae, who was studying her closely.

"Not really what you came around for yesterday, hey?"

Shae chuckled softly as she pulled her knees up to her chest and rested her coffee on top.

"I was hoping for just a conversation, and I woke up in your bed. It was a win in my books."

It had been three lonely weeks since Shae had spoken to her, and she had missed the flirting as much as she imagined Shae had missed her strong batch of coffee beans. Before Shae had shown up at her practice yesterday, she was reasonably certain that she would never again be on the receiving end of one of Shae's dazzling smiles, and yet, there sat Shae wearing exactly one of those. Life surely proved to be unpredictable these days. She felt like she was treading uncharted territory and she didn't know what the way forward would look like, but clearly it would entail that serious conversation Shae had intended to have the day before.

"I don't know if I can do it on an empty stomach," Adrian said.

"Whoa! I mentioned a conversation and you're offering me morning sex? Behave yourself, Dr. Ramsey."

"I was actually referring to the conversation. Don't flatter yourself, Miss McPherson."

They spent a moment just sipping on their drinks and staring at each other. In that moment, Adrian could almost pretend that Devon Nelson was still the faceless boy that had haunted the love of her life instead of her father's illegitimate son.

"Toast and eggs?" Shae asked.

"I can probably only handle the toast."

Adrian met Shae in the sunroom where she had buttered some toast for Adrian and heaped some scrambled egg and grated cheese on her own slice of toast. She had also sliced up an apple, promising that it was just the thing to settle Adrian's stomach. They ate in companionable silence, sharing tentative smiles from time to time.

"You know you keep dodging that elephant in the room, right?" Shae asked as she drained her glass of orange juice.

"I have no idea what you're talking about," Adrian said.

Shae dusted some breadcrumbs from her chest and crossed her feet at the ankles. She gave Adrian a look that said "I can wait here all day." Adrian took a deep breath before she turned to face Shae.

"This is such a fucking mess that I don't even know where to start."

"Let's start right at the beginning. How did I end up in your consulting room, Adrian?"

Adrian's brows shot up as she leaned forward, not even hesitating to take Shae's hand.

"Shae, you have to believe me. I had nothing to do with that. I didn't know who Devon was. When you walked into my office, I didn't know anything about you other than the fact that you were forced by Mr. Foster to seek treatment."

Adrian rubbed her thumb across Shae's knuckles.

"When you mentioned the picture you had found in my father's wallet, I rushed over there and confronted him. Apparently my father had an affair—or at least a one-night stand—and Devon was conceived. He confessed to my mother at that time, and she forgave him. Hillary contacted my father and sent him that picture right after you paid her that visit. She told him how their son had died, and when he did the research, he realised that you were the teacher Devon had attacked."

Shae sighed deeply and leaned back in her chair but didn't pull away when Adrian shifted closer and rested a hand on her thigh.

"My father didn't breathe a word to me, not even when he realised that I had fallen in love with you. He and my mother had decided long ago that the affair was no one else's business but their own to deal with privately. They are so proud of their marriage and the work they both put into it. Hell, Dad was even giving you and Leonard lessons. And when it came to the fact of Devon and what he had done...all of that was already in the past when they found out. I can't say I agree with their decision from my perspective, but I understand the inclination. It pains me so deeply, my darling, to know that I am related to the source of your affliction. I am so unbelievably sorry that you had to suffer at the hands of someone that turned out sharing my DNA."

Shaking her head profusely, Shae cupped Adrian's face.

"Just stop, Adrian. Please don't apologise. You did nothing wrong. I am the one who needs to apologise."

Shae dropped her hands to Adrian's lap where she took both of her hands in her own.

"I never should have doubted you. We spoke about love, trust, respect, and passion—our recipe for perfection. Unfortunately, I didn't inspire much faith when I failed to trust you the very first time our tree house rattled in a storm. I am so sorry. You've never given me reason not to trust you. I should have come to you instead of making my own stupid assumptions."

Adrian lifted their joined hands to her lips and kissed Shae's fingers.

"I am so sorry, Adrian. You must have felt so betrayed and frustrated."

"I imagine you felt the same way, darling," Adrian said.

Shae stood and pulled Adrian into her arms, and within seconds the world righted itself, flipping right back onto its axis, spinning slowly...much like Adrian's head.

"Shae, can we head back to bed? I'm a little dizzy."

Together, they climbed back under the covers, but this time Adrian settled into the crook of Shae's arm and draped her thigh across her stomach. She rubbed her nose against Shae's neck and snuggled as close to her as she possibly could. With her hand on Shae's heart, she closed her eyes and smiled her first real smile in three weeks. Shae gently pulled her fingers through Adrian's hair, kissing her forehead.

"We'll survive this, right?" Adrian asked softly.

"Figlet, I cleaned up your vomit yesterday. I can survive absolutely anything."

Adrian laughed heartily, rolling onto her back and clutching her stomach. It didn't take very long for Shae to roll on top of her. She traced her index finger across Adrian's dark brows, down her temple, and across her chin.

"You are exceptionally beautiful."

"You don't look at me and see Devon?" Adrian whispered softly.

Shae covered Adrian's mouth with her own in a kiss that started out softly and slowly but quickly escalated once Adrian slipped her tongue into Shae's mouth and dragged her nails across her back. When Shae groaned, Adrian slipped her leg between Shae's and rested her thigh snugly against her crotch. Adrian ran her one hand up Shae's back, curling her fingers around her shoulder while the other snuck into the front of her underwear. She clutched Shae's shoulder while she slipped two fingers into Shae's wet folds.

Shae broke their kiss and rested her forehead against Adrian's shoulder as she rode her fingers slowly, arching her back from time to time. She sucked one of Adrian's nipples into her mouth and flicked her tongue across it. When Adrian's breath caught, Shae rubbed her thumb across Adrian's clit through soaked underwear, which resulted in Adrian picking up the pace, thrusting her fingers into Shae faster and deeper.

"Touch me, darling," Adrian moaned.

Within seconds of pushing her fingers into Adrian and raking her teeth across a hardened nipple, they crashed into oblivion together with racing hearts and trembling bodies. When Shae caught her breath she rolled onto her back, pulling Adrian into her arms.

"So you missed my coffee, hey?"

"Yup, it's the coffee. I am here for the coffee."

EPILOGUE

Audrey swore out loud when she absentmindedly grabbed the edge of the hot pan that held the honey-glazed, baked carrots. The perfectly grilled chicken and a vast array of salads were already arranged on the table on the patio. Adrian had also roasted a pork belly. Now that she was teaching, she had loads of time, and she chose to spend a good deal of that time in the kitchen.

Today marked Audrey's one-year cancer-free anniversary, and the patio was aptly decorated in racy decorations that Fiona and Easton had either found at a sex shop or made themselves. There were breasts in all shapes, forms, and sizes. They dangled from the ceiling, were wedged between candleholders, and bound to the legs of every chair and bench, celebrating the fact that Audrey had two healthy breasts.

"Hi, fam. I come bearing booby cupcakes," Easton said.

She slipped a tray of cupcakes that indeed resembled breasts, complete with Jelly Tots nipples, onto the already-crowded table. She nudged Shae with her hip and kissed Adrian's cheek in passing.

"These are fucking sick!" Jax shouted as she posed with a cupcake in front of each of her breasts, making Andie blush profusely.

"Don't play with the food, Booger. I swear you could have been Fiona's long-lost love child," Shae said.

She clasped a hand over her mouth immediately, realising that she had made yet another reference to illegitimate children. She now regularly, unwittingly, referenced any and all topics that should rather be avoided, from adultery to illegitimate offspring. Obviously she only possessed this superpower in the presence of Norman, his wife, or his children.

"Oh, don't feel bad, Shae. Easton calls me Hefner sometimes." Norman winked.

It had been an awkward few months since the day that Adrian stormed into her parents' house confronting them with that picture of Devon, but true to their nature the Ramseys had stuck together and worked through all of it. Norman had apologised for not telling them about his transgression. He had planned to reveal the truth about Devon to all of them, but Ally had asked him to just give Adrian and Shae some time to settle into their relationship.

Shae finding that photograph when she did had upset that apple cart, and instead of settling into their relationship, Shae and Adrian had to climb their first mountain together. With stern motivation from Ally, the girls had forgiven their father. Although Adrian and Norman's relationship still needed some work, they had made some headway already.

"Goodness knows, living in one house with all of these Ramsey females certainly sounds as demanding as being Hugh Hefner," Leonard chipped in, earning him a death stare from Avril and a slap on the back from Norman.

Avril had moved in with Leonard after a very intense argument with Norman shortly after the big reveal, and she hadn't moved out since. Jayden and Jonah now called him *Daderd*, which Easton had suggested since she had graduated him to semi-father. He was now a combination of Dad and Leonard. Norman was quick to remind Avril that she needed to tell her boys the truth, but she couldn't help making a pot/kettle reference.

"No Janice today?" Shae asked.

"She'll be joining us later, thanks for meddling—I mean asking," Easton replied.

It turned out Easton wasn't sleeping alone when she crashed on Janice's couch, and the two had been inseparable ever since.

"Can you all please start paying attention to me? Am I not the one who puked so much that the enamel on my once gorgeous teeth is now a little dodgy? Did I not lose my lovely locks and, worst of all, my libido? Did I or did I not kick cancer's ass and earned myself a handsome toy boy at the chemo centre?" Audrey said to no one in particular.

Shae nodded slowly, with raised brows. "You did indeed. You also didn't lose your modesty, thank goodness."

"Great. Now, let's eat. My toy boy has a curfew and we're meeting for drinks," Audrey said.

Standing behind Adrian, Shae wrapped her arms around her waist and kissed her softly on her ear, causing a delicious shiver down Adrian's back. Despite any fears that Adrian might have had, the invisible band of energy keeping her tethered to Shae McPherson was firmly intact, and Shae was utterly grateful for it. Together they embodied the definition of strong force.

"Is everything okay, Figlet?" Shae whispered in her ear.

"All is exactly as it should be, darling."

Bella Books, Inc.

Women. Books. Even Better Together.

P.O. Box 10543
Tallahassee, FL 32302

Phone: 800-729-4992
www.bellabooks.com